EXTREME FORCE

A ROGUE NOVEL

HARRY BROOKS

Reflected Moon Publishing

COPYRIGHT

OTHER TITLES BY HARRY BROOKS

The ROGUE Thriller Series

Hard Choices (Book 1)

Check for new titles at

www.harrybrooksauthor.com

To the authors of the many books that
I read in my youth, and since.

Those adventures planted the seeds
that inspire me to write.

Thank You

"Let your plans be dark and impenetrable as night, and when you move, fall like a thunderbolt."

Sun Tzu, The Art of War

Chapter 1

Webb had a cigarette between his lips long before he passed through the first set of sliding doors. As the outer set opened, he flicked the wheel on his lighter and lit up. Three steps onto the pavement, he stopped and inhaled deeply from the Marlboro Red. As he exhaled, he felt the knot of tension in his stomach releasing. He took another long pull as other arrivals to Zurich's Kloten airport flowed out behind him and divided like a river, then merged again onto the pedestrian crossing.

As Webb looked for a taxi, Coburn appeared in his peripheral vision. He also stopped, lit up, and filled his lungs. Webb headed for the taxi rank, the cigarette receding towards his lips. He paused at the first empty car, an Opel Insignia. After sucking a last hit of nicotine, he extinguished the butt into a metal bin, then dropped into the front seat and shut the door. Out of the corner of his eye, he watched Coburn saunter along the pavement as if he'd all the time in the world.

Webb had been looking forward to the trip for weeks, ever since he'd negotiated the deal with Meerkat, a hacker based in Zurich. On the evening before the flight from London, Webb went to the Black Hammer Bar to meet Goran Savik and collect the money for the purchase, twenty thousand pounds in cash. Savik represented the interests of Dimitri Mitrovic, a self-titled businessman whose movements and operations were of constant interest to the police, especially the Drug Squad.

When Webb arrived at the bar, Savik was at his regular table in a quiet booth close to the rear exit. During previous meetings, Coburn had sat a short distance away on a high stool. From there, he had monitored everyone who came into the bar through the front and rear entrances. However, on this occasion, Savik instructed Coburn to join them at the circular table. Webb knew little about Coburn, only that he was Savik's driver and bodyguard. When Savik announced that Coburn would also travel to Zurich for the meeting with Meerkat, Webb's enthusiasm dropped a level. He tentatively suggested that Coburn's presence might spook his contact, but the tone of Savik's response ended the debate.

At one point, Savik moved to the next table to take a brief phone call. Webb's attempts at light conversation with Coburn were met with short answers that told him little about the man or his interests. Throughout the two-minute exchange, Webb had the impression he was being studied, like a specimen in a lab jar. When the meeting finally ended, Savik and Coburn left through the rear door. Webb slumped back in his seat, deflated and a little uncertain. He was confident of his technical skills, but in their presence, he had felt insignificant. He moved to a high stool at the bar and drowned his sorrows, eventually concluding that their opinions didn't matter once he and his crew got paid. Savik was bankrolling the job and if he wanted to protect his investment by sending Coburn as a babysitter, so be it. Webb would focus on the bigger picture, that of making some money for Karnage, the hacker group he and Stella had started some years earlier.

The taxi driver clicked home his seat belt and shifted the car into gear. "Where are you going?"

Webb dropped his backpack to the floor and pointed at Coburn. "He's coming too."

The driver shrugged. According to the licence taped to the dashboard, his name was Henri Grossman. The image beneath the name resembled a police arrest photograph. Crew cut, deeply furrowed brow and penetrating eyes. He didn't look the chatty type, thought Webb, which was a pity. Coburn had kept to himself during the two-hour flight from London. He didn't read or use headphones, just sat there staring at the seat in front. Whenever Webb had tried to start a conversation, the older man gave single-word responses that were clearly intended to shut Webb up. Since the plane landed in Zurich, Coburn had uttered exactly twelve words and seven of those had been to Passport Control. As Webb struggled with the seat belt, Coburn stopped outside the taxi and began tapping the screen of his phone.

"We're going to the MegaTron Arena," Webb informed the driver. "It's near Technopark. Do you know it?"

"Of course. In the Kreis 5 district."

"How long will it take to get there?" asked Webb.

The driver typed their destination into the satnav and started the meter. A map filled the screen and displayed an aerial view of a plaza surrounded by tall buildings. Names hovered over the shapes like characters in one of Webb's computer games. Technopark, Hotel Ibis, Pulse5, Bar Grooves. The scene was familiar to Webb. He'd studied it on his laptop the day before, using the street view to follow a route across the square and up a side street to MegaTron. When the driver tapped the screen again, the map panned out to show the quickest route from the airport, with the distance and estimated journey time detailed underneath. Just over ten kilometres, a nineteen minute drive.

Webb made another attempt at conversation. "Are you from Zurich?"

He shook his head.

"I've heard it's a cool city, lots to see," said Webb.

Coburn opened the rear door of the taxi and climbed in without a word. The driver muttered something about tourists, then flicked on the indicator and pulled into the flow of traffic. When another car pulled out in front of him, he braked hard, blew the horn and yelled through the windscreen. As they moved off again, he turned up the volume on the radio, filling the car with jazz music and ending any possibility of conversation. The taxi bounced over the speed ramps as they left the airport complex and joined the A51 motorway for the city.

Webb stared out through the side window, but it offered little to distract him. It was already dark outside and all he could see was his own face reflected in the glass. He sat back with a resigned sigh. As his eyes followed the tail lights of an articulated truck, his gut tightened, gripped by a familiar anxiety. The buzz of the previous few days had long since evaporated. Travel didn't suit him at all. His only previous trips abroad had been to gaming conventions in Seville and Antwerp. They'd been intense weekends spent in front of consoles, with little time for anything else. Once he'd survived the outbound flights, it'd been easy to convince his brain he was still at home. After two full days of competition, he was so exhausted that the flight home was a blur of alcohol and sleep. Apart from those trips, he preferred to experience the world through the hi-tech setup in his apartment.

As the taxi sped along the motorway to the city and the cool breeze tugged at Webb, he wondered if he'd made a mistake. He shifted in the leather seat and lowered the window halfway. He was much happier in front of his computer, cracking passwords and breaching firewalls. Maybe Ringo or Danny should have taken the trip to Zurich, not him. They'd both have jumped at the chance. And they wouldn't be wussing out just because Coburn wasn't being all buddy-buddy. What did he expect from Coburn? He was just one of Savik's enforcers and probably couldn't tell a PlayStation from an air conditioner.

Webb slid the phone from his pocket and checked for messages. The last one had been from Stella just before he'd boarded the plane in London. 'U got this Jay' followed by two yellow fists. Straight and to the point. It had been Stella's idea to start Karnage, a team of hackers for hire. She'd approached Webb first, then Danny and Ringo. Brooke joined a year later. Over the past three years, their tight group had gradually built up a reputation on the dark web. This latest job with Savik was their big break. It could, would, lift them to the next level, where they could command huge fees. The deal in MegaTron was the first step towards that dream and Webb felt the entire weight of it on his slim shoulders.

When the taxi slowed abruptly, Webb looked up and saw they were leaving the motorway. He glanced at the satnav and was surprised to see only three minutes remaining of their journey. His contact had chosen Megatron as the venue for the exchange. They had a chain of twenty gaming arenas throughout Europe, operating twenty-four hours a day, three hundred and sixty-five days a year. Webb was a member of the London branch.

MegaTron Zurich was in the Kreis 5 district, an area sandwiched between the Limmat river and a swathe of railroad tracks. In the early nineties, the district had been a deserted industrial wasteland, home to squatters, drug dealers and seedy clubs. Since then, it had been transformed into one of the most hip and popular centres of art and culture in Europe. Restaurants and disco bars lined both sides of the streets, spinning bands of coloured light into the night air. A steady beat drifted in through the open window of the taxi, increasing in volume as they drove deeper into the district. Webb began to come alive, energised by the music. The taxi followed the curve of the streets, then stopped along an open square. The driver flicked on the interior light and tapped a few buttons on the digital meter.

"Fifty-five francs." His voice was barely audible over the music.

"He'll pay," said Webb, jerking a thumb into the back seat. He stepped out onto the cobbled pavement and rolled his shoulders. Despite the chill in the evening, he peeled off his jacket and slung it over his shoulder, letting the temperature flush some of the anxiety from his body. The maps he'd studied were accurate, but they hadn't come close to conveying the atmosphere that swept over him as he gazed across the square. He let his eyes wander, absorbing the array of eateries and bars. Cafe Jaxx, Grooves, Maag, Pulse5, Club Orb. Names he'd only seen on a computer screen now beckoned to him, promising anonymity and pleasure.

Webb's stomach rumbled. He hadn't eaten since a bacon sandwich earlier that afternoon. He checked his watch. Twenty-five minutes left before their meeting. His hunger pangs would have to wait. The flashing sign of the Ibis Hotel on the far side of the square caught his attention. Savik had reserved a twin room for them, but as far as Webb was concerned, Coburn could have it to himself. Webb intended getting every ounce from the few hours he had before their early morning return flight. He could sleep on the plane. He turned and looked back at the taxi. It was empty. Coburn and the driver were standing at the back with the boot open. Webb wondered what they were doing. Apart from small backpacks, they had brought no luggage.

He wandered over to the car. "What's going on?"

Coburn extracted a twenty from his wallet. "Just some insurance."

Webb watched as the driver reached into the car and produced a wheel brace. Coburn folded back the left side of his jacket and slid the long section of the L shaped tool into a custom made sleeve. Then he folded a Velcro strap over the shorter end and zipped his jacket up halfway.

Coburn nodded to the driver. "Cheers mate."

The driver pocketed the cash and got back into the car.

"Bit over the top, isn't it," said Webb. "I know the guy we're meeting. He's cool."

Coburn watched the taxi drive off. "I've heard that before," he said, pointing to an old scar along his temple. He fished a packet of Marlboros from his pocket, shook out one, and put it between his lips. He returned the packet, produced a lighter, and lit up. His eyes narrowed as he scanned the square.

Webb turned away, dug out his own cigarettes, and lit one. He wondered what went on in Coburn's brain. They were both working for Savik, albeit temporarily, in Webb's case. They were on the same side, just with different jobs.

"This rat guy we're meeting," said Coburn. "What's his story?"

"His name is Meerkat. That's his handle, his code name."

"You got one of those handles?" Coburn flicked his cigarette ash at Webb's feet.

Webb cleared his throat and kicked one boot against the other. Savik had entrusted Coburn with the money for the deal. Otherwise, Webb would lose him and do the job alone. "Meerkat works for VerKoll, the software company who developed the security system we've been trying to crack. He acquired a set of access codes from a contact he has in their development hub. Without those codes, Mr Savik's grand plan will remain just that, a plan."

"So this guy is the middleman," said Coburn.

"Yeah. That a problem?"

"We'll see." Coburn tugged the last of his cigarette, dropped the butt onto a waste can and set off towards the opposite corner of the square.

Chapter 2

Coburn seemed to know where he was going, which surprised Webb. He followed, but had to quicken his pace just to keep up. The square was busy, forcing them to weave between groups that stood around chatting or sitting on a bench. When Webb finished his cigarette, he flicked the butt towards a trash can, but miscued and sent it into the path of a young woman. She shrieked and frantically knocked ash from her sleeve.

"Franz, look," she complained, pointing to a smudge on her beige jacket. She glared at Webb. "You could have set me on fire."

Webb raised his middle finger and kept walking. Seconds later, his shoulder jerked back. He staggered, found his balance, and turned around. The guy who had grabbed him looked considerably younger than Webb's twenty-nine years, similar in height but broader and muscled, like a boxer.

"Apologise to my girlfriend," said Franz.

She was a few steps behind him, being consoled by two girls and a couple of guys. Webb's arm tensed by his side, and he curled his hand into a fist. Before he could reply, a hand gripped his shoulder. He whipped around. It was Coburn.

"It was an accident," Coburn said to Franz.

Webb tried to pull free, but Coburn's fingers dug into Webb's muscle like steel hooks.

"Apologise to the lady," said Coburn. Although he was talking to Webb, he was watching Franz and his friends closely.

Webb took a swing at Coburn with his other hand, but Coburn dodged it easily. Pain scorched along Webb's arm as Coburn increased pressure on a nerve. A wave of nausea rose from Webb's stomach and the colour drained from his face. Coburn reduced the pressure, and the intensity subsided a little.

"OK," said Webb, his voice strained. He looked past the boyfriend, to the girl. "Sorry, it was an accident."

Franz, surprised, looked from Webb to Coburn, unsure how to proceed.

"Are we OK here?" said Coburn.

Franz stared back at Coburn, his mind processing what had just happened, his eyes finding the scar on Coburn's forehead and the tattoos that snaked around his neck. Franz relaxed his stance and nodded.

"Good," said Coburn.

As Franz turned back to his girlfriend, Coburn hauled Webb away and disappeared into the crowd.

Webb tried to look back, but Coburn blocked his view and pushed him on. As they passed a narrow alley between two bars, Webb stopped dead and faced up to Coburn.

"What was that about?" said Webb. "I can handle myself. I don't need you sticking your nose in."

Coburn circled one hand around Webb's throat, placed the other on his chest and drove him into the alley. Checking he hadn't attracted any unwanted attention, Coburn pushed deeper into the shadows of a fire escape. "We're here to do a job. That means staying focused and not drawing attention to ourselves. If you'd started something back there, the cops would be on us in minutes. Would you be OK explaining to the boss why we spent the night in a cell, not to mention how his twenty Gs of cash got diverted to the police charity fund?"

"I'd have floored that guy and been gone before anyone called the old bill," said Webb, stepping forward.

Coburn slammed Webb back against the brickwork. He jammed his forearm under Webb's chin and swept his legs out from under him with a deft flick of his foot, leaving the younger man suspended by his neck. "Wrong, whizz kid. There's seven security cameras in the square and an unmarked Polizei van parked thirty metres from where the taxi dropped us off. I spotted two plain clothes guys in the crowd, most likely drug squad."

Webb wheezed, the supply of air through his windpipe reduced to a trickle. His backpack fell to the ground as he tried in vain to prise Coburn's arm from his throat. Coburn eased off, wary that a passerby might notice their confrontation. He waited for Webb to find his feet, then gave him some space. Webb doubled over, hands on his knees, and gulped fresh air. He coughed a few times, spat out, then leaned back against the wall, his breathing quick and shallow.

"I know you're pissed," said Coburn.

Webb's eyes flared, but he didn't move.

Coburn glanced up the alley, making sure they weren't drawing attention. "Whether you believe me or not, we're on the same side, which is good for you, because Mr Savik is not a tolerant man."

Coburn waited for his words to sink in, then continued. "Do this right, we all get paid, everyone goes home happy." Coburn stepped right up to Webb and lowered his voice. "But screw up, the boss gets angry, and it's game over. No second chances."

Coburn was intimidating, but Webb also detected a slight twitch over the man's lip that he hadn't noticed before. He looked into Coburn's eyes, past the arrogance and recognised a sliver of fear. A chill sliced through Webb, like a ghost had crept beneath his skin. He tried to pull away from Coburn's eyes but couldn't. Instead, he found himself nodding.

Coburn stepped away, rubbed one hand over his mouth and gazed off towards the square. After clearing his throat, he returned his attention to Webb. "Are we good?"

Webb took a tentative step, testing his legs. "Yeah."

Coburn straightened his jacket and waited until Webb appeared ready. "Right then, let's go."

As they left the plaza, Webb pointed to a corner building further up the street. "That's the place."

A purple neon sign pulsed the name MegaTron over the entrance, with 'eSports Arena' in smaller lights underneath. A line of ten or twelve people were queueing to get in. Webb hadn't been to a MegaTron outside England before, but he had watched their tournaments streamed live from all over the world. The venues in Munich and Stockholm were enormous, twice the size of MT-London. They had VR booths with a wide variety of configurations, including battle scenes from Webb's favourite Star Wars movies where you could choose Rebel or Empire ships, cruisers or fighters. Standing outside the club, he felt a trickle of excitement returning. He took a couple of photos and uploaded them to the MegaTron app. His mates back home would be dead jealous.

As they waited in the queue, Coburn noticed that the guys ahead of him had ID cards bearing the purple and gold MegaTron logo. Webb pulled out his wallet and extracted his own card.

"What's the deal here?" asked Coburn.

"Apart from the odd open event, it's members only," said Webb. "I can bring you in as a guest, but you'll have to pay."

As the queue edged nearer the steps, Coburn became aware of music thumping out onto the street. It sounded like there was a disco going on inside. He didn't recognise the tune or even the style, but the predominantly young people in the queue were swaying to it as they chatted. Even though Coburn was only in his early forties, music had evolved beyond the few classifications he had grown up with. His best guess was rap or hip-hop. He took out his wallet. "How much?"

"Back home, it's fifteen quid an hour, forty gets you four hours. Probably similar here."

"So, how much is a year's membership?"

"Costs me three hundred. I've got silver, gold costs five-fifty."

"That's less than six quid a week," said Coburn. "How can they charge fifteen for one hour!"

"I pay three hundred a month, not a year," said Webb, shaking his head.

Coburn's jaw dropped.

"You better pay for at least two hours," said Webb.

"Why, we're meeting him at ten."

"This isn't like a meeting with your bank manager."

"So?" said Coburn.

"So, Meerkat is a gamer." Webb shrugged. "He'll show when he shows."

Coburn ran his fingers through his hair, but said nothing. He estimated most of the people in the queue were between seventeen and mid-thirties. They wore hoodies over t-shirts and baseball caps with logos he didn't recognise. Coburn's polo neck and leather jacket wouldn't blend in very well, but there was nothing he could do about it now.

They climbed the steps and entered a narrow hallway. Two guys wearing dark purple t-shirts under black hoodies were scanning the ID cards. The word 'GateKeeper' was emblazoned in gold letters across their chests. Built like wrestlers, their job was to weed out potential troublemakers. A poster on the wall listed prices under a variety of categories, including member and guest rates. An adult guest cost twenty francs per hour or fifty for four hours.

Webb swiped his ID card against a scanner and asked for a two-hour guest pass. The first Gatekeeper took payment from Coburn and handed them wristbands, purple for Webb and neon yellow for Coburn. Then they proceeded through a turnstile and double doors into a large, dimly lit lobby, lined on either side with booths selling a vast array of gaming merchandise. Shirts, hoodies and caps hung from long rails while posters, badges and figurines decorated tiered shelves.

Webb and Coburn weaved through the crowd to a set of swing doors that led into the main gaming zone. As they pushed through, a torrent of noise and light hit them. Coburn had never experienced such an assault on his senses and instantly felt disoriented and agitated. The vast arena was simultaneously midnight dark and dazzling bright, the absence of overhead lights replaced by multicoloured flashes from dozens of computer screens that pierced the gloom, then plunged it back into a shadowy blackness. Row upon row of computer games filled the floor space, all blasting their own unique sound effects. The clatter of machine guns and lasers echoed off the walls, making it impossible to tell which direction they came from. Music boomed from speakers mounted on tall pillars, as giant plasma screens suspended from the ceiling displayed live coverage of tournaments from other Megatron arenas.

As Coburn's vision acclimatised to the erratic lighting, he scanned the surrounding space. He counted seven MegaTron staff patrolling the area. They wore similar uniforms to the muscle in the lobby, but had Sentinel emblazoned on their chest instead of Gate-Keeper. CCTV cameras hung from the ceiling at regular intervals, no doubt relaying everything to a central office upstairs. The areas further away from Coburn were darker, making it difficult to gauge the correct size of the place. Three tiers of polished wooden steps led down to the main floor. Parallel rows of computers with high-backed seats stretched from the base of the stairway, as far as he could see. Gamers occupied every seat and the adjoining screens bathed their faces in constantly changing streams of colour. Groups of spectators crowded the aisles, shouting warnings and encouragement to the players.

As they descended the steps, Webb relaxed into the mayhem of noise and lights. His earlier anxiety quickly disappeared as he soaked in the atmosphere and feasted his eyes on the games and excitement surrounding him.

"Where are we meeting Meerkat?" shouted Coburn. When he got no response, he punched Webb hard on the shoulder.

Webb stumbled sideways, then regained his balance. "What the hell!"

"Meerkat, where are we meeting him?"

Webb rubbed his shoulder vigorously for a few seconds, then said something while pointing into the distance.

"What?" said Coburn, shaking his head. He moved closer to Webb.

"In the Battlefront compound," said Webb.

Coburn stared blankly back at him. Directly above them, music boomed from an oversize speaker. Webb moved off to one side and gestured for Coburn to follow.

"We're meeting in the Battlefront section, over there somewhere." Webb pointed across to the west side of the arena.

Coburn could see screens suspended from the ceiling playing Star Wars movie clips on a continuous loop. Webb descended the steps and stood, hands in his jeans pockets, watching a guy playing Duke Nukem, a retro game from the nineties.

Coburn stepped in front of Webb, blocking his view of the game. "What's he look like? Have you got a photo?"

Webb shook his head. "No idea. We've only met in chat rooms and online games." He went to step around Coburn, but was yanked back.

"You've never met him before! You said you knew him."

"Calm down, man." Webb nodded his head to the right. "Those guys don't take any crap."

Coburn followed his gaze. A MegaTron Sentinel was standing nearby, but facing the opposite direction.

"Anyway, I know Meerkat for years. He's cool."

"Listen up," said Coburn. "Deals like this can go sideways. Why do you think the boss has me here? It wasn't to carry your coat and wipe your ass. Have you ever done anything like this before?"

Webb said nothing.

"I didn't think so," said Coburn. "This isn't a computer game where you get three lives, then start over. It's real guns, real bullets and real pain."

"You're some paranoid dude, you know that," said Webb. "Look around you. The only guns here are plastic ones."

Coburn noticed the Sentinel was now watching them. He smiled at Webb, then broke into a laugh. "Let's check out this game over here."

Confused by Coburn's change of mood, Webb allowed himself to be guided to a bunch of guys cheering at a team deathmatch.

"So how will we recognise this guy?" said Coburn, one eye monitoring the Sentinel.

"Every member has a handle, a unique codename," said Webb. "His is Meerkat. It's coded into the chip on our ID cards."

Webb pulled out his phone. "The MegaTron app shows who's in the club and what game they're playing."

He scrolled through an alphabetical list of names and showed it to Coburn.

"I presume you can search for a particular person?"

"Of course, but better than that, I've added an alert," said Webb.

Coburn showed no sign of understanding.

"When Meerkat scans his ID on the way in, I'll get a notification on my phone," said Webb.

"But we'll never find him in this crowd."

"He'll DM me. Same as a text message."

Webb showed Coburn a list of older messages he'd received. As Coburn read them, an alert popped up.

"Meerkat has checked in," said Coburn, pointing at the screen. "You go to the BattleFront area and wait there. If he sends you a message, don't respond for at least the next three minutes. I want to see if he's brought anyone with him, intentionally or otherwise. Understood?"

It was Webb's turn to stare blankly at Coburn, but the older man didn't wait for an answer, just marched off towards the lobby.

Chapter 3

Coburn took the steps two at a time and pushed through the doors into the lobby. He didn't know what Meerkat looked like, but that didn't matter. If Webb was right, that he could trust his contact, then the biggest threat to their mission would be somebody following Meerkat. That somebody would be a professional, paid by VerKoll. Coburn was confident he could spot a tail with little difficulty.

There were twenty-five to thirty people in the lobby, browsing the stalls, chatting in groups and taking photos. Coburn stopped beside a kiosk, picked up a catalogue and pretended to read it while he assessed the crowd and placed each person into one of three categories—regulars, newbies and misfits.

Coburn tagged two-thirds of them as regulars. They wore purple wristbands, knew their way around and were only there for the games. They quickly dodged around everyone else in the lobby and vanished into the arena.

The second lot, the newbies, were the direct opposite. They were keen to see everything and took their time to browse each stall before moving on. Coburn put seven in that category.

It was the final group, the misfits, that Coburn was most interested in. They looked out of place. He spotted three of them and memorised their faces. The first was a middle-aged man wearing a shirt and tie, and carrying a briefcase. A salesman, for sure. He approached a door marked Staff, pressed a button and waited to be admitted. Next was a beefed up gym addict. Like Coburn, he was five foot ten or eleven, but that's where the similarity ended. The guy was solid muscle from the neck down, probably interviewing for a job as a bouncer. He exchanged a handshake with a MegaTron Sentinel, then they both walked into the main arena.

The final candidate wore typical gamer attire. Grey hoody, ripped jeans and black trainers. Older than most of the other gamers, he looked pale and undernourished. A purple wristband confirmed him as a club member. Despite that, he appeared jittery and uncomfortable. He wedged himself between two stalls and began thumbing the screen on his phone, his eyes darting left and right every few seconds. If it was Meerkat, he was probably composing a message to Webb.

Coburn scanned the crowd again, checking for newcomers. There were five. The first three had purple wristbands and quickly disappeared through the double doors as they elbowed each other over who would pay for the drinks later. Coburn tagged the remaining two as trouble. Wearing identical bottle green jackets over matching shirts and black ties, the two men craned their necks as they searched the lobby. They didn't look like police, which left private security. They might have nothing to do with Meerkat, but Coburn didn't believe in coincidences. If they were after Meerkat, then that meant trouble for Webb as well.

Coburn manoeuvred his way closer. The taller man said something to the shorter bearded one, who then took out his phone and consulted a photograph. Coburn glanced at the screen and saw a head shot of Meerkat standing at a blank white wall. It was a typical employee identification photo. Coburn moved back across the lobby and paused at a stall from where he could see both Meerkat and the two men that were after him.

Meerkat hadn't moved from his hiding place, tucked between two stalls selling shirts and hats. He unscrewed the cap from a bottle of Coke, took a few sips, then replaced the top. Half way to his pocket, he opened the bottle again and drank some more. When the phone in his hand lit up, the bottle slid from his grip, bounced on the floor, and rolled under a stall. He tapped the screen and read the message, then pushed through the doors into the gaming arena.

The two green jackets had split up and were moving through the crowd, searching for their target. They regrouped at the double doors, exchanged a few words, then proceeded through. Coburn followed close behind. The two men had paused on the top step.

"We'll never find him in this crowd," said the bearded one.

"You take the left, I'll go right. Meet me at the rear wall in five minutes," said the taller man.

As they descended the steps and merged into the crowd, Coburn took a direct route to the BattleFront area. He needed to complete the deal before the green jackets found Meerkat. After that, they could do whatever they wanted with him. Coburn didn't care.

For the first time since leaving London, Webb was alone and free. Coburn had totally ignored him on the flight over, but since they'd arrived in the city, the guy had turned into a wanna-be secret agent and a total control freak. Webb had no intention of waiting anywhere. While he had never actually met Meerkat in person, he had corresponded with him online over the previous six months on gamer and hacker forums. Meerkat was cautious by nature, and the two of them had planned the exchange meticulously. In Webb's opinion, Coburn was just being paranoid.

Webb continued towards the Battlefront section. As he squeezed through excited spectators, their passion and intensity seeped into his bones and increased the temptation to join in. He kept going, knowing he could enjoy himself once he completed the deal with Meerkat. Half way across, Webb's phone buzzed. It was a message from Meerkat to meet at console BF714 in three minutes. Webb replied with a thumbs-up. He wouldn't let Coburn destroy the opportunity of a lifetime. He would get the device from Meerkat, test the access codes, and close the deal himself.

The BattleFront compound was a hive of activity. Access was through an open archway ringed with pulsing red and white lights. Through the entrance, Webb could see seven screens, each occupied by two gamers perched on high stools. Webb squeezed his backpack and made sure he had the equipment necessary to test the codes. It was then he remembered the cash for the transaction. He didn't have it. Savik had given it to Coburn.

Webb sagged against the arch, ran his hands through his hair, and tugged at it with frustration. As much as he wanted to complete the deal alone, he needed the money. He clicked into his contacts and scowled at Coburn's number. Indecision bounced around his brain, screaming at him to find Meerkat. He tapped the number, but instantly regretted it. He began pacing, short erratic steps, as he squinted into the flashing darkness, expecting Coburn's surly face to materialise.

After twelve paces, the ringing stopped. Webb's finger hovered over the redial button, twitching anxiously. Three minutes had already passed since Meerkat's message. Webb was late.

The phone in Webb's hand jumped. It was another message from Meerkat. 'Where R U—I'm leaving in 5'. He was getting jittery.

To hell with Coburn, decided Webb. The priority was the access codes. Without them, Savik's plan would get no further and Webb's dreams for Karnage would be over. As he walked through the arch, the music changed to the Star Wars theme. Above each screen was a plaque showing a console number, running from 701 to 707. BF714 would be in the next row. As Webb pocketed his phone, a hand seized him from behind and spun him around.

"I told you to wait," hissed Coburn.

Webb wrestled free of Coburn's grip and turned to face him. "Meerkat's about to leave. He got spooked when I didn't show."

"Where is he now?"

"Further back, console 714."

Webb held a hand out. "I need the cash."

"Then what?" Coburn kept looking back through the arch into the main arena.

Webb shifted impatiently. "You know the plan. It hasn't changed. I test the codes, give him the money, then we fly home."

Coburn didn't respond, just stood watching people come and go through the arch.

Webb tried again. "We're out of time. Did you hear anything I just said?"

"Rat Man was followed by two guys in security uniforms," said Coburn.

Webb tilted his head in disbelief.

Coburn held up his phone, displaying a photograph of the two men from the lobby. "In the next sixty seconds, one of these guys will march in here and search for this guy." He swiped to the next image. "Before he reaches number fourteen, you need to get Meerkat out of here."

Webb couldn't help but stare at the phone. It was the first time he'd seen Meerkat. Webb had expected someone his own age, but the man in the photo looked twenty years older, his face pale and angular under several days of patchy grey stubble.

At that moment, one of the green jackets ducked under the arch.

"Go, now!" ordered Coburn.

"I need the money," said Webb.

"Get Meerkat away from here, then phone me," said Coburn between gritted teeth.

Webb glared at Coburn. "Without the cash, he'll walk."

Despite his scepticism, Webb found it hard to ignore the green bomber jacket. The guy was methodically moving through the busy enclosure, taking more interest in the people than in the games. Occasionally, he paused and glanced at a photograph on his phone.

Coburn took an envelope from his inside pocket and handed it to Webb. "Here's half. Now go."

Webb wondered how Coburn conveniently had exactly half the agreed amount in an envelope. It wasn't ideal, but if Webb spent any more time arguing, it would be too late. He snapped the envelope from Coburn and took off.

———•———

Webb hurried to the second row. Seven X-Wing flight simulators stood end to end. They were low profile enclosed units, equipped with recliner seats and noise cancelling headsets. All of them were occupied, their pilots twisting and turning as they engaged in fierce battles with enemy ships, oblivious to the outside world. Clusters of spectators stood watching the screens, eagerly waiting for their turn. Webb couldn't see numbers over any of them, but he noticed the occupant of the last simulator peering out, looking up and down the aisle. As Webb drew nearer, he recognised the guy's face from Coburn's photograph.

"Meerkat?"

The pilot glanced up at him suspiciously but said nothing. BF714 was etched in gold over the cockpit.

"I'm Spider," said Webb, revealing his gaming handle. He leaned closer to the simulator. "We need to get out of here. You were followed!"

Meerkat lifted himself out of the seat, his thin frame looming over Webb. A grey hood cast a shadow over his face, but couldn't hide the gauntness of his features.

"In the darkest dungeon?" said Meerkat. His voice was low and difficult to hear through the blasts and explosions all around them.

"What?" Webb was confused.

"How do I know who you are?" said Meerkat, jabbing an index finger.

A switch flipped in Webb's head and he remembered they'd agreed on a pass phrase, but his mind went blank, refusing to retrieve the information from his memory. Even though Coburn had shown Webb a photograph of Meerkat, Webb was still shocked by the man standing in front of him. His appearance was all wrong, nothing like the image Webb had formed in his mind during their online conversations.

Two girls who'd been watching them moved closer. "You finished here?" said one of them, pointing at the simulator.

Meerkat nodded and stepped aside. "Well, you got an answer for me?" he growled at Webb.

The harder Webb tried to remember the pass phrase, the more his brain refused to cooperate.

Meerkat pulled a phone from a pouch on his belt and consulted the screen, checking that Spider's location on the MegaTron app matched where Webb was actually standing. "Last chance Spider. In the darkest dungeon."

Suddenly, the word 'dungeon' sparked a trigger in Webb's brain. He blurted out the answer. "We spawn the savage beast." He stared open-mouthed at Meerkat, waiting and hoping.

"You're late! Where's my money?"

Webb wiped his sweaty hands on his trousers. "Didn't you hear what I said? You were followed. Two blokes in green jackets and shirts."

Meerkat frowned. "No one else knows about this." He prodded Webb in the ribs. "Who did you tell … "

Meerkat stopped mid-sentence, distracted by something behind him. His face turned from recognition to fear. Webb twisted around. The green jacket was gradually making his way down the aisle.

Webb turned back to Meerkat. "You know him, don't you?"

Coburn appeared alongside them. "Of course he does."

Meerkat's expression confirmed it.

Coburn stepped in front of them, shielding Meerkat from the guard's view. "Get going and watch out for that guy's partner."

"Where's my money?" demanded Meerkat.

"I have it," said Webb, "but first I need to see the merchandise."

The guard had stopped a short distance away. He was holding a phone to his ear and was watching the three of them.

"Go, I'll deal with him," said Coburn.

Meerkat nodded. "I know a place."

Webb followed Meerkat, resisting the temptation to look back. They left the BattleFront compound and half walked, half ran, towards the far side of the building. Meerkat surprised Webb with his speed and agility as they ducked through a warren of dark turns. As they rounded a bend, Meerkat jarred to a stop, stepped between two vending machines and yanked Webb in front of him. The second security guard from Coburn's photograph flew past, a phone pressed to his ear.

"Nearly there," said Meerkat as he pushed Webb aside, rounded a corner and stopped outside a row of VR booths. Taking his MegaTron card, he jammed into a card reader. When the door slid open, he stepped inside and hauled Webb after him. Meerkat tapped a sequence of numbers on a keypad beside the door. It beeped three times and flashed red. Meerkat tried again, forcing himself to slow down. The door closed and locked. Although Webb was relieved to have escaped the guards, he felt trapped. Instead of leading them to freedom, Meerkat had locked them in a dead end.

Chapter 4

Meerkat sagged against the chrome panels inside the virtual reality booth. Gripping his head with both hands, he clamped his eyes shut. His lips formed shapes, but no sounds emerged. Across the room, Webb's heart was pounding and his head swam as a headache crept along his temples.

Webb dropped to his hunkers and waited for the dizziness to clear. "Who were those guys? Why are they after you?"

Meerkat's head bobbed left, then right, his brow deeply furrowed.

Webb studied him. It looked like Meerkat was concentrating, working out something. Webb stood up and inched a little closer. "Do they know about me?"

Static erupted from the furthest corner of the booth. It was dark inside and much quieter, as if sound proofed. As Webb's eyes adjusted, he discovered it was the same size as his single bedroom back home. The layout resembled the cockpit of a spaceship. A large conical screen beyond the two pilot seats reminded him of the Millenium Falcon from Star Wars. A deep red glow illuminated the pilot's instrument panel and the VR headsets hanging from the low ceiling. Beeps and flashes called for attention from small screens imbedded in the console.

One screen in the centre caught Webb's attention. It was showing a live video feed from outside the booth, switching to various parts of the arena every five seconds. He watched closely, hoping to see the two men who were looking for them. The image flickered, and the view changed. He glimpsed Coburn walking towards the camera before two MegaTron Sentinels blocked his view. The first jabbed a fist at Coburn, then the second swung a baton, catching Coburn in the ribs. The video switched to another part of the arena before Webb could see any more.

Webb staggered back in shock, then turned to Meerkat, gripped both sides of his hoody and shook him. "Snap out of it, man."

Meerkat's eyelids jerked open. He stared wide-eyed at Webb. "I have a plan, Spider dude." He prised Webb's hands away, hurried to the console and began tapping buttons. Abruptly, he swivelled around and pointed accusingly at Webb. "Who was that man you were speaking to?"

"His name is Coburn, he's got the rest of your cash." Webb had the words blurted out before he realised it.

"You were supposed to come alone. That was our agreement," said Meerkat. "What's that guy's story? Is he a gamer?"

Webb massaged his temples, trying to shake off the worsening headache. "The guy funding this project is paranoid, doesn't trust anyone with his money, so he sent Coburn as insurance."

Meerkat was quiet again, his eyes semi vacant, deliberating.

Webb threw his hands up. "It's no hassle, man. He came in handy back there, didn't he?"

"I don't like changes to my plans," said Meerkat. "I'm only dealing with you cause you're trusted on the forums. You know what I'm sayin'?"

"OK, so I should've warned you, but ... well ... I wasn't thrilled to have him tag along either," said Webb, jerking his thumb towards the door. "But business is business, right? We do what we gotta do. If this goes well, there could be more money in it for both of us."

"Don't mess with my head dude, this is my turf, my rules," said Meerkat.

"Hey, we're on the same side, but now we're stuck in here like fish in a barrel," said Webb, looking around the confined space.

"There's another way out," said Meerkat absentmindedly. "What about my money? That other guy has it?"

Webb felt the deal slipping away. Meerkat was going to abandon the whole thing. Webb pulled out the envelope Coburn had given him and opened it, letting Meerkat see the wad of notes inside. "There's ten grand there. That's exactly half of what we agreed. Coburn has the other ten. Once I verify the access codes, it's all yours."

Meerkat stared at the money, flicked his eyes to the exit door, then back to the scrolling video feed. Webb could almost hear the cogs turning in the guy's brain. Without warning, Meerkat stood up, snapped the envelope of cash from Webb's hand, folded it in half and shoved it inside his jeans pocket. Webb held his breath, watching and waiting, hoping he had made the right call. Meerkat lifted up his shirt to reveal a canvas pouch secured to a belt around his waist. From the centre pocket, he removed something the size and shape of a smart phone but without a screen. He balanced the dark rectangular unit on his palm and grinned.

"This little baby is the VerKoll Decryptor version 3-17."

Webb reached for it, but Meerkat closed his fingers around it. Turning over the device, he pressed his thumb on a small black button until an orange light began flashing in one corner. "It's also known as the DX3, or the DEX3 by the nerds in the production hub."

After a few seconds, the flashing light settled to a steady green. Only then did he offer it to Webb. "It may not look very impressive," said Meerkat. "But treat this baby with respect. One of these will grant you a clear path through the labyrinth of encrypted gateways that VerKoll claim is impenetrable, namely their Data Maze."

It was lighter than Webb expected, half the weight of his phone. On the back, the letters VK-DX3 were etched in silver beneath the VerKoll name and logo. Along one edge, a string of numbers in a tiny font was barely legible. Webb let out a sigh of relief. For the first time that day, he felt one step closer to his goal. With the DX3 in his possession, Savik and Karnage had the power to hold Anchor BioTech to ransom and lift the hacker group several rungs up the dark web ladder. But first, he had to test it. He slid off his backpack, extracted a tablet computer, and powered it up.

"There's a USB port at one end," said Meerkat. "It also supports Bluetooth and Wi-Fi, but you'd need the VerKoll DX app to use those."

Webb took a cable, plugged one end into the tablet and the other into the DX3.

"There's a file on it called Dex3017. Run it," said Meerkat.

Webb clicked the file. "It's asking for a password."

"With great power," started Meerkat.

"Comes great responsibility," finished Webb.

Meerkat nodded. "The second letter of each word is uppercase, no spaces between the words. Three wrong attempts and it deletes everything."

Webb carefully typed in the password and looked to Meerkat for confirmation before he clicked the 'enter' key, then waited while the program loaded. A green box appeared on the screen showing three strings of numbers, each containing ten digits.

Webb stiffened. "I only see three access codes. I thought we were getting five."

"What you see is one thirty digit code broken into three segments," said Meerkat.

"How do I see the other four?" snapped Webb.

"Relax dude, it's loaded with five codes. Each time you press the power button, it reveals a different one. After five, it cycles through the same codes again."

Webb nodded slowly. "I need to test one."

"We don't have time for that. It won't take those security grunts long to find us in here."

"If it was up to me, fine, but no way will Coburn hand over the rest of your cash until I complete a test."

"You know each code only has one life, right?" said Meerkat. "Once you use it, it's dead."

"I remember. But I'm willing to sacrifice one to be sure it works," said Webb.

Meerkat looked at his watch. "Five minutes max, then I'm outta here and I'm taking the DX3 with me."

Before Webb could respond, Meerkat spun the seat around to the console, planted his elbows on either side of the video screen and stared at the feed from the arena. Webb dragged his focus back to the mission. He needed an internet connection for his tablet. Since he didn't want to risk using the MegaTron Wi-Fi, his best alternative was his phone. Thankfully, it showed a strong signal. He perched the phone on his knee and enabled the personal hotspot, the option that allowed another device to access the internet through his phone. Back on the tablet, he typed in the address to a computer belonging to Anchor BioTech. Based in London, the multinational corporation specialised in medical implants and other less publicised technology for the government.

"This won't take long. Their so-called firewall is a joke," said Webb.

"No details please," said Meerkat. "Less is more in the world of pleading ignorance."

"What's happening outside? Any sign of Coburn?"

"If he's smart, he'll lie low and avoid the VerKoll security guards. There's four of them now."

Webb stopped typing and glared at Meerkat. "Those guys are from VerKoll? When were you going to share that piece of information?"

"Forget about them. Just focus on what you're doing. They probably couldn't hit a barn door with a bazooka."

"Are you saying they're armed?" Beads of sweat lined up on Webb's forehead and his heart started thumping again.

"Taser sticks and batons." Meerkat kept his eyes glued to the monitor. "Let's hope your bodyguard keeps them busy until we're done here."

Webb had serious doubts. Meerkat was treating everything like a game. The last thing Webb wanted was to be slung in a prison cell for stealing security software, but his options were limited. Continue according to the plan or bail out. Meerkat wouldn't let him leave with the Decryptor until he got the rest of his money. And Webb didn't fancy explaining to Coburn, or worse, to Savik, that he'd abandoned the deal because he got scared.

Meerkat swivelled around to face Webb, who was staring into space. "Your batteries low or something?"

"What?" said Webb.

"The clock's ticking, Spider dude, get to it," said Meerkat, pointing at the tablet balanced on Webb's lap. "Those guys may be dumb, but eventually they'll check the security cams and come looking for us."

In that moment, Webb realised VerKoll wouldn't just want Meerkat. Recovering their software was a priority, but they'd also want to know who wanted to buy it and why. He turned his attention back to the job in hand and tried to block out the panic building in his gut. The Anchor computer he had connected to was an old machine used for stock control in one of their basement storage rooms. It had escaped the usual software upgrades and was easy for him to hack into. From there, he navigated to a server in the Research and Development Department. It prompted him for an access code.

This was the moment of truth.

Assuming Meerkat had stolen the right codes, Webb was about to gain access to Anchor's MIG, their Medical Implant Governor. From there, he could interact with thousands of medical implants throughout the world; pace makers, defibrillators, spinal cord stimulators. Webb read the first five digits from the DX3 and typed them into the flashing box on the screen. He repeated the process in chunks of five until the full thirty digit code had been input.

Webb's finger hovered over the Login button, trembling. He trusted Meerkat, but nothing about the deal was going according to plan. What if it didn't work? Since the VerKoll guards had followed Meerkat, they knew exactly what he was selling. What if they'd known all along and the codes he had stolen were duds? Webb clicked the button. A small amber rotating circle appeared. It was processing, validating the access code.

He held his breath and fixed his eyes on the rotating disc, afraid to even blink. He'd never got past this step. Every member of Karnage had spent weeks, day and night, trying to hack into the Anchor server. Part of him expected to see the annoying 'invalid credentials' message yet again. Banishing that memory from his mind, he leaned in closer to the screen, willing it to give him access. He could feel Meerkat watching him, his nose making a strange whistling sound as he exhaled.

A harsh ringing shattered the tension. Webb jumped and sent his phone crashing to the floor. The connecting cable shot after it, disconnecting the phone from the tablet. Webb glared at the phone and the caller's name flashing back at him. Coburn. He turned his attention to the tablet.

The rotating amber circle was gone, replaced by a message that said 'No internet connection'. He reached for the phone, rejected the call, and slotted the cable back into the tablet. It had been without a connection for four seconds, possibly five. Webb held his breath and willed the program to resume where it had left off. He waited, but nothing changed on the screen. He groaned in frustration.

His phone rang again.

"Answer that blasted phone or turn it off. Just stop it ringing." Meerkat was standing again and clearly agitated.

Webb answered the call.

"Webb?" Coburn's voice battled through a wall of noise.

"What?"

"Where are you?" snapped Coburn.

Webb looked up at Meerkat. "Where exactly are we?"

Meerkat leaned over the phone. "Go to the rear wall. You'll see a row of ten VR booths." He glanced up at a panel over the door. "We're in number three."

"What's your status?" said Coburn.

Webb gritted his teeth. "We're testing it."

"Right. I'm on my way," said Coburn.

"Make sure you're not followed," growled Meerkat, but Coburn had ended the call before he had finished his sentence. Meerkat began pacing the floor, the soles of his trainers squeaking.

"Stop pacing. I can't concentrate," said Webb.

"If they follow him here, I'm bailing out."

"He knows what he's doing. Just sit down."

"And I'm taking those codes with me."

Webb stopped to look up. "I've already paid you half. Ten grand."

Meerkat's face was glistening with sweat, his eyes flicking erratically. "You don't understand," he said, way louder than expected. "Money isn't everything."

Webb placed the tablet on the floor and stood up. "What are you not telling me?"

Meerkat shrunk back, his lips quivering.

Webb shoved him against the wall, hard. "Spill it."

"VerKoll. It's not ... they're not a private company," said Meerkat.

Webb threw his arms in the air. "What does that even mean?"

"It's run, owned, by the military." Meerkat swallowed hard. "The Russian military."

The cogs in Webb's brain turned slowly, reluctant to translate the implications of Meerkat's words into reality. But his stomach had already reacted, tightening and rising into his chest. Then images flooded in. Innocents dragged from their beds in the middle of the night. Brutal interrogation scenes in remote Siberian prisons. Bodies tortured beyond recognition, discarded in open graves. Bile burned its way up his throat.

Webb backed away from Meerkat and took a fit of coughing, eventually spitting globs of mucus onto the floor. He pulled a bottle from his pack and sat down, his breathing shallow and heavy. In between sips of water, he used his sleeve to wipe sweat from his face.

He watched Meerkat, waiting for him to say something else. Not that anything could change the hell hole he'd dropped Webb into. But he wanted an explanation. A reason, even an apology. The gamer he'd known and trusted had evaporated in twenty turbulent minutes. As much as he hated to admit it, Coburn had been right. Webb should have been more cautious.

Meerkat said nothing, just looked down at his feet. Webb was on his own. With that thought, the panic returned, spreading from his chest to every extremity. Russian military. Even if he made it back to England, he'd wouldn't be safe. He'd always be looking over his shoulder.

Two deafening thumps rattled the door. The bottle fell from Webb's grip and crashed to the floor. Visions flooded his mind of being dragged from the booth by his ankles and tossed into the back of a secret service van, never to be seen again. His body froze to the chair, consumed by fear. On the floor, he watched water tumble from the bottle and form a pool. As the liquid found an escape route between the tiles, Webb's shoulders slumped in despair.

Chapter 5

"That's your bodyguard banging on the door," said Meerkat, standing over the monitor.

Jolted from his nightmare, Webb rushed over to the screen. Coburn's face filled the screen, but Webb's stomach dropped when an arm wrapped around Coburn's neck and jerked him backwards, lifting him off his feet. Two men stood over Coburn, both armed with batons. A third man, wearing a MegaTron shirt, approached the door to the booth and thumped it with his fist.

Webb dropped his head. "We're trapped. It's only a matter of time before they break in here."

Meerkat backed into the furthest corner, wrapped his arms around his head and groaned like a wounded animal.

Webb advanced on him. "You said there's another way out of here."

Meerkat stared at him vacantly.

"Where is it?" said Webb as he scanned each wall. "I don't see another door."

Meerkat's eyes locked on a panel behind Webb. He took a penknife from his pocket and stumbled across the cramped space, knocking Webb out of his way. Hunching down, he began undoing a column of screws. As each screw dropped to the floor, he moved to the next. When he'd undone the left side of the panel, he switched to the right. Webb was mesmerised by Meerkat's speed.

Something heavy pummelled the door. Webb returned to the video screen. There was a brawl going on outside. As multicoloured lights flashed over the chaotic group, Webb picked out Coburn and several guards, but also two gamers swinging punches at the guards. Coburn was using his wheel brace against two green jackets, both armed with batons. More purple shirts arrived and quickly subdued the gamers who had joined in, leaving Coburn on his own. Backing off a little, the guards quickly worked their way around Coburn, encircling him like a pack of wolves. Coburn spun, swinging the wheel brace at arm's length, but he was fighting a losing battle. As one coordinated unit, the circle closed in and smothered him with blows.

Webb felt sick watching from the safety of the booth. A torrent of emotions swept through him. Revulsion, guilt, fear. A part of him wanted to help Coburn, but it was too late. One guard was on the floor, cradling his jaw. Coburn lay slumped against a vending machine, his face covered in blood, his body limp. A cold sweat rippled down Webb's back as he looked away from the monitor.

Meerkat dropped the last screw to the floor, ripped off the chrome panel and cast it aside. He jammed the penknife in behind a thin sheet of board and tried to prise it from the wooden frame. It only separated a little. Webb couldn't see any nails holding it, just layers of some tacky gunge. Webb gripped the sides further up and together they prised the panel away. Cool air flooded in from outside. Through the gap, Webb could see a dirty brick wall and a narrow alley of some sort running behind the booth. Meerkat grabbed his hoody, shoved Webb aside, and stepped through the gap.

Webb reached out and gripped Meerkat's arm. "Hey, you leaving me here?"

"If those VerKoll guys catch me, I'm screwed. Hell, I'm probably screwed anyway. So yes, I'm leaving." Meerkat jerked free of Webb's grip and disappeared.

Behind Webb, the door cracked, then bulged. The entire booth shook from a second assault. The bottom of the door buckled, but the hinges and locks somehow held firm. Webb knew it wouldn't survive a third attack.

He stuffed the tablet and the Decryptor into his backpack and hurriedly pulled on his jacket. Then he half ran, half stumbled into the passageway. He searched for Meerkat up ahead but couldn't pick him out in the gloom. In the distance, lights burst, then died, like fireworks. The familiar sounds of the arena filtered down the corridor to Webb, lasers and explosions, shouts and cheers. Then he spotted a silhouette as it bobbed and weaved. It had to be Meerkat. Webb called after him but against the noise, his words fell away to nothing.

Unable to see the ground clearly, Webb shuffled forward, wary of cracking an ankle. Cables dropped along the walls like vines in a jungle, and every few steps he was forced to clamber over a wooden beam or a water pipe. Up ahead, the shadow of Meerkat rapidly disappeared. Webb bellowed after him, but it was a waste of energy.

Something crashed loudly behind Webb. He squinted into the blackness, but couldn't see a thing. It took a second before he realised the guards had broken into the booth. Reluctantly, he increased his pace, sliding his hands along the walls to steady himself. His shin smacked hard against a crossbeam and he toppled forwards, blinded by the pain. Frantically, he reached for something, anything, to stop his fall. As the raw concrete ripped the skin from his fingertips, his head bounced off a wooden joist and he collapsed in a heap. He rolled onto his back and prayed that he hadn't split his head open.

As he rubbed his forehead, a beam of light erupted above him. It played back and forth, searching. His heart thumped inside his ribcage and every impulse screamed at him to get up and run, but his muscles refused to move. He pressed into the floor and remained still. With any luck, the guards wouldn't notice him wedged between the timbers. As the light probed the shadows and the ache in his head from the fall subsided, he knew that hiding was a stupid decision, a waste of precious seconds. They knew how he had escaped from the booth and they would follow him into the passage.

The darkness returned, but for how long? Webb crawled forward, reminding himself to stay low. Light streamed over him again, probing. Then a voice shouted. He couldn't make out the words. He didn't need to. The torch light was bouncing erratically, its owner now in pursuit.

Webb stood up. With the extra illumination, he could see the obstacles and increase his pace, but each second seemed like an eternity and the end of the row never seemed to get any closer. As he staggered along, he couldn't stop himself from looking back, needing to check how close the guard was. It was a poor decision. Blinded by the beam, he missed a loop of cable, snagged his head through it and crashed to the concrete.

His heartbeat thumped in his eardrums, muffling every other sound. Sweat seeped into his eyes, blurring his vision. He tried wiping it away, but the dust and grit on his sleeve made it even worse.

In that moment, Webb felt like giving up. The guards outnumbered him, and his chances of escaping were slim. Maybe if he surrendered the DX3, they'd let him go. What could they charge him with? Strictly speaking, he had stolen nothing. He could plead ignorance, say he understood the DX3 was Meerkat's own creation. But Meerkat's words flooded back to haunt Webb.

VerKoll isn't a private company.

Run by the military.

The Russian Military.

Images of labour camps filled Webb's thoughts. He couldn't survive prison. He'd rather split his skull in this forest of cables and timber than die in some salt mine in Siberia. He started forward again.

Meerkat had said there were ten booths in the row and they had been in number three. Webb tried to count how many he'd left behind, guessing at least four, possibly five. As he progressed, the sound of lasers and explosions grew louder. Voices and laughter drifted towards him. Gritting his teeth against the pain, he surged ahead, stumbling and colliding, until he reached the end of the passageway.

Pausing for a breath, he searched for Meerkat, but deep down, he knew he was alone. In some ways, he was better off without him. The guards had followed Meerkat to MegaTron. It was him they wanted. Then Coburn had intervened. If the guards caught Meerkat, they might leave and forget about Webb, but that was a big 'if', one Webb couldn't depend upon. The stakes were too high to gamble on luck. He needed to push on and use every ounce of his experience to find a way out of MegaTron.

Meerkat knew the arena like the back of his hand, every twist and turn, nook and cranny. It was his playground. Even if the guards had help from the Sentinels, they didn't think like Meerkat, like a gamer. He was probably long gone already, through some old forgotten exit in a disused part of the building. Webb was a gamer too, but it was his first time in MT Zurich. He rubbed the dust from his face and wiped himself down. Sure, he was on his own, but he wasn't out of the game yet.

He squeezed into a group of lads watching a tournament on the big screens and tried to get his bearings. It was even busier than when he'd first arrived, thronged with players and spectators. It was a perfect cover, but hard to make progress as nobody wanted to give up their spot. He tried another route and suddenly found himself in a small clearing. On the far side, a pair of MegaTron Sentinels appeared.

Webb turned and ran, ploughing through a group of spectators. He bounced off a pillar, tripped, and went sprawling.

A pair of powerful arms lifted him off the floor. Webb balled his hands into fists, ready to resist.

"Are you OK bud?" It wasn't a guard.

Webb steadied himself, uncurled his fingers. "Yeah, thanks mate, I just got distracted. Could you point me towards the lobby?"

"Sure, over that way, under the green exit sign."

Webb thanked the guy and hurried to the steps, avoiding open spaces and MegaTron staff when possible. As he reached the top step, the semidarkness was flooded with bright lights. Webb shielded his eyes and pushed at the double doors. They rattled but wouldn't open. He leaned into them, but they held firm. Through the clear glass, he saw MegaTron staff blocking anyone else from entering the arena.

Webb turned back around in time to see two VerKoll guards in the crowd, one pointing directly at him. He took a second to scan the walls on either side, searching for neon exit signs and an alternative escape route. The guards were getting closer, but were hindered by the crowd, who had reacted to the lights coming on and were streaming towards the double doors.

Away to his right, Webb noticed a cluster of people beneath a fire exit. A glimmer of hope penetrated the growing fear in his gut. He bounded down the steps and was quickly engulfed by a confused, restless throng looking for a way out. The music had stopped, replaced with shouting and growing hysteria. Webb caught snatches of panicked conversations, some suggesting a drugs raid, others a fire. A few parents with young kids tried to lift them to safety, holding them tight in their arms.

Webb considered joining the surge, hoping the doors would collapse under the volume of people, but there were several MegaTron Sentinels in the lobby. He decided to try for the fire exit instead.

The crowd moved in waves, heaving forward, then losing ground, advancing bit by bit. With careful timing, Webb took advantage of the backward movements, and made progress towards the far side of the building. Emerging from a knot of people, two young guys lying on the floor blocked Webb's path. One was moaning, reaching out an arm for help. The other lay motionless.

Webb tried to avoid stepping on them, but was shoved from behind and slammed against a drinks dispenser. He lost his balance, toppled sideways, and slid to the floor between two consoles. Just in time, he dragged his legs under him before they got trampled on. Webb sat there in a daze, watching people milling by, aimless and chaotic.

The two guys on the floor resembled discarded mannequins from a movie, their bodies askew and faces bloody. After escaping from the booth, Webb's fear had gifted him an adrenaline shot, but now he was running on empty. He was injured, traumatised and exhausted. If the guards appeared in that instant, he didn't have the willpower to run. That realisation churned around his stomach, then spread to his chest. He felt like vomiting, but that would signal the end, the ultimate surrender. If he allowed his body to crumble, his last grains of resistance would dissolve too.

He tried to focus on the positives. First, he had the DX3. Second, Coburn still had the other half of the money, so Savik was ten grand up on the deal. Webb manoeuvred onto his hunkers and let the energy of the melee wash over him. It reminded him of a zombie game and the frenzied attempts of the players to avoid increasing hordes of the undead. Webb thrived in those games, his quick reactions always keeping him one step ahead of the other players. If this were a game, he'd gear up and fight his way out.

All around him, bags and clothes lay abandoned on the floor. Peeling off his denim jacket, he pulled on a brown fleece and jammed a navy baseball cap down firmly on his head. A change of appearance might improve his chances of avoiding the guards. He spotted a half bottle of Coke and downed the contents, grateful for the cool liquid on his dusty throat and the expected caffeine hit. Then he stood up, took a deep breath and dived back into the hysterical mob, determined to escape.

Pressing forward, Webb shoved and dragged less determined members out of his way. Finally, he glimpsed the fire exit. A pair of doors had opened onto an alleyway. The closer he got, the tighter the sea of bodies as they funnelled into the bottleneck. Webb was sure the VerKoll guards weren't far behind him. Worryingly, he'd hardly moved forward at all in a full minute, nobody willing to give way in the crush to freedom.

A voice yelled in his head, a sixth sense warning him of danger. He whipped around in time to see two green jackets within striking distance. Then the signs of recognition on the first guard's face.

Webb cursed himself for turning back, nullifying his attempt at disguising himself. The guard, a tall, beefy man, called to his companion as he forced his bulk through the crowd like an icebreaker. Strong, determined, and relentless.

Webb needed to do the same, but didn't have the same stature or the strength. "Bomb, there's a bomb," he screamed, "get out, quick, bomb."

Word spread like wildfire and the ocean of people moved as one, some dropping helplessly to the ground. Webb tripped over a trailing foot, collided with a pillar, and fell to the floor. His chances of escaping were diminishing by the second. He thought of the DX3. If they caught him with that, his story of innocence would be useless. But he wasn't prepared to just throw it away.

He crawled around the pillar, extracted the Decryptor from his backpack, and scanned for a hiding place. Two girls collapsed down beside him, victims of the desperate charge for the exit. He was running out of time. He crawled to the nearest game machine, popped open a service door on the side, and tucked the DX3 inside. Once he'd closed it again, he snapped photos of the console as a reminder to himself. Then he stepped over the moaning bodies and rejoined the throng trying to escape.

If he could just reach the emergency exit, his odds of escape would increase tenfold. More bodies pushed up behind him, driving him forward. He seized the coat of a giant in front of him, knowing he'd be swept underfoot otherwise.

The surge stopped as suddenly as it began and Webb was crushed in the pileup, his arms pinned to his sides. The guy in front of him half turned and caught Webb on the forehead with his elbow.

As Webb's vision blurred and pain seared through his skull, the noise receded into a dull murmur. Knowing he was about to lose consciousness, he tried to fight it, to focus on the alleyway only a few metres away, but his legs lost their power and folded under him. As he slid down, he felt something grip the collar of his fleece.

"You're mine," were the last words Webb heard before he drifted into oblivion.

Chapter 6

The Eaux-Vives quartier of Geneva was quiet at 6 am. Only the bakers started working that early, firing up their ovens around five o'clock, so the fresh bread and pastries would be ready for the locals on their way to work, and the tourists setting out for a day of sightseeing.

Rogue liked the early hours. The air was fresh, having cleansed itself of the fumes from the city's traffic during the night. Unfortunately, the hours of darkness didn't do the same for her. Dreams and nightmares interrupted her sleep, and she rarely woke up feeling refreshed. Early morning runs were her cleanser, her rejuvenator. She jogged slowly at first, winding along the narrow paths of Parc la Grange. The paving was damp with dew and a little slippery in places. Exiting the park onto Quai Gustave-Ador, she followed the promenade along the East shore of Lake Geneva and let the crisp breeze wash away the remains of her restless night.

Agnetha was still asleep. Rogue had looked into her niece's bedroom before sneaking out of the apartment. Agnetha had thrown off her bedclothes during the night and lay askew with her arms wrapped around her head, her blonde hair covering her face like a net curtain. The girl—correction, young woman—was a constant reminder of her mother. Tasha had often slept in the same position, like a mime artist frozen in the middle of a performance.

Tasha's bubbly smile flashed into Rogue's mind. Then, just like in Rogue's nightmares, Tasha's eyes filled with dread and overflowed, staining her cheeks with rivers of black. Clenching her fists, Rogue shook her head and stopped the reel before the bullet hole formed on Tasha's forehead. Agnetha's resemblance to Tasha was joy and pain, all at once. Rogue had hoped her nightmares would stop once Tasha's killer, Viktor Kaznov, was dead. He'd haunted Rogue for six long years, always staying out of her reach and always a threat to Agnetha's safety. Three years and four months had passed since the shootout in London, since Rogue had shot him dead, but her nights were still haunted with accusations and guilt.

Rogue quickened her pace as she approached a large sports centre. Her calf muscles felt tight, not surprising considering all the walking she and Agnetha had done the previous afternoon, wandering through boutiques and shoe shops. Rogue hated shopping, but spending time with Agnetha was heaven compared to the daily grind of her security business. She stopped at the 5km mark and purchased a bottle of flavoured water from the vending machine outside the yacht club. As she savoured the tangy lemon, she wandered over to the jetty.

Gazing out over the lake, she marvelled at the view, a welcome contrast to the stifling streets of London. As she leaned on the railings, Rogue sighed and considered for the hundredth time whether she could leave her old life behind and start afresh. Possibly in another few years, she told herself. Her agency wasn't thriving, but if she could secure a few more contracts with MI5, she would have enough money saved to provide for herself and Agnetha.

As she sipped from the plastic bottle, a rainbow formed across the lake. Agnetha loved rainbows and always considered them good omens. Whenever one appeared, she made a wish into her palm, then blew it into the sky. Rogue refused to believe in omens. She'd witnessed too many operatives panic when they lost a lucky charm, believing their missions were doomed to fail.

After draining the last drops of water, Rogue tossed the empty bottle in a waste bin and started back. The holiday in Geneva was a welcome break from her work, an opportunity to reassess and plan her future. Agnetha had finished her second-level schooling, and they had another week together before she started at her new college. After that, Rogue planned to drive further up the lake and spend a few days on her own.

Before she knew it, she was passing the Parc la Grange again. Her stomach rumbled, reminding her to pick up some provisions for their breakfast. As she ran along the side streets towards the apartment, her watch beeped twice, signalling that she'd completed ten kilometres. She slowed to a gentle jog, letting her body cool down and her heart rate return to normal.

She stopped off at Pfister's Deli and collected some fresh baguettes, a platter of Swiss cheese and some Westphalian smoked ham. At the checkout, the cashier was unpacking a wooden box of strawberries. The sweet red fruit reminded Rogue of the weekend she'd spent in Florence with Tasha and Agnetha. They'd stopped at an open market and bought strawberries in wafer cones, topped with fresh cream. Agnetha, only six years old, had never tasted the fruit before and declared it her 'favourite food for ever-ever'. Rogue added a punnet to the other items and paid for them.

A few minutes later, she stepped through the open doorway of their apartment building and climbed the stairs to the two-bed they had rented. She planned to have a shower, then wake Agnetha. After breakfast, they'd take a cruise up the lake to Yvoire.

As she left the stairwell, Rogue reached into her pocket for the key and swung left to her apartment. Instantly, she noticed the lock had been ruptured. Spikes of painted timber protruded from the frame like daggers. Fear coiled itself around Rogue, crippling her reactions. All she could think of was Agnetha. The wail of a police siren from the street jolted Rogue back into action. She burst through the door, calling out to her niece.

Every instinct told Rogue to be cautious, that the intruders might still be in the apartment, but she had to find Agnetha. She dropped the groceries and tore through the short hallway, her eyes seeking the bedroom door on the opposite side of the living room. Her soles slid and crunched on the tiles, her running shoes failing to get a grip. She grabbed for a wooden shelf and found her balance. Yellow and red shards littered the floor, broken pieces of the wine glasses they'd used the previous evening. As she rushed across the living room, her peripheral vision scanned for threats. A wooden stool was lying on the floor, one leg askew, broken. Her eyes were drawn to the knife rack on the counter. One slot was empty.

The chrome handle on the bedroom door was askew, the screws ripped from the timber. Bloody hand prints smeared the woodwork and a pool of dark red oozed under the door onto the cream tiles. Rogue's chest tightened, squeezing the air from her lungs. As the blood crawled towards her, she knew that whoever it belonged to was beyond help. Rogue went to push the door open, then stopped, almost afraid to go inside, terrified of what she'd see. She pressed one hand to the wall as her legs threatened to buckle beneath her and prayed that the blood didn't belong to Agnetha.

Seconds passed in a blur until Rogue heaved, her lungs demanding oxygen. She'd hadn't realised that she'd been holding her breath. Without thinking, she kicked the bedroom door open, slamming it back against the wall. Inside, the flower patterned lino was smothered with blood. At the foot of the bed lay a body. His hair was short and dark, with a bald patch in the centre. Rogue exhaled a sigh of relief.

Holding onto the slim chance that Agnetha was hiding somewhere, Rogue tore through the apartment, calling her name. She whipped open every cupboard and wardrobe door and checked behind every piece of furniture. Apart from the man lying dead on the floor, the apartment was empty. Careful to avoid getting blood on her soles, Rogue returned to the bedroom and tried to piece together the sequence of events.

There were clear signs of a struggle. The reading lamp was lying on the bed, the shade askew. The bulb was gone, pieces of opaque white scattered across the bed and the floor. One diamond shaped fragment was stained with blood. Water from an overturned glass on the dressing table had soaked makeup and jewellery as it seeped towards the edge. The clothes Agnetha had worn the previous day had been knocked off the chair and lay in a crumpled heap on the floor. Her red backpack lay open in the corner. Inside the flap, Rogue could see Agnetha's purse and the new tan coloured handbag she had bought at the local market.

Rogue stabbed the screen on her phone and rang Agnetha's number, hoping her niece had fled the apartment during the break-in. Muffled ringing came from somewhere in the bedroom. Rogue followed it and found the phone nestled under a pillow. Frustrated, she cancelled the call, sank onto the bed and scrolled through the activity on Agnetha's social media apps. The most recent entries were from the previous evening with her friends. It was all lighthearted chat, nothing to suggest she might be in any kind of trouble.

Whoever had been in the apartment hadn't taken jewellery or money, which ruled out a robbery. They'd lost one man, which meant they'd started with at least two, maybe more. It could be human trafficking, but why now? Agnetha had lived in Geneva for the past few years and the city was full of young women. There were far easier places to abduct someone that didn't require breaking into an apartment in broad daylight.

Rogue turned her attention to the corpse. The missing kitchen knife protruded from a deep wound on the side of his neck. The man wore all black, including the balaclava that lay discarded beside him. Bloody footprints surrounded the body, some bearing the wide thread of a boot, others a narrower pattern from a shoe. Mixed amongst them, Rogue found the impression of a smaller foot, which she guessed was Agnetha's pink runners. There was no sign of them anywhere in the room.

Rogue jumped as Agnetha's phone burst to life on the bed beside her. She snatched it up and answered.

"Yes."

"Rachel Olsson Garde." A deep, raspy voice. Male.

"Where's Agnetha," snapped Rogue.

"She is safe ... for now."

Rogue leapt off the bed. "If you harm her ... "

"You are not in a position to threaten me," he said, raising his voice.

Rogue held her breath for a count of three, then exhaled silently. When she spoke, the words came out much quieter than she had intended. "I want to speak to Agnetha."

"So, first we talk business." He had a European accent, possibly Hungarian.

"What business?" Rogue ran to her own room, found her travel bag, and tipped the contents onto the bed.

"I have a job. Complete this, and I let your adopted niece go free."

His words stung Rogue. How did he know Agnetha wasn't a blood relative? Over the years, she had got used to being called Aunt Rachel. She had become part of Tasha and Agnetha's mini family. "You could have just hired me like anyone else."

"Of course, but my contacts, they say you need motivation, the extra incentive."

Rogue placed the phone on the table and switched on the speaker so she had both hands free. She selected a cable from the items on the bed and used it to connect Agnetha's Samsung to her own phone. Then she started a tracking program and watched as it traced the source of the call. It would need at least two minutes, but probably more. "These contacts. What else did they tell you?"

"That you worked for the British MI5. That you would agree to my orders, but then you will ignore them and try to find me."

"Sounds about right. And yet here we are!"

"Tasha Ryll, she is dead because of you. Maybe this time can be different. You can learn from your mistake, yes?"

Rogue's gut twisted and tightened as the air was sucked from her lungs. Dropping to the bed, she dug her fingernails deep into her palms and steadied her voice. "You know nothing about Tasha. Or me."

"I know this much. Tasha, she is dead because of you. Her daughter, she has no mother because of you. So, this time, will you be selfish once more and let Agnetha die also?"

Rogue grabbed a vase of flowers from the windowsill and launched it across the room. It disintegrated against the wall, showering her dressing table in glass and rose petals. Who the hell was this guy? How did he know about Tasha? Names and faces spilled through Rogue's mind. It was a waste of energy. He could be one of dozens.

"So, your famous Rogue temper. You will control that if you wish to see the pretty Agnetha again," he said.

Rogue stared at the phones on her bed, urging the tracker to speed up. Thirty-five seconds had passed and the red line was still bouncing off cell towers all over Europe. That meant he was using computer software to prevent his call from being traced. He was no amateur.

"Let me talk to Agnetha, I need to hear her voice." Rogue closed her eyes and strained her ears for any background noise, any clue of the caller's whereabouts. They had abducted Agnetha some time in the previous hour, so she couldn't be too far away.

"This is my game. I make demands, not you."

His accent was from further south, Croatia or Serbia. Two names sprang to mind. One was in hiding, the other was dead, but had a family rooted in crime. Both had reasons to come after Rogue.

"How do I know she isn't already dead?"

"If you need proof, I can cut off a finger. You can hear her scream." The sound of heavy footsteps, boots, echoed across a rough concrete floor. "Bring the girl here," he bellowed. More echoes. A large indoor structure, like a garage or a warehouse.

Rogue jumped to her feet. "No, no, enough, don't hurt her."

"So. Now I speak, you listen. First, you drive to Zurich, Kleiner Technology Campus beside the A1 motorway. Arrive at twelve noon, park at Migrol petrol station. Do not be late."

"Then what?"

"I call you again with extra instructions."

Rogue thought of the bloody corpse lying on the bedroom floor. "I need more time. I don't have a car and I need to clean up the mess your men left behind."

"Be on time or I will shoot your niece and dump her body in some landfill. Arrive alone, no backup, understand?"

Two minutes and seven seconds had passed. The tracker had drawn a line through several cities in North America, then dropped to Mexico. It was pointless. "What's the job? What equipment will I need?" asked Rogue.

"You are wasting time Rachel Garde, such valuable time. Forget about tracing my phone call. Remind yourself whose life is at stake."

She heard a click, and the call ended. 'Connection Lost' appeared on the screen of her phone. Rogue pressed her forehead against the cold windowpane and squeezed her eyes shut as she struggled to process what was happening. Visions flooded her mind of Agnetha cowering in a cold, dark room at the mercy of some lunatic. Guilt burned its way up Rogue's throat. Why had she gone out running that morning, leaving Agnetha alone? She should have stayed in the apartment, or better still, not come to Geneva at all. She knew the dangers. Wasn't that why she rarely visited, to minimise the risks? What if they hurt Agnetha? Or worse.

She trudged into the bathroom, flicked on the cold tap and massaged water into her face, gentle at first, then harder, but the voices and accusations in her head just got louder. Every fibre of her being wanted to find Agnetha, but instead, she was being forced into some crazy mission. As Rogue towelled herself dry, she caught her reflection in the mirror. All she could see in the eyes that stared back was dread. She was responsible for whatever was happening to Agnetha in that exact moment, and the next and the next after that.

Two sharp beeps called her back to the bedroom. There was a message on Agnetha's phone. GPS coordinates for the Migrol service station on the outskirts of Zurich. The phone beeped a second time. Rogue stabbed at the screen and a photograph opened. It was Agnetha, dressed in the navy pyjamas with gold stars that she'd worn the previous few nights. Hunched up on a chair, Agnetha's ankles and hands were bound with rope, her blonde hair partly covering her face. Despite the poor light of her surroundings, Rogue could see dried blood under Agnetha's nostrils and below her mouth. Her lips were set in defiance, but Rogue recognised the fear in her eyes. Rogue dragged her focus away from Agnetha's face and scrutinised the rest of the image, searching for clues, but there was nothing. The room could be a garage or warehouse anywhere in the world.

Rogue sagged against the wall. She had absolutely nothing to go on, and it went against all her rules to blindly follow the instructions of some psycho kidnapper. As her mind spiralled back down into a pit of self-recrimination, she noticed the abandoned groceries strewn along the hallway. The bright red of the strawberries, Agnetha's 'favourite food for ever-ever', were enough to halt Rogue's slump into despair. She pushed herself up, left the bedroom, and began picking up the fallen fruit. It was time to make a plan and get Agnetha back.

Chapter 7

Rogue's mind ran through multiple threads, all of them vying for her attention but none of them getting enough to make any concrete decisions. Agnetha was her priority. She was the only reason Rogue had kept going since Tasha's death. Now Rogue needed to do everything in her power to find her. Only then could she plan revenge on the man who had so violently invaded their lives.

Rogue considered phoning her contacts and call in whatever favours were necessary, no matter what it cost her personally. But it was pointless with no leads, at least none solid enough to identify the man responsible, or the location where Agnetha was being held. With the right resources, she could trace the origin of the phone call or identify the dead body in the bedroom. But for that, she'd need to persuade her old boss in MI5 to lend her the Operations Team in Section D. Even if she somehow did that, it would take too much time.

Among all the unanswered questions, there was one scratching louder than the rest, demanding to be heard. Rogue picked up Agnetha's phone and opened the call history. The last call was from the kidnapper, labelled 'unknown'. In that moment, the nagging puzzle in her brain jumped clear. The phone had rung when Rogue was in the apartment. There were no missed calls before that. How had he known that she was in the apartment at that exact moment, that she had returned from her run?

There was only one explanation. The answer chilled its way up Rogue's spine. He had seen her enter the building, given her enough time to absorb the enormity of what had happened, and then made the call. Her apartment was being watched.

She spun around to face the living room windows. He was probably still out there, waiting for her reaction. She stepped up to the glass and scanned the pavement opposite the apartment block. It was getting busy with a steady flow of pedestrians going in each direction. She ignored the people going about their daily routine and instead scrutinised the few who were stationary. A man in a light blue suit stood smoking a cigar while he chatted with a coffee vendor. Two women with shopping bags were blocking progress while they selected vegetables outside a grocery store. A courier took a package from his bike and went into an estate agent. None of them looked in her direction. The only vehicles parked on that stretch were two delivery vans and a taxi unloading a young couple with a baby. Because of the trees that lined both sides of the road, only someone at street level would have a clear view of the entrance to her apartment building.

Rogue considered other angles. What if they weren't watching the entry point? What if they had a view directly into her apartment? Rogue scanned the upper levels of the block, checking each window and balcony for anything out of place. The second floor units were commercial, each filled with desks and filing cabinets. There was no activity in any of them yet. The third and top floors were residential—net curtains, kitchen tables and televisions. In some of them, the occupants were getting dressed or having breakfast. The other apartments were obscured by curtains or blinds.

Rogue wondered where she herself would choose to monitor a target. Somewhere overlooking the apartment, with easy access and escape routes. Not inside the building, but outside on the roof. She inched closer to the window and lifted her gaze beyond the balconies of the top floor and over the parapet. It was a bright morning, and she had to squint against the sun. She panned left, but the only breaks in the skyline were chimneys and aerials. She switched back to the right, losing hope that whoever had been watching would still be there. Even if they were, they had the advantage of knowing where she was and would vanish before she picked them out.

She stopped. Was that a person's head above the parapet? It was hard to make out. The shape moved, became larger, taller. It looked like a figure had just stood up. Judging by the silhouette, it was a man. He raised himself to full height, his hands on either side of his head. He appeared to be holding something. His right arm extended forward, then his fingers touched his temple, like a salute. After a few seconds, he turned and disappeared from view. The cogs in her brain clicked into place. He had been watching her through a pair of binoculars and had exaggerated the salute for her benefit, mocking her.

She sprinted from the apartment and flew down the stairs, taking two and three steps at a time. As she burst out onto the street, she screamed at tourists gathered on the pavement, then plunged through them and vaulted the bonnet of a parked car. A taxi screeched to a stop, blaring its horn. A tour bus swerving to avoid her mounted the pavement. Rogue ignored them all.

When Rogue reached the opposite pavement, she realised there were several routes the man could take from the roof. She had to choose one, and fast. Most people would take the stairwell down into the building, but he might use the fire escape or cross the rooftops to the next block. If she were in his place, she'd have transport waiting in a nearby side street, ready for a quick escape in case the mission blew up and the police arrived.

From her apartment window, she'd seen an alley beside the grocery store that would lead to the rear of the block. Leaving the busy street, she sprinted along the alley, dodging dumpsters and cardboard boxes until she reached a left turn at the end. From there, the alley stretched for three hundred metres, then exited on to a side street. She looked up, searching for the fire escape. There were two, thirty metres apart. Both were deserted. She had gambled and now had to hope her decision paid off. Whoever she was up against was a professional. He had sent three men to her apartment and posted a lookout. Leaving the dead man behind as an acceptable loss showed that he was cold and methodical. In Rogue's mind, that meant he would complete his mission and not leave any loose ends. Even if she cooperated, he would kill both her and Agnetha. To have any chance of survival, she had to go on the offensive from the start.

Rogue proceeded cautiously along the alley, checking every door, listening for any movement. Damp smoke plumed from a large vent, carrying the taste of laundry detergent. Bulging black sacks and cardboard boxes slouched along the walls. The steel steps of a fire escape snaked their way down from the roof, with the last section folded up. She searched for a weapon and found a short length of steel poking out from under a trash can. It wouldn't stop a bullet, but it was better than nothing. Half way along the alley, she paused and scanned buildings for movement, but as the seconds passed, doubts picked away at her plan. The smart move was to cut her losses and focus on getting to Zurich by the deadline.

A short distance ahead, angry voices carried through an open door, followed by the sound of crashing pots and pans. As Rogue drew nearer, a man wearing a leather jacket and trousers hurried out, shouting and shaking his fist at someone inside. Rogue couldn't tell if he was the man from the roof, but her gut instinct urged her on. She ducked around a parked van and ran up the inside. When she emerged, he was walking away towards the street. Rogue had to engage him before he reached the other end, but she needed somewhere out of sight to interrogate him. Further along, she spotted a transport container. The steel doors gaped open, revealing stacks of folded chairs and tables.

As the man raised a hand to light a cigarette, Rogue saw the telltale bulge of a gun in his left armpit, which also told her he was right-handed. He walked with a swagger, confident he was in no danger. Observers would say he was well built, but Rogue noticed specifics. His shoulders were rounded and hunched forward, the result of too many hours pumping weights. His balance was slightly off and he favoured his left leg, possibly the result of an injury to his right knee. Rogue's fingers tightened around the steel bar. She wanted to smash his cocky skull with it. Agnetha's abduction could leave her scarred for life, mentally and physically. Fury swelled inside Rogue, but her heart needed Agnetha back safely. Rogue's priority had to be information, not retribution.

She slowed her pace a little, taking time to get her balance right. As she closed in, she prepared to ram the bar into his kidney area beneath his favoured right arm. She'd follow with a sharp kick to the back of his weaker leg, then swing the bar into his face. It didn't matter if she broke his nose, as long as he remained conscious and she could interrogate him.

Too focused on her plan, Rogue missed a flattened tin can on the ground. Her foot kicked one end and sent it skittering across the concrete. He spun around. Rogue reacted quickly and targeted his midriff. He dropped the cigarette, parried the blow, and followed with a sidekick to her chest. She deflected it, moved in close, and sunk her knee into his groin. He folded over, but caught her with a head butt. Pain ripped through Rogue's temple, destroying her vision and balance. Disoriented, she dropped the steel bar and staggered back, trying to get out of his reach. She had only seconds to stop him from pulling his gun. Every instinct screamed at her to attack, but her limbs refused to cooperate. Closing her eyes, she shut down the primal part of her brain designed to protect her and charged forward.

As his hand reached inside his jacket, Rogue stabbed two fingers at his eyes. Her stronger middle finger glanced off the side of his nose, but her other one found its target. He screamed and blinked furiously as his eyes filled with water. Rogue followed with a reverse punch to the side of his head, sending a shock wave through his ear canal. He dug in and propelled her back with both hands, his superior body strength launching her off her feet. Landing heavily, she rolled to avoid a follow up attack, but when she got to her feet, he was pointing a Sig pistol at her chest. At a distance of four metres, he couldn't miss. His lips curled into a snarl as his trigger finger tightened.

Rogue cursed herself. She'd done the hard work of finding him, then carelessly thrown away her advantage. Now he was pointing a Sig pistol in her face. She had nowhere to run and nothing to bargain with. She considered rushing him and catching him off guard, but the odds were stacked in his favour. Instead, she tried to predict his next move. The muscles in his face twitched as he fought to keep his damaged eye open. He glared angrily at her, but she could see his mind working, trying to figure out something.

"You can't shoot me, can you?" she gambled. "Your boss needs me."

He frowned but said nothing.

Rogue figured he'd pulled the gun on instinct. He wanted to kill her, the skinny little female who had bruised his body and his ego. But he had orders. Observe and report back, but do not engage. "Now what?" she said, taking a stride towards him. The odds had flipped in her favour.

"Stay back. I can't kill you, but I can still shoot you." He shifted his aim from her chest to her shoulder. "It will be much harder for you to operate with one arm, don't you think?"

Rogue stopped in her tracks.

He stepped back towards the street.

Desperate for information about Agnetha's whereabouts, Rogue needed to keep him in the alley and force him into making a mistake. If the distance between them increased, that option would evaporate.

"You're bluffing," she said, keeping pace with him. "You're under strict orders from your boss and, like a good little boy, you'll do exactly what he tells you. Isn't that right, little boy?"

He glared back at her. The knuckles of his gun hand went white as he fought the urge to pull the trigger. She'd hit a sore spot, and she knew it. This was her opportunity. He paused, clearly conflicted. Maintaining eye contact with him, she slowed her pace to a crawl. They were three metres apart when a door crashed open. A young woman reversed out of a hotel kitchen, pulling a cart of food waste. She was wearing headphones and was oblivious to their presence, the sound of rap music audible to both of them. The gunman's eyes flicked between Rogue and the woman. Rogue could almost see the options playing like a film reel across his face. Rogue closed the gap between them, forcing him to focus completely on her.

He switched to a two-handed grip. "That's far enough."

Rogue planted her feet wide, hands on her hips. She didn't want to involve an innocent bystander, but the information she needed about Agnetha's whereabouts was more important. "So, are you going to shoot her, too?"

His eyes flicked to the woman. She continued reversing towards them until she had cleared a pair of large rubbish skips either side of the doorway. Then she began a slow ninety-degree turn. As she completed her manoeuvre, Rogue came into her view. The woman jumped, put her hand to her chest, then smiled. Pinned to her white full length apron was a tag. Her name was Tayanah. Rogue returned her smile, hoping she would continue on down the alley to safety without seeing the gunman.

Instead, the woman pulled down her headphones, a look of concern on her face. "Are you OK?"

Rogue's smile hadn't convinced her. There was only one way Rogue could guarantee the woman's safety. Walk away. Back away and let the man leave. Once the woman was safe, Rogue could chase after him again. In that split second, she saw the change in the man's expression and knew that he had arrived at the same conclusion. Three quick strides brought him behind the Tayanah. He circled his left arm around her throat and yanked her slight frame back, dragging her feet along the ground. The muzzle of the Sig under her chin forced her head upwards.

Rogue watched the inevitable sequence run its course. First the shock in the woman's eyes and her futile attempts to prise his arm from her throat. Then she opened her mouth to scream, but he was squeezing so tight that no sound came out. She gasped for air, her eyes bulging with terror.

"Your move," he said to Rogue. "Back off or I kill her."

Rogue knew he would do it. She'd seen that killer look before, and it had always ended badly. Injury to an innocent was sometimes unavoidable, but cold-blooded murder was not acceptable. She nodded and backed away.

In one flowing move, he slid the barrel of the gun down along the woman's neck to her shoulder. Then he pulled the trigger. The bullet seared through muscle and bone, then burst out through her white apron in a spume of red mist.

Chapter 8

The gunman released Tayanah and let her fall to the ground. She landed in a crumpled heap, her chest heaving, every muscle in her slim frame trembling. Rogue watched as he pointed the gun at Tayanah's forehead.

"Enough," demanded Rogue. She held her palms up and stepped away. "Let her be."

He switched his aim to Rogue, backed off a few paces, then turned and ran. Rogue started after him, then stopped dead. She desperately wanted to catch him, but she was conflicted. Tayanah had rolled onto her back, blood streaming from her wound. She was coughing, each convulsion sending shock waves through her shoulder. She had been in the wrong place at the wrong time. It wasn't the first time Rogue's presence had been the trigger for an innocent's misfortune. Rogue watched as the gunman reached the end of the lane, rounded the corner, and disappeared. She let him go.

Two men ran out through the kitchen door, one wearing a chef's hat, the other a porter's uniform. They saw Tayanah on the ground, but kept their distance.

"It's OK, he's gone," said Rogue. She crouched down beside Tayanah. Music still flowed from the headphones hanging limply around her neck. Rogue took them off and tossed them aside. If Rogue hadn't challenged the gunman, the woman would still be happily going about her work. Rogue wouldn't let her die in a dirty back alley.

The two men moved closer, wide eyed and speechless. The chef was holding a kitchen towel in one hand. Rogue reached up and snatched it from him. She folded the towel in four, then wedged it underneath Tayanah's bullet wound. Tayanah stared up at Rogue, her face contorted in confusion and agony.

"You'll be OK, hang in there," said Rogue.

"What happened? Was she shot?" asked the chef.

"Place your hand here." Rogue pointed at the bullet's entry point. "And press down hard."

He pulled back, scared.

"If you don't, she will bleed out and die," Rogue shouted at him. "Do you want to save her or not?"

The porter hunkered down and gently placed his palm on the woman's bloody uniform. Rogue leaned on his hand, then grabbed his other one and pressed it on top of the first. Tayanah's back arched and tears streamed down the sides of her face. The porter eased off, not wanting to hurt her.

"Keep the pressure on, dammit, you need to stem the blood flow," said Rogue, leaning on his hands. "It's the only way to keep her alive."

He closed his eyes and nodded. "I can do it."

Rogue turned to the chef. "Phone for an ambulance." He nodded and ran back to the kitchen.

The wail of sirens echoed up the alley from the street. Rogue whipped around, expecting to see a police vehicle. None appeared, but she knew they were close. She stood up and retrieved the length of steel pipe she had dropped during the fight. It was time for her to leave. She couldn't risk being detained for questioning.

The chef returned, but kept his distance, his face ashen. "The ambulance, it's coming. Is she … "

"Her pulse is steady and the blood flow has slowed," said Rogue.

Several more kitchen staff emerged and circled around them. The porter looked up at Rogue as blood oozed between his fingers from Tayanah's wound. "Will she make it?"

Rogue could see the anguish on his face, but she couldn't answer that question. There were too many unknowns. He knew that too, but he needed hope. A small silver cross peeped out through an open button on his shirt. Rogue had noticed a matching one around Tayanah's neck.

"It's up to you … and God," said Rogue, the last word catching in her throat. She coughed. "Just keep the pressure on until the medics arrive."

Tyres screeched as an ambulance stopped at the entrance to the alley. Rogue slipped through the growing circle of onlookers. As she hurried away, she spotted a pile of old rags spilling from a plastic bag. She grabbed the cleanest looking one and began wiping Tayanah's bright red blood from her hands. Sunlight reflecting off something on the ground caught her attention. Lying next to the rags was a clear plastic wallet with a photograph visible through the cover. Something about it compelled her to look closer. As she bent lower, her stomach flipped. The face in the image was Agnetha's.

Rogue seized the wallet and slid out the photo. Agnetha was posing in front of a circular flower bed, an ice cream in one hand, her sunglasses in the other. In the background, Rogue recognised the flower clock from the Jardin Anglais. They'd visited the park earlier in the week. Rogue drew out the remaining two photographs. The first was a head and shoulders shot of Rogue as she and Agnetha waited for a tram. Rogue shivered. Someone had been following them for days. Maybe longer.

The last photo was a closeup of Agnetha, also captured at the tram stop. In it, she looked happier than Rogue had seen her in the ten years since her mother died. Agnetha had transformed into a woman and during the past two weeks, she'd enjoyed a reversal of roles where she'd been the tourist guide showing Rogue around the cafes and tourist spots in Geneva.

But now, Agnetha had been snatched from her new home, the one place she'd felt safe. Rogue had been crazy to think she could just forget her past and start a new life with Agnetha.

Attracted by the sirens, three teenagers came racing into the alley, one holding a camera, all of them eager to see what had happened. Rogue dropped to one knee and fiddled with the laces on her running shoes until they passed by, then stuffed the photos into her back pocket and ran in the opposite direction. As she emerged onto the street beside the grocery store, a police bike screeched to a stop. The officer dismounted and removed his helmet. Rogue went to step around him, but he blocked her path.

Looking her up and down, he narrowed his eyes and frowned. "What happened to you?"

Rogue followed his gaze and saw a long smear of blood and grit down her leg. "I tripped over a stupid dog. It came out of nowhere. Not that his owner cared, she just laughed."

The officer took a notebook from his shirt pocket. "I need your name and photo identification."

Before Rogue could provide a fake name and address, a microphone wielding reporter and a cameraman pushed between them, knocking the notebook from the officer's hand. He raced after them, grabbed the cameraman, and yelled at the reporter to stop. Rogue took advantage of the distraction and hurried away. Police cars had blocked the traffic at either end of the street and officers were questioning pedestrians before letting them through. As more sirens approached, people emerged from doorways, eager to see what had happened. Rogue quickly dodged through the line of cars and disappeared into her apartment block. She needed to gather her things and clear out quickly before the entire area was locked down.

Rogue sprinted up the stairs to her apartment. She'd left the door wide open. Anybody passing could have wandered inside, all the way to Agnetha's bedroom and the bloody corpse lying on the floor. She stepped inside, eased the door closed against the frame, and listened. It was quiet. After checking that each room was empty, she returned to examine the front door. The kidnappers had shattered the lock, rendering it useless. She realigned two broken pieces of the wooden frame as best she could and slid across the bolt on the inside. It wouldn't stand up to scrutiny from a passerby, but from a distance, it might go unnoticed.

She went to the kitchen and lifted a glass from the shelf over the sink. Filling it under the cold tap reminded her of the broken fragments in the hallway. Agnetha must have been in the kitchen when the kidnappers forced their way in. After throwing the wine glasses at them, she must have taken a knife from the rack and locked herself in the bedroom. Rogue smirked, then tensed. Agnetha was spirited, but her captors wouldn't tolerate that for long.

Rogue abandoned the full glass of water and typed Zurich into the map application on her phone. The fastest route was along the A1, but it would still take three hours and seven minutes. Her watch showed 8:37 am. That left her only sixteen minutes to vacate the apartment and find transport. If traffic was light and she pushed the speed limits, she could probably shave fifteen minutes off the journey once she wasn't pulled for speeding. Chasing the man in the alley had been reckless, squandering precious time that hadn't been hers to waste. She hurried to the bathroom and scrubbed the remaining blood from her hands. After cleaning dirt from the gash on her knee, she quickly applied a plaster from the first aid kit. As she towelled her face dry, she felt the beginnings of a bruise on her forehead. Luckily, he'd missed her eye.

Back in her bedroom, she stuffed a change of clothes into her travel bag. She could change from her running gear when she got to Zurich. In Agnetha's room, she selected a top and jumper from a drawer, grey ripped jeans from the wardrobe and a pair of trainers, all items she knew Agnetha would find comfortable. Bringing fresh clothes also boosted Rogue's own belief that she would rescue Agnetha and that they'd both survive the ordeal.

As she packed the travel bag, a framed photograph on the dressing table caught her eye. Tasha and Agnetha were huddled inside a photo booth, laughing uncontrollably. Agnetha was only six or seven years old in the photograph, but was already a mirror image of her mother. Rogue recognised Tasha's handwriting in one corner of the photo. "The best birthday yet Neta, Happy 7th. Love, Mum." Rogue smiled as she remembered Agnetha's early attempts to pronounce her own name. In the end, they'd settled for Neta. Rogue added the frame to Agnetha's bag, zipped it closed, and surveyed the room.

Time was running out fast, but she had one more job to do. Careful to avoid stepping in the blood pool, she leaned over the corpse and searched his pockets. She found a receipt for petrol dated two days earlier, a cafe loyalty card and some cash in a trouser pocket. A set of Volvo car keys, a Sig 9mm pistol, and a spare magazine in his jacket. No wallet and no phone. Nothing to identify him. She slid the gun and spare ammo into her backpack, then slung it over one shoulder. It was time to go.

There was no way of locking the front door from the outside, so Rogue took the only alternative, a fire escape that dropped between her apartment and the next one. There was a risk that someone would see her from the building opposite, but it was a chance she had to take. She opened the window and stepped out on the tiny balcony, then drew the curtains closed behind her and pulled the window tight against the frame. From there, she descended the steel steps and dropped the final few metres to the ground. Flashing red and blue lights filtered down the alley from the main street.

Rogue turned and headed in the opposite direction. Her next challenge was to find transport, and fast.

Rogue pushed open the glass door into an OrbitCar office she'd seen during her morning runs and was relieved that there were no other customers.

"Hi, can I help you?" said the barely twenty-something girl behind the counter.

"My account number is PL78147. I need something fast and high end." Rogue placed a passport on the counter under the name Miranda Baker.

The girl produced a wad of forms. "Why don't you fill out these at the table by the window while I see what we have available?"

Rogue didn't want to be remembered by the girl if the police questioned the local businesses about the shooting in the alley, but neither did she have time for long-winded procedures.

"You must be new, Allison," said Rogue, reading the girl's name badge.

"No, I've been here six months ... "

Rogue held up her hand. "I have an Orbit Platinum-78 account. That means I pay a premium for rapid service, with no forms and no questions."

Allison shook her head. "Oh, I don't know. I've never come across anything like that!"

Behind Allison was an office marked 'Manager'. Through the frosted window, Rogue saw the silhouette of a man holding a document of some sort. The door was partly open.

"Can I speak to the manager?" said Rogue loudly, hoping to catch his attention.

"Let me just call up your account. Seven, eight, one—what was the rest of your account number?"

"PL78147," repeated Rogue impatiently.

Allison frowned at her, then hit a sequence of keys and stared at the screen.

Rogue drummed her fingers on the counter as valuable seconds ticked by. She was about to abandon the rental idea and risk stealing a parked car when a man walked out of the manager's office and marched over to the counter.

"Miss Baker," he said, glancing at the passport open on the counter. "Are you being … " He quickly interpreted Rogue's expression and sensed her urgency. "I'm Joel Baumann, the manager. What do you need?"

"SUV or MPV, something high end and fast, whatever you have right now."

He walked to an open cabinet and scanned the rows of keys.

"I have a red BMW X5 Auto or a black Audi Q5 manual, both three litre."

"I'll take the Audi," said Rogue, relieved.

Baumann photocopied Rogue's passport, then placed it and two identical keys on the counter. "Anything else I can help you with?"

Rogue grabbed two bottles of water and a handful of protein bars from a small fridge on the counter. "Add these to my bill."

"They're on the house, Miss Baker. The Audi is parked out back. You can come through this way." He lifted the counter and led Rogue down the corridor and out to a small private car park.

Allison looked after them, her mouth gaping.

Chapter 9

At eight minutes past nine, Rogue had cleared the Geneva city limits and joined a steady stream of traffic headed north. She typed the coordinates for the Migrol service station into the SatNav. It calculated the distance and showed her estimated arrival time in Zurich to be 12:17 pm. Agnetha's kidnapper was due to call again at noon. Rogue moved to the fast lane and pushed down on the accelerator, determined to reach her destination on time.

Traffic on the A1 to Zurich was light. Rogue kept the needle ten kph over the one hundred kilometre speed limit, only slowing down when she approached major junctions where traffic police might be lurking. She'd have preferred a bike to the Audi, something like the Kawasaki Ninja she had back in London. Rogue did her best thinking with the wind roaring around her as she carved a path through the traffic, but the car gave her more flexibility for surveillance, storage and sleep.

Rogue pulled the plastic wallet from her back pocket that she'd found in the alley. Emptying the photos onto the passenger seat, she selected the one of Agnetha in the Jardin Anglais and propped it up on the dashboard. Agnetha had the biggest grin on her face, excited to be playing tourist guide for Rogue. It was ironic how many cities in the world Rogue had been to, yet hadn't really seen any of them, always on a mission. The trip to Geneva was a holiday, but also a trial run. During the three-week break, Rogue pretended she had retired from the business of espionage and gave her mind permission to explore some possibilities. It had been challenging, but by the end of the second week, a few ideas had surfaced. Then reality struck. Now it was clear that she could never really leave that world behind. As much as she dreamed of providing Agnetha with a tiny piece of what she'd lost when her mother died, it seemed that Rogue and Tasha's past would haunt them forever.

"I'm coming Neta baby, just hold on." She brought her fingertips to her lips and transferred a kiss to the photograph.

Rogue leaned on the pedal a little more and started to form a plan. First, she needed to clean up the mess she'd left behind in Geneva. She'd booked the apartment under an alias, but her and Agnetha's faces had been recorded daily on the street cams close by. She didn't want Agnetha to have a police record this early in her life, especially one linked to Rachel Olsson

Garde, ex MI5 assassin. Scrolling through the contacts on her phone, she selected her go-to man for supplies and services in Europe, Arnold Hunter. She hit the connect button on the Audi's steering wheel and waited.

Hunter was a cautious man who insisted on protocol and procedure. He understood emergencies required fast action, but believed that most of the time, a calm approach and organised planning were even more important. His methods had served him well in his nineteen years as a Major in the Royal Engineers. He reluctantly retired from the army in 2012 after being injured while disarming an IED in Afghanistan. The last time Rogue had worked with Hunter was on a rescue mission in the Ukraine. Despite the conditions, he'd been immaculately turned out. He confided in her that, for him, his morning rituals were essential for his sanity as a bomb disposal engineer.

Rogue's phone call answered after three rings.

"Hello."

Hunter would have recognised Rogue's phone number, but always waited for a sign that she was not calling under duress.

"How's life since Novoazovsk?" asked Rogue.

"Do you recall our last meal?"

"Cold beans and spiced Medovukha," replied Rogue. "A lethal combination."

"How are you, my friend?"

"Well enough. How's business?"

"Thriving, which is good for me but a sad reflection on the state of the world," said Hunter. "So, is this a social call or can I provide you with some assistance?"

Rogue had never phoned Hunter for a social call and couldn't imagine him relaxing with a few beers over a pizza. "I need a cleaner for an apartment in Geneva."

"Condition?" asked Hunter.

"There was a surprise party which got a little out of hand. One of the gate crashers is still there."

"Location?"

"Twenty Rue de Monthasel, unit three-zero-one."

"Geneva is a lovely city," said Hunter. "What is that area like?"

"Normally quiet, although there was a shooting across the street this morning, so I guess you never know," said Rogue, meaning there'd be police in the area.

"I see. What about parking?"

"There's an alley at the side with access via a fire escape. I noticed a door in the alley too, maybe to a boiler room."

"Will you be returning?"

"No. It was a holiday rental, we were due to leave it next Wednesday. Put our stuff into storage. And the front door needs a carpenter."

"Understood."

"I've an appointment in Zurich this morning," said Rogue. "I'll need some supplies later today. Can you recommend someone?"

"Of course. Send me a list of what you need."

"Will do. Talk soon."

Rogue trusted Hunter completely. His high personal standards extended to his business, and he ensured those he employed reached the same levels. His reputation depended upon it. If he failed in that regard, his clients would make certain he never let them down again.

The cleaner that Rogue had requested was not the type of housekeeper you'd find in your local directory. A team of two or three would enter the Geneva apartment unnoticed and leave the same way several hours later. During that time, they would sanitise the entire place, erasing all traces of blood, saliva, hair, and skin. The dead body would be removed and disposed of, never to be seen again. They would repair the front door and remove any food from the premises, including the groceries from Pfister's Deli. Rogue and Agnetha's belongings would be carefully packed and moved to a secure storage facility, and the keys to the apartment which Rogue had left on the kitchen table would be returned to the letting agency along with ample compensation to cover the cost of any breakages. The cost of Hunter's service was considerable, but well worth it. Agnetha lived and studied in Geneva. It was important that she didn't come to the attention of the police.

Approaching intersection seventeen at Écublens, the traffic slowed as drivers made last-minute lane changes and trucks joined the primary route to the north of the country. Rogue ripped open a protein bar with her teeth and chewed it as she waited impatiently for the traffic to sort itself out. Playing back the sequence of events from that morning in her mind, nothing seemed to make sense. How did the kidnappers know she was in Geneva? She'd booked everything under an alias and taken a circuitous route to get there. She was damn sure she hadn't been followed, and apart from Marcus, nobody else knew she had planned the trip. Rogue let out a heavy sigh, her breath condensing on the windscreen.

The motorway absorbed the extra commuters, and the fast lane opened up again. Rogue pushed closer to the car in front, a rental saloon with three kids in the back, cruising at eighty kph. Rogue hated driving slow. Her thoughts meandered aimlessly, in never ending circles. At speed, she was forced to focus, to deal with facts only and make quick decisions with no emotional conflict. She flashed her headlights and was about to blow the horn when the driver switched to the slower lane.

Back at one hundred and ten kph, Rogue replayed the phone conversation with the kidnapper over the car's stereo system. He'd used her full name, Rachel Olsson Garde, and knew that she had worked for MI5. But so did a thousand other people. He also knew that Agnetha was her adopted niece and had alluded to the circumstances surrounding Tasha's death during her final mission. He had to be someone from Rogue's past. Tasha had gone to great lengths to hide Agnetha; even the few people who knew she existed did not know where she lived or under what name. So someone must have given the kidnapper that information. If Rogue could figure out who, then she might have an edge.

Half an hour from Zurich, Rogue eased off the speed a little. She'd pulled the estimated arrival time back to 12:03 pm, and she was confident of shaving a further five or six minutes off the journey time. As her back muscles relaxed into the seat, she gave her analytical mind a rest by memorising car number plates. When she tired of that, she counted vehicles with sun roofs, then makes of truck. Anything to shove the worry and guilt into the far corners of her brain.

Shortly after Lenzburg, the traffic bunched up. As the cars ahead slowed further, Rogue glanced at the SatNav. A red line of congestion snaked as far as Birrhard, five kilometres away. Her estimated arrival time in Zurich jumped from 11:59 am to 12:05 pm, then pushed further to 12:11 pm. Brake lights came on up ahead and the cars in front of her came to an abrupt stop. In the distance, a plume of black smoke drifted across the motorway. As the traffic moved along in fits and starts, Rogue watched the minutes creep by. There was no way she would reach the coordinates on time.

Just before the next junction, Rogue discovered the source of the traffic jam. Fire trucks had surrounded an incident on the runaway at Birrfeld airfield. The smoke appeared to be coming from a light aircraft, and both sides of the motorway had slowed to stare at the scene. In Rogue's rear-view mirror, she could see the blue flashing lights of the traffic police. As she crawled past the airport, the pace picked up again, but Rogue had lost valuable time. Between Birrfeld and the outskirts of Zurich, she tailgated, lane swapped and pushed the speed limits, desperate to reach the Migrol service station by noon.

She was still in the fast lane as she neared her turn off, with the GPS registering an arrival time of 12:01 pm. Up ahead, trucks and buses were filling the slower lanes, and the cars stuck behind them began switching into the fast lane, forcing Rogue to brake constantly. The overhead signs told her the turnoff was two kilometres ahead. Rogue checked the rear-view mirror and noticed a gap opening in front of a car transporter. She pulled in ahead of him and floored the accelerator, passing five cars on her outside. If she could gain another minute, it might be the difference between success and failure. There weren't any police patrols in her mirror, but they usually appeared at precisely the wrong time. She forced her way back into the outside lane between a Lexus and a Mercedes, the latter blowing her out of it. She surged past a procession of trucks, then slowed again. The GPS announced in a calm voice that she should take Exit 58 for Dietikon in one kilometre.

In the lane beside her, the driver of a Volvo had a cup of coffee in one hand and was operating the entertainment system with the other, only glancing at the road every couple of seconds. She shimmied towards him, hoping he might drop back a little and let her in, but he was oblivious. She swerved again and blew the horn. He jumped and squeezed the paper cup too hard. The lid popped off and coffee overflowed onto his clothes. He shook his fist at her and mouthed a string of expletives. The car behind Rogue blew the horn, but was wise enough to keep a safe distance. Rogue tried again, signalling to the Volvo driver that he should let her in, but he stuck up two fingers. She pulled the dead kidnapper's Sig pistol from her pack, slid down the passenger window, and pointed the gun at the driver. He braked hard and vanished from her view. She switched lanes into the gap and took off, but quickly used up the free stretch of road ahead of her and had to slow down.

Desperate to make up time, Rogue swapped lanes again, nipping in front of a Lexus. They briefly hit one hundred kph, then dropped back to seventy. The GPS piped up again. She was running out of motorway. After passing an articulated truck on her inside, she indicated and just squeezed in ahead of him. The sound of sirens reached her from a distance behind, possibly a result of her tussle with the coffee spilling Volvo driver. Her exit loomed up ahead, but the inner lane was jammed up and going nowhere.

Rogue spotted a pair of motorbikes in the exit lane, in front of a bright red Jaguar XJS. As the traffic came to a stop, she braked alongside the sports car, slapped on her indicator and looked across. The driver was a balding fifty something, his passenger easily half his age, all blond hair and fake tan. When the bikes moved off, Rogue eased towards the gap, but the Jag leapt forward to fill the space before the procession stopped again. Rogue gritted her teeth and inched slightly ahead of him. As the bikers moved off again, Rogue blew the horn to attract the Jag driver's attention and simultaneously floored the accelerator, aiming the Audi into the narrow gap. The Jag reacted quickly and burst ahead, but Rogue kept going. She felt a thud as his bumper connected with her side panel. The steering wheel jolted in her hands, pushing her back into her own lane. Gripping tight, she swung hard. Glass shattered as the Jaguar's headlight crumpled, but Rogue held her course and shoved the sports car out of her way. Abruptly, the resistance dropped off and the wheel became free again in her hands. Reluctant to engage with her any longer, the Jag had dropped back. Rogue sped off, watching her mirror for any sign of blue flashing lights. There were none. At least not yet.

At 11:59 am, Rogue drove through a red traffic light, her eyes fixed on the Migrol sign in the distance. When the time changed to 12:00, Agnetha's phone screamed to life. Rogue snatched up the phone and hit the answer button.

"You are not where you're supposed to be," said the kidnapper.

"There was a traffic jam near Birrfeld, a plane crash," blurted Rogue.

"For every action, there are consequences."

Rogue froze. Her eyes snapped to the photograph of Agnetha resting on the dashboard.

Chapter 10

Rogue's Audi bounced over the ramp into the service station forecourt and screeched to a halt. The digits on the dashboard clock showed 12:02 pm.

"I'm here now." Her throat was dry, her voice croaky. She dried her palms on the edge of the seat.

There was silence on the other end of the line. Then fragments of another voice.

Rogue scanned the other vehicles parked around her, wondering if the kidnapper was there, watching her. There was a black BMW and a deep red Peugot at the pumps, their drivers gone to pay for fuel. In her rear-view mirror, she counted five people at window seats in the cafe, most eating, one on a phone. Half a dozen cars were parked either side of Rogue, but nobody was paying her any attention.

"Across the road from Migrol is the Kleiner Technology Campus," said the kidnapper. "There is an office building named VerKoll. They have a prisoner.

His name is Jason Webb. You will free him tonight and bring him to me."

"That's crazy, I need time to plan an extraction like that," said Rogue.

"You will arrive here in Basel at eight o'clock tomorrow morning. I am sending you a plan for the office."

The Samsung pinged several times. Rogue swallowed a mouthful of water and scrolled quickly through the images, each one showing the layout of a different floor in the office block. The final one was a driver's licence bearing the name Jason Webb, born first of September, 1991. "Floor plans are not enough. He could be anywhere in that building. It's four levels over a basement."

"The office opens at 8 am, closes at 6 pm," he continued. "After that, the building is empty, except for security personnel. It should not be difficult for someone with your skills."

"This isn't Basra or Kabul, I can't blast my way in there with frag grenades and an Uzi," said Rogue.

"That is not my concern. I want Webb and I want the device he is carrying. Arrive in Basel tomorrow morning, otherwise he is of no use to me. Do you understand what that means?"

Rogue understood too well. If Webb was expendable, then so was Agnetha. "Let me speak to Agnetha."

"You will speak to her tomorrow when you complete your mission."

Rogue bit her tongue and counted. One … two … three. "Eight o'clock tomorrow morning. Where in Basel?"

"Drive across the border into France and wait at the EuroAirport. I will ring you again."

The line went dead. Rogue pounded the dashboard, venting her anger. A woman walking past the Audi, dressed in a business suit and heels, faltered, regained her balance, then glared through the windscreen. When Rogue revved the three litre turbo engine, the woman scurried on and didn't look back.

Rogue slumped in the seat and stared at her phone. The tracker app had stopped when the call ended. As before, it had failed to trace the source. She played back the phone conversation, listening beyond the voice to the spaces behind it, hoping for a clue. There was nothing. No traffic horns or whirring machinery. No kitchen sounds or intercom announcements. The call must have been made indoors from an office or storage room. Either that or he had created a sanitised space for the call that would mask the sounds from the environment. Rogue decided it didn't matter. She had no way of mounting a rescue unless she knew his exact location and even then, it would be too risky.

As she absentmindedly scrolled back through the photographs on the phone, it stopped on the image of Agnetha—tied up, terrified, and lost. Rogue's chest tightened and sweat gathered on her face. The smell of pine needles from the air freshener was suddenly overpowering and smothered her in panic. She opened the car door, stumbled out, and gasped for air. Clamping her eyes shut, she focused on the cold breeze entering her nostrils and waited for the attack to subside. After what seemed like forever, the spasm gripping her lungs eased off and she breathed freely again.

After opening all the windows, she tossed the air freshener away, then slumped into the driver's seat and sipped some water. She needed to keep moving, doing, otherwise her mind would run riot and drive her insane. For now, focusing on the mission would give her a sense of purpose.

The immediate priority was to get more information. She scrolled through her contacts and rang Marcus Walker, an ex colleague in MI5 and a good friend.

"Rach, how's it goin'? I thought you were taking a break," said Marcus.

Alarm bells rang until Rogue remembered Marcus was the one person she had confided in. "I was. I am. It's a long story. I need your help, Marcus."

"Of course. What's happened?"

"Agnetha's been kidnapped. I'm uploading two phone conversations to my shared folder, see if you can get something from them—a voice match, a location, anything useful."

"I'm on it. What do you know so far?"

"Very little. If I want to see Agnetha again, I have to break out someone being held prisoner here in Zurich, then drive him to Basel."

"Who's the guy?"

"His name is Jason Webb. I've uploaded his driver's licence and plans of the VerKoll office block where he's being held."

"VerKoll. That name rings a bell," said Marcus.

"It's in Zurich, the Kleiner Technology Campus."

"Europe, that's good, we have teams there. Have you told the Chief?"

"No, don't tell him. This is between us."

"Dent would do anything to help," said Marcus, "you know he would."

"Just get me anything you can on VerKoll. Security personnel, rosters, and find out exactly what their business is."

"I'm looking them up now. They're a software company specialising in corporate security. I'll see what else I can get, but it might take a while to get into their servers."

"I'll call you back in an hour."

"I was thinking more like six."

"I don't have that long, Marcus," snapped Rogue. "I'm going in there tonight."

"I'm on it, Rach, but less time means taking more risks. It's gonna be harder keeping it under the radar."

"Just do whatever you can."

"Of course. Try not to worry, you'll get her back."

"Call as soon as you have anything."

Talking to Marcus reminded Rogue of the old days when she worked in D Section. Every member of the team possessed skills essential to the execution of a mission. Some, like Marcus, were based in the Operations Centre. Rogue and Tasha hated indoor jobs and preferred to be on the front line. Regardless of their individual roles, Rogue understood the importance of the team and knew she wouldn't have survived some missions without the backup and intel provided by Marcus and his colleagues in the Ops Centre. Rescuing Agnetha was arguably the most important mission of Rogue's life. Having Marcus at her back, even without the full resources of her former employer, injected her with a much needed dose of confidence.

Rogue left the car and walked across the forecourt to the roadside. From there, she had a clear view of the Kleiner Technology Campus. Facing her was a row of car showrooms, each with an array of highly polished vehicles on view through the giant windows. Some distance behind them, she could see the office blocks of the campus. Further examination revealed that access to the campus was protected by a perimeter fence. The only way in was through a barrier manned by security guards.

She opened the maps on the phone and zoomed in. The campus was laid out like a tall tree, with a main road running from the security gate to the top. Narrower roads branched out from the sides, each home to one or two multi-storied buildings.

VerKoll was three branches in from the front and occupied the front half of the building. A company called Astro Logistics had the rear. According to the street view, VerKoll was a standard three story office block. On one side was a car park, divided into sections by hedgerows. At the front, a set of wide steps led up to glass doors. Rogue navigated to the far end of the building used by Astro Logistics. It looked totally different. Loading bays with tall sliding doors spanned the front aspect. A large yard out front provided ample parking space for vans and trucks.

Rogue looked at her watch. It was 12:41 pm. Below the time, the display showed the distance she had run that morning in Geneva, reminding her she was still wearing her running gear. That gave her an idea.

She popped in a set of ear buds, stuffed the phone into her pocket and locked her car. Then she jogged along the pavement outside the car showrooms until she reached the entrance to the campus. Outside the security cabin, a guard holding a clipboard was talking to the driver of a truck, arguing over a bunch of documents in the driver's hand. A pedestrian gate on the near side of the hut was closed. Rogue could see a magnetic card swipe mounted on the wall beside the gate.

She slowed her pace, then hunkered down and pretended to remove a stone from her running shoe.

Climbing over the railings wouldn't be difficult, but it would attract unwanted attention. She considered hiding in the back of the waiting truck, but the rear doors were in full view of passing traffic. Inside the campus, she spotted two women approaching the pedestrian gate. If Rogue timed it right, she could pass through as they exited.

The truck driver and the security guard had finished their discussion. While the driver climbed back into the truck, the guard waved at the security hut and the barrier lifted.

Just inside the pedestrian gate, the two women stood chatting. One had a card in her hand, ready to swipe it and open the gate.

At the barrier, the truck proceeded through the security check and the guard turned his attention to Rogue. As she pulled on her shoe and tied the laces, he ambled over to her. She could see he was concentrating, searching for her face in his memory.

"Do you work in the campus?"

Rogue nodded, then removed her other shoe and fumbled inside it.

As the woman swiped her card and pushed the gate open, another truck pulled up at the barrier and applied the brakes.

"Show me your identification," said the guard.

Rogue pretended she couldn't hear him, pointed to her ear buds, then looked at her watch and feigned shock.

The driver of the waiting truck blasted the horn. The guard jumped and dropped his clipboard. Flaming red, he glared at the truck, retrieved the clipboard, and marched off.

Still holding her running shoe, Rogue hurried to the gate. As the two women walked through, Rogue slipped inside.

Chapter 11

Rogue jogged at a steady pace and swung onto the third side road without hesitating, as if she ran that same route every day. The entrance to the VerKoll reception area looked bright and inviting, but a closer inspection revealed multiple security cameras mounted at regular intervals outside the building and in the car park. There were several cars parked out front, surprising for a Saturday. Through the smoked glass windows, Rogue could make out two people standing in the lobby.

She continued along one side of the building and noted two emergency exits, also monitored by cameras. Close to each exit were signs marked VerKoll Assembly Point V1 and V2. As she jogged along the footpath, the second door opened. A man emerged and quickly lit a cigarette. His uniform matched that of the guard she had encountered at the security barrier. Three hundred metres further on, a tall hedge marked the end of the VerKoll section of the block and the beginning of the Astro Logistics premises. Rogue rounded the northwest corner and stopped outside the gates. Five loading bays opened into a large warehouse. To the right was a small office. As with VerKoll, there were security cameras mounted high on the walls. As she watched, a truck came around the corner, drove through the gates, and reversed up to a vacant bay. Rogue moved on before anyone got suspicious.

The road ended in a large circular cul-de-sac. As she started back, Rogue upped her pace to a sprint, so that she was sweating and panting hard by the time she reached the VerKoll entrance. She mounted the steps and pushed through the glass door. A man and a woman, both wearing headsets, sat behind a reception desk. At one end, a security guard stood watching a computer screen. Rogue doubled over, wheezing hard.

"Are you OK, miss?" asked the guard.

Rogue pressed one hand to her chest and steadied herself against a pillar. "Some water, please."

The guard left his post and approached her.

"Asthma attack, forgot my inhaler," said Rogue as she moved to a seating area, plonked onto a leather sofa, and dropped her head between her knees.

The guard's jaw seemed to relax a little. He called over to the reception desk and asked them to bring some water, but remained standing beside Rogue. The man from the reception desk hurried over with a plastic bottle, unscrewed the cap and handed it to Rogue.

She sipped the liquid and slowed her breathing a little. "Thanks."

"Do you require a medic?" asked the guard.

Rogue shook her head. "No, I just need a minute." She finished the water and handed back the bottle. "Thank you." She stood up, feigned some light-headedness, then looked around. "Can I use your toilets, please?"

The guard hesitated.

Rogue placed her hand on her abdomen, bent over a little, and grimaced. "Please?"

He paused, looked around, then relented. "OK, follow me." He led her to a bank of body scanners, picked up a plastic tray and held it out to her. "Place your belongings on this, please. Phone, watch, headphones."

Rogue feigned surprise. "I just need a toilet. I won't be long."

"No one is exempt," he said, his voice less friendly.

She shrugged and dropped the specified items into the tray.

"The toilets are that way, on the left," said the guard.

"Thanks," said Rogue. She walked down a corridor at the side of the reception desk. A door directly ahead of her was protected with an electronic swipe and retina scan. Before that, doors on the left were labelled Ladies and Gents. She entered the first one, glancing back towards the elevators. The guard stood there watching her.

Inside the Ladies, a woman was using a hand dryer. She had an ID badge and a swipe card clipped to the belt of her trousers. Rogue could have taken it without the woman noticing, but given the level of security, its loss would soon be noticed and the badge would be cancelled.

When Rogue emerged from the ladies', a female guard was waiting for her. She wore a name badge with R. Heschler printed in black.

"Are you OK now?" said Heschler. "My colleague said you were unwell."

"I'm fine now, just overdid it a bit," said Rogue.

Heschler nodded and gestured towards the exit. Rogue followed her, taking in every detail of her surroundings.

"The security is very high here," said Rogue as they returned through the security scanner. "Problems with staff taking stationary?" She smiled at Heschler, hoping to glean some inside information.

"It impresses our clients," said Heschler. "And the owner is a little paranoid," she added, lowering her voice.

Rogue collected her belongings.

"Might see you around," said Heschler. "I sometimes take a run between shifts. What company do you work for?"

Rogue was caught off guard and looked at her blankly.

"I assume you're based here in the business park?" said Heschler.

"Oh, no, I was just passing and came this way for some variety."

"That's not a good idea." Heschler's eyes narrowed into a frown. "They should have stopped you at the barrier."

"What's so special about this park? Why the tight security?"

"Most companies in the park have government contracts, domestic and international."

"Everything alright here." It was the male guard from earlier.

"Yes sir," said Heschler, taking a step back from Rogue. "She's fine now, was just leaving, Sir." Heschler stared firmly at Rogue.

Rogue took the hint and left. She hadn't found a way in to Verkoll, but she had learned that her mission would be a lot more difficult than she'd expected.

Back at the service station, Rogue opened the boot of the car and shoved a change of clothes into a bag. Next, she examined her phone to ensure the VerKoll security guard hadn't tried to access it while she'd been in the toilets. To any observer, it resembled a regular smartphone, but it was protected by tamper proof software she'd acquired from Marcus in MI5. Anyone trying to hack the phone would be blocked by three layers of encryption. If they managed to breach the first two, every piece of data on the phone would be destroyed before the third level was crossed. Once Rogue was satisfied that it hadn't been tampered with, she proceeded into the cafe.

At the counter, she ordered a large Americano, and a spiced beef roll to-go. While that was being prepared, she used the toilets to change out of her running gear. She'd have loved a shower, but it would have to wait. After paying for the food, she returned to the car. As she inhaled the rich aroma of the coffee, she felt hunger pangs surfacing. Apart from a protein bar, she hadn't eaten anything since the previous night.

She peeled back the foil on the hot roll and took a mouthful. While she ate, she worked on a plan. After finishing the roll, she compiled a list of the items she'd need for the mission. Arnold Hunter had weapon caches all over Europe, guaranteeing delivery to any major city within a six-hour window. His depots stocked everything from handguns to RPGs, night vision goggles to tear gas. Once you had the money, he had the equipment. Rogue delayed sending the list until she heard back from Marcus. Based on the information he might provide about the security in the Verkoll building, she might need to change her order.

It was less than two hours since Rogue had spoken to Marcus Walker, but she rang him anyway. Anything he had discovered about VerKoll might influence her plans and therefore her equipment order for Hunter.

"Rach, I was just about to call you," said Marcus.

"What have you got?"

"Nothing on the voice recordings, I'm afraid. There was no match on our system. I even hooked into the Interpol and US databases."

"It was a long shot," said Rogue. "At least I know I'm not dealing with some psychopath from an old mission."

"That company you asked me about—VerKoll—they specialise in security systems. There are lots of software houses providing antivirus and firewall applications, but these guys are a couple of levels above the others."

"What do you mean?" Rogue slid the window down a little as the car began fogging up.

"When I got into their servers, I came up against some surprisingly high end resistance," said Marcus.

"Meaning what, they're a cover for a government agency?"

"Not exactly. If you look at the public records, VerKoll is a private company owned by a couple of tech prodigies who came up with the right product at the right time. But once I got through their firewalls, I got the sense they were into way more than data protection. Quite the opposite, in fact."

"So they're professional hackers, stealing from the rich and selling to the crooks?" said Rogue.

"Looks that way, except they're only selling to one customer, or rather, one master."

"Since they're based in a neutral country, I'm guessing it's not us or the Yanks."

"Exactly," said Marcus, letting out an audible breath.

"I hope you don't catch any flak for this," said Rogue.

"Don't worry, I'm covering my trail. But it puts a totally different slant on your mission. That's not just any software house you're looking at. Their security personnel are probably ex-military. Getting in is one thing, but get caught and you'll disappear for a long time."

Rogue filed away the information, knowing she couldn't afford to let it change her plans. If she wanted to see Agnetha again, she had no choice but to carry out the mission she had been given. "What did you find out about their security setup?"

"You're not gonna like this," said Marcus. "First off, they man the place twenty-four seven. Three eight-hour shifts, starting at 6 am. The day shifts have a full complement of fourteen guards, but the night shift, which starts at 10 pm, only has eight. The general staff keep to normal office hours, nine to five, but looking at the electronic time sheets, a handful occasionally get in earlier or stay later."

"What about fire exits and access to the roof?" Rogue reckoned she could handle the guards, as they'd be scattered throughout the building. She just needed to avoid triggering the alarms.

"All external doors are protected by ... a combination of sensors and infrared beams ... and that includes the roof."

Rogue knew by his staggered speech that Marcus was still logged onto the VerKoll system and scrolling through data. "Don't stay in there much longer, Marcus. If they notice you, it'll put them on alert. That's not what I need right now."

"Good point. One thing that might help, the rear fire exit on the west side opens twice every night, always around the same times, 1 am and again at 4 am."

"How long does it stay open?" said Rogue.

"Only three to four minutes max."

"Smoke break, I'll bet. I saw a guard there about an hour ago."

"That's a possible entry point, but they have cameras in every corridor. I'm sending you a copy of the floor plans now. Do you know where Jason Webb is being held?"

"No. What about those cameras? Can you hook into them?"

"Maybe, but it'll take time," said Marcus. "Piggy-backing the video feed should be easy, but I don't want to set off any alarms, more for your sake than mine."

"Start with the basement. It's the most likely place, well away from the general office population."

"Right. I gotta go. I'll call if I find anything."

Rogue heard voices in the background. "Thanks Marcus."

She sat back and downed the dregs of the Americano. She'd only have one shot at getting Webb out of the VerKoll stronghold. After that, the guards would be on high alert. They might even move him to another location. Gaining access to the building would be relatively easy, despite the surveillance cameras and guards. Finding the target and extracting him in one piece would be the difficult part. Experience told her that the odds of them escaping unnoticed were low.

The office plans that Marcus had sent her were identical to those she received from the kidnapper. If Webb was her prisoner, Rogue would definitely keep him in the basement. It was away from the general staff and an ideal location for interrogating someone. A basement would also be difficult to escape from. If she got cornered down there, her only option would involve bullets and explosives. Once that started, she'd wouldn't have much time before reinforcements arrived and surrounded the building.

She zoomed in on the schematics and followed the corridors, mentally recording the routes to and from the basement. There was an elevator off the reception area that would require a security card, but she didn't like using elevators. It was too easy for a security team to shut them down and trap her inside. She counted four stairwells. One was behind the reception area next to the elevator shaft, with a second one against the south wall that divided VerKoll from Astro Logistics. The other two hugged the east and west external walls next to the fire exits. If the guard took his smoking break, she could get in without setting off the alarm and take the stairs to the basement. Whether they'd catch her on the internal cameras or not would be down to luck.

She opened the image of Jason Webb's driver's licence and enlarged his face. He looked pale and undernourished, as if he didn't see regular daylight. She wondered how long he'd been captive, and what condition he was in. Would he be able to run or even walk? And then there was the mysterious item he had in his possession that was so important to the kidnapper. Given the circumstances, Rogue had to assume it was a piece of technology that Webb had stolen from VerKoll. As Webb was imprisoned, he wouldn't have the tech on his person. Recovering it would also impact her escape plans.

Next, she brought up a map of Zurich and began studying it, familiarising herself with the routes available to her if things got heated during their escape. After twenty minutes, she had decided on a selection of rat runs designed to lose one or more pursuers, including places to lie low for short periods and likely locations to switch the Audi for another vehicle. Finally, she opened the list of equipment she wanted to order from Hunter. After changing a few items, she emailed it to him. Apart from weapons, there were also a few other supplies she needed, things she could easily pick up herself. She used her phone to search for a nearby retail park, then pulled out of the service station and took the ramp onto the motorway.

Chapter 12

The skies were murky and troubled when Rogue emerged from the Crater Outdoor store. She just managed to reach the Audi before the heavens opened. As she peered out at the deluge, she checked the forecast. She needed it dry for the night ahead, both for her own comfort and that of the security guard on his smoke break. A throbbing that had started behind her temples half an hour earlier had developed into a blinding headache. She looked in the mirror and saw an angry bruise on her forehead, a souvenir from the fight in the alley. A patch of blood had stained the plaster over her eye, but the wound appeared to have stopped leaking.

Rogue did a mental check on everything she needed for the night ahead. The two Crater bags in the back seat contained the clothes and footwear she required, along with some other necessities. Hunter's contact would provide the weapons. Her next task was to find accommodation where she could prepare for the mission. As she started the car, the phone rang. Rogue hit the green answer button on the steering wheel. "Hunter."

"Rogue. What's your status?"

Even though she'd used his name, he waited for a confirmation that it was safe to talk.

"Planning the usual holiday stuff, like breaking into a top security facility in the middle of the night."

"Your order will be ready at 5 pm. The supplier's name is Odette. I'm sending you her phone number along with the coordinates to a supermarket car park half an hour south of Zurich. When you arrive there, ring her for further instructions. The collection window is one hour."

"How far is the pickup point from the supermarket?"

"Less than fifteen minutes. Do you need a drop off?"

Rogue had planned little beyond the VerKoll mission. She could dump whatever equipment she had left, but she'd rather use Hunter's disposal service. Her fingerprints and DNA were registered with many of the European security databases since her days with MI5.

"That depends on how tonight goes," said Rogue. "A clean vehicle might be useful too, somewhere outside Zurich on the principal route to Basel."

"Understood. I'll have both on standby. Ring when you know and we can arrange a suitable location."

"Perfect."

"The cleaners have started on your apartment."

Hunter rarely gave updates, unless there was a complication. On those occasions, he'd get straight to the point.

"Is there a problem?" asked Rogue.

Hunter cleared his throat.

Rogue knew he was searching for the right words. She waited.

"Agnetha was in the apartment with you."

A lump formed in Rogue's throat. "I was out running." In her head, it sounded like an excuse.

"Do you know where she's being held?"

"No. They want me to do a recovery job. Here in Zurich."

"I can gather a team, whatever you need."

Rogue preferred to work solo, especially on a mission so personal. Apart from that, Hunter had rules. The first was that he never got involved in his client's missions. Rogue didn't want to compromise that rule, even though she knew he was making an exception because of his history with Tasha—she had saved his life and his business not once, but twice. Even though Tasha was gone, Hunter wanted to repay that debt and would do anything to help rescue Agnetha.

"I appreciate the offer, Hunter."

"They won't get in the way. Your terms."

"The intel points to a solo op."

"Understood," said Hunter. "Keep in touch."

At 5:07 pm, Rogue arrived in Menzingen, a small town thirty kilometres south of Zurich, and pulled into the car park outside Lehmann's supermarket. It was busy, every slot occupied by a car or a pickup. She cruised along the aisles, braking every few seconds for over-loaded trolleys and distracted children. An attendant in a high viz jacket waved to her and pointed towards the furthest corner. Sure enough, she found a few vacant spots there and reversed into one facing an exit. With the engine still running, she dialled the phone number Hunter had sent her. It answered after three rings.

"Hello." A woman's voice. Hard to detect any accent from the single word answer.

"Can I speak to Odette," said Rogue.

"I am Odette."

"You have an order for me."

"Who took the order?" said Odette.

"Buccaneer." It was Hunter's codename.

"Are you driving a black Audi Q5?"

Rogue whipped her head around, searching. She was confident she hadn't been followed. "Yes."

"My cousin will show you the way."

A man appeared in front of the Audi and casually waved at Rogue.

"He doesn't say much, but he can handle himself. You understand?" said Odette.

"I do. Follow his directions. Don't ask any questions." Rogue nodded at the man through the windscreen.

The cousin opened the passenger door and climbed in. A mass of hair and an overgrown beard made it difficult to put an age on him. He slammed the door closed, rocking the Audi.

"That way." He pointed at the exit, then off to the left.

Rogue eased out of the car park and joined the traffic as a fine drizzle spattered the windscreen.

"Left, then next right." His voice was a forced whisper, every word an effort.

After another right turn and two lefts, they left Menzingen and followed a narrow road across a grassy plain devoid of features except for an occasional wooden cabin. The car soon filled with a heady mixture of sweat and garlic. Rogue lowered the window halfway, preferring the light rain to her passenger's body odour. Now and then, he looked in the wing mirror. Rogue couldn't help but do the same, but there was nothing else on the road. A few kilometres further on, the land rose toward a forested area. Despite the presence of her silent companion, Rogue found the drive peaceful and calming after the chaos of the motorway. Soon they were climbing along tree-lined roads with occasional gaps, offering glimpses of the town they'd left behind.

"Slow down now. Real slow," said her passenger as they approached a tight bend overshadowed by low-hanging branches.

Rogue dropped to a crawl. As they crept around the hairpin, the tarmac abruptly ended, replaced by a muddy track with a grass ridge down the centre. A dozen metres further on, an old log blocked their path.

"Keep going, just take it easy."

Rogue eased over the log and repeated the manoeuvre half a dozen times along a winding route through the dense forest. The Audi had a sports suspension and took the many dips and bumps in its stride, but Rogue maintained a slow speed, just in case. Finally, they cleared the obstacles and rumbled over a cattle grid. The track split, one fork leading to a two storey log cabin, the other veering away to a barn. Odette's cousin unclipped his seat belt and instructed Rogue to stop the car. After getting out, he told her to drive to the barn and wait in the car. Then he slammed the door and trudged off towards the house. Rogue parked outside the barn doors and switched off the engine. Two German Shepherd dogs appeared from nowhere and took up sentry duty, one on each side of her car, both emitting a low growl. Rogue closed up her window and waited. A woman emerged from the barn and approached the car, stopping at the driver's door.

Rogue lowered the window again. "Odette?"

"That's me. Don't worry about these fellas. Once you behave yourself, they'll leave you alone." She waved a hand towards the dogs. They sat back but remained alert, watching Rogue intently.

"Good to know," said Rogue. She opened the door and got out slowly, trying and failing to appear relaxed. She liked animals, but having had some terrifying experiences with security dogs, she'd rather take her chances with an armed human any day.

"This way." Odette set off towards the barn. One dog followed her, the other stood and waited.

Rogue followed a few strides behind. The second dog trailed behind her, keeping its distance. Odette was older than the image Rogue had formed in her mind. Her voice on the phone had suggested late thirties or early forties. Her silver hair and weathered look added at least twenty years to that estimate, but her movements were balanced and purposeful. Not a woman to be underestimated.

"How long do you know Buccaneer?" asked Odette as she pushed into the barn.

"Quite a while," said Rogue. "Close to fifteen years."

"I got that impression. He said to give you whatever you needed."

"The list I gave him should cover it," said Rogue.

Odette shut the doors behind Rogue, then flicked a switch on the wall. Fluorescent tubes buzzed overhead and ignited one at a time, spilling a dull yellow light into the barn. Stalls lined the right-hand side of the large space. There were horses standing in two of them, but the remaining four were empty. On the left, rectangular bales of hay were stacked to the roof.

"This way." Odette walked halfway along, then turned through a gap in the bales. She continued to the side wall of the barn, then slid her hand behind a wooden panel. More lights came on, low wattage bulbs, just enough to show the way. As Rogue followed, her nostrils were invaded by the stench of manure. A little further on, she found the source. Three barrels with steam rising from their open tops. The dog behind her growled deeply, urging Rogue on, seemingly oblivious to the smell. She quickened her pace along the narrow corridor, which soon opened out into a wide expanse. From outside, the barn had looked the same size as the house. Once Rogue's eyes became accustomed to the brightness, she discovered the building stretched way back into the trees.

Odette approached a wall of steel drums several metres long. Rogue heard the whirr of a motor and the wall swung open, the row of drums moving as one. The area beyond was filled with steel cabinets and heavy wooden boxes, some marked with model numbers and acronyms familiar to Rogue. Off to one side, a black holdall sat on a bench. The items Rogue had ordered were neatly arranged beside it, like groceries on a supermarket conveyor belt.

"Everything you asked for is there, but I'd prefer you check it for yourself."

Rogue surveyed the tools of her trade, mentally ticking them off the list in her head. They were grouped by category. Weapons, explosives and wearables. She lifted the first gun, a Glock 17. The gun bore a few scratches and dents, but appeared to be in good condition. She tested it for balance. It wasn't the latest Gen5, but that was fine. Rogue had used the older Gen4 since its release in 2010 and trusted it. As her fingers folded into the grooves, the handle nestled perfectly into her palm and a familiar confidence infused her whole body. After ensuring that the chamber was empty, she ran a few basic checks. Racked the slide, tested the trigger action, and ensured the sights lined up. She could have stripped it down completely into its component parts, inspected them and reassembled it, but that would be considered an affront to a respected arms dealer like Odette. And besides, Arnold Hunter trusted her, and that was good enough for Rogue.

She'd chosen another 9mm Glock as her backup, the smaller G26, also known as the Baby Glock. It was perfect as an ankle weapon. It came with a compact ten round magazine, but when concealment wasn't an issue, she could use the larger capacity magazine of the G17. The mag would protrude a couple of centimetres from the G26's grip but added a valuable seven rounds. Beside the guns, Odette had laid out two stacks of magazines, four for each weapon.

"There's one P+ magazine for each gun. I've glued a ridge to the base," explained Odette.

Rogue inspected the magazines on the bench and, sure enough, she could feel a narrow line on the last pair. The P+ cartridges travelled faster and were more explosive, perfect for more stubborn obstacles.

"Try them out," offered Odette.

Rogue looked over at her, surprised.

"This way."

Rogue picked up the G17 and a full magazine. At the back wall, Odette flicked a switch. A section of the wall moved sideways, revealing a pair of black target silhouettes. They were mounted on padded chipboard and suspended from the ceiling on cables.

Odette pulled on a pair of ear defenders and handed a second set to Rogue.

"Can you move the targets further apart?" asked Rogue.

"Sure, they're on pulleys. I can add some more if you wish." Odette moved off to one side and rotated a handle. The leftmost target slid away.

"That's perfect," said Rogue when they were a car's length apart. She stepped twenty metres back and slotted home the magazine. As she racked the slide to pull in the first round, both dogs growled. One crept towards Rogue, while the other positioned himself directly in front of his master. Odette snapped a single word in German and both animals went quiet. The dog nearest Rogue stopped, glared coldly at her, then reluctantly returned to Odette's side, looking back several times. The other one remained between his master and the stranger, but sat down. Odette waved at Rogue to proceed.

Gripping the Glock single handed, Rogue took aim at the target on the right. She squeezed the trigger three times in quick succession, panned left, and repeated the sequence. She lowered the weapon and considered the cluster of bullet holes in the silhouettes. Both were center mass, exactly where she had intended. Satisfied with the gun's performance, she nodded to Odette.

Back at the bench, Rogue scanned the remaining items. An MK3 Navy combat knife and a pair of slim Gerber boot knives. An open box holding four grenades, two stun and two smoke. Next, four olive coloured Mylar pouches, each containing a square block of C4 plastic explosive. Beside them was a cardboard box labelled EDD. She opened the lid and counted eight electronic delay detonators. Each was essentially a blasting cap attached to a small electric timer. All eight were individually covered in bubble wrap. Then two holsters, a shoulder model for the G17 and an ankle strap for the smaller G26. A gun cleaning kit, fence cutters, binoculars, and a pair of head torches completed the order.

Maybe it was overkill, but experience had taught Rogue to expect the worst. She carefully packed the items into the holdall, which was divided into compartments of varying sizes, then turned around to Odette. "All good."

"Your order included ten thousand euro in cash," said Odette. "You might want some of that in Swiss francs?"

Rogue raised an eyebrow. Then it clicked. Most outlets accepted euro but charged high commissions and gave the change in Swiss francs. If she needed cash to open doors, local currency would be preferable. Having said that, she didn't know if Basel would be her final destination. "Good point. Make it five of each."

Odette opened a cupboard door off to one side. The contents were hidden from Rogue's view, but she heard the familiar beeps of a keypad as Odette accessed a safe. After locking it and shutting over the cupboard door, Odette handed two stacks of used notes to Rogue. "You know how to contact me if you need anything else."

Rogue dropped the money in the holdall and hefted it off the bench. "Is there another way back to the motorway?"

A frown crossed Odette's brow. "Did someone follow you to Menzingen?"

Rogue shook her head. "No, definitely not. I just prefer to vary my routes where possible."

Odette's expression relaxed. "There are trails that go deeper into the forest, then exit on the far side, but you'd need an ATV and a guide. Too many dead ends."

"ATV?"

"All Terrain Vehicle. Wide tyres, extra ground clearance, independent suspension."

Odette led Rogue back through the barn, escorted by the dogs. Rogue suspected they'd had military or body-guard training. Back outside, she eased the holdall inside the boot of the Audi and covered it with a picnic blanket she'd bought in the outdoor shop.

"I presume you can find your way back?" said Odette.

"Yeah, no problem." Rogue sat into the Audi and started the engine.

Odette was already walking back into the barn as Rogue pulled out of the yard.

Chapter 13

Rogue's next priority was to organise her weapons and equipment for the night ahead. Before joining the motorway outside Menzingen, Rogue parked at the side of the road and used her phone to search for a hotel on the Basel side of Zurich. She sorted the results by cost, reasoning that the cheaper establishments would have less security. All the better if she could get from the car park to her room without having to pass through the reception area. After evaluating five possibilities and studying the aerial views, she decided to check out two of them.

It took her half an hour to reach the Breitfeld in Baden. According to the satellite image on Rogue's phone, the hotel car park was bordered by a wood, with no buildings overlooking the rear of the hotel. When she arrived, she immediately saw that the map was out of date. All the trees had been cleared, replaced by warehouses and a brewery. The stench of hops wafted in through the Audi's air vents. There were only a handful of cars and vans outside the hotel, much too quiet for Rogue's liking.

She continued to the second candidate, the NeuWald, ten minutes away. Outside, tour buses were busy unloading passengers and luggage. Larger and older than the Breitfeld, the NeuWald had been extended on either side, the new wings stretching away from the main building. Rogue found a parking spot at the side of the hotel under the cover of an aged oak tree. The exterior of the building badly needed repainting, and only half of the lights in the car park seemed to work. Confident that the hotel would serve her needs, Rogue left the car and headed inside. The reception area was crowded and disorganised. Some areas were cordoned off, where men in overalls were repairing the ceiling.

Rogue managed to reach the reception desk before a noisy group of tourists and asked for a room. The manager apologised as the only rooms available were in the old wing, which faced the overflow car park at the back of the hotel. Rogue feigned disappointment, but said it would do as she only needed it for one night. The manager placed a registration form and pen on the desk, but couldn't make himself heard over a swarm of American accents that invaded the lobby. Mumbling under his breath, he scrunched up the document, handed Rogue a key and wished her a pleasant stay.

Rogue's ground floor room had recently been painted, but despite the fresh cream walls, it triggered unpleasant memories of the orphanage where she had spent her early years. There was barely enough space for the two single beds that were shoved into opposite corners. The window facing the rear car park reluctantly allowed slivers of evening sunlight through the grimy glass. Old-fashioned cream wallpaper with wood chips trapped under fresh magnolia paint did nothing to lift the mood of the room.

She walked into the cramped bathroom and turned on the shower. Water spluttered from the head as it struggled through clogged pinholes. The pipes hidden behind the wall rattled and chugged, then settled into a steady hum as hot, steaming water sprayed onto the off-white tray below. Small mercies. On a corner unit opposite the shower, she found an ample supply of clean towels alongside miniature bottles of shower gel and shampoo. On the bottom shelf was an aerosol can of lemon air freshener. She switched off the water, returned to the bedroom, and forced open the window.

Kicking off her boots, Rogue collapsed onto the bed. It was firmer than most people liked, but suited Rogue perfectly. The pillow lacked enough filling to serve its purpose, but it didn't matter; she wouldn't be spending the night. She stared at the ceiling and chased the twisted loops etched into the plaster. She had a couple of hours to kill, too many for her liking. Already her mind was running wild, finding endless reasons to blame herself, twisting her deeper and darker in ever tightening knots. To break the cycle, she snapped her eyes tight, then popped them open again before her persistent nightmares crept in. She looked back at the ceiling, selected a complete circle, and exhaled slowly as she traced the circumference. When her eyes returned to the top of the circle, she forced the remaining pockets of air from her lungs. Then she remained still. And waited. No breath in, no breath out. Eventually, her brain stuttered to a halt. All her problems and doubts were replaced by one priority—the need for oxygen.

As Rogue allowed her lungs to fill with cool air from the open window, she restarted the journey on the ceiling, circling slower this time. The distractions returned, but with less intensity, less power. Her lungs filled, paused, emptied, waited. As she repeated the sequence, she noticed the sound of a pigeon outside. The bird's soft cooing followed the rise and fall of her chest. Gradually, the muscles in her back eased out and sank into the bed beneath her. The tangled thoughts in her mind loosened, allowing some stillness to seep in. She could have easily drifted off to sleep, but she needed to prepare for the night ahead. She took one final deep breath, let it out, then sat up and swung her legs off the bed.

First stop was the bathroom where she splashed cold water on her face and rubbed the fatigue from her eyes. In the mirror, she could see a crescent shaped swelling over her left eye, a combination of violet and blue. Back in the bedroom, she tossed her jacket on a chair, took out her phone, and opened the office plans the kidnapper had sent her. There were five images, one for each floor in the VerKoll building, including the basement. She zoomed in and examined each section up close, panning vertically and horizontally until she had built a clear picture in her mind, one she could draw upon when she was inside. Each floor had a standard layout, one Rogue had encountered many times before.

The main entrance faced north and led to the reception area she'd visited earlier that day. Immediately behind the reception desk was an elevator and a stairwell. Beside them were toilets, a small kitchen, and two storage rooms. Next was a corridor that spanned the width of the building from east to west, giving access to various sized offices. A similar corridor hugged the rear wall of the building. These two east-west corridors were connected by two more that ran from the reception area to the rear wall. Most of the offices were labelled sales or marketing, but one caught her attention. It was marked 'Security Control (SC)'. Rogue made a note of it, marking it with a red star on her mental map. That would be her target.

If the scale of the map was accurate and nothing had changed, she could reach the Security Control room from a fire exit on the west side in less than a minute. The SC could provide her with several things she needed for a rapid extraction—the location of the prisoner, the security roster and a pass which would grant her access to stairwells and offices. However, there was a downside. The SC was the nerve centre, coordinating the security team members and providing them with real-time intel. Once it was compromised, the team would lock down the building and converge on that room. Rogue needed to get in and out of there fast. She would need a diversion, something to draw the guards to the east side of the building, as far from the control room as possible. It might only buy her a few extra minutes, but every second counted.

The upper floors of the building were laid out similar to the ground floor, with additional offices instead of the reception area. The top floor had a large board-room on the west side. Rogue pulled up the basement plan. Apart from the stairwell and elevator shaft, it appeared to be one large, open area. It was probably just used for storage.

Rogue's phone pinged. It was an email from Marcus with a more recent set of building plans and a profile of Jason Webb. In the new diagrams, the basement had three small rooms in one corner, close to the rear stairwell. It was an excellent location for a prisoner, away from the general office population, where no-body would hear cries for help. The photograph in Jason Webb's profile confirmed his appearance. Aged twenty-nine, he was born in Manchester, had a brother two years younger called Thomas and a sister Jessica, who was only nineteen. Webb was employed by Cross-fire Analytics in London for the past five years as a software developer and shared an apartment with a guy called Matt Brennan who also worked at Crossfire. Apart from a couple of parking tickets, Webb had a clean record.

Rogue took an iced tea from the minibar, drank half the can, then sat on the bed with her back pressed up against the headboard. She closed her eyes and visualised herself slowly walking through the corridors of VerKoll. Pausing at each junction, she imagined how it would look and where each route would lead to. Her mental map would be an essential item in her toolkit and could be the difference between evading the security guards on her way to an exit, or finding herself trapped in a dead end. A stealth approach was her preferred option. That meant relying on the smoking guard to open the fire exit for her. If he failed to appear, she'd have to force her way in. That's why she needed the C4 explosives.

She closed the curtains, turned the key in the door and flicked on the lights. Then she emptied her purchases from the Crater Outdoor shop onto the bed and divided the items into two groups. The clothes for the mission were all black. Cargo pants with Velcro pockets, t-shirt, a fitted softshell jacket, lightweight hiking boots, socks, a beanie hat and a balaclava. The other pile included a small black backpack, a pocket torch with spare batteries, a polythene ground sheet, duct tape, cable ties, first aid kit, surgical gloves and a roll of plastic food bags. She'd left a second bag in the

Audi with a spare pair of trousers, two more t-shirts, socks, underwear and a rain jacket.

During the next hour, Rogue checked and prepared every piece of equipment she required for the mission. After donning two pairs of surgical gloves, she covered the spare bed with the groundsheet and then laid everything out in the sequence she would need it. Weapons first—guns, ammunition and knives. Then explosives—C4, detonators and grenades. Finally, the extras—head torch, fence cutters, duct tape and the first aid kit.

Using the combat knife she purchased from Odette, she cut each block of C4 in half and placed them into individual plastic zipper bags. Each chunk was powerful enough to blow a fire exit door wide open. They were also extremely pliable and could be moulded into any shape, so she could quickly change the blast size if needed. The electronic detonators included a timer mechanism and a blasting cap. Rogue gently arranged these in another bag, separated from each other with a square of foam she cut from the original packaging. C4 is very stable and insensitive to most physical shocks, so dropping it onto the tiled floor of the hotel room wouldn't cause an explosion. The detonators were a completely different matter, as the blasting caps contain a small amount of explosive material, which can be easily ignited. Dropping one, or a box of eight, had the potential to cause Rogue serious injury, not to mention setting off the hotel's fire alarm. With luck, she wouldn't need to blow up anything, but experience had taught her that Plan A only worked seventy per cent of the time. The C4 was her Plan B.

Next, she turned her attention to the guns. As she stripped and cleaned both Glocks, the smell from the gun oil crept into her nostrils. At that moment, she was transported back several years to the MI5 Ordinance Centre, where she and Tasha prepared for missions together. Standing on opposite sides of an aluminium topped bench, they'd blindfold each other and have a race stripping and rebuilding a row of weapons, from compact Sig pistols to H&K submachine guns. Nine times out of ten, Tasha would finish first, but in the year leading up to their last mission together, they'd shared the honours, namely a takeaway from Maximo's Bistro. Rogue's stomach rumbled at the thoughts of the chef's famous Fettuccine Alfredo. She shook the memories from her mind and resumed brushing the slide of the Baby Glock. After reassembling both weapons, she loaded them with full magazines and added a bonus round to the chamber of each. Then she tried on the holsters, adjusting them to suit her preferred fit and position.

After Rogue had completed the equipment check, she arranged specific items inside the black backpack. Anything she wanted to carry on per person, including the guns, knives and two grenades, she placed in the holdall. Once she had parked the Audi somewhere near the technology park, she could gear up. After stowing everything away, she pulled back the curtains. The room reeked of oil, mostly from the C4, but also from the gun cleaner and lubricant. She sealed the gloves, wrappers and cloths in a double plastic bag, and zipped the holdall shut to prevent any further fumes escaping into the room. A healthy breeze blew in from outside.

Satisfied with her work, she headed for the bathroom. It had already been a long day, and she'd missed her usual shower that morning. The hot water quickly found cuts and bruises from her fight in the alley. After scrubbing off the sweat and grime, she let the water cascade through her hair and onto her shoulders, waiting for the heat to seep into her muscles. When her thoughts strayed back to Agnetha, she stepped out of the shower before her imagination tied her body in knots again.

Ten minutes later, Rogue had dressed in clean clothes and felt much better. At least physically. Emotionally, she was anxious, afraid for Agnetha, but otherwise, she was ready. She gathered the bags at the door and did a last sweep of the room. The breeze seemed to have cleared the odours, but just in case, she aimed a few blasts of the lemon air freshener into the corners and around the beds. At 10 pm, she left the NeuWald Hotel unnoticed through a rear service door and drove off.

Chapter 14

Rogue pulled into the Migrol service station for the second time that day and looked across at the Kleiner Technology Campus. In contrast to the bright lights of the car showrooms, the windows of the office blocks seemed grey and lifeless. After topping up the Audi's fuel tank, she headed into the cafe. It was going to be a long night, and she didn't know when she'd get a chance for proper food again. The menu was limited, mostly fast food or sandwiches, but she settled for a steak baguette, which came with a portion of deep fried onion rings, potato wedges and coffee. A table by the window gave her a good view of the forecourt and the entrance to the technology park. While she devoured the food, she ran through her plan.

Extractions came in two flavours, stealth and hard strike. Both had advantages and disadvantages. Stealth was easier to plan and was more predictable. It used minimal personnel and equipment and resulted in fewer casualties. The downside was that it required reliable intel with plenty of detail. That included knowing the location and physical condition of your target, security arrangements, and knowledge of the entry and exit points. Because of their cautious nature, stealth missions required more time to complete.

With the second option, a hard strike, the goal was to distract and confuse the enemy, allowing you to locate and rescue your target before they regrouped. However, this approach instantly alerted security personnel, making them more difficult to overcome. A hard strike had to be executed quickly, before the guards identified the source of the disruption.

Rogue's team of one reduced her options. She could only carry a limited amount of equipment and was vulnerable to attack from every direction. Not knowing exactly where Webb was being held meant she'd have to use the stealth approach. If that failed, she'd switch to all guns blazing and hope that the security guards on duty would run for cover.

Her plan was to park the Audi on a maintenance track along the west side of the campus. According to the satellite view, dense trees lined one side of the track, interspersed with clusters of hedging. There were plenty of gaps to hide a vehicle from prying eyes, and the Audi's black paintwork would blend in easily. From there, she'd cut a gap in the wire fence, make her way to the VerKoll building and wait for the smoking guard to appear at 1 am.

While Rogue finished her meal, she noticed several trucks pulling in, some for fuel, others on food breaks. Among them were a few with the Astro Logistics logo, a silver star inside a red triangle. When each truck left, they drove directly into the technology campus. A few minutes before 11 pm, Rogue left the cafe and drove the Audi along the maintenance track. A hundred metres before the spot she'd selected, she killed the headlights and covered the remaining distance at a crawl. She nudged the car onto a soft patch between two large hedges, then reversed in behind the first one, hiding the vehicle from view.

Once her vision adjusted to the darkness, she used the binoculars to survey the area around the Astro Logistics depot. All the delivery bays were open, and floodlights bathed the forecourt in a hazy yellow light. It reminded her of a military base, but without the armed guards. The spot where she had parked was shrouded in darkness, and she doubted anyone could see her from the depot. There were two trucks reversed up to the warehouse. She recognised one man standing on the forecourt, laughing with an Astro employee holding a clipboard. The driver had come into the Migrol cafe earlier for a takeaway.

Rogue pulled on the black beanie hat and tucked her hair underneath. Then she crept over to the fence and used the wire cutters to make two incisions, one horizontal, the other vertical midway along the first. The four corners that met in the centre folded back easily to reveal a gap large enough for her to pass through. She returned to the car and geared up. Shoulder and ankle holsters first, then the Glock pistols. Extra magazines split between two pockets. MK3 combat knife at her waist, Gerber boot knife strapped to her right calf. Everything else went into the backpack. As she started her equipment check, the screech of tyres and a thunderous crash shattered the stillness.

Dropping low, she pulled the boot lid down as an explosion of light penetrated the trees. Voices carried through the night air, hectic and urgent. Rogue squeezed into a hedge until she could see through the other side. In the distance, two beams of yellow lights, one above the other, flooded the grassy area inside the wire fence. She squinted against the glare and gradually picked out the shape of a truck lying on one side. A shadow appeared on top of it, a man trying to open the cab door. More shadows and voices gathered around the front of the stricken vehicle. The driver must have taken the bend too fast and overturned the truck. It wasn't any of Rogue's business, but it impacted her plan. Going through the fence was no longer an option, not with all that activity and bright light. If the driver was hurt, there'd soon be an ambulance and maybe police.

She extracted herself from the foliage and examined her options. She considered cutting another gap in the fence further back, but that stretch was well lit by street lamps. Going in the other direction was no good either, as she'd have to pass Astro Logistics in order to reach VerKoll. She needed another option. She looked back at the lights of the service station. While she'd been in the cafe, an Astro truck had pulled in every fifteen or twenty minutes. If that frequency remained constant, at least for the next hour or two, it might provide her with a way in.

Rogue completed her equipment check and was about to lock the car, but changed her mind. If she lost the keys during the mission, it would cost her valuable time. Instead, she pocketed one key and shoved the spare under the mat behind the driver's seat. Then she hurried back to the service station, keeping in the shadows. Once inside the forecourt, she walked casually along the row of parked vehicles, watching for one bearing the Astro logo. She was out of luck, but it was still her best option, so she ducked behind a billboard and waited.

Shortly after midnight, an Astro van arrived and reversed into a parking spot. The driver went into the cafe and Rogue saw him examining the sandwiches in the fridge. There was no one else in the van, a Ford Transit. She'd have preferred something larger, ideally an artic, but time was running out. Staying clear of the forecourt floodlights, she made her way to the van. Inside the cafe, the driver had reached the cash till and appeared to be waiting for a coffee. Rogue twisted the handle on the rear door of the van and pulled.

It opened easily. She shone her torch inside, hoping it was fully loaded, with just enough space for her to hide behind the cargo. Stacks of brown cardboard boxes reached the roof of the van, with a clear path up through the centre. Placing one foot on the bumper, she grabbed the other door and hauled herself up. A scratching noise came from behind the boxes, followed by a deep growl. As a pair of eyes rose from the floor and advanced towards her, the growling increased. Rogue's torch illuminated an enormous dog glaring at her, shoulders hunched and teeth bared. She dropped back to the ground, gently closed the door and turned the handle. Barking erupted, shattering the silence. Rogue hurried behind a row of trucks, startling a pair of cats who tore off across the forecourt. She looked at her watch. 12:14 pm. If she wanted to take advantage of the smoking guard's first break at 1 am, it was essential that she get inside the campus soon.

She reconsidered her original plan of breaching the fence and decided to select the best spot she could find and take a chance. As she turned to leave, she heard voices, two men chatting. They were close by. She'd been so lost in her thoughts that she'd missed them as they'd approached. She looked up at the sides of the two articulated trucks she was standing between. One had the name GenPharm, the other Muller Electronics. She'd seen a pair of Muller trucks stopped in the Astro Logistics gateway earlier that day. Most likely, their next destination was the Astro depot, but she needed to make sure. She moved closer to eavesdrop on the drivers. They were discussing an exchange of some sort.

"I couldn't get it, they've stepped up the security in R&D," said a gravelly voice.

"Damn, I said I'd have it this time. He's already paid me," said the second guy, a fast talker.

"I need to get going, gotta be at the Astro depot in the next ten minutes. You dealing or what?"

"Yeah, fine, you can have the Fentanyl, but you owe me. Next time, you better bring that VR kit."

The voices faded as they moved to the far side of the Muller truck. Rogue heard a metal door grind open and a man clamber inside. This was her chance. The Muller driver would depart shortly and she'd be outside the VerKoll building with time to spare. She sidled up to the cab and tested the handle. It turned freely. She listened, then pulled. The door swung open silently. Rogue climbed into the driver's seat and gently closed the door. A laminated ID card clipped to the dashboard showed a passport sized photo of a bearded man. His name was Gerhard Ziegler. She turned her attention to the area behind the seats. There was a set of plain black curtains separating the sleeping quarters from the front. She slid them apart. It was a basic setup, with storage units underneath a single bunk. A navy striped blanket lay draped over a pillow directly behind the driver's seat and a half rolled up sleeping bag sat at the bottom of the bed. Electronics magazines and brochures littered the floor.

The cab rocked from the vibration of the rear door being slammed shut. Rogue scrambled between the front seats onto the bed and slid the curtains closed. She stashed her backpack in a cupboard underneath the bunk, then tucked herself into a ball directly behind the driver's seat, pressing her back against the side panel of the truck. Taking the Glock from her shoulder holster, she rested it on the pillow beside her. The cab door opened and Ziegler got in. Then there was silence. No sound of keys jangling or the seat belt clicking into place. Rogue tensed.

Seconds passed, five, ten, fifteen. As she focused on slowing her breathing, she detected the smell of fried onions. At first she assumed it was from Ziegler, then remembered the onion rings she'd eaten at the cafe. She lowered her head and breathed into her jacket, hoping the odour wouldn't make its way forward.

Rogue jumped when the curtain lifted and Ziegler's hand reached in, stretching towards her. His fingers were twice the size of hers, the skin hard and calloused. He was a big man, well over a hundred kilos. She couldn't afford to wrestle with him in the close quarters of the cab. He'd crush her. She realised the curtains were still closed. That meant he was just looking for something and didn't know she was hiding there.

She stood upright, planted her feet wide and snatched up the Glock an instant before Ziegler's hand dug under the pillow. He probed left and right, stretching to his limits. Rogue tried to shrink back into one corner, her back pressed up against the ceiling in the small space. When Ziegler dragged the pillow to one side, she saw what he was looking for. A plastic bag of tablets lay just beyond his reach. Carefully, Rogue nudged it closer until his fingers wrapped around it and he whipped it away.

Rogue relaxed a little, but knew her ordeal wasn't over yet. As she listened to the bag rustling, she visualised Ziegler dropping the Fentanyl capsules he'd bought from the GenPharm driver into the plastic bag and wondered what his next move would be. With a little luck, he'd stow the bag of drugs somewhere up front, but chances were he'd want to return them and the pillow to their original locations. That meant opening the curtains and partly crawling inside the bunk area. She pointed her gun at the gap between the front seats. If Ziegler pulled the curtains apart, he'd come face to face with the muzzle of the Glock.

The anticipation of a close quarters confrontation with Ziegler dumped adrenaline into Rogue's bloodstream. As her heart pumped faster, raising the temperature, moisture seeped from her fingertips, compromising her grip on the Glock. In the confines of the cab's sleeping quarters, the heat from her body and smell of fried onions from her breath had nowhere to go. She hoped the Ziegler was too busy to notice.

The curtains parted. Not fully, but enough for a head to pass through. Rogue braced herself against the side of the cab. Ziegler's hand darted through, grabbed the pillow, and tossed it back to the head of the bed. It collided with Rogue's leg and landed on its side against her shin. She nudged it, urging it to fall over, but it refused to cooperate. Ziegler stretched back with the plastic bag, feeling around for the pillow. Rogue gripped the Glock with both hands. Ziegler shifted in his seat, twisted his whole body around, and stuck his head partially through the curtains. He still couldn't see the furthest recesses of the sleeping area, only the end of the pillow furthest from Rogue. He lunged for it and missed. He tried again, failing by millimetres. Rogue knew a confrontation was inevitable. She adjusted her posture, ready to ram the muzzle of the Glock under Ziegler's chin.

Chapter 15

Outside, a horn blasted twice from a nearby truck. Ziegler's hand, still holding the bag of drugs, hovered in mid-air. He withdrew a little and sounded his own horn in reply. Rogue heard him mumble something about being late. Ziegler lifted the edge of the mattress, shoved the bag underneath it, then withdrew. The cab shuddered as he started the diesel engine and shifted into gear. As the truck lurched forward, Rogue eased down onto the bed and allowed her lungs to breathe again, then wiped the sweat from her hands and allowed herself a half smile. Luck was on her side. Hopefully, it was a good omen for the night ahead.

From the moment she'd arrived back at the empty apartment that morning and discovered that Agnetha was missing, Rogue had felt out of control. The kidnapper was pulling all the strings. As the truck left the service station, some of her old resolve and determination returned. It was a relief to be taking the initiative and doing something decisive that would bring her closer to rescuing Agnetha. She pressed the cold barrel of the Glock against her cheek and visualised herself striding through the corridors of VerKoll, calmly taking out anyone standing in her path.

Ziegler slowed the truck when they reached the gates into the Kleiner Technology Campus. The whine of the brakes jolted Rogue from her daydream. Realising where her thoughts had strayed, a wave of guilt crept over Rogue. She was looking forward to the night ahead, to the adrenaline rush and the action. Her head dropped to her chest as she sent Agnetha a silent promise.

The truck banked as it turned off the road and stopped at the security barrier. A hint of cool breeze wafted between the curtains as Ziegler lowered his window. Rogue heard him exchange greetings with the guard as he handed over the required documentation. The guard could decide to search the truck, but it was unlikely. It wasn't a customs post. If a driver had no paperwork, the guard might ring ahead and verify their credentials. Even if he decided on a rare spot check, it'd be the cargo space in the back and not the cab that he'd be interested in.

The cool air receded as Ziegler closed the window. The engine revved, and they moved off again. As Ziegler shifted through the gears, Rogue started planning her exit from the cab without being seen. The trucks she had spotted parked in the Astro depot earlier that day had all reversed up to the bays.

The drivers then left and disappeared into the office with their paperwork. Rogue checked the time. 00:43 am. She needed Ziegler to park and leave the truck promptly if she was to make it to the VerKoll fire exit before the guard appeared for his smoking break. The truck slowed, then turned in through the gates of Astro Logistics. Ziegler made a half circle before reversing up to a vacant bay. He got it right the first time and killed the engine.

Rogue stiffened when she remembered the drugs Ziegler had stashed under the mattress. With a little luck, he'd leave them there, but she couldn't take a chance. She rose onto her knees with the Glock ready. She didn't need Ziegler any longer. If he confronted her, she'd disable him and be long gone before anyone discovered him. The sound of rustling paper came from the driver's seat. Ziegler was taking forever. Finally, the cab door creaked open.

"Have you got the manifest?" bellowed a voice.

"Hang on," said Ziegler. More rustling of papers. "Here it is."

"OK, I only need the top sheet. Take the rest over to the office."

"How long to unload?"

"Forty minutes should do it."

"Right, thanks." The cab shifted a little as Ziegler jumped down from the truck and banged the door shut.

Rogue forced herself to wait two full minutes in case Ziegler came back for something he forgot. She heard the rear doors open as the depot staff began unloading the cargo. Finally, she eased herself between the front seats and paused, letting her eyes adjust after the darkness of the bunk area. Using the wing mirrors, she could see activity at the rear of the truck. The forecourt was lit by powerful lamps, but thankfully, the path to the gates was deserted. Rogue reached under the bed and retrieved her backpack. Opening the cab door gently, she dropped to the ground. She didn't want to leave the door swinging open, but shutting it fully would require force and noise, so she compromised and clicked it into a half closed position. Moving around to the front of the cab, she checked there was nobody looking in her direction, then walked swiftly across the forecourt and through the open gates.

Opposite the entrance, a crew was preparing to lift the overturned truck using a mobile crane. Floodlights illuminated the underside of the truck, reminding Rogue of a wounded animal in a wildlife documentary. She spared a thought for the driver, then turned away and followed the railings towards VerKoll. When she reached the row of hedges that marked the border between the Astro and VerKoll properties, she stepped off the path and listened. No footsteps followed her. No voices called out. Her watch showed 00:56 am.

Rogue quickly scaled the barrier, found a gap in a row of hedges, and hunkered down amongst the branches. It wasn't comfortable, but she didn't expect to be there for more than a few minutes. If the smoking guard failed to show at his usual time, she'd switch to her backup plan. A fine misty rain covered the grass verge and the pavement leading to the fire exit a few metres away. She tugged stray branches from each side to provide additional cover, but once released, they sprang back.

Rogue studied the fire exit. A canopy sheltered it from rain and spiders had strung webs from the canopy to the surface of the door. She relaxed a little, confident the door hadn't been opened recently, and the guard hadn't taken an early break. She swapped her beanie hat for the balaclava, then positioned the head torch snugly around it. As the seconds ticked by, her thoughts strayed to Agnetha. Rogue couldn't help wonder where she was being held and under what conditions. Scenarios invaded Rogue's mind, each one more terrifying than the last. Before long, she was visualising Agnetha lying beaten and dying in a deserted basement. Rogue swore to herself that she'd hunt down each of the men responsible and deliver each a slow, painful death.

A rustling sound to her left startled Rogue back to reality. Her hand wrapped around the hilt of the combat knife on her belt as she held her breath and strained her ears. As a shadow moved into her peripheral vision and stopped, a pair of green eyes stared at her. It was a cat, jet black. Satisfied it wasn't in any danger, it resumed its patrol. Rogue released the knife and exhaled.

She checked her watch, careful not to let any light reflect off it. 00:59 am. Just one more minute. She knew it would feel like a hundred and one. She moved a little and stretched each leg alternately to ward off any stiffness or cramp. Waiting wasn't usually a problem for Rogue. She'd been on many stakeouts and surveillance ops during her time. She knew how to zone out, shut down her systems to conserve energy, while remaining alert and observant. But this was different. It was personal. Agnetha's life was at stake. Rogue felt responsible and knew that if she screwed it up, it would destroy her. She couldn't let Tasha down again.

So she waited. And hoped that everything aligned. That Marcus was right about the fire exit opening twice a night, that the smoking guard would remain loyal to his addiction, that the door she was staring at would soon swing open. Then she would shift gears and use her pent up energy to get Webb out instead of letting it gnaw away at her insides.

The black cat reappeared and plonked down outside the door. Maybe it was expecting the guard as well. Rogue's watch pulsed three times against her wrist, signalling 1 am. She watched the exit door, expecting the sound of a key turning or a bolt sliding open. She'd run the most likely scenarios through her mind and knew exactly how she would take down the guard, regardless of whether he stood in one spot or paced around. Marcus has said that the fire exit never remained open for more than four minutes. Somebody in the security control room was covering for the smoker, but for whatever reason, four minutes was the maximum they could give him. Or maybe he knew that nobody monitored the cameras at 1 am for those specific minutes. Either way, Rogue needed to move fast and get inside before the control room raised the alarm.

Twin lights in the distance caught her attention. As they grew brighter, she realised that it was a truck taking the road to Astro Logistics. It would pass right by her position. Damn it, she thought, why now? She couldn't risk disabling the guard in full view of the truck's driver. She tried to estimate the distance and speed, to calculate how long it would take before the truck passed her by. He was crawling along, wary of a sequence of speed ramps. She turned her attention back to the fire exit. It remained shut. She stared at it, shielding her eyes from the approaching headlights. Eventually, the truck glided past, and she was alone in the darkness again. The cat also watched the door, occasionally emitting a meow. It looked like they would both be disappointed.

1:04 am.

Rogue waited for another six minutes, then slid off her pack and opened the flap. It was time to execute Plan B.

Chapter 16

Webb blinked his eyes open, then shielded them with his arm from the intense white light. The thin blanket did little to keep him warm or to soften the concrete floor beneath him. At least it was dry, not damp, like the forest in his recurring nightmares. As he rolled off his back and eased himself into a sitting position, cable ties bit into the raw skin on his wrists. Lifting the tail of his blood stained t-shirt with both hands, he wiped the sleepy sweat from his face. Then he inched back into the small corner alcove, the only part of the room that offered some respite from the overpowering bulbs the guards had installed overhead. Propped against the wall, he waited for his heart to stop thumping.

For days, he'd been trapped in the same never-ending cycle. Fatigue led to sleep. Nightmares jolted him awake, lathered in sweat. He'd throw off the small blanket, drift off again, only to wake up shivering from the cold. The only interruptions were the unscheduled visits from the guards, sometimes to bring food, but usually to ask the same incessant questions about Meerkat, the Decryptor and who Webb was working for.

Escape was impossible. They'd locked him in a basement room with only one way in and out. There were no windows, no air ducts, no slivers of hope. On his first day of captivity, Webb had searched every part of the room for a tool or weapon of any sort, but the guards had been thorough. There was nothing he could use. The floors were bare concrete, the boarded walls sealed tight. He guessed it was a storage room, but the only items that remained were a couple of chairs, plastic over aluminium frames, and some low wooden shelving bolted to the wall.

At first, the guards had gone easy on Webb. They tried psychology, telling him how much trouble he was in, that he'd end up in prison for industrial espionage, that his only chance was to cooperate. After a day or two of playing nice, they'd deprived him of food and sleep. That had no effect on Webb. He'd often gone days with nothing but cold pizza while playing online games, refusing stubbornly to concede defeat to adversaries halfway across the world.

Then they'd got physical. Only the guard called Steinbeck had the stomach for it. The others left the room while the German used Webb as a punchbag. Steinbeck was a bruiser. Taller and wider than Webb's slim frame, he'd legs like tree trunks and could lift Webb off the floor with one giant hand. He approached

Webb slowly, grinning through his beard, enjoying himself. When Webb heard the crunch of a tooth coming loose, he'd yielded, giving Steinbeck the information his boss had asked for, or rather a modified version of it. After another volley of punches, they'd left him curled up on the ground.

Webb wrapped the blanket around him again. As the terror of his nightmare ebbed away, the aches all over his body returned. He dabbed his left side gingerly and winced. He knew nothing about first aid, but suspected they'd fractured one or more of his ribs. With luck, it might only be severe bruising. He opened and closed his jaw slowly, wincing with each movement.

His memories from the night in MegaTron were sketchy. After he'd passed out in the stampede, he vaguely recalled a bumpy ride in the back of a van, but had lost consciousness again. He woke in the small room where he'd been ever since. It felt like he'd been there for a week, but the stubble on his chin told him it was only three or four days. His backpack, phone and other belongings were gone, even his favourite Doc Marten boots.

A key turning in the locked door signalled the return of the guards. Webb straightened up a little as two men entered the room. One was the boss, a man called Gantz. Webb didn't recognise the other guy, but he wore the same uniform as the others.

Gantz scrutinised Webb's bruised face before addressing his colleague. "The van will be here in an hour. Have him cleaned up and ready to go before then."

Webb tried to speak but only managed a croak before he got a fit of coughing. When it subsided, he'd left a splatter of bloody mucus on the concrete.

"And get him a change of clothes." Gantz stepped away, holding his nose.

"Where are you taking me?" asked Webb, his voice still a little croaky.

"You're not my problem anymore, but I'll give you some advice. What we did to you here was nothing." Gantz paused and shook his head. "The man in charge of this operation? Let's just say he's not as patient as I am. He always gets what he wants, one way or the other."

The look on Gantz's face chilled Webb. He scrambled off the floor. "I told you everything I know. I gave you what you asked for!"

"You sent us on a wild goose chase, wasted hours of my time." Gantz headed for the door.

"Wait, I'll tell you where it is, then you can hand me over to the police," pleaded Webb.

Gantz stepped into the corridor.

"Wait, come back," shouted Webb. He tried to run after Gantz, but his legs were still asleep and couldn't support him. He stumbled and landed in a heap. The second guard kicked Webb's feet out of his way and followed Gantz into the corridor. The door slammed shut.

As the key turned in the lock, Webb crawled on all fours to the door and thumped it with his fists. "It's in MegaTron, I'll show you." He pressed his ear to the timber, but the footsteps became fainter. He shouted after them, but knew he was wasting his energy. His head swam and his stomach lurched. He retched, but only managed dribbles of dark green bile. Every heave hurt his stomach and burned the lining of his throat.

He lay on the cold concrete floor and waited for the nausea to subside. His eyes focused on a discarded sandwich carton from his first day as a prisoner. The lingering smell of the spiced beef sandwich reached his nostrils and triggered a fresh round of retching, dry this time, but equally painful. He craved a drink, something cool and soothing. He looked around the room, more in hope than expectation. The air inside was heavy and suffocating. Heat radiated from one wall, possibly from a boiler or hot-water pipes on the far side. Steinbeck had taunted him the previous day, sipping from a plastic bottle of sparkling water while he questioned him, licking his lips to emphasise the pleasure of it. Yet again, Webb's eyes locked on the empty bottle on the floor, mocking him. He closed his eyes and drifted into another restless sleep.

<hr />

The door jolted open and pulled Webb from a fresh nightmare. Webb looked around, simultaneously hopeful and afraid. His spine chilled when he saw Steinbeck's bulk fill the gap. Webb backed into the corner.

Steinbeck swaggered in, stood over Webb, and kicked him in the ribs. "Get up."

Another set of boots trudged in after the big man. "Hey, that's enough. Wedge that door open, get some air in here."

Webb squinted up at the new arrival. It was Hermann, the guard that had accompanied Gantz earlier.

"Some water," said Webb. "Please."

Hermann righted the upturned chair and set down a first aid bag. He unzipped it, found a bottle of water, and rolled it across the floor. Webb snapped it up with both hands, unscrewed the cap, and swallowed the cool liquid in gulps. Then he poured some over his scalp and face, rubbing the sweat and grime away with his hand.

Hermann moved the first aid kit to the floor and snatched the bottle from Webb. "Sit on the chair."

"My boss, he's loaded. If you help me get out of here, you can name your price," pleaded Webb.

Hermann selected a few items from his bag, looked at Steinbeck and nodded towards Webb.

"Where are you taking me?" asked Webb.

Steinbeck crossed the room in three strides. He grabbed Webb by the throat, effortlessly hoisted him off the floor, and planted him in the chair. He grinned at Webb and laughed. "A one-way trip, to hell, that's where."

Hermann assessed his patient, poured some antiseptic on a cotton swab, and began wiping a gaping cut under Webb's left eye.

Webb jerked back. "What the hell was that?"

"Antiseptic. It prevents infection," said Hermann. "Hold him."

Steinbeck moved behind the chair and pinned Webb's shoulders back.

"What's the point?" said Webb. "You're going to kill me anyway."

Hermann began treating the cuts on Webb's face again, ignoring his protests. Webb tried to pull away, but Steinbeck's grip allowed no leeway.

"How come you're playing nursemaid?" sneered Steinbeck.

"I'm the First Aid Officer," said Hermann. He stuck a plaster under Webb's left eye and another one over the right, then applied antiseptic cream to Webb's split lip.

"You give massages?" Steinbeck emitted a deep, heaving laugh.

"Anything broken?" asked Hermann.

Webb pulled up his shirt. "Maybe a few ribs."

Hermann traced the bones with his fingers, pressing as he went until Webb yelped, and then explored that area more closely.

"So why you?" said Steinbeck.

"There was an opening, and it came with an extra allowance," said Hermann. "I'd spent two years as an ambo driver."

Steinbeck grunted.

"Only bruises, no breaks," said Hermann.

"Why bother with all this?" said Steinbeck.

"I just follow orders. Why don't you ask Gantz next time you see him?"

"And get another telling off?"

"The boss said question him, not pummel him to death."

"My fists don't understand the difference," said Steinbeck with a smirk.

Hermann handed Webb two painkillers and the water. "Take these."

"Only two!" said Webb, looking at the pills in his hand.

Hermann closed the first aid bag and stood up.

Webb swallowed the tablets and finished the remains of the water before they could take it from him. "What about food? I haven't eaten in days!"

Steinbeck came around the chair to face Webb and showed him his clenched fist. "Shut up or I'll undo the nurse's good work!"

Webb looked at Hermann, hoping for some sympathy, but the medic was already on his way to the door. Static erupted from the radio clipped to Steinbeck's belt. A panicked voice delivered a few words Webb failed to catch, then Steinbeck rushed past Hermann, almost knocking him over. Hermann followed, but stopped long enough to lock the door after him. Webb was left alone again, with only his vivid imagination for company.

Chapter 17

It was Dejan Reissman's seventeenth year working for VerKoll GmbH. After spending the first fifteen in software development, he decided it was time for a change. When an opportunity arose in the security department, he indulged his midlife crisis and opted for something different. As a long serving employee of the company, familiar with their computer systems and security protocols, he was a good fit. Being an active member of the fire brigade in his local town turned out to be a bonus.

Every alternate month, Reissman took the night shift from 10 pm to 6 am. It was an easy stint as very few VerKoll employees worked through the night, only those on the international support team, and occasionally a few developers putting in extra hours on a major upgrade. Even during the day, the security personnel were rarely called into action. Reissman's boss, Marler Gantz, ran a tight ship and was a stickler for procedures, but once his team completed the scheduled checks to his liking, he allowed them some leeway. Reissman's computer experience meant that Gantz usually stationed him in the control room, watching the multitude of cameras and sensors throughout the offices and car parks.

At 1:30 am, as was his custom, Reissman lifted his flask and lunch box onto the desk. He opened his phone and started his favourite music playlist, a selection of classical pieces. Taking a bite of a roast beef sandwich, he carefully poured a cup of carrot and coriander soup that his girlfriend had made. As he savoured the first mouthful, an angry klaxon burst from the rack of computers mounted on the wall.

Reissman shoved his lunch to one side and rolled his chair closer. The security system automatically sent every alarm notification to each guard on duty, including the boss. At most, Reissman had thirty seconds to assess the situation before Gantz buzzed him on the radio. The centre screen showed a three-dimensional model of the building with a blue square flashing on the west side. The square represented an external door. Blue was a ground floor alarm. It was probably another faulty sensor, but it could also be one of Gantz's impromptu fire drills. Either way, Reissman had to follow protocol. He clicked the flashing square to get more information. It showed the door's status as 'unknown' and the alarm sensor as 'offline'. That ruled out a drill. It could be a fault, but the chances of both the alarm and the door sensors failing at the same time were low.

Reissman swivelled to face an adjacent monitor and clicked through a list of video feeds until he found the zone where the alarm had gone off. The corridor was empty, but the door hung open. As he zoomed in closer, he realised that a chunk of the door was missing where the lock should have been. He picked up the radio to call Gantz, but was unsure exactly what he would say. If he suggested an explosion and he was wrong, his colleagues would never allow him to forget it. Before he could decide, the radio buzzed in his hand. Reissman dropped it and knocked his mug of soup on its side.

A command barked from the radio speaker. "Romeo, this is Golf." It was his boss, Marler Gantz.

Reissman cursed, then wheeled away from the desk, letting the thick yellow liquid flow onto the floor. He snatched up the radio and pressed the button to reply. "Romeo here, go ahead Golf."

"Status check," bellowed Gantz.

"Sensor activation of Blue One-Seven, video feed shows the door open with damage along one side," blurted Reissman. "The corridor is empty."

"Describe the damage."

"Looks like it was … burnt … by a flame or something."

"Dammit Romeo, I want a threat assessment, not a school report," roared Gantz.

"No sir. Copy that sir. It looks like a detonation blew out the locks," said Reissman, holding the radio away from his ear.

"And you're not in the army, Reissman. One sir is enough. I am en route to the target. Send Hotel to meet me there. Out."

A long burst of static plunged into Reissman's ear, intentionally sent by Gantz whenever he vented his rage.

Reissman buzzed Hermann, code named Hotel.

"I'm on my way down to you, Romeo. You got the kettle on?"

"Boss wants you at Blue One-Seven. There's been a breach. He's en route there now."

"Damn it, probably one of his stupid drills. Where the hell is Blue One-Seven?"

"Rear fire exit, ground floor, west side," said Reissman.

"I'm on my way."

"Roger that."

"Out," said Hermann.

Reissman put down the radio and stared at the soup dripping from the desk. Before he could mop it up, another alarm screamed at him. He turned back to the monitors. Another fire exit, also on the west side, this time towards the front aspect of the building. He switched the video to Blue-16. The image was almost identical to Blue-17. The door swung open, charred and disfigured. He grabbed the radio and buzzed Gantz.

"Report," said Gantz, without waiting for Reissman to announce himself.

"Sensor activation of Blue One-Six, video image matches Blue One-Seven."

"Initiate ground floor overwatch, internal and external. Notify me of any intruders."

"Affirmative."

"That means cameras on all floors, Romeo, on five second rotations using three screens. Understood?"

"Copy that, sir."

"Out," said Gantz.

Reissman exhaled. The shift wasn't going well for him. He knew how to run an overwatch procedure better than the rest of the team. Except Gantz, of course. Reissman didn't need it explained to him. He whipped open a cabinet door and was relieved to see a stack of napkins. Grabbing a handful, he wiped the desk dry, then set about configuring the surveillance system. He switched all the screens to video mode, then allocated each one a specific range of camera IDs. Finally, he set the intervals to five seconds and kicked off the rotation. Each screen showed video from four cameras simultaneously. He dimmed the lights in the room, making it easier to focus on the screens, particularly the cameras outside the building. He was hell bent on showing his boss that he was up to the job. Two minutes later, his radio buzzed.

"Romeo, this is Golf. Report."

"All cameras are clear, sir." Reissman stood up and leaned in closer to the screens.

"I'm proceeding outside to start a perimeter check," said Gantz.

"Copy that," said Reissman, relieved he hadn't been given yet another job to do.

"Keep your eyes on all squad members. Make contact if anyone drops off the grid. Out."

The radio clicked, and Reissman was alone again. He remained standing, but relaxed a little. It was clear, at least to him, that someone had used explosive charges to breach the exits. So far, he had seen no one on the cameras except other members of the security team. Hermann was still at Blue-17 and Gantz had assigned security personnel to sweep each floor of the building. Gantz had served as a drill sergeant in the army. The other members of the security team jumped when he spoke, but he did not intimidate them. Every time Gantz asked Reissman to do something, he overcompensated and got flustered. All he could do now was follow orders and let the boss call the shots.

He risked a glance at the floor. His boots had spread the spillage across the centre of the room. He longed to clean it up, but he wasn't prepared to abandon the cameras, even for a minute. He'd rather endure the bosses' reprimand over the condition of the office than miss something on the videos. Even though he'd been made a permanent member of the security department, he knew that counted for nothing if Gantz decided otherwise.

There'd been something else nagging at the back of Reissman's mind since the first alarm had activated, but he'd been so busy, he hadn't been able to identify it until now. Documented protocols existed for every situation, all printed and stored in ring binders on a shelf behind him. He'd studied them all during the induction training, but that had been two years ago. Once he'd started the job, he'd focused on memorising the daily routines and making sure he recorded everything according to the regulations. He'd encountered nothing exceptional, certainly nothing close to a perimeter breach.

Indecision taunted Reissman yet again. He reckoned Gantz trusted him with the Security Control Centre, otherwise he'd have sent one of the other team members to take over. But that trust brought a weight of responsibility. What would Gantz do in this situation? He'd be decisive and follow his gut instincts. Reissman turned to the first screen and quickly checked the feed from every camera. Then he started a five second countdown in his head, during which he searched the shelves for the Security Procedures folder.

He found it with one second remaining and darted back to his desk just in time to see an eruption of light on the first monitor. This time it was a fire exit on the east side of the building, designated as Blue-4 and was only fifty metres down the corridor from the Control

Room where Reissman was stationed. The last thing he saw was the fire door sailing towards the security camera, before the screen filled with white noise. He switched to a camera further along the same corridor, just in time to see a shadow pass beneath it. His radio buzzed, startling him.

"Romeo, this is Golf. What the hell was that?"

"The door at Blue Four has been destroyed and the video feed is down."

"Get Hotel and Tango to the west side of the building, to exits four and three," ordered Gantz.

"There's something else, sir. I think an intruder entered through Blue Four."

"Say again, Romeo."

"I saw something in the main corridor, like a shadow. I think whoever breached the door is inside the building."

"Seal off the upper floors and initiate a System Lockdown. Out."

Reissman froze. He was out of his depth, overwhelmed with responsibilities and suddenly feeling very much the newbie. What should he do first? Looking down at the desk, he saw the security folder he'd pulled from the shelf. Procedures. He worked best when following a predetermined sequence. What had Gantz told him to do first? Get Hotel and Tango over to the west side of the building. Before Reissman picked up the radio, he heard a clunk on the far side of the control room door. He stood up, expecting to see Gantz walk through. Instead, a deafening roar assaulted his ears. A chunk of timber erupted from the door and hit Reissman in the face. Stunned, he stumbled backwards into the wheelie chair. As it rolled away and he toppled to the floor.

Chapter 18

When the smoking guard failed to appear at the fire exit, Rogue switched from her planned stealth approach to a hard strike. Her new objective was to surprise the security guards and cause confusion. She knew the benefits of a shock attack wouldn't last long. Exactly how long depended upon how experienced the guards were, so speed was critical. Rogue set explosives at four fire exits, two on the east side and two more on the west. They were timed to detonate at sixty-second intervals. She set the third rig to blow the door closest to the security centre, hoping the fourth a minute later would draw attention to the furthest corner of the building.

Even before the smoke cleared at Blue Four, Rogue barged past the smouldering door and sprinted along the corridor, turning left, then right, the route fresh in her memory. Outside the control room, she extracted a C4 rig from her pack and attached it to the door. Using her knife, she cut away half of the explosive block.

The internal doors were lighter than the heavy fire doors and she needed whoever was inside to remain conscious. She stepped to one side and detonated the charge, then drew her Glock and kicked the door in. Robbed of its magnetic locks, it surrendered easily. Inside the room, a guard lay on his back, cradling his head, conscious but disoriented. Sidestepping him, Rogue dragged a wooden coat stand and used it to jam the door shut. She wasn't happy being trapped in the small office, but it was her best chance of finding Jason Webb quickly. She set a two-minute countdown on her watch.

As Rogue turned back around, the guard came at her, unsteadily swinging a fire extinguisher. She spun out of his path and let his momentum carry him into the wall. Then she stepped forward and unleashed a vicious kick to his knee. The joint ruptured, and he fell against the shelves. As his feet slid from under him, he frantically tried to regain his balance. When his right leg didn't respond, he looked down and saw his foot hanging limply. His face turned white, and he collapsed to the floor.

Rogue scanned the room and found the security roster pinned to a notice board on the wall. There were six names on the night shift. D. Reissman was assigned SC duty. She swapped her Glock for the combat knife, knelt down beside him and pressed the serrated edge of the razor-sharp blade against his cheek, the tip hovering millimetres from his left eye.

"You must be Reissman," said Rogue. "What's the D stand for?"

He looked up, puzzled, then whispered. "Dejan." His eyes dropped back down to stare at his injured leg.

"I'm short on time, Dejan, and even shorter on patience," said Rogue. "The prisoner, Jason Webb, where is he?"

Reissman was in a daze, unable to look away from his mangled knee. Rogue snatched a jacket that had fallen from the coat stand and flung it over his leg. Gripping his jaw, she twisted his head around to face her and eased the tip of the knife into the bone below his eye. As blood trickled along the blade, Rogue's watch pulsed. Thirty seconds had passed since she'd breached the Security Control Centre.

A voice erupted from the radio on the desk. "Romeo, this is Golf."

Barricaded in a tiny office with only one exit was suicide, but Rogue searching the entire building was out of the question.

"Reissman, me and my knife are out of time. Where is Jason Webb?"

Reissman looked back at her. She could see that he was in shock, but not so much that he didn't understand her question. Cogs were spinning in his head, debating, fight versus flight, buy time or save himself.

The radio buzzed again. "Romeo, this is Golf. Report."

Rogue switched her grip on the knife and hovered it above his thigh. "If you want to keep your leg, now is the time. When this blade slices your femoral artery, it's all over. Five ... four ..."

His eyes locked on the weapon and saw the blood smeared on the tip. His fingers instinctively dabbed at the sticky wound on his face. He bit his lip, willing himself to be strong, praying that one of his colleagues would come and rescue him.

"Three ... two ... one ..."

Rogue rammed the knife down.

Reissman clamped his eyes shut, screamed, then buried his face in his hands. "He's in the basement, the basement."

"Where exactly?" demanded Rogue.

Reissman opened his eyes and looked down. Rogue's blade had sliced through his trousers and pinned them to the floor, missing his flesh. Drowned in sweat, he sagged against the wall, resenting himself and the woman who had seen right through him.

Rogue punched him in the jaw and yelled in his face. "Where is Jason Webb?"

Reissman spat at her, his drool landing on her jacket, and stared back defiantly. Thumping erupted on the control room door, followed by shouts to open up. Rogue's peripheral vision caught the door handle turning rapidly, but the coat rack held firm. She could hear urgent voices outside the door and knew she only had seconds before they forced their way in. She glared at Reissman's and plunged the combat knife deep into his thigh. Agony tore through every nerve in his leg, removing any doubt of further trickery. His lungs heaved mouthfuls of air, robbing his ability to scream. Rogue smacked his skull against the cabinets and forced him to look at her.

"What section of the basement? Front or rear?"

No reaction.

"Where is Webb? The three rooms at the back?"

A spark of recognition in Reissman's eyes.

A coordinated roar from outside signalled an attack. Rogue leaped up as the door burst in and propelled the coat stand into Reissman's injured leg. He screamed. Rogue grabbed the wheelie chair and rammed it against the door, crushing an arm that had reached in, then wedged the coat stand back in place. Her watch beeped again, but time was irrelevant now. She dragged Reissman into the centre of the room, then grabbed the fallen fire extinguisher and hid behind the door.

As she kicked away the coat stand, the door burst in, followed by a security guard. Unable to slow down, he tripped over Reissman and crashed into the desk. When he saw Rogue, he raised his baton, but she was too quick and pounded the fire extinguisher into his face, shattering his nose in a sickening crunch. As he fell backwards, his eyes flicked to something behind her. She ducked and turned, but was too late to avoid a second guard. Her lower back screamed from the impact, robbing power from her legs.

Dropping the extinguisher, she stumbled forward, demanding her legs keep her upright. She reached for her Glock but a blow to her shoulder paralysed her arm and her hand fell empty by her side. Desperate to get out of the guard's reach, she snatched a smoke grenade from her hip pocket, took a deep breath, and extracted the pin. A cloud of green billowed around her. The guard would have to either back off or come through the smoke hard and fast. Rogue dropped the open cannister and ducked sideways, listening for the sound of footsteps, but all she could hear was Reissman groaning.

"Golf, this is Tango. SC under attack, repeat, SC under attack." The voice was heading for the door.

Rogue drew her Glock, followed his voice, and fired through the smoke. She heard a heavy thud. Rogue found him writhing on the floor. She had intentionally aimed low and two of her four bullets had caught him in the thigh. He'd live. Crouching down, she took his radio, then stepped out into the corridor.

The nearest stairwell was tucked in between the elevators and the reception desk. Rogue left the injured guards on the floor of the control room and headed for the front of the building. As she hurried along the corridor, the radio in her pocket buzzed.

"Security team, code red, switch channels, over."

Whoever was in command was acting fast to regain control of the situation. Rogue tossed the radio into a potted plant; it was useless to her now. She couldn't waste time trying different frequencies, hoping to hit the right one. She quickened per pace, rounding the corners without slowing, holding the Glock two handed in front of her. Lights came on in the dimly lit corridors as she progressed, activated by motion sensors. Fifty metres before the turn into the lobby, voices carried along the corridor from behind her. Then the screech of boots on the polished tiles. She'd lost the advantage. Reissman would have informed them she was after Webb, so they knew exactly where she was heading next. Compared to the upper floors with windows and emergency exits, the basement would offer few options to escape, possibly none. She was effectively setting her own trap and walking into it willingly. It wasn't the first time.

Rogue paused at the last bend and peered around. On the left were the elevators. Opposite them, the door to the stairwell. A dozen paces beyond, the rear panels of the reception desk obscured her view of whoever was on duty there. It was eerily silent. Then Rogue heard a low humming. On the panel over the elevator doors, the floor numbers ticked down—four, three, two. She darted into the lobby as the elevator bell rang and the doors slid open. A four-wheeled trolley laden with bottles and brushes rolled out, propelled by a woman nodding to a lively beat in her headphones.

Rogue yanked the vehicle into the open and heaved it over. Containers tumbled and bounced away. Buckets toppled onto the tiles, spilling waves of suds into the path of two guards as they charged around the corner. The trolley's owner unleashed a string of curses at Rogue, finger jabbing each word at her. When Rogue raised her Glock, the woman retreated, redirecting her finger at the panel of buttons inside the elevator, desperate to shut the doors.

The first guard, a bruiser, couldn't slow down. He skidded into the fallen trolley and slammed his face into the tiles. A handgun spun from his grip across the floor. The second guard dodged to the left but stepped on a rolling brush handle and fell down between the closing doors of the elevator. Inside, the cleaner, still prodding the buttons, screamed as the guard's head was hammered by the doors. The first guard extracted his limbs from the trolley and tried to stand, but his soles failed to grip the soapy tiles and he slid sideways.

Rogue felt a breeze whisper along her cheek from behind. She dropped low and spun around in time to deflect a blow to her head from a female guard who had emerged from the stairwell. The baton hammered into Rogue's wrist, paralysing the muscles in her arm. The woman followed up with a kick to Rogue's kneecap, then an elbow to her temple. Rogue staggered back as her vision hazed. Her assailant surged forward, eyes wild and teeth bared, her baton raised for the kill. Rogue dug in her heels, propelled herself forward, and rammed the barrel of her Glock into the woman's solar plexus. She grunted and doubled over. Rogue followed with a head butt into the woman's jaw.

The odds were against Rogue now. It was only a matter of seconds before the other guards joined the fight and overpowered her. She had to get to the basement. She made for the stairwell, but was yanked back by the straps of her backpack. The woman was injured but determined not to let Rogue escape. The two male guards were back on their feet and advancing fast. Reluctantly, Rogue slipped off the shoulder straps and let the backpack drop away. Her left arm came free, but the other one was trapped.

She twisted around and saw her Glock snagged in the straps of her pack. The female guard was bigger, stronger, and easily held Rogue in place. She cursed and let go the Glock. Once her arm was free, Rogue crashed through the door into the stairwell.

She took the steps two at a time and swung around a u-turn down to the next flight. A guard yelled after her, threatening to shoot. She leapt onto the railing and slid the remaining distance, reducing his angle of fire. Bullets exploded into the walls, peppering her with plaster and paint. As she dropped off the end of the rail, her momentum carried her into the shallow recess of a doorway. She yanked it open and ducked through as more shots hit the tiles and ricocheted past her.

Rogue couldn't understand why they were shooting at her. She was outnumbered and they could easily secure all exits from the basement. Their eagerness to kill her changed everything. Descending footsteps echoed from the stairwell behind her. She needed to buy time. She slid the backup Glock from her ankle holster, regretting the loss of the more powerful G17 and the backpack. Her difficult mission had transformed into an almost impossible one.

Chapter 19

It was dark and uninviting inside the basement. Rogue flipped on the head torch and panned left, then right. Tucked against a wall, she found a four wheeled trolley, laden with office chairs. As she approached it, overhead fluorescent lights flickered on, triggered by sensors. She heaved the trolley around and parked it tight against the door to the stairwell. Behind the rear wheels, she locked down a pair of metal brakes. It wouldn't keep the guards out for long, but it might buy her enough time to find Webb.

She got her bearings and hurried towards the rear of the building. As she passed under more light sensors, the tall grey shadows morphed into rows of shelving, many of them jammed tight with storage boxes. The building schematics had shown three small rooms on the southeast wall, close to the rear stairwell. Rogue ran down the nearest aisle. The tall shelving soon gave way to an open plan area. Rogue passed boxes of electronics stacked on wooden pallets, followed by benches laden with office supplies and, beyond those, a section containing vacuum cleaners, mops and other cleaning products.

She paused and listened. It was unexpectedly quiet. The odds were that the guards chasing her had remained in the stairwell, cutting off her retreat. Others would be sent to the rear exit. Before long, the bulk of the security team would approach from one end and chase her into a dead end like a pack of wolves.

Rogue stopped outside a large room on a raised platform and peered through one of several small windows. The walls were lined with banks of tall cabinets, some with digital displays, others fed by cables that snaked down from the concrete ceiling. Fans whirred overhead, extracting the heat generated by an array of computer, telecommunications and electrical equipment. She shoved in the door and stepped up to the raised floor. The first few cabinets contained racks and switches for the building's computer network. Ignoring them, she tugged open the aluminium doors on the last three cabinets and gazed at the array of digital readouts and switches. Her eyes glazed over and she cursed herself for skipping the electronics briefings during her MI5 training.

If she could kill the power, it would plunge the entire building into darkness. There was probably a backup generator somewhere, but the distraction would buy her valuable time and maybe pull one or two guards away from her escape route. The only piece of equipment she recognised was a heavy duty fuse board. A C4 rig would have been perfect, but she'd lost her backpack during the fight at the elevators. Remembering the stun grenades, she patted her pockets and was relieved she hadn't put everything in the pack.

Rogue left the computer room, ran over to the bench of cleaning products and grabbed two over-sized containers of disinfectant and an aerosol spray. Back inside the room, she sprayed the fuse boards with the aerosol, squirting liquid into every crevice. Then she poured bleach over the cables and dials inside the other cabinets. She unscrewed the top from the second bottle of bleach and emptied the contents on the floor as she reversed back out to the basement. Once outside, she yanked the pin from a stun grenade and tossed it inside. After slamming the metal door shut, she hid behind the nearest block of shelves and covered her ears.

When the grenade exploded, the noise was largely contained within the electronics room, but the blinding flash lit up the basement like a fireworks display. Seconds later, the white light faded, replaced by flames that quickly swept up the electrical equipment, invading switch panels and melting cables. One by one, fuses blew, until the basement was plunged into darkness.

In the gloom of the farthest corner, Rogue spotted a cluster of small rooms. The first was open, home to a coffee stained pool table and a few swivel chairs. A row of shelves on one wall contained flavoured drinks and a selection of snack bars. Under the table, a cardboard box overflowing with used paper cups and empty food wrappers served as a trash can. Rogue cracked open a bottle of strawberry water and took a few mouthfuls as she moved to the next room. She forced the door opened with a rasping groan. In the centre was a table and chairs, but instead of coffee stains, the square table was smeared with dried blood. A broken tooth lay abandoned on the floor, close to a red backpack. Rogue hoped Webb was mobile, at least able to walk. Beside the pack, a brown fleece lay draped over a pair of Doc Martens.

Dull thuds in the distance told Rogue the guards had regrouped. It wouldn't be long before they breached her makeshift barricade. She moved to the last room and turned the door handle. It was locked. She could pick the lock, but it would waste precious seconds. She thumped the door twice and yelled a warning to get clear, then swapped the standard 9mm magazine for the more powerful P+ and fired half a dozen rounds into the area between the keyhole and the door frame. Standing back, she kicked at the lock. The door burst open and clattered against the wall.

In the light of the head torch, she picked out a plastic chair with tubular steel legs. Her nostrils winced at the stench wafting from an overturned bucket lying in one corner. A figure huddled under a blanket against the furthest wall.

"Jason Webb?" Rogue moved closer, half watching the covered shape on the floor, half listening for the guards.

A head lifted slowly and squinted back at her. Rogue clicked a button on the torch, reducing the glare of the beam, then squatted down for a closer look. Despite the plasters, bruises and mass of tangled hair, the face before her matched the photograph of Jason Webb on her phone.

Webb dragged the flimsy blanket up around his shoulders, flinching as the restraints bit into his wrists. Cowering further into the corner, his bloodshot eyes pleaded to be left alone. Rogue had witnessed that same dread before, in prisoners who expected to die during their next round of torture. She needed to mobilise him fast, but knew he wouldn't cooperate until she had gained his trust. Holstering her gun, she rolled the balaclava up onto her forehead, giving him a full view of her face. She unsheathed her knife and reached for his wrists, but at the sight of the steel blade, he shrunk back further.

"Your boss sent me to get you out of here," she said. "But we need to move fast. Can you walk?"

He blinked and raised one swollen eyebrow. For a moment he seemed to consider what she'd said, then cast it aside. Rogue knew what he was thinking. He thought she was one of his captors trying to trick him into revealing whatever information they were after.

She sat down crossed-legged in front of him. "Your name is Jason Webb, you work for Crossfire Analytics in London, share a two bed with Matt Brennan and have two unpaid speeding tickets. You were born on the first of September ninety-one, which means your birthday is the day after tomorrow. What say we get you home for that, eh?"

Webb raised himself up onto one elbow. "Who are you?" His voice was croaky and deep. He coughed, held his stomach, then rested his head against the wall.

Rogue unscrewed the cap from the bottle of water and offered it to him. He sipped from it, then coughed some more.

"My name is Rogue. I've been … recruited to get you out of here." She stood the bottle on the concrete and gestured with the knife again.

This time Webb didn't move, just watched. The blade sliced through the plastic bands and they dropped away. He rotated his joints gingerly, then manoeuvred himself into a seated position and let the blanket fall away.

"Can you stand up?" asked Rogue.

Webb gathered his legs under him and stood up, resting one hand on the wall. "My boss sent you?"

"You sound surprised," said Rogue, as she stood back to assess him.

"He's not the sentimental type."

Webb took another fit of coughing, then spat a mixture of phlegm and blood onto the floor. As he tugged his shirt up to wipe his mouth, he saw Rogue looking at the bruising around his ribs.

"Did you give them what they wanted?" she asked.

Webb laughed, then groaned and held his side. He rolled down his shirt and shrugged. "Not really sure. My memory's a little sketchy."

Rogue knew he was holding back, still not sure about her. "What about the piece of tech you came for?"

He looked sideways at Rogue. "The DX3, that's all Savik really cares about."

"Where is it?" said Rogue.

Webb flexed his legs to get the blood flowing. "See my boots anywhere?"

"In the next room. Where's this DX3?"

Webb half grinned, then winced and cradled his jaw in one hand. "I stashed it in the city when these guys showed up."

The sound of boots pounding down the rear stairs echoed into the small room.

"Time to get moving." Rogue rolled the balaclava down over her face, turned off the torch, and hurried to the door.

The basement was still in darkness. Rogue could hear Webb behind her, his socks scuffing the concrete floor, his legs stiff from confinement and dehydration. She peered around the door frame in time to see a guard clear the last step of the rear stairwell. He paused, torch in one hand, gun in the other, sweeping both in a broad arc. In seconds, his light would reach the open doorway and they'd be trapped inside. Rogue signalled Webb to stay put, then she ducked out and into the next room. Shadows rose and fell against the walls as the torch swept past her temporary refuge. She pressed herself against the wall and peeked out.

The guard came closer, his torch focused on the open door of Webb's cell. When his radio buzzed, he swapped the torch to his gun hand and tugged the radio from his belt. "Affirmative. Looks like the prisoner's gone. Door has been bust open."

Rogue couldn't hear the response, but a burst of static reached her from the opposite end of the basement. The security team had broken through her barricade and was closing in. She had to act fast. The guard closest to her finished his radio call. He had the torch and gun in one hand and was struggling to clip the radio back onto his belt. Rogue saw her chance and rushed at him.

Startled, he fumbled and dropped both the torch and the gun to the floor. Plunged into darkness, he charged at Rogue, fists raised and roaring. Rogue stepped sideways and tripped him as he flew by. He crashed but recovered quickly, rolling away from her. She closed in and stamped her boot into his face as he got up. He grabbed blindly for her leg, but she was already behind him. The butt of her Glock crashed into his skull and he slumped to the floor, unconscious.

Rogue turned back to find Webb and saw multiple torch beams approaching from the opposite direction.

She counted three figures, moving slowly, each one probing a different aisle. The remaining two aisles were clear. Even with Webb in tow, she could probably pass unnoticed along either of them. The guards wouldn't expect her to double back. But it was too risky. If they'd posted a man in the stairwell, he could hold her off indefinitely.

Rogue peered into the room where she'd left Webb, but it was empty. The approaching lights were brighter now, closer. She swept the area all around her, looking for him. Nothing.

"Webb, where are you?" she shouted.

At that stage, it didn't matter if the guards heard her. She strained her ears for an answer. The torch beams bounced, moving faster. She hurried away from the cluster of small rooms and hid behind a stack of cardboard boxes as a guard emerged from the aisles. He crouched down and fired at her. She needed a distraction.

Dragging a cardboard box onto the floor, she tipped it over, selected a pair of wireless mice and launched them towards the rear stairwell, followed by another pair. Multiple shots rang out, this time aimed at the stairwell. Rogue stood up, selected the largest of the three shadows, and fired. He howled and scrambled back for cover. The other guards returned fire, but retreated with the injured man behind the shelving.

A light flicked on in the middle room. It was Webb, using a torch. Rogue fired a continuous volley at the guard's position as she sprinted back across to the three rooms. The guards returned fire, but she stayed low, and in the poor light, their shots flew over her head. When she reached Webb, he was holding the boots and jacket she'd seen earlier. In the distance, Rogue could hear chatter on a radio.

"Come on, we need to move," said Rogue, grabbing Webb's arm.

He staggered and reached for the wall.

"Are you OK? Were you hit?" Rogue looked him up and down, checking for blood.

He shook his head slowly, deliberately.

She pressed him back into the room, took the torch from him and switched it off. "Get your boots on, fast."

Webb dropped the Doc Martens and stepped into them. While he tied the laces and pulled on his fleece, she scanned him again for bullet wounds. He seemed unhurt, just pale and weak.

"Stay close behind me. When I stop, you stop. When I move, you move. Understood?"

He glanced at the gun in her hand and nodded.

She handed him back the torch. "Keep it turned off. Only use it for emergencies."

He laughed nervously. "What would you call this?"

"Me risking my life for a complete stranger. You ready now?"

"Yeah, ready."

They left the protection of the small room and ran for the rear stairwell. En route, Rogue retrieved the gun dropped by the guard during their fight. As they neared the steps, the basement was flooded with the sizzling light of multiple flares. The guards behind her were launching an attack.

Chapter 20

The emergency lights in the rear stairwell cast a shadowy gloom. Rogue raced up the first flight of steps as far as a u-turn and hunkered down. She guessed there'd be one or two men stationed on the next level. Their orders would be to avoid engaging the intruders, rather to block the escape route and wait for their colleagues to close in from below.

Webb trudged up behind Rogue and leaned against the wall. She studied his face. His breathing was easy, but his eyes glazed over. She took a gel shot from her pocket, tore off the top, and handed it to him.

"Eat this."

Webb stared at the slim pouch, trying to read the name.

"It's energy gel, mix of glucose and caffeine," said Rogue.

Webb scrunched up his nose. "I hate bananas. Got any other flavours?"

She pressed it into his hand. "Just swallow it."

The murmur of urgent voices echoed off the walls in the basement. The guards were closing in fast. Rogue hadn't time to check the Sig pistol she'd taken from the dead guard, but even half a magazine would be enough. She'd either overcome whatever opposition was waiting for them up ahead or be dead herself.

Rogue turned to Webb. "Stay close to me."

She rounded the bend and surged up the steps, her index fingers lightly pressed on the triggers of both guns. Hugging the wall as she climbed, Rogue craned her neck upwards. The expected barrage of gunfire never came. As she mounted the last few steps, she heard a quick burst of muffled static. The double doors leading to the ground floor corridor were locked, and she could see nothing through the small windows. With the butt of the Sig, she smashed the glass, but the pieces didn't fall away, just slid slowly down. Carefully reaching through the broken glass, she realised the guards had blocked the doors with something tall and heavy, maybe a filing cabinet. Her escape route back to the fire exit was blocked.

Webb came up behind her and rattled the door handles. "It's locked! Now what?"

A menacing sound grabbed Rogue's attention. The sliding action of a handgun receiving a fresh magazine.

"Get going," she hissed at Webb, shoving him towards the next flight.

He was slow to react. "What ... I thought we ..."

A muzzle snaked around the rail below them. Rogue launched herself at Webb, lifting him into the air. Bullets ploughed into the plastered walls, assailing their ears and showering them with debris. Keeping low, Rogue returned fire. Webb sat looking at her, hands clamped over his ears. She gestured frantically and shouted at him to go on ahead, but he didn't budge. She holstered the Sig, grabbed a fistful of his shirt and heaved him up. Still firing the Glock, she urged Webb forward, eventually punching him in the back to get her message across.

They reached the next floor, but the doors were also barricaded, the same as the previous level. Rogue guessed the exits on the remaining floors would be the same. The guards were driving them to the roof. If Rogue was alone, she'd be confident of finding a way out. But with Webb in tow, the odds were stacked against them. He was already running on empty. Another fifteen minutes and he'd be useless.

Webb sat down to rest, but Rogue urged him on, promising a breather at the next level. He got up straight away and launched himself at the stairs, surprising her with his determination, but at the next set of locked doors, he doubled over, gasping for air. Rogue gave him another gel shot, knowing it wouldn't work fast enough but hoping the psychological effect might help.

She took a few steps back down to the previous floor and waited, listening for any giveaway sounds. Shapes played on the lower walls and grew larger as the guards gradually drew nearer. Being above them, Rogue had the advantage. They knew that and were cautious. The pursuing shapes morphed into human shadows, one with an outstretched gun. It fired twice, the rounds drilling into the steps beneath Rogue.

Webb didn't need any encouragement from Rogue. He took off up the stairs. Rogue returned fire, then followed Webb. They continued past the top level, up the last flight to the roof. The door was equipped with a push bar, standard for an emergency exit. As Rogue stepped out onto the roof, she heard police sirens in the distance. As her odds of success plummeted, her stomach tightened and flooded with doubt that she would complete the mission. Her body shuddered with dread and the certainty that she would never see Agnetha again.

Webb squeezed past Rogue, ran to the roof's edge, and peered through the rain at the dimly lit roads of the campus. "Cops, lots of them, and fire trucks." He turned to face Rogue. "I really hope you have a plan!"

She checked her bearings and pointed towards the distant motorway. "Go that way, onto the next building. Find the exit from the roof. Hurry!"

Webb wiped the rain from his face and squinted across the darkness. All he could see were shapes and outlines, but her plan made sense. He pulled up his hood and limped across the rooftop, using the torch to pick a safe route.

Rogue slammed the stairwell door shut and looked around her for something to jam it with. The concrete expanse was devoid of the usual debris left behind by maintenance crews. No cables, no steel bars, nothing. She slid the nylon belt from her trousers, looped it through the door handle and secured it to an air conditioning unit. It wouldn't hold for long, but an extra ten seconds might mean the difference between escape or death.

She crossed a low wall between the VerKoll and Astro buildings, and skirted a network of skylights that spanned most of the area. She found Webb wrestling with the rooftop door. It rattled but wouldn't open. The ground was littered with cigarette butts, a sign the door was used regularly. It was locked from the inside. Rogue searched for a makeshift tool, something to force it open, but the Astro rooftop was the same as VerKoll's, devoid of anything useful.

"They're coming," screamed Webb. "Hurry."

Rogue turned and saw three figures emerging onto the VerKoll roof. They fanned out, scouring the expanse for their prey. When one shouted, they started running towards her, their shapes growing larger.

"Find something to get that door open," said Rogue as she reloaded both guns. "And turn off that damn torch."

"Give me a gun," said Webb as he fumbled to switch off the torch.

"We need a way down from here. Find one," demanded Rogue. She sprinted back towards the dividing wall, but halfway there, she diverted between rows of skylights and crouched down behind the perspex domes. At the highest point, they provided just enough cover. Through a mixture of bird droppings and algae, she glimpsed stacks of boxes in the warehouse below.

Off to her right, a guard hopped over the dividing wall. He aimed at Webb and shouted something, but his words were whipped off the roof by the wind. Rogue needed to buy time for Webb to find a way into the building. She fired a few rounds at the lead guard, just over his head. He crouched down and continued firing. The other guards moved along the dividing wall, one stopping midway, the others scurrying across to the left flank. It wouldn't be long before they advanced, taking turns to pepper her with bullets. Using both guns, she fired a cluster of rounds at each position, encouraging the guards to remain where they were.

The chambers in both Rogue's weapons clicked empty. She reloaded and looked for Webb. He was using a length of pipe, trying to force it into the door frame, but it just slid off the metal in the rain. He kicked at it in frustration.

A bullet whizzed past Rogue's ear, fracturing the skylight panel behind her. She ducked just as another flew over her head, then scurried along the narrow passageway on all fours. She knew the guards would move and close in. Switching to a low squat, she popped up, picked the first man and fired both weapons. He staggered sideways, then fell over.

Rogue ducked low as a barrage of bullets sought her out. As she crawled back a few metres, she replayed the scene, trying to pinpoint the location of the other gunmen. She popped up and fired a volley, but the guards had already moved. Her jacket sleeve jerked as a bullet carved a hole through it. A second round found its target, drilling through her upper arm. She grunted, more in frustration than pain. Encouraged by Rogue's reaction, the guard jumped up and came at her, shooting wildly. Rogue calmly took aim and planted a single bullet in his chest, then hunkered down and gritted her teeth as fire seared through the nerves in her arm. She'd been shot before. Pain was something she could work with once it didn't disable her. A quick examination revealed blood leaking inside her sleeve, but not enough to suggest any major damage. The sooner she and Webb got off the roof, the better.

"Webb, Webb, are you in yet?" shouted Rogue.

Seconds ticked by. Had he gone on without her? She tried again. "Webb!"

"It's locked, I can't get …" His voice trailed off, lost in the night.

Rogue ran through the options in her head. Her intended escape route was out. If she hadn't lost her backpack, a wedge of C4 would have blown through that door easily. Doubling back through the VerKoll building was out of the question now that the police had arrived. A fresh hail of bullets thudded into the concrete and skylights. The perspex dome behind her exploded, showering her with splinters. She returned fire, shooting blindly in a wide arc until her guns were empty.

As she loaded the last magazine into the Glock, she got to her knees, ready to engage shooters from both sides. There was a man to her left, bent over another, preoccupied with his injured colleague. Rogue swivelled right in time to see a figure run across to another injured guard. She took off and raced around the shattered skylights to the door. Webb was flat on the ground, hands over his head.

"Get up." Rogue jabbed him in the hip with her boot.

Through the shattered skylight, she could see towers of cardboard boxes. The tallest was only three metres from where she stood. Webb was on his knees, staring across the rooftop.

"Come on, now's our chance," said Rogue.

Webb looked up at her, then followed her gaze down. "You're mad!" he said, shaking his head. "No way, forget it."

"You'd rather take your chances with those guards?"

Webb glanced back across the roof. More figures had emerged from VerKoll. The guards that had retreated with the injured man had regrouped and were advancing again, this time with reinforcements. Webb grimaced, but said nothing. He stood up, bent over, and looked down.

"Just go," urged Rogue. "Land on your back, protect your ankles."

Webb shuffled sideways and hesitated.

"Police, put down your weapons." At least six men had crossed the divide and were closing in on both sides.

Rogue gripped the collar of Webb's jacket and propelled him over the edge. "On your back," she called after him.

His arms and legs flailed erratically, but she didn't wait to see him land. Holstering her Glock, she dived after him. The VerKoll guards fired, their bullets flying over her boots as she disappeared from their view.

Chapter 21

Webb shut his eyes as he plummeted towards the mountain of cardboard boxes, terrified that he'd break an arm or a leg. The first box caught him in the chest and blew the air from his lungs. As he crashed down through the stacks, the sharp corners stabbed his arms and legs like spears, until he landed on a long roll of industrial plastic and slid to the floor. As he lay there stunned and bruised, he opened his eyes in time to see Rogue dive through the shattered skylight above. Her arrival started an avalanche of boxes tumbling towards him. He scrambled back into a corner and barely avoided the oncoming landslide.

In the poor light, the shadowed stacks flew at Rogue like a frenzied computer game. She landed on her side, the impact crushing her like an articulated truck. The temptation to rest and wait for the pain to subside was interrupted by her brain screaming at her to move before the guards opened fire.

Wrapping her arms about her head, she rolled and let gravity toss her down one side of the cardboard mountain. She came to a sudden stop, wedged sideways between a concrete wall and a pile of bulging sacks. She heard gunshots, but couldn't turn around to get her bearings. Bullets thumped into the surrounding bags, then stopped. She reached for something to pull herself free. Her fingers found cold metal protruding from a ruptured box. It was the head of a claw hammer. She gripped the handle, swung, and felt the claws dig into something. As she pulled on it, agony ripped through her injured arm. Gritting her teeth, she tugged harder. Slowly, her upper body lifted clear, and she was able to use her free hand to come onto her knees.

Dim yellow light filtered into the room from the corridor, giving the room a ghostly aura. As rain fell through the cloud of dust, Rogue spotted Webb slouched in a corner, his head resting against the wall. He wasn't moving, but neither was he showing any signs of injury. As long as he could walk, they still had a chance. Rogue felt the Glock still secured in her shoulder holster, but the head torch was gone, ripped from her head during the fall. She felt like a jackhammer was drilling inside her head, and every time she used her injured arm, a spasm shot through the nerves in her shoulder. On the plus side, the bleeding had slowed to a trickle.

Heavy pounding penetrated through the ringing in her ears. The guards on the roof were trying to gain access to the stairwell. As Rogue half climbed, half crawled across open and damaged boxes, the mountain shifted and her legs shot from under her. Her torso followed as a river of wooden panels dragged her along. Seconds later, the wave pinned her to the floor.

Webb struggled to his feet and shuffled over to her. "Are you OK?"

Rogue opened her eyes and tried to lift herself up. "Get me outta here, quick."

Webb dragged several lengths of timber off her chest until she could sit upright. She pulled her left leg free, but her right foot was wedged tight. Voices up above caught her attention. A guard perched over the shattered skylight, his legs dangling down. He was looking for the best place to jump, with the least risk of breaking a leg. Webb tried to dislodge the rubble pinning Rogue's foot, but it wouldn't budge. Each time he tugged, more items slid down, adding to the mound. He dropped to the floor, his face pale and dejected. Rogue could see he was exhausted. When they'd left the basement, he'd summoned whatever energy he could, believing that they would escape. But the fight on the roof and their crazy descent through the skylight had drained him.

Above them, the guard stood up, moved a few steps along, then eased his legs over the ledge again, carefully avoiding the jagged perspex. Reluctantly, Rogue came to a decision. Webb was her only leverage to free

Agnetha, so the priority had to be his safety, even if that meant temporarily losing him.

"Webb, get out of here," said Rogue. "I'll catch up with you later."

Still on the floor, he looked at her in disbelief and shook his head. "There's too many of them."

Reaching forward, she pulled him closer. "You can stay here and wait for that guard to drag you back to the basement where you'll die an agonisingly slow death. Or you can pull on the Astro jacket hanging in the hallway, walk down the stairs and out the front door to freedom. It's your choice."

Webb glanced into the hallway and saw the jacket. Then he looked up at the VerKoll guard as he turned over, grabbed the ledge, and lowered himself down. He recognised the man by his bulk. It was Steinbeck, the guard who had enjoyed torturing him.

Webb pulled his shirt free of Rogue's grip and stood up. "Do you have a car?"

She nodded. "Opposite the entrance gates to this building, there's a gap in the fence. Beyond that, in the hedges, there's a black Audi."

Above them, Steinbeck released his grip and plunged into the chaos of boxes below.

Webb's face paled. He stuck out his hand. "Give me the keys."

"Wait for me there," demanded Rogue.

"Of course, just give me the keys." Webb bounced from one foot to the other, his eyes darting between Rogue and Steinbeck.

"It's not locked. The key is under the mat behind the driver's seat."

Webb turned and ran, whipped the jacket from the hook, and disappeared into the stairwell.

Boxes tumbled and bounced all around Rogue as Steinbeck clambered free. From her position on the floor, he looked huge, a man mountain. Her Glock was empty, and she'd used the last spare magazine up on the roof. Her fingers reached for the knife on her belt, but only found the torn loop of the leather case—the combat knife was gone. She slid her hand down her leg and hoped the backup was still there. She tugged at her trouser leg, trying to pull it clear from the Gerber's handle, but like her foot, her trousers were wedged tight. As Steinbeck loomed over her, she whipped around, searching left and right for a weapon. She launched a series of chisels and hammers at him that had spilled from a broken box, but he swatted them away easily.

"Enough!" He pulled a gun and aimed it at her face, then planted his boot on her chest and pinned her back against the wooden floor.

"This is your handiwork," he said, pointing to his blood-soaked shirt. "It would have been better if you had killed me."

He tugged the empty Glock from her holster and tossed it across the room, then wrapped his meaty fingers around her throat. Rogue kicked out, aiming for his kneecap, but she couldn't turn enough and her heel only glanced off his thigh. Grinning, he jammed the muzzle of his Sig through the bullet hole in her sleeve and twisted it back and forth against the bleeding wound in her arm. Rogue gritted her teeth and locked onto his eyes, while her free hand scavenged for something sharp. Steinbeck drew back and repeatedly jammed the butt of his Sig into her flesh.

Rogue screamed, using the energy to reach further. Her fingers found a nest of tools. She whipped her head around, praying for a knife, but only found screwdrivers and chisels. She hadn't a clear path to his throat, so she rammed a long screwdriver up between his legs. He growled like a wounded bear and retreated. Rogue braced her free foot against the pile of timber and pulled her trapped leg. It moved a little, but not enough to get free.

Steinbeck charged in, stamping at Rogue in a frenzied attack. "I am going to rip you apart!"

She twisted away and took the blows on her back, waiting for an opportunity to retaliate. When he switched his attention to her trapped foot, she lunged at him with the screwdriver, skewering his leg several times. Taking a step back, he holstered his gun, gripped the sheets of timber holding her in place and hauled them from the pile of debris, releasing her foot.

"Get out here," he bellowed. "Fight me." He was incensed, his cheeks swollen with rage, his eyes bulging.

Rogue flexed her leg and rotated her ankle, testing it for mobility. He stomped across, locked his fingers around her ankle and dragged her across the rain soaked floor like a rag doll. Then he stood back and waited for her to get to her feet. As she struggled up, Steinbeck kicked her in the chest, catapulting her across the room. She crashed into a stack of crates as shock waves rippled through every bone and organ in her body. Steinbeck closed in and stooped down to drag her into the centre of the floor. Rogue grabbed an aerosol, knocked the cap off, and sprayed it in his face. He blinked, slowly at first, then more urgently. His eyes squirmed and twitched, blinding him. Rogue read the label on the can. It was bleach. As the liquid burned, Steinbeck lurched away from her, howling and swearing, trying to wash his eyes with spittle from his mouth.

Rogue clambered up, staggering from the numbness in her foot. With one eye partly open, Steinbeck charged at her. Rogue dropped sideways against the wall, hooked his ankle with her foot, and sent him sprawling. She followed up with a body slam, landing elbow first on the back of his neck. He swiped blindly for her, but she rolled off him and whipped the gun from his holster. He charged at her on all fours. Rogue fired at the only target she had. Bullets drilled into Steinbeck's shaved scalp, but he kept coming at her.

He lifted Rogue off her feet and slammed her to the floor. Steinbeck's weight collapsed on top of her, his head askew on her stomach, his body motionless. From above, Rogue heard a crash. The guards on the Astro rooftop had broken through the door. Soon they'd be pounding down stairs, hellbent on revenge.

Chapter 22

Rogue twisted onto her side and hauled her body from under Steinbeck's bloody corpse. Her soles skidded on the rain soaked floorboards and she collided into the door frame. Letting her momentum carry her out into the hallway, she bounced her way along the corridor, pushing herself off the walls with her good arm. Boots pounded down from the roof as she half-ran, half-fell down the stairs. Needing both hands to steady herself, she forced Steinbeck's pistol into her holster and hurried down.

A confusion of sounds ricocheted off the stone walls. It was impossible to pinpoint their origin, but she guessed the security guards were close behind. They had guns, and they wanted blood.

As she reached the last flight, her instincts told her to slow down, but that was not an option. She jumped from the third last step and found herself with a choice of doors. The first two were locker rooms lined with benches and clothing rails. Rogue guessed the third door led to the warehouse.

Reaching through the nearest doorway, she whipped a navy blue Astro Logistics work coat and a matching cap from a hook. As she put on the coat, two men emerged from the opposite locker room.

They stood there, engaged in a heated debate, blocking her path as two guards thundered down the stairs behind her. Rogue kept her back to them and pulled on the cap.

"Down on your knees, now!" bellowed the first guard.

Rogue elbowed her way between the two Astro employees, using them as cover as she tried to reach the exit door.

Two shots boomed around the small space. "Get down now," ordered the guard.

The two men cowered down and wrapped their arms around their heads.

Rogue turned around slowly, running the options through her mind, calculating distances and judging angles. She could use the men as interference, risk their lives to save hers and Agnetha's, but the exit was a problem. It opened inwards. She needed time, and space, to pull the door open and escape without catching a bullet.

The guards cleared the bottom step and closed in, a man and a woman, side by side.

"On your knees, all of you," demanded the woman.

The two Astro employees obeyed silently, eyes on the floor.

As Rogue lowered into a squat, she inched a little closer to the exit.

The woman moved towards them, keeping clear of her partner's line of sight.

"Get on the floor," she bellowed, all the time aiming her Sig at Rogue's chest.

Rogue lowered down and let her knees come to rest, but kept her toes tucked under her feet.

"Remove the gun with your left hand," said the guard.

Rogue drew back her jacket and used a thumb and forefinger to remove Steinbeck's gun.

"Place it on the floor, real slow."

Rogue complied, resting the weapon on the ceramic tiles.

"Now, hands intertwined behind your head."

As Rogue followed the guard's instructions, she heard muffled laughter seeping in from the warehouse behind her. And voices. Two, maybe three. The volume increased rapidly, getting closer. As the woman noticed it too, uncertainty filled her eyes. The door swung in, just managing to clear the soles of Rogue's boots.

Still chatting to his colleagues, a tall bearded man reversed through the doorway. His heels collided with Rogue's. As he fell back, he reached out and grasped his colleague's jacket, trying to steady himself.

Rogue, her arms still behind her head, stretched back, grabbed his coat with both hands, and heaved. He toppled over her and landed in a heap between Rogue and the female guard. The second man staggered through the doorway, but kept his balance.

Rogue snatched her gun from the floor and bounced up. She jammed it under the second man's chin and manoeuvred around him, using him as a shield.

"Shoot her," the male guard screamed at his colleague, his own line of sight now blocked.

Rogue reversed over the threshold, pulling the confused hostage with her. The woman followed, altering her aim, trying to get a shot. The male guard pushed her aside and fired twice, the bullets ripping into the innocent man's thigh.

Rogue returned fire but missed, her aim hampered by the injured man slumped against her. The open door obscured the woman's line of sight, but her male colleague trampled forward through the chaos of bodies on the floor. Rogue fired again as bullets drove into the timber door frame. The guard lurched as a round punctured his collarbone. He continued firing, but his arm lost power and dropped. He stood his ground and switched to his left hand, but his aim was off. Rogue stepped clear of the doorway and ran.

She hoped nobody had heard the gunfire over the warehouse sounds and that she could blend into the workforce, but she soon realised that wouldn't be so easy. Red and blue strobes of light washed over the towers of crates that filled the vast warehouse. She was cornered. Police cars were waiting in the forecourt, and the remaining VerKoll guards were close behind her. Ducking into the shadows, Rogue zigzagged between crates and barrels until she reached a dusty corner piled with broken boxes and pallets. She released the Sig's magazine. It was empty.

A chilling breeze swept in through the giant loading bays and crawled its way around the jungle of boxes to find her. As her body cooled down, Rogue suddenly felt alone and weary. She was floundering from one disaster to another, each step drawing her closer to failure. Everything that had happened during the previous twenty-four hours felt distant and surreal. All she knew for sure was that Agnetha was in danger.

Rogue caught her reflection in a chunk of broken glass and a shiver of guilt coursed through her, rattling her confidence. She'd screwed up, made the same damn mistake again. She should have called for help back in Geneva. But that would have meant asking, and her big ego just wouldn't allow that. Not before and not now. Probably never. Rogue's stubborn selfishness had cost her on previous missions, but they'd been faceless strangers, acceptable losses. This time was different. It wasn't just another round of spies and villains. Agnetha was family. How had Rogue not seen that before. And what if she'd left it too late.

The crunch of a trolley colliding with a concrete pillar startled Rogue. She wondered how long she'd been standing there, second guessing her decisions. What felt like ten minutes was probably only thirty seconds, but the police could have locked down the entire building during that time. She squinted at the surrounding aisles. They were dark, but voices ricocheted around the warehouse, impossible to place. As she wedged the empty pistol under a pile of boxes, she discovered a roll of packing tape. She slid her injured arm out of the Astro coat and wound the tape tightly around the blood stained hole in her jacket. It served to both hide the damage and stop the bleeding. With some difficulty, she struggled back into the coat, then hurried towards the front of the building.

Away to her right, voices and slivers of light leaked through the stacked aisles. She buttoned the coat all the way up and tucked her ponytail under the cap. Sliding up the leg of her trousers, she removed the Gerber knife from its sheath and slipped it into a pocket, her fingers wrapped comfortingly around the rubber handle. Snatches of conversations drifted on the breeze, but echoes bouncing around the warehouse made it difficult to gauge how close they were to her and if they belonged to Astro workers or police.

She kept one eye out for Webb. In the best-case scenario, he had escaped unnoticed and was waiting at the Audi. Worst case, he had been caught and returned to the basement in VerKoll. The odds favoured something in between. Rogue tried to ignore her biggest fear, that he'd driven off without her and contacted

Savik. If that happened, it was game over, as Savik would have no further use for Agnetha. Rogue needed Webb. He was her only bargaining chip.

As she reached the end of the tall stacks, she paused. Between her and the loading bays, powerful fluorescent tubes suspended from the ceiling illuminated every nook and cranny. There was nowhere to hide. Forklift trucks glided along the lanes, expertly pivoting as they loaded and deposited bales of anonymous items. Even at four in the morning, it was a hive of activity.

Rogue left the safety of the aisle and walked purposefully through a maze of pallets, trying her best to blend in. In the distance, she saw vans and trucks parked at the loading bays with their rear doors open, like giant beasts waiting to be fed. Beyond them lay the entrance gates. Now and then, she heard someone shouting instructions, trying to be heard over the din.

Rogue unhooked a clipboard from an empty trolley, tucked it under her arm, and guided the trolley towards the loading area. She hadn't noticed any women on the warehouse floor, so she modified her gait, grateful for the large work coat which concealed her figure. The loading bays were the busiest part of the complex. A few men, who she assumed were drivers, stood chatting while forklifts sped around like bumper cars along designated routes. Rogue felt that whichever path she took, she was in danger of being in someone's way or on a collision course with a load.

Off to one side was an office. A man and a woman stood inside a wide hatch, one speaking on a phone, the other sifting through forms. As Rogue reached the loading bays, two uniformed policemen approached the hatch. They exchanged words, then the woman pointed towards the stairwell at the back of the warehouse. Rogue abandoned the trolley and proceeded along the platform, away from the office.

Shouting erupted behind her, urgent and commanding. Rogue quickened her pace and used every available obstacle as cover. When she reached the last bay, she jumped down from the platform into the relative darkness of the grass verge and darted into the safety of the hedges. She risked a quick look back. There was a Verkoll security guard at the opposite end of the platform, talking animatedly into a radio. He was facing her direction, but she couldn't tell if he had recognised her.

Rogue peeled off the Astro coat, rolled it into a ball and stuffed it into the undergrowth. Beyond the line of trucks, flashing lights from two police cars doused the forecourt in blue and red. Keeping low, Rogue hurried along the row of hedges. As she drew closer to the gates, a third police car and a security patrol van arrived. As their headlights swept across Rogue's location, she squeezed back into the bushes, grimacing as twigs and branches stabbed her hands and face.

The police car continued to the warehouse and screeched to a halt outside the office, but the security van stopped just inside the gates, partly blocking the exit. The guard lowered the window and lit a cigarette.

Rogue knew the police would soon begin searching the area. The hedges behind her were tall and dense, impossible to penetrate without a machete. She studied the security guard in the van parked at the entrance. Some distance behind him, she could see the truck that had keeled over onto the grass. Beyond that was the wire fence and her route to the Audi. Through the fence, a ray of light caught her attention. As she watched, the single beam turned into two. As the lights swept over the expanse of grass, she realised they belonged to her rented Audi. Webb had found it.

The headlights completed a one hundred and eighty degree turn onto the maintenance road, then sped off. Webb had left without her.

Rogue stepped out of her hiding place to get a better look at the red taillights disappearing into the distance, her brain refusing to believe that he had abandoned her. The significance of his departure hit her like a bullet between the eyes. Without him, she had nothing of value, no bargaining chip for Agnetha.

As the gravity of her situation sunk in, the forecourt lit up like an airport runaway. It was too late to retreat. Rogue had to make a run for it.

She took off towards the gates, targeting the gap between the security van and the nearest pillar.

The guard inside the van leapt out and ran to intercept her. He was short and stocky, built for strength, not speed.

Rogue waited until the last moment before changing her direction. The guard tried to turn and follow her, but he slid on the gravel and landed in a heap.

Rogue jumped into the van. Through the windscreen, she saw two police officers sprinting towards her, guns drawn. She hit the accelerator and flew through the gates as bullets pinged the bodywork. In the rear-view mirror, she watched the police run out onto the road, but she rounded the corner and lost them.

Thirty seconds later, she approached the security checkpoint and slowed down, giving the man inside the hut the impression that she was about to stop. Just before the white line, she floored the accelerator, ploughed through the wooden barrier and screeched out of the Kleiner Technology Campus. A short distance down the road, she took a ramp onto the motorway.

Chapter 23

After Webb left Rogue in the Astro storage room, he'd made his way through the warehouse and found the Audi exactly where she told him it would be. Once he found the keys and started the engine, he turned on the heat and debated whether he'd wait for Rogue or go meet Savik on his own. In the safety and warmth of the car, he soon dozed off. The sound of police sirens woke him with a jolt, as two patrol cars screeched through the gates into the Astro yard. Webb panicked and drove off without Rogue.

Exhausted both mentally and physically, he followed the signs for the centre of Zurich. He was confident the city would have a myriad of small streets and laneways where he could lie up, and an all-night bar where he could get a stiff drink or five to calm his nerves and dull the throbbing pain in his head. As he cruised along the quiet streets, flashing blue lights grabbed his attention like alarm bells. He hit the brakes too hard, but managed to shift gears before the Audi cut out. He pulled into a dark side street and turned off the lights as an ambulance flew past.

The relief he'd experienced after escaping from VerKoll in one piece had quickly drained away, replaced by a creeping vulnerability. The Audi's heater was on, but Webb was shivering. He turned the temperature up to the highest setting and switched on the heated seat. Every couple of minutes, he shuddered uncontrollably. His joints and muscles ached, but the throbbing in his head was the worst. He needed painkillers and maybe something hot to eat. Then he'd be able to think clearly and plan his next move.

Webb left the side street and followed the road along the Limmat river until he saw a service station with a sign for a cafe. He parked, then sat there, soaking up the warmth from the heated seat. His eyes wandered to the digital clock.

Sunday 4:41 am.

More than three days since he'd left London. For the first time since finding the Audi, Webb looked around the inside of the interior. A half bottle of water and an empty coffee cup stood in the centre console. He twisted the top off the water and sipped from it as his eyes wandered. He found a box of ibuprofen in a cubbyhole and popped two, then added two more. A set of headlights blinded him as a van turned into the forecourt. The driver parked opposite Webb, got out and walked stiffly across the forecourt to a cafe. Webb noticed that the cafe and the shop next door were both open twenty-four seven.

Webb knew his body well. Stodgy carbs would settle his stomach, but his nerves needed a stimulant to keep the tremors at bay, at least until he got back home for a fix.

Thoughts of home reminded him he didn't have a passport or plane ticket. Getting out of Switzerland might be difficult. After the shootout on the roof, the police would be on the alert for him. It depended on whether the security guards told the authorities the complete story or not. They had imprisoned and beaten him illegally. The guards might keep that piece of information to themselves. That and the fact that a DX3 had been stolen. If that went public, it could send VerKoll clients and shareholders running. Webb's stomach rumbled. Food first, he reminded himself, then he could worry about getting home.

Webb got out of the car and instinctively patted his pockets for his wallet and phone. He found neither. He looked back at the Audi. Rogue was well organised, so maybe she'd left some extra cash in the car.

He sat back in the driver's seat, opened the glove box, and dragged the contents onto the floor. A user manual, some maps, tourist guides and a small torch. A receipt from OrbitCar revealed that Rogue had rented the Audi in Geneva. Webb reached under the passenger seat. Nothing. He flicked on the overhead light and twisted around to the back seat. It was empty. The rear shelf was clear too, but maybe he'd have better luck in the boot.

He got out and lifted the rear lid. There were several bags inside, including two bearing the name Crater Outdoors. A dark green rain jacket peeked out of the first one. His own clothes, ripped and stained with sweat and blood, stank like he'd worn them nonstop for a year. He'd have loved a shower, but a change of clothes would be the next best thing. Tipping over the first bag, he found a couple of t-shirts and a pair of trousers, all brand new. He held a shirt to his chest, but it was too small. The second Crater bag was no better. It only held a jumble of crumpled and sweaty running gear.

Disappointed, he shoved the clothes aside and turned his attention to a large black holdall. He yanked back the zip and prised the sides open. Instead of more clothes, he found an assortment of household items. Duct tape, cable ties, a first aid kit, a packet of surgical gloves, some food bags and a small torch. He lifted those aside, peeled back a folded polythene sheet, and opened the bag wider. Light from the powerful forecourt lamp glinted off a handgun.

Webb had never held a real gun, only the imitations that came with some computer games. Knowing the pistol facing him was real, he was both excited and apprehensive. Next to the gun was a spare magazine, a head torch, and a black box with an outline of a hand grenade on the cover. Tentatively, he probed deeper.

Spotting a knife, he picked it up and slid it from its plastic sheath. It was short, the blade not much longer than Webb's middle finger. Despite its size, the black rubber handle and tapered blade gave it a menacing appearance.

A hiss of air brakes exploded behind Webb. He whipped around, banged his head off the open door, and dropped the knife.

Cursing, he quickly picked it up and threw it back into the boot. A truck on the far side of the forecourt released another gasp of air and pulled out onto the road.

Webb's heart pounded. He whipped up the knife and fumbled it back into the sheath. He was about to return it to the holdall, but paused, then tucked it into his belt instead and pulled his shirt down over it. His eyes strayed back to the gun. It would give him more protection, but he wasn't confident enough to carry it, afraid that in his fragile state he'd end up shooting himself.

Webb sifted through the remaining items in the bag. The grenade box was empty. Underneath, he found a clear plastic bag containing slabs of a putty type substance. Beside it, another bag held some kind of electronic timer devices, with strips of wire connected to small brass rods. He lifted it out and turned it over. Slowly, the combination of items came together in his head. Plastic explosive. A timer. A detonator.

Webb's hands shook, and the packet tumbled from his grip. He leaped back, expecting to be blown to hell.

Seconds passed and nothing happened. Scenarios swept through his brain. He'd driven the Audi for several miles, oblivious to his cargo. What if the police had stopped him? And why on earth would that woman leave a gun and explosives in the car?

He wiped a layer of sweat from his forehead, picked the fallen bag with his fingertips and replaced it in the holdall. He zipped it shut and was about to move it aside when he noticed a separate pocket at one end. Gently, he prised it open and peered in.

Several wads of cash stared back at him. He lifted one out and flicked through it. A mix of fifties and hundreds, at least a thousand euro. The next one was Swiss francs. He peeled off a couple of hundred of each currency and stuffed them into his jeans pocket, then dropped the rest into the bag. In the distance, a door creaked open and two guys walked across the forecourt carrying takeaways. Webb closed the boot, locked the Audi and trudged across to the cafe.

As he stepped inside, the intoxicating smell of fried food swept over him. It stirred hunger pangs in his stomach, reminding him of Sunday morning brunches back home. It surprised Webb to see the cafe half full, with most of the customers tucking into large plates of breakfast. He looked back out into the forecourt and found a row of trucks parked in the shadows off to one side. He'd missed them when he'd pulled in, lost in his own world of exhaustion and indecision.

At the far end of the cafe, Webb spotted a sign for toilets. As he opened the swing door into the gents, he caught his reflection in a mirror. At first, he thought it was someone else that had come in after him. The man that stared back from the mirror reminded Webb of a convict on the run. Matted hair poking out at random angles, a dirty plaster peeling over one eye, one cheek smeared swampy brown. Apart from his fleece, Webb's clothes were crumpled, stained, and torn.

After using the toilet, he hung the fleece and t-shirt on a hook, and used damp paper towels to wash his face and upper body. Then he ran some liquid soap through his hair and quickly rinsed it off with warm water. He dried it using a combination of paper towels and a few minutes under the hand drier.

His grey t-shirt had seen better days, but most of the damage was on the front, so he flipped it over and pulled it on backwards. The plaster had fallen off his face, but the wound looked much better than Webb expected, given how much it stung. After pulling the fleece back on, he stood back and took another look in the mirror. Apart from his trousers, he looked respectable, certainly good enough to pass for a tired and dishevelled trucker after a long shift.

Back in the cafe, he joined the queue and surveyed the food on offer. He decided on a full breakfast, which included bacon, eggs, hash browns, mushrooms, and toast. He added a mug of hot chocolate and a glass of water, then found a table near the window.

As Webb munched through his food, he wondered how best to proceed. As money was no longer an issue, he could decide to return to London. He didn't have a passport but figured he could drive cross-country and get a ferry from Calais or Le Havre. He didn't know if some form of identification was required to cross the European borders. That was something he'd need to find out.

A second option was to contact Savik. Webb's stomach clenched at the thought. Savik had a short fuse. When things didn't go according to his plans, he liked to make an example of those who failed him. If Webb returned to London without the DX3, Savik would find him and end his career before it got started, permanently. Webb's only option was to return to MegaTron and recover the Decryptor.

The big problem would be getting back into Mega-Tron. After the trouble he and Meerkat had kicked off, Megatron had probably cancelled Webb's membership. He could buy a guest pass, but the bouncers paid particular attention to non-members, checking each face against a list of troublemakers they'd banned from the arena. Either they'd refuse him entry, or worse, lock him up and call the cops.

Half way through his breakfast, Webb's stomach lurched. He slid the plate away and swallowed some water, praying he wouldn't throw up.

To distract himself, he stared out the window and thought about the reason he'd come to Zurich. Apart from the money Savik had promised, Webb wanted to further the cause of Karnage, the hacker group he'd formed with Stella. The trip to Zurich was the first step in his ambitious plan. Savik hadn't revealed the full details of his scheme to Webb, not yet, but Webb had heard enough to be impressed. Being part of that would promote Karnage up the rungs of the international hacking ladder. Not to the top tier, but certainly within reach of it, close enough to get high-paying jobs. Webb knew he should phone Ringo and Stella, and tell them what had happened, that he was OK. They could help him figure out a plan to retrieve the DX3 without being caught.

He watched as a few more trucks pulled into the car park, each with its own unique display of lights mounted on the roof and the grill of the cab. The drivers dropped onto the tarmac and fist bumped, probably celebrating the end of their respective long trips. They chatted easily while a couple of them rotated cramped necks and backs. Then, almost telepathically, they began walking towards the cafe, joking and laughing. Webb looked around at the groups already inside, chatting over food and coffee. Sitting by himself, he felt alone, cut off and very much out of his depth.

Back in London with his crew, he had been excited about the trip. He was the leader of Karnage. All the gang were great techies, but none of them had the drive to lead the group, to get up from their computer screens and go canvas for business. Truth be told, they'd be content to play games all night and celebrate the odd hack into some government agency now and again. A few months back, they'd replaced a flu vaccination awareness promo on the Health & Safety Authority's website, with a video of a prominent politician's colonoscopy they'd found while hacking into the servers of a local hospital. But like Webb, they all felt unappreciated at their day jobs and knew they'd still be writing boring business software at fifty years of age.

After that, they'd be replaced by younger, more energetic programmers fresh out of college, overflowing with naïve enthusiasm and keen to show off their skills to their new employers. Even worse, Webb could find himself replaced by robots and artificial intelligence. He wanted excitement and a big payday, and eventually retire to an island in the sun. He hated the thoughts of growing old in a damp apartment somewhere, his only outing an arthritic shuffle to collect his government pension in the local post office once a week.

A sharp jab erupted behind his eye. He was somewhat refreshed after the breakfast, but his head still pounded. He needed something stronger than ibuprofen. Other parts of him hurt too, mostly from the beating that hulk of a guard had given him. He hoped Rogue had killed Steinbeck. Webb felt a little guilty, leaving her trapped under that landslide. But his staying wouldn't have made any difference. And anyway, it had been her idea for him to leave.

The cafe door swung in and cracked against the wall. Two men entered, stood in the doorway, and scanned the room. Webb's body ran cold as their eyes landed on him. One of them looked scarily familiar. Webb dropped his shoulders, hunched over his plate, and lifted the mug of coffee to his lips.

The first man called out, then both men continued past Webb's table to a group of truck drivers just behind him.

A trickle of sweat ran down Webb's back and he instantly regretted coming into such a busy cafe.

After wiping his brow with a napkin, he slid out of the seat. As he headed for the exit, he got a shooting cramp in his lower back. He was at least ten years younger than most of the men in the cafe, but moved like he was their senior.

As he hobbled out through the door, the pain in his head throbbed harder, almost blinding him. Resting a hand on the wall, he waited for the early morning air to clear his senses. An adjacent door led into a general store. Through the glass panel, Webb glimpsed a fridge laden with beer. He pushed the door open and walked in.

Chapter 24

After the buzz of the cafe, the aisles of the shop were eerily quiet. Only the faint hum from a flickering fluorescent tube broke the silence. Webb scanned the signs hanging over each aisle and caught the gaze of the cashier reflected in a wide angle mirror. The man nodded. Webb acknowledged with a head tilt of his own, then looked away and tried to remember what he'd come in for.

He wandered down the first aisle past a limited selection of tinned and dried foods, then looped around into confectionery, sweets and soft drinks. He selected a family pack of crisps, just to have something in his hands, and resisted the urge to look up at the mirror again. A fridge in the next row had a choice of beer and a few bottles of white wine. The chilled bottles of Corona were very tempting, but they wouldn't give him the hit he needed. Instead, he took a half bottle of Bell's whiskey from the next shelf and a bottle of soda.

The first aid section had the usual supermarket array of pain killers, plasters and vitamins, but nothing stronger than the Ibuprofen he'd found in the Audi. He took a large box of antacids and followed the last aisle to the cash desk. Beside the till, a glass case displayed a handful of mobiles. He scanned the price tags, looking for the cheapest, and decided on a basic model for forty-nine francs. Then he remembered the wad of cash in his pocket and pointed to an iPhone. It came with a small amount of credit, which he knew wouldn't last long, so he added an extra hundred.

Back in the Audi, Webb extracted the phone from the sealed plastic casing, attached the cable, and plugged it into the car's USB port. While it started up, he poured a healthy measure of whiskey into Rogue's empty coffee cup, added some soda, and took a mouthful. Then he sat back and savoured the familiar heat as the liquid slid down and warmed his stomach. When the phone came to life, he clicked through the start-up instructions. As it began downloading data from his cloud account, he mulled over who he would call.

The only people he fully trusted were the other founding members of Karnage. The rest of the group got on well together, but they hadn't earned his total trust yet. He pictured his two partners in crime, Ringo and Stella. Considering the trouble he was in, he needed someone logical who would see the big picture and help him choose a path that wouldn't come back to haunt them in the future. By the time the phone had synced with his Apple account, he had decided. He took a mouthful of the whiskey, opened the contacts list on the phone, and selected Stella's name. He decided on a video call. Stella talked through her face more than her voice. Her expressions were world class whether she was overjoyed or heart broken. Even seeing her animated face would give him the boost he needed to keep going.

The phone purred for several seconds before a soft voice answered.

"Jay, is that you?"

Webb could see Stella's sleepy eyes peering through a mop of curls.

"Yeah, it's me Stel, sorry for waking you."

He saw a hand, then an arm, before a light flickered on. Stella gathered her hair back from her eyes. She was a welcome sight, the first friendly face Webb had seen in what felt like weeks. They'd never been romantically involved, but in that moment he suddenly felt very alone and would've given anything to have her beside him.

"God Jay, you look like crap," said Stella, rubbing sleep from her eyes. "Savage told us you'd been ambushed by security guards from VerKoll. What happened?"

"I'm alright," said Webb, a smile forcing its way through at the mention of Savage, Stella's nickname for Savik. Webb cleared his throat. "Just a little banged up.

It's been a rough few days." He massaged his forehead and cracked the window open a little.

"We were worried sick." Stella's face disappeared for a moment as she settled into a more comfortable position. "Where are you now? Savik said he was sending a team to break you out."

"A team," exclaimed Webb. "He sent one person, a woman. No offence, Stella, but it turned into a firefight on a rooftop, bullets flying everywhere. It was crazy."

"God, were you hurt?" exclaimed Stella.

"Nothing major, but I've an impressive collection of cuts and bruises."

"Wow. And what about the woman who rescued you?"

"Rogue? No idea. We got separated. We'd agreed to meet at her car, but then the cops showed up. There was no sign of her, so I took off." Webb grimaced and looked out the window of the car.

"Have you spoken to Savik?"

"No, only you." Webb took a deep breath, then blurted out all his troubles. "I don't know what to do next, Stella. Savik's money is gone, I don't have the Decryptor, the VerKoll guys took my passport and I'm in bloody Switzerland after screwing up the deal of a lifetime."

"Jay, take a step back. It isn't all on you. We agreed to this as a team. You took point, but we've got your back."

Webb forced himself to look Stella in the eyes. "Yeah, but I'm the one who screwed up and now it's gone beyond fixing."

At the back of his mind, Webb knew exactly what he needed to do, but he was so shattered that he just wanted to disappear for a few days and come back when everything was sorted.

"You're halfway there Jay," said Stella. "So far, anything that's gone wrong has been out of your control. You are not to blame. Are we agreed on that much?"

He said nothing.

Stella shifted closer to her phone so that her face filled the screen. "Well, Jay?"

"Yeah, suppose so." Webb could never hide his true feelings from Stella. It was as if she had the answers before he even worked out the questions.

"There's no 'suppose so' about it. Listen to me Jay, it's important you get this."

Stella waited for a sign that Webb was paying attention, not gone off into his head, where he'd spiral into a pit of self-recrimination.

He switched the phone to his other hand and shrugged the tension from his shoulder. "OK, I'm here. Hit me."

"Savik put Coburn in charge of the trip, so he was calling all the shots. If anyone has to answer to Savik, it'll be Coburn. Where is he, anyway?" asked Stella.

"Last time I saw him was in MegaTron, getting beaten up by the security guards." It suddenly dawned on Webb that he hadn't thought about Coburn once during the escape from VerKoll. "I completely forgot about him."

"Don't worry," said Stella. "He got away. It was him who told Savik where you were. Wasn't Coburn part of the rescue?"

"Like I said, there was no team, only that woman, Rogue."

"What about Coburn. Does he know where the Decryptor is?" said Stella urgently.

Webb shook his head. "No, last I saw him, he was fighting with the guards. Meerkat bailed, and I went after him, or tried to. When things got hairy, I stashed the DX3. Soon after, I ran into an elbow and it was lights out."

"You sure? Could he have followed you and seen where you hid it?"

"Coburn? No way. What are you getting at—do you think he's already has it and left me here? Did you hear something Stella, is there something you're not telling me?" Webb was getting panicky.

"No, forget it. I just thought it odd that he hasn't linked up with you since you broke out, that's all."

Webb had enough going on in his head without worrying about Coburn. "I need a plan, Stella, one that gets me back in the game."

"We need a plan," said Stella. "Not you, we. Team Karnage, remember?"

An image flashed into Webb's mind, a photo of him with Stella and the rest of the crew at the MarsCon games convention a year earlier. They'd been in second place with one round to go. Ringo and Danny had struggled and were in foul humour, furious at themselves for letting the team down. Webb wasn't much better, though he'd played well, keeping Karnage within striking distance of the leaders. But it was the girls, Stella and Brooke, that got them fired up again. They won the competition the following night. After that, 'Team Karnage' was their rallying call. Webb felt fragments of self-belief creeping back.

"Let's focus on the priorities," continued Stella. "One, get the DX3 and two, get you back home. That's it. Two steps."

"From where I'm sitting, they are two enormous steps," snorted Webb.

"Which is why we're going to break them down. We play this like a game Jay, you and me double-teaming. We've done it before, we can do it now. You with me?"

"Yeah," sighed Webb.

"Say it Jay, are you with me?" Stella did her 'I'm watching you' routine. She pointed two fingers at Webb, turned them back to herself, then pointed at him again.

Webb shifted from his slouched position on the car seat. "Yeah, OK, let's do this. What's the plan?"

"First, where exactly did you stash the Decryptor?"

"It's in the main arena, behind a console panel. It was crazy in there, Stella. I panicked, thought I wouldn't make it out."

"Good call, as it turned out," said Stella. "Next, what are the obstacles to getting it back?"

"In theory, I can go back there and get it, but Mega-Tron security will have me flagged. Even if I manage to avoid them, the VerKoll guards will have figured out that I hid it somewhere inside MegaTron. They'll be waiting for me to show up. After what happened last night, they'll do whatever it takes to get the DX3 back." Webb reckoned the VerKoll guards would also be hellbent on finding him and Rogue, but saying that aloud was too terrifying.

"It's way too risky for you to go back in there," said Stella, shaking her head. "Chances are you'd get in OK, they'd wait for you to retrieve it and then bang, you'd disappear for good. It'd be a suicide mission."

"True. Well, maybe we can use that somehow. I get in, pick up the DX3, and then ... "

"Then what Jay? You need a plan, one that will work. I won't let you walk into a trap and hope for the best," said Stella, frowning.

"Pity you guys aren't here," said Webb. "They don't know your faces."

"Yeah, wish we were too, Jay. It would be exciting, teaming up on a mission like that."

Webb closed his eyes and massaged his neck.

"Hey that gives me an idea." Stella's eyes lit up as she pulled her phone right up to her face. "Do you remember at JamCon, when we were short two players?"

"Yeah, two years ago, we got Marko and Fran to make up the numbers," said Webb.

"Exactly, the guys from Fierce Dragons. They were missing a few of their crew as well. But between us, we had a full team and almost won the trophy."

"So, what, you thinking of bringing them in on this? Aren't they based in Edinburgh?"

"Not them, stupid, but someone else that might already be in Zurich. There's a tournament on there this week. I bet you anything we've played with some of them."

"Probably several, but not at this hour," said Webb.

"The MegaRun is on this weekend, dude. It's an all-nighter, remember?"

"It is? Right. Sorry Stella, I'm running on empty."

"You need help Jay. We've already agreed you can't go back in there yourself. They'd recognise you," said Stella. "And you're running out of time. Those guys from VerKoll will be looking for you."

"I know, I know, but after the last few days, it's difficult for me to trust anyone. Apart from you, of course."

"What about the woman that broke you out? Rogue. What's her story?"

"She said very little, but made it abundantly clear that she wasn't doing it by choice."

"Savik must have something on her," said Stella.

"Anyway, I doubt she even made it out in one piece."

"And if she did, she'll be mad that you bailed without her," said Stella. "Is that her car you're sitting in?"

"Yeah, all her spare gear is in the back. There's a gun, ammo, an empty grenade carton and a couple of grand in cash. She must be special forces or something."

"Damn Jay, you should've waited for her. You could really use her right now!"

"Hindsight Stella, hindsight. Anyway, I rang you for help, not a telling-off."

"Fair point. So, back to our plan. Here's what I'm thinking. You drive to MegaTron and use the club's app to see who's in there."

"Then what? I casually message them and say, hey dude, do me a favour?"

"No dumbass, you use some of that cash you found to motivate them," said Stella.

Webb thought about it. The bottom line was he had very few options. Either try to get the DX3 back or else go back to London without it and face Savik.

"Right, let's do it," said Webb, starting the car before he changed his mind. "I'll call you when I get there."

"Watch your back Jay."

"Will do."

Chapter 25

The nearer Webb got to MegaTron, the less he liked the plan Stella had come up with. Enlisting the help of strangers was a bad idea. The trouble was, he was too tired and sore to think of anything better. It took all his concentration just to focus on his driving. He made it to the Turbinenplatz in one piece and parked where the taxi had left Coburn and himself only a few days earlier. So much had happened in that short space of time. He felt like a different person and not in a good way.

He opened the MegaTron app on this phone and held his breath as he logged in. He fully expected so see an access denied message, convinced they'd have suspended his account. The MegaTron logo spun around and after several seconds, the welcome page appeared. Equal measures of relief and suspicion washed over Webb. He clicked the members' section and selected the 'friends near you' option. The screen filled with a map of the immediate area, stretching for a few blocks in each direction around him. It marked his parking spot with a blue triangle in the centre of the map. Red dots showed the locations of MegaTron members that Webb was connected to. These included names from his friends' list and anyone he had played with, either online or in person. Five dots formed a cluster on the screen. All five of them were in the MegaTron building itself. Webb scrolled through the list, hoping to see a name he could trust. Three were gamers he'd met at competitions. The other two were designers he'd worked with in the past, but didn't know on a personal level.

Webb's phone rang. It was Stella. He clicked the speaker option so he could still see the screen while he spoke to her. "I'm parked near MegaTron. I've five members on my radar, but none jump out as candidates."

"No problem, I've eighteen on my list," said Stella. "I've already messaged three of them. Chances are, at least one will be free to link up with you."

Webb could never figure Stella out. On one hand, she was like himself, a computer nerd, a gamer and a hacker, an introvert. But she knew a crazy number of people, not only in London, or England, but everywhere. Unlike him, she loved travelling, which is how she made so many friends.

"Great Stella, but remember, I can't actually go inside MegaTron. Won't they think that's odd?"

"Be creative. Tell them you had a run in with a bouncer and got banned for twenty-four hours. Happens all the time in clubs."

"Are we crazy trusting someone else with the DX3? What if they decide to keep it for themselves? It's worth a fortune."

"I've got a reply from Isabelle, says she's heading to a bar called Deck 5 in a few minutes and can meet you there."

Webb began searching through the list of members. "Isabelle who?"

"de Bruin. You met her before, last year in Manchester, remember?"

"You know me and faces Stella." Webb found Isabelle's profile. The photograph revealed a smiling round face covered in freckles, squeezed into a viking helmet. Webb sent off a friend request. If Isabelle accepted, she'd appear as a red dot on his map and he'd see her walk into Deck 5.

"You're nearly there Jay. Call me, I'll be waiting to hear, OK?" said Stella.

Webb peered through the windscreen of the Audi, trying to read the names over the various bars and restaurants around the square. "Yeah, of course."

Having Stella coordinating things increased Webb's confidence a hundred-fold. She was outside the danger zone and could think more clearly than him. Even though there was little she could do if he got in trouble again, it felt like she was his protector, watching his back, and that he was no longer alone. After washing down two more painkillers with a mouthful of whiskey and soda, he searched for Deck 5 on the map. It was wedged between a cafe and an Italian restaurant directly opposite Megatron. He clambered stiffly out of the car, opened the boot and took some more cash from the holdall, then headed across the square. The side street was pedestrianised and lined with trees on both sides. As he drew closer to Deck 5, Webb used the cover of the trees to avoid being seen by the two bouncers stationed outside MegaTron. As he opened the door to the bar, his phone pinged. An icon on the screen showed Isabelle's photo. She had accepted his friend request and sent him a message. 'C U 5 min'. Webb replied with a thumbs up.

In many respects, Deck 5 was like MegaTron. Dark interior sporadically illuminated by flashing lights and game soundtracks pumping from wall mounted speakers. Memorabilia adorned the walls and replicas of weapons hung down from the ceiling. The seating area was carved into zones of different shapes and sizes, reminding Webb of quest games where, once you entered, you found it almost impossible to find your way out. Small groups occupied half a dozen tables, some chatting over beers about the tournament across the street, other staring into phones or tablets. A couple of lads had surrendered to tiredness and stretched out on benches along the wall.

Webb made his way to the bar and ordered a bottle of Cardinal, then perched himself on a high stool with a clear view of the entrance. As he sipped the drink, he opened the photo album on his phone and downloaded the images he'd taken in MegaTron a few nights earlier. He'd hidden the DX3 behind a console panel. What if somebody was playing that game when Isabelle arrived there? She'd have to wait until they'd finished before she could risk opening it. The more that Webb thought about Stella's plan, the more he doubted their chances of success. He switched back to the MegaTron app in time to see a red dot appear in the street outside Deck 5. A moment later, the door opened and two girls stepped inside, but in the semidarkness, it was impossible to match either of them to Isabelle's profile photo.

The tallest of the two strode confidently up to Webb, climbed onto a stool, and pulled it in close to him. "You're Jason Webb," she announced.

It was a statement more than a question. She stared at him, her face revealing no emotion, friendly or otherwise. Webb, hypnotised by her dark penetrating eyes, struggled to form a coherent reply.

The girl's friend nudged her. "Don't be mean Izzy, the poor lamb looks terrified."

A smile broke over Isabelle's face and she laughed. "I'm sorry, there's a cosplay competition on tomorrow night. We've been practising our poses all weekend."

Webb breathed a sigh and grinned back. "You got me."

Isabelle sat back. "Formal introductions. I am Isabelle and this is Sofia."

Webb nodded. "And I'm Jay."

"I recognised you from your MegaTron photo," said Isabelle.

A tall guy in a green camouflage jacket came up behind the girls and stood there, watching. When Webb noticed him, he jumped, and the colour drained from his face. The guy resembled one of the VerKoll guards, but Webb couldn't be sure.

Isabelle continued talking, but Webb couldn't concentrate on what she was saying. She waved her hand in front of his eyes. "Are you there Jay?" Then she turned to see what had distracted him. "That's just Hugo, Sofia's boyfriend."

Sofia elbowed Hugo, who forced a momentary smile, then removed it again. "Just ignore him. He's in a huff, wanted to stay gaming all night."

Webb relaxed a little and took a mouthful of beer. "Can I get you guys a drink?" he said.

"G&T, two lemons," said Isabelle. She looked at Sofia. "Same?"

"Yeah. He'll have a Heineken," said Sofia, tilting her head towards Hugo.

While they waited for their order, Webb let the girls chat. Even though Stella had vouched for Isabelle, Webb knew he couldn't afford to lose the DX3 for a second time. He needed to get comfortable with Isabelle and Sofia first, before he was prepared to trust them. The presence of the broody Hugo did little to ease Webb's jitters, but his only alternative was to risk going back into MegaTron himself. They chatted about gaming and MegaTron until their drinks arrived, then Webb guided them to a quiet alcove near the back. Sofia and Hugo sat on one side of a square table, Webb and Isabelle on the other.

"Now, what's this mysterious thing you need help with?" asked Isabelle.

Webb glanced around, making sure nobody else was within earshot, though it would have been difficult for anyone to hear above the music.

"I left something in MegaTron a couple of nights ago. I'd go back myself, but the thing is, I'm in their bad books right now."

Isabelle leaned over the table. "I'm intrigued. What is it?"

"Just something I've been working on, a piece of electronic kit."

"Game jammer?" suggested Hugo. "I've seen a few of them around lately. That would get you barred."

"It's not a jammer, is it?" said Isabelle. "I hate cheaters, prefer to win using my skills."

Webb shook his head. "No, it isn't. Anyway, I'd be grateful if you guys could get it back for me."

"Where did you leave it?" said Isabelle.

"There's a section full of Millenium Falcon consoles," continued Webb. "It's against the side wall, about halfway along."

"Yeah, over on the right, near the drinks kiosk," said Isabelle.

Webb nodded. "Go to the last simulator in the row. You'll need to remove a panel on the side." Taking out his phone, he scrolled through the photos he'd taken. "It looks like this. There's two clips. Flip them sideways and it'll slide off."

"I know how they work," said Isabelle. "But why did you hide it inside a console?"

"Long story. I was under pressure, needed somewhere safe," shrugged Webb.

"Is that when you got those bruises?" said Hugo.

Webb took a mouthful of beer, wondering how much he should tell them. He needed their help, but didn't want to scare them off. He rested the bottle on the coaster and rotated it, still thinking.

"If you want our help, you must level with us," said Sofia.

Webb looked at Isabelle.

She folded her arms. "I'd like to help but I'm won't risk losing my membership for something dodgy."

"I guess that's fair," said Webb. "A few nights ago, I met a bloke in MegaTron, a gamer called Meerkat, to buy some gear off him. All was going fine until a couple of heavies turned up, said he owed them a ton of money. The two of us took off, but I lost Meerkat in the crowd and found myself trapped in a dead end. I'd already paid him for the gear and didn't want to hand it over, so I hid it."

"Meerkat. I've seen his name on the forums," said Isabelle.

"Like I said, he's a gamer, pretty good one too."

"What happened next?" prompted Sofia.

Webb shrugged. "There was a scuffle, and I got knocked out. When I came to, they questioned me, wanted to know where they could find Meerkat."

"They, who?" said Isabelle, looking confused. "Who questioned you? Did they give you those cuts and bruises?"

"Security guards. They work for the same software company as Meerkat." Webb had to tell some truths in case the VerKoll guys turned up in MegaTron. Isabelle needed to avoid them. "It was no big deal. They were more interested in Meerkat than me." He took a slow drink from his beer, wondering how the two girls would react.

"Exciting stuff," said Sofia.

"Sounds dodgy to me," said Isabelle. "What if those thugs are still around?"

Webb shook his head. "That was Wednesday night. I doubt they'll hang around MegaTron every night, hoping for Meerkat to turn up."

"Still, tampering with a console in there is risky."

"She got docked a thousand credits for spilling drink over a keyboard during a duel a few months back," said Sofia, elbowing Isabelle.

"It was an accident." Isabelle tried to keep a serious expression, but quickly broke into a broad smile.

"Stella said there might be some cash in this for us," said Isabelle. She shrugged. "We're a little short at the moment."

"Yeah, no problem," said Webb.

"How much?" asked Hugo.

"I can give you a couple of hundred."

Isabelle held up a silver bum bag, no bigger than an A5 notebook. "How big is this gizmo? Will it fit in my bag?"

"Easily. Imagine two packs of cigarettes, side by side." Webb held his hands apart, palms facing each other to show the size of the DX3.

"We'll do it for four hundred," said Hugo.

Webb wasn't keen on the idea of Hugo going into MegaTron. If a gamer or staff member challenged him while removing the console panel, Webb reckoned that Hugo would pick a fight rather than bluff his way out of it.

Webb turned to Isabelle. "It'd be better if you and Sofia went in. If somebody is playing at that console, one of you could distract them."

Hugo lifted his Heineken. "You're right," he said, pointing at Webb. "The girls would look less suspicious. But two people will cost you double."

Isabelle looked a little uncomfortable with Hugo's demands for money but busied herself by checking her phone.

Webb's energy levels were dropping fast. The surge he'd got from the food back at the cafe had worn off and he was feeling a little nauseous. He pulled the wad of notes from his pocket and, doing his best to conceal it under the table, peeled off five. He placed the money on the table and looked at Isabelle. "Five hundred, as long as you go now," he said, keeping one hand over the cash.

"Drink up girls, time is money," said Hugo, reaching for the notes.

"And where do you think you're going?" said Isabelle. "That's our money. If you play nice, maybe, just maybe, we'll buy you something later."

Webb steered the five hundred euro towards Isabelle. He was reluctant to pay them the full amount in advance, but Stella trusted Isabelle and Webb badly needed her.

"Hey, I was only going to mind it for you," said Hugo defensively.

Isabelle scoffed. "Sure, and by the time we got back, you'd have spent it on weed." She stuffed the notes into her jeans pocket. "We'll meet you back here," she said to Webb. "Last console in the Falcon corner, right?"

"Yeah, the last one," confirmed Webb. He pulled out his phone. "I'll send you a photo."

Isabelle knocked back her G&T.

Sofia pulled on her jacket. "You guys play nice while we're gone."

When the girls were out of earshot, Hugo leaned over the table, too close to Webb for comfort. "So this little black box, what's it do?"

"Like I said, something I've been playing with. It's still in the R&D phase, lots of issues to figure out."

"Pull the other one," said Hugo. "You've been jittery all evening. You need that gizmo, bad enough to pay five hundred smackers for it without even blinking."

Webb's hand went to his knee to stop it from jumping. Who wouldn't be jittery in his circumstances? He needed to hold it together until Isabelle and Sofia returned. Then he'd hit the road and get as far away from Zurich as possible. He looked left and right, hoping nobody could hear them. The bar was busier now than when he'd first come in, mostly gamers, judging by the logos on their clothes and caps. Two guys plonked down at a table nearby. One of them produced a tin box and began rolling a cigarette. That's what I need, thought Webb. A little blast to take the edge off.

"So, what's the full story?" prompted Hugo.

"I'm wrecked, man. Been pulling all-nighters for the past few weeks." Webb continued to watch the guy at the next table as he patiently arranged the flakes, licked the paper's edge, and folded it in. When it was done, he handed it to his friend, who slid it into his shirt pocket.

"You want some?" asked Hugo.

Webb turned back, surprised. He took a gulp of his beer. "Hmm?"

"Gummin' for a hit?" Hugo rummaged in his jacket pocket, pulled out a brown leather pouch with an elastic band around it, and slid it across the table to Webb. "Help yourself."

Webb sprang back. "In here?"

"No, stupid. Outside. There's no smoking in the pubs here," said Hugo, smirking.

Webb looked at his watch. "Let's wait for the girls to get back." They'd only been gone five minutes, but it already felt like twenty-five.

"They're both careful. They'll scope the place out first. Come on, we've time for a quick one."

Hugo lifted the pouch and stood up. "You coming?"

Webb checked his watch again, knowing less than a minute had passed since the last time he'd looked. What the hell, he thought. He needed something to calm himself down.

Chapter 26

After leaving the Kleiner Technology Campus, Rogue took the A1 towards the city, then branched off onto the A3 and headed south. It was early morning, still dark, but there was enough traffic that she didn't feel exposed on the motorway. For the first few kilometres, her eyes spent more time watching the rear-view mirror than the road ahead. As she gradually relaxed and unclenched her fingers from the steering wheel, her thoughts switched to her next priority. The security van she had stolen was a beacon, easily spotted, both visually and electronically.

She tapped the LCD console on the dashboard and selected the maps. The evening before, she'd earmarked locations in the suburbs of Zurich where, if needed, she could acquire a replacement car. A few minutes later, she took the exit for Urdorf-Nord and followed the directions through a sequence of residential streets until she reached the train station. It was a small suburban setup. A converted cottage with shuttered windows served as a shop and cafe. Outside, sheltered seating and a car park faced the train tracks. As Rogue drove into a spot, two men in suits marched towards the open door of the cafe, no doubt eager for their daily coffee before the next train arrived.

Rogue hopped out of the van and opened the back. It was stuffed with a variety of safety gear and traffic control equipment. As she pulled on a high viz jacket, a silver Volvo S60 screeched into a parking spot a few spaces away from her. Rogue looked on as the driver, a middle-aged man in an expensive three-piece suit, climbed out, cursing loudly into a mobile phone wedged under his chin. He opened the rear door and grabbed a briefcase, then tucked several books and folders under his arm. As he stretched across the seat for his coat, the public address system announced the imminent arrival of the next train. The man slammed the car door, then slid the phone and car keys into his pocket. As he half walked, half ran towards the platform, the jumble of items under his arm slid around, threatening to fall.

Rogue grabbed two stacks of orange traffic cones from the back of the van and strode towards the footpath, timing her arrival perfectly. As the man drew level with her, she feigned a trip and dropped the cones into his path. He stood on one and, in a desperate effort to keep his balance, let the books and files tumble to the pavement. Rogue collided into him with a sufficient force that he didn't fall, but was distracted enough that she slipped her hand into his pocket and removed the car keys. He pushed her away and screamed abuse, threatening to report her to the authorities. As his train arrived, Rogue apologised profusely and helped him to gather his belongings. He snapped them from her and hurried off to the platform. As Rogue collected the cones and dumped them back into the van, she kept one eye on the man, to make sure that he boarded the train. Then she locked the van, dropped the keys in a trash can and drove off in the Volvo.

As she woke up the SatNav, a flashing blue light appeared in the rear-view mirror. She took an immediate right turn, followed by a sharp left, then another right. When the road behind her remained empty, she plotted a route to the centre of Zurich, making sure to avoid the motorways. With a little luck, the owner of the Volvo would be away all day and wouldn't notice his keys missing until that evening.

Rogue's next task was to find Webb. Since she knew almost nothing about him, it made her chances of predicting his next move more difficult. He had no money, phone or passport, but he might have friends or contacts in Zurich who would help him. There was also a good chance that he'd find the rest of the money she'd left in the Audi. His priority would be to retrieve the device, then contact Savik and find a safe way back to London. Rogue needed to keep herself in the game. That meant finding either Webb or the device, otherwise it was all over. Savik would tie up any loose ends, kill Agnetha, and disappear.

Rogue went over everything that had happened since finding the dead kidnapper at the apartment. The call from Savik, the fight in the alley and the brief conversation she had with Webb in the VerKoll basement. Unfortunately, she had no clue when Webb had obtained the DX3 or where the VerKoll guards had apprehended him. As she waited impatiently at a red traffic light, she reviewed the previous few hours, hoping for inspiration, but all she could see were her mistakes. Losing the backpack with the C4 meant she wasn't able to blow the rooftop door into the Astro building. If she'd been more careful jumping through the skylight, maybe she wouldn't have got her leg trapped and been forced to let Webb go on alone. She should at least have planted a tracker on him or on the Audi. She whacked her fist against the dashboard, then punched it harder. The throbbing in her knuckles felt good. She thumped it again with both hands, screaming her anger at the windscreen. She was about to head butt the steering wheel when a sharp beeping startled her. In the mirror, a bearded man glared at her from his Ford pickup. The traffic lights had turned green. Resisting the urge to get out and confront him, she pulled into a side street and stopped.

Rogue lowered the window and sucked in lungfuls of damp morning air. Every cell in her body wanted to retaliate, to charge into Savik's lair and destroy him.

But the emotions hiding beneath her aggression were scared to death of how the next few hours would play out. Her hands started shaking. That was all it took, one half moment of looking her worst fears in the eye. She gripped the steering wheel with both hands, dug her nails into the soft leather and tried to inhale slowly, but instead of calming her nervous system, the air choked her up. Tears gathered behind her eyes, threatening to destroy whatever control she had left. Why did she always find it so difficult to find the balance, that sweet spot between unbridled rage and emotional collapse.

She abandoned the holistic approach and probed around the gunshot wound near the top of her arm. Risking further blood loss, she stuck her index finger into the damaged muscle, sparking a torrent of stabbing pain. She dug in further, using the hurt to refocus her mind and recharge her resolve. She recalled the image of the dead man in her apartment, the photo from Savik of Agnetha bruised and frightened, the pale face of Tayanah bleeding out in the alley, and the triangle of bullet holes she had put in the security guard's skull. Rogue's fears faded away, replaced by a renewed determination to rescue Agnetha, and a vow to destroy the man responsible for the torment of the previous twenty-four hours.

Her first step was to find Jason Webb, but time was critical and she couldn't afford to spend hours driving around in circles, trying to guess where he'd turn up next. She needed to play the odds, pick the most likely option, and run with it. The dashboard clock showed 4:47 am. London was two hours behind, but Rogue needed information. She picked up her phone.

Marcus answered Rogue's call after ten long rings.

"Yeah?" A groggy voice.

"Marcus, wake up."

"Rogue, that you?" Muffled sounds drifted down the line. "Hang on."

Rogue could almost see Marcus reaching across a stack of books for the bedside lamp. She'd been to his apartment a few times, crashed in his bedroom once when her own place had flooded. He'd slept on the couch, insisted she take his bed. The small bedroom was like an obstacle course, every available space covered with computer books, music magazines, and a variety of notepads.

"Are you there Marcus?" said Rogue impatiently.

"Yeah, just about. Do you know what time it is?" he called, the phone some distance from his mouth, probably askew on the bed as he fumbled for his glasses. Marcus was extremely short-sighted and found it impossible to think straight without his specs.

"Get to your computer. We need to find Webb."

"What happened at VerKoll? Did you get him out?"

"That's a long story. Short version is he took off. In my car." Rogue heard the scraping of a chair on the wooden floor, followed by tapping on a keyboard.

"You rescued him and then he bailed on you! Ungrateful sod."

"I have very little time, Marcus," said Rogue, an edge in her voice.

"Right. Let's start by tracing his phone. Do you have his number?"

Marcus' voice was stronger now that he was fully awake. Rogue could tell he had switched to a hands-free headset.

"He'd no phone when I found him, so forget that. I assume the guards took it."

"So, what do we know?" asked Marcus.

"Webb flew to Zurich to get an electronic device called a DX3. At some point after that, they captured him and brought to the VerKoll offices. I found him in a basement room where they'd roughed him up. He stashed the DX3 somewhere before they nabbed him."

"I assume he didn't tell you where?"

"No."

"Any idea where he collected it?"

"That's what I need you to figure out," said Rogue.

"We could try social media. We know he's a gamer, so odds on he was using at least one platform. I'll start with the most popular apps."

Rogue suddenly felt drained, physically tired. Her mind was running at full speed, but after her exertions in VerKoll and Astro Logistics, her energy reserves were desperately low. Apart from a half bottle of orange standing in the driver's cup holder, the interior of the Volvo was spotless, totally devoid of the typical driver bits and pieces. Rogue explored the storage compartments, hoping for some painkillers or something to eat. All she found was the owner's manual and an ice scraper. It had all the hallmarks of a rental car.

"OK, I found some activity on his Instagram account," said Marcus. "The last post was 10:07 pm. It's a photo showing the inside of a gaming event. It's tagged as MegaTron Zurich. There's nothing more after that."

Rogue unscrewed the bottle of orange and wiped the top with the inside of her shirt. "What's Megatron?"

"A chain of gaming arenas. There's two here in London. They're also a major competition sponsor. Far as I know, MegaTron Zurich is hosting the world gaming championships next year."

"That's probably where Webb completed the deal." Rogue drank the remains of the orange. There was no fizz left in it, but she was glad of something to wash the dryness from her throat.

"Then whoever he met must have been followed by the VerKoll guys," said Marcus.

"Webb's contact probably stole the DX3 from VerKoll."

"Considering the calibre of clients those guys have on their books, that raises the stakes considerably."

"Where exactly is MegaTron?" said Rogue.

"I'm sending you the coordinates now. Do you think Webb will go back there?"

"Let's hope so. Right now, it's the only lead I have." Rogue's phone pinged. She opened the message from Marcus and clicked the link. MegaTron was less than ten kilometres away.

"It would make sense," said Marcus. "Let's assume Webb's meeting was in MegaTron and a couple of VerKoll security guards followed his contact. They waited until the exchange took place, snapped a few photos as proof, then grabbed Webb and the other guy."

"Webb makes a run for it," added Rogue. "But security lock down the exits. Webb gets jittery and stashes the DX3 somewhere inside MegaTron, then gets caught trying to leave."

"Even if we're right, he'd be crazy to return to Mega-Tron now."

"He may not have a choice. If he completed the deal, then he's minus the cash and the product," said Rogue.

"True. If it's some kind of decryption unit, we're talking twenty to thirty grand minimum."

"According to Webb, all Savik cares about is the DX3. If it's his money on the line, there's no way Webb will return home without the device."

"My guess is that Webb's contact works for VerKoll," said Marcus. "I'll crosscheck the VerKoll employee database with MegaTron's member list. That might throw up something."

Rogue could hear the keyboard clacking away in the background. "Check his social media accounts for the past week. There might be a clue about where he's staying."

"So far, it's just gaming banter, no mention of travel arrangements, or anything like that."

Rogue shifted in the seat. She had to find Webb, but didn't know where to look. There was no point going to MegaTron and wasting time hoping he might turn up. "What about my car? I rented it from OrbitCar. Can you trace its current location?"

"Officially no. Unofficially, if I was at the office, then probably."

"Come on Marcus, give me something concrete to go on."

"Hang on. Webb took some photos on the street outside MegaTron on Wednesday evening. Looks like he's queueing to get in. There's a guy standing close to him who doesn't look at all happy."

"Send me a copy." Rogue's phone pinged before she had finished the sentence. She opened the message.

"It's dark, and a little blurred," said Marcus. "Want me to clean it up?"

"No need." Rogue recognised the man glaring at Webb. It was the same man she'd seen on the roof opposite her apartment in Geneva, the same man she fought in the alleyway. "I need to know who he is."

"I'll run it through facial recognition. Anything you can tell me about him that might speed it up?"

"Not much. Hired gun, Manchester accent, an old scar across his right temple. I assume he works for Savik."

Rogue drummed her fingers on the steering wheel. Every minute she did nothing was a minute that Webb got further away from her, either to freedom or recapture. She hated being out of control, unsure what to do, but this was worse. For all she knew, Webb was already on a train heading for the border.

"We're getting nowhere, Marcus. I'll go check out MegaTron while you work on the rental car and that other guy in the photo." Rogue searched for MegaTron on the Volvo's SatNav.

"Hang on, Rach, I might have something. I'm scrolling through any social media posts tagged MegaTron, not just Webb's. There was some kind of disturbance there on Wednesday night. A few photos show a fight. Looks like your guy from Manchester took a beating. Other posts talk about a stampede and the place being locked down."

"If he was there, then so was Webb. I bet that's where the VerKoll guards nabbed him, so he must have hidden the DX3 there too. What time does MegaTron open up?"

"There's a tournament on this weekend, so they'll be open twenty-four seven."

"Why didn't you say so earlier?" yelled Rogue. She slammed the Volvo into gear and screeched out of the side street, narrowly missing a taxi coming the opposite way. She ended the call with Marcus and hit the start button on the SatNav.

"You will reach your destination in twelve minutes," said the automated voice.

"Try half that," said Rogue as she leaned on the accelerator.

Chapter 27

Webb followed Hugo out of Deck 5. A little further up the street, they ducked into the shadows of a bicycle shelter. Looking back, Webb still had a view of the steps into MegaTron.

Hugo selected two reefers and a lighter from his pouch. He handed one to Webb and offered him the flame. Webb's eyes followed the trail of smoke wafting from the tip of the joint between his fingers. Still unsure, he waited. Hugo lit his own, took a long pull, and inhaled deeply. Satisfied, Webb sucked in the vapours, then rested back against the concrete wall, waiting for the hit.

The past few days hadn't gone as he'd expected, but if he could recover the device and get back home in one piece, he'd consider the trip a success. He'd even have a few stories to brag about to his hacker buddies, boosting his reputation and adding to his profile as someone who got the job done.

"Good stuff, yeah?" said Hugo.

Webb opened his eyes, startled. He'd drifted off a bit. He looked at the joint. "What is it?"

"Bazooka." Hugo grinned. "Coke and marijuana cocktail, top grade."

Webb hoped so. The last thing he wanted was a kickback from some dodgy mix.

"Want a few more?" Hugo took the pouch from his pocket and held it open. Inside, Webb counted four perfectly rolled joints.

Hugo took out two. "Keep you going until you make it back home."

The throbbing in Webb's ribs had already receded to a dull ache. Maybe it was the placebo effect, but he didn't care. He reached out. "Thanks, man."

Hugo snapped his hand back. "They'll cost you. Like I said, top grade stuff."

"How much?"

"Twenty five each. I'm only making a tenner on the two, straight up."

Webb had paid more in London and wasn't exactly short of cash. He extracted a fifty from his pocket. "Throw in the lighter?"

"Why not?" said Hugo, handing it over.

Webb's phone pinged. He read the message, took a long draw on the Bazooka and extinguished the remains under his boot.

"That was Isabelle. They got it. On their way out now."

Webb led the way back down the street and, without thinking, continued across the cobblestones towards MegaTron. All he could think of was getting the DX3 to Savik. Only then would he completely relax.

Half way across the street, he stopped, his eyes locked on the faces of two bouncers outside MegaTron. They were watching him as well. The taller bearded man consulted his phone, said something to his colleague and nodded in Webb's direction. The two of them started down the steps.

Webb shouted one word to Hugo. "Run."

When he reached the cover of the trees outside Deck 5, Webb veered left and raced along the pavement. As he dodged between pedestrians, his head swam, blurring his vision. He bounced off a trash can and slipped on the cobblestones, but somehow stayed on his feet. He wasn't sure if the MegaTron guys were following him, his ears deafened by the pounding in his head. Up ahead, he saw the plaza and remembered the Audi, but his legs were giving out, so instead he ducked into an alley and doubled over, wheezing.

"What gives man? Why'd you take off like that?"

Webb jumped when he heard the voice beside him. Hugo wasn't even breathing hard.

"The bouncers," wheezed Webb. "One of them ... he recognised me."

"And why is that a problem?"

Webb sneaked a look into the street. He tried to follow the voices, but couldn't see any movement in the shadows. He rubbed his hand across his face and retreated deeper into the alley. "If they catch us, we're dead meat."

Hugo took a few steps back. "What do you mean, we? This is nothing to do with me."

Webb chewed on his lower lip, trying to figure out his next move, but his nerves were buzzing and he struggled to think straight. He jumped when his phone rang, the ringtone bouncing off the walls.

It was Isabelle. "We're back in Deck 5. Where are you guys?"

"Down the street towards the plaza," whispered Webb.

"We've ordered a round of drinks."

"I can't go back in there. Meet me out here."

"What? I can hardly hear you. Sounds like you're underground or something."

"Isabelle, are you there?"

"Hang on Jay, I can't find my credit card."

"Isabelle, you need to leave there now."

There was a clunk, and the line went dead.

"Where is she?" said Hugo, one foot in the alley, the other back on the pavement.

"They're in the bar," groaned Webb. "She hung up on me."

"I need a drink, man," said Hugo, shaking his head. "This is way too intense. You coming?"

Webb squinted along the pavement. Every shadow was a threat, but his options were limited. Either trust

Hugo to get the DX3 for him, or risk going back to Deck 5 himself. Neither appealed to him.

Hugo walked off without waiting for an answer. Keeping close to the buildings, Webb followed him in spurts. As they neared Deck 5, he spotted a man in a green jacket bearing the same lightning bolt on his shoulder as the VerKoll guards. Webb darted behind a parked van and hissed at Hugo.

"Now what?" Hugo sauntered back.

"That guy outside the bar, on the phone."

"What about him?" Hugo stepped onto the street for a better view. "There's two of them now. Hang on, one has just gone into the bar."

"Damn it, there's no way I can go in there now. They'll kill me."

"I'll go meet the girls. You wait here in the alley."

Webb took a step closer to Hugo. "No, it's too risky. They might have seen you with me. Phone Isabelle, get her to come out here."

"Don't worry, I'll only be a minute." Hugo took off before Webb could stop him.

Webb pressed his forehead against the cold window of a van. Nothing was going according to plan, nothing. He didn't like Hugo, and he sure as hell didn't trust him. But like everything else so far, Webb was forced to rely on other people. First Coburn and Meerkat, then Rogue, now Isabelle and Hugo.

Webb left the cover of the van and inched towards Deck 5, ducking from one shadow to the next. When the guard turned around and Webb recognised his face, he froze. It was Bruhn, a member of VerKoll's day shift with an evil streak.

Webb pressed into a doorway and held his breath as the crunching of the guard's boots drew nearer. Webb ran back into the alley and kept running, bouncing off bins and plastic sacks. When the light from the street disappeared completely, he crouched behind a stack of empty beer kegs, gasping for breath. Further down the alley, all he could see was blackness. No lights, not even a breeze to suggest another way out.

He was trapped.

Footsteps from the street broke the unbearable silence. A street lamp outlined Bruhn's shape at the mouth of the alley. He stood motionless, watching. Webb inched backwards, using his hands to feel his way around the obstacles.

Something crunched under his foot.

Broken glass.

He froze as the sound bounced off the walls. Crouching low, he watched the silhouette of the guard. A light came on, a powerful torch which ripped through the gloom and moved slowly towards Webb's location.

Judging by the number of waste bins, several businesses had access to the alley. Webb squinted, searching for a door or window to escape through. He had a torch on his phone, but using it would give away his position.

Agonisingly slow, he crept further down the alley, terrified that he'd step on something and give away his location again.

The slow crunch of Bruhn's boots drew closer, echoing in the darkness.

Webb paused beside a large dumpster. He considered climbing inside and waiting until the guard went by, but it would make too much noise. Instead, he continued until he found a pair of doors facing each other across the alley. The handle on the first turned but wouldn't budge. He tried the other one, but it was also locked.

The beam from the guard's torch swept left and right, patiently checking every nook and cranny.

Webb looked for something he could use to defend himself, then remembered the knife he'd taken from the Audi. He pulled it from his belt and slid the blade from its sheath. It felt strangely familiar and reassuring. Sequences played in his mind of knives and swords, swipes and stabs, not from real life, but from endless hours and days playing games on his computer. This was no game, he reminded himself. Could he use a knife against a real person, stab and kill them? If his life depended on it, then maybe. He shoved it back into his belt until that time came.

The guard's torch beam widened as he drew closer.

Webb squeezed in further between the dumpster and the concrete wall. The footsteps paused. Webb guessed that Bruhn was level with the far end of the dumpster, but the sound of Webb's heart thumping seemed louder than anything else. He tried to calm down, but his chest tightened even more.

The torch swept around the alley, the light bouncing off bins and plastic refuse sacks. Webb spotted a narrow gate in a far corner and grunted in frustration that he hadn't seen it sooner, then caught himself and clamped his mouth shut.

Light and boots swooped on his position until he was drenched in a blinding glare. Webb shielded his eyes and tried to make out the figure behind the torch.

"I found him. He's in the first alley after the bar." It was Bruhn, talking into his phone.

Relief descended on Webb. He wasn't about to die, at least not right away.

"Yeah, he's cowering in a corner like a spineless rat."

For the second time that night, Webb felt a knot of shame turn in his gut. Hugo had scoffed at him earlier when he ran from the bouncers, and now this guard was having a go. Ever since Webb had left Rogue at the mercy of Steinbeck, he'd been running scared. His shoulders sank as he waited for his fate.

"Reverse the van into the alley and wait there. I'll bring him up when I've finished with him," laughed Bruhn.

As Webb slumped against the dumpster, the handle of the knife dug into his ribs. A hint of anger rose through his self-contempt, the weapon injecting a fragment of defiance into his veins. Twisting sideways, he slid the knife out, but kept it hidden under his fleece.

"Get out here," Bruhn bellowed, gesturing his torch away from the dumpster.

Webb didn't fancy taking another beating, or worse, being hauled back to the basement to rot. His only other option was to fight, or at least try. If nothing else, he might leave his mark and die with a little self-respect. He stepped out from his hiding place.

Bruhn balanced his torch on the dumpster lid, angling it so it illuminated the rear wall of the alley. Then he turned to Webb. "You and that bitch caused us a ton of trouble. The cops are all over us looking for answers, and the chief took it out on us." The guard rolled up his sleeves. "Which means I'm going to take it out on you."

Chapter 28

Lights glinting at the top of the alley gave Webb some hope until he realised they belonged to the security van.

Bruhn closed in. "Anything to say before I beat you to a pulp?"

Webb tried to imagine himself in a computer game, armed with swords and daggers, facing some crazy ogre. He searched the guard's upper body for a vulnerable spot, knowing he'd only get one chance.

"You're all talk. I'm not tied to a chair this time." Webb's voice lacked strength, but he hoped his words might rile the bigger man.

"You little punk, you really think you've a chance with me? I'm going to enjoy every minute of this."

"Come on, let's see what you've got," taunted Webb.

Bruhn moved fast. His right hand clenched into a massive fist and the light behind him cast a monstrous shadow over Webb. As Bruhn charged, Webb chose his target and lunged, urging the knife home before the guard's fist connected. Unable to adjust his angle, Bruhn overshot his target. He grunted, recovered quickly, and wrapped Webb in a crushing bear hug. Webb failed to react. He was in shock that Bruhn hadn't even notice the knife rammed into his side. Webb still had his hand wrapped around the hilt, but his arms were pinned to his sides. He channelled all his remaining energy into twisting the knife, pivoting the blade through the guard's organs. As Bruhn tightened his bear hug, Webb felt warm liquid ooze along his fingers.

Bruhn slammed Webb into the steel doors, stepped back, and charged again. Webb collapsed, feeling like a truck had hit him. As the guard targeted Webb's skull with his steel-toed boot, he stopped dead. Bending down, he looked closer at the blood-stained knife in Webb's hand, denying the conclusion his brain had arrived at. Even when Bruhn pulled back his jacket and saw the blood soaking his shirt, he was astonished that Webb had stabbed him.

Webb rolled onto all fours and clambered up the wall, his legs reluctant to support him. Bruhn glared at his prey, his eyes bulging with hatred. Ignoring the widening blood patch, he pulled a gun and stuck the barrel firmly between Webb's eyes. Webb froze. He wasn't afraid of dying, just terrified of being shot, of the unbearable agony. His mind wanted to retaliate, to die fighting, but his body was crushed. A voice called out in the distance, but to Webb, the words were an underwater mumble. Bruhn looked around and yelled a reply, then whipped back, his mouth gaping in agony. Webb looked down at his own hand and saw that he'd stabbed the guard again, without even realising it. Some part of him, desperate to survive, had taken control. Bruhn lashed out, smashing Webb's hand into the wall. His knife clattered to the ground. Two meaty hands seized Webb's throat, smacked his skull back against the concrete and dragged his face along the stony surface.

"I could kill you right now. Nobody would give a damn," growled Bruhn. "Hell, I'd be doing the world a favour."

Webb sucked in shallow breaths and tried to stay conscious.

"Give me what I want," said Bruhn. "Then maybe you won't die in this stinking alley."

Webb tried to speak. His lips formed the words, but no sound emerged.

"What?" Bruhn eased his grip on Webb's throat.

"It's here. I can get it," said Webb.

"Where's here? No more games."

Webb's head swam, and his vision blurred. Bruhn's face morphed into a monster. Four eyes bulging with rage, lips curling away from snarling teeth. Webb's stomach churned and erupted, regurgitated food spewing into the other man's face. Webb smirked, an involuntary nervous reaction.

Bruhn pulled a sleeve across his face to wipe it clean, then roared at Webb. "You think this is funny?"

A fist caught Webb in the jaw, followed by a volley of punches to his ribs and gut. Every organ in his midsection screamed for an end to the agony. In that moment, he'd have welcomed a bullet. His stomach convulsed again and emptied onto the ground.

As Bruhn backed away to avoid his boots being splashed, his phone rang, the tone an alien sound in the dark hell of the back alley. He stepped further back from the spreading pool of vomit and answered it.

When Webb's head cleared a little, he was shocked to be alive, but that shock was quickly replaced by a burden. Dead, all his problems would be over, with no choices to make, but alive, it was back to the basement cell and most likely, a slow agonising path to an unmarked grave. He twisted away from the smell of his own vomit and saw the knife. As he closed his fingers around the handle, he thought about ending it all himself, right there. Simply ram the blade through his shirt, into his gut and bleed out. Or slice the carotid artery in his throat. It sounded so easy, but deep down, Webb knew he couldn't actually do it, couldn't inflict that kind of pain on himself. He just wasn't able.

Bruhn's voice got louder as he ended the call. Webb slid the knife under his thigh, trapped in a nightmare of his own making.

"You finished puking your guts up?" Bruhn limped over, his breathing laboured.

Webb cleared his throat and spat out a mixture of saliva and blood. He kept his head lowered, expecting a boot in the face or a bullet in the head. He wished for the latter.

"Get up. The chief wants to question you."

Webb glanced at the guard, still waiting for another blow, but none came.

Bruhn grabbed Webb's arm and wrenched him off the ground. "Let's go. He doesn't like to be kept waiting."

As he straightened up, Webb lunged forward, leading with the blade of the knife. Bruhn tried to pivot, but Webb stayed with him, jabbing the blade like a crazed animal. Bruhn rained blows onto Webb's back, but his fists lacked power. Webb sensed the change and thrust harder with each attack, ignoring his own exhaustion. Bruhn's legs buckled and the two men toppled over.

Webb couldn't move. His brain sent instructions to his limbs, but nothing happened. So he waited for the inevitable. Seconds passed and all he heard were his own ragged breaths. He rolled onto his side and came face to face with the guard. Bruhn was breathing hard, his eyes blinking as if trying to see clearer. Blood bubbled from his lips and formed a growing pool in the dirt. As Webb looked on, a raspy growl escaped from the guard's throat, then his whole torso convulsed. Webb pushed himself back out of reach. Bruhn stopped shaking and lay still. The eyes that stared back at Webb were hollow and lifeless.

Webb slumped back down on the cold concrete. He had survived. The Gods he didn't believe in had given him another chance. And he had killed a man. Nausea swirled in his stomach and spread upwards. He closed his eyes and tried to focus, to stay conscious. Cold sweat drenched his face and his ears filled with an eerie static. If he passed out and the other guards found him, he was finished. Clenching his fists tight, he counted aloud and focused on the numbers, determined to stay awake. Eventually, the spinning in his head abated. Voices and music drifted around him from somewhere far away. He rolled on to his hands and knees, and looked at the corpse again. It hadn't moved. The guard really was dead.

Webb grabbed the dumpster and hauled himself upright. Footsteps approached, but Webb couldn't drag his eyes from the handle of the knife, the blade buried deep in the guard's stomach.

"What the hell, man? Is that your handiwork?" Hugo's eyes flicked back and forth from Webb's bloodied hands to the uniformed corpse.

Webb leaned over and wiped his hands on the dead man's trousers.

"We need to leave here right now," said Hugo. "Before anyone sees us."

Webb nodded.

Hugo took a few steps and waited. "Shift it dude, come on. Isabelle and Sofia are waiting for us."

Webb started walking, slowly at first. The mention of the girls reminded him why he was there, what he had come for. He quickened his pace and followed Hugo back along the alley. As they neared the street, Webb saw a van with the VerKoll insignia on the back. He pulled up his collar and hurried past the van. Inside, he heard the driver laughing, oblivious to what had happened to his colleague.

A minute later, Webb realised they had reached the square. He stopped at a doorway and looked back towards the bar. "Where's Isabelle?"

"What happened back there?" said Hugo. "You stuck that guy pretty good."

Webb started shivering again.

"You don't look too good, man. Are you hurt?" asked Hugo.

Webb's head spun. He grabbed the door handle to steady himself.

"The girls are in a cafe up here," said Hugo. "Just around the next corner."

Webb had only one thought in his mind. Get the DX3 and leave Zurich before he passed out. "What about my stuff from MegaTron?"

"Don't worry, I have it." Hugo patted his jacket pocket. "Come on, you look like you need a drink."

Hugo took off before Webb could argue with him. Webb quickly forgot the dead guard and focused on keeping up with Hugo. Webb was one step closer to leaving Zurich, but a bad feeling in his gut told him that Hugo wouldn't give up the Decryptor easily.

The further they got from the alley, the safer Webb felt. Even though he knew police sirens would soon flood the street, emerging into the early morning sun from the damp and depressing alley made it easier for him to shove the images of the dead guard into the deep recesses of his mind. As his heart rate settled, he started to believe he would get home soon, but his body hit back with savage pain, first in his stomach and then at the base of his skull. Hugo was several strides ahead of Webb, with the Decryptor buried in his jacket pocket. Webb struggled to keep up and called out for him to wait, but Hugo ignored him. Terrified of losing the DX3 for good, Webb forced his pace. Without warning, Hugo disappeared. Webb panicked and stumbled after him, his legs heavy and unstable.

At the spot where Hugo had vanished, Webb found a narrow lane. One side was lined with abandoned cottages, the windows boarded up and scrawled with graffiti. A blank wall faced them, rising several stories high and blocking the first shards of the early morning sun. As Webb's eyes adjusted to the poor light, he spotted Hugo perched on a window ledge.

"What happened back there? Why'd you kill that guy?"

Webb shook his head. "Doesn't matter. It was him or me, that's all."

"He was wearing a uniform. He wasn't nobody." Hugo stood up and scowled at Webb. "And what about me? There's street cameras back there. You need to fill me in so I can stay out of trouble."

Webb slid down the wall and sat on the pavement, his legs no longer willing to hold him up. "OK, the short version." He hesitated, trying to decide on how much he would tell Hugo. "I came here to buy that device in your pocket from Meerkat. Turns out he'd stolen it from a software company. The security guard in the alley worked for the same company. That's their van parked on the street."

Hugo listened, taking it all in. He took the Decryptor from his pocket and turned it over in his hands, as Webb continued with his explanation.

"When I met Meerkat in MegaTron, the guards were waiting. I panicked and hid the device just before they grabbed me. They locked me up, beat the crap out of me, wanted to know where they could find Meerkat. Eventually they let me go and I came back here to get my gear. You know the rest."

"So this gizmo, it must do something pretty cool?" said Hugo.

"Like I said, it's an R&D project. So far, it does very little."

"VerKoll," said Hugo, reading the name on the back. "Don't they sponsor tournaments at MegaTron?"

"Yeah."

Hugo tossed the DX3 in the air, let it slip through one hand and caught it with the other.

Webb jumped up. "Don't mess around Hugo. If that gets damaged, I'm a dead man."

Voices seeped into the lane from the street. A group of lads passed by in high spirits, chatting and jostling each other.

Webb fished two hundred euro from his pocket and offered it to Hugo. "Thanks for helping me out, Hugo. Here's a little extra, OK?"

Sirens sounded in the distance. Police or an ambulance, thought Webb, probably both. Soon, they'd close off the area.

"I know you're not telling me the full story about this," said Hugo, still examining the device in his hand. "That's alright, I guess, but it's worth a lot more than a couple of hundred quid. And it seems to me, you're not exactly short of cash."

Webb knew it would come down to money, probably everything he had. But he was in no position to argue. He was out of time and about to collapse. He took out five hundred in folded notes and fanned them out. "That's it, everything I've got. But first, you give me the device."

Hugo glanced up to the street, then knocked Webb against the boarded-up window, grabbed his wrist and tried to force the notes from his hand. Webb let the money go and took a swing at Hugo. His fist connected with Hugo's jaw, but lacked any power. Hugo shouldered Webb back against the window, then followed up with a left hook and a head butt. Webb fell back and sagged onto the ledge. Hugo rifled through Webb's pockets, finding the rest of the money Webb had taken from the Audi, more than a thousand euro.

Webb tried to resist, but he hadn't the will or the strength. "Fine, take the money, take it all. Just give me the device."

Hugo flicked through the bundle of notes before shoving them and the DX3 into his jacket.

"We had a deal," pleaded Webb.

Hugo smirked. "Things change. That was before you stabbed that security guard."

Webb felt dizzy as his stomach churned again. Not for the first time in the past couple of days, he'd made the wrong choice. He reached a hand to the wall to steady himself, then hunched down to clear the dizziness. The noise of the sirens, much closer, penetrated his brain again, reigniting the headache.

"You want your kit back? Get me another five grand," said Hugo.

Webb's head spun and he collapsed onto the pavement. There was no point fighting any longer. He rested his head on the ground and watched helplessly as Hugo backed away.

Chapter 29

Rogue reached the North corner of the Turbinenplatz in nine and a half minutes, without causing any accidents. According to the map, the MegaTron arena was halfway down a side street on the opposite side of the square. She drove around in a clockwise direction, watching out for her rented Audi. As she rounded the South corner, she glanced up the side street towards MegaTron and almost missed the Audi tucked in beside a camper van. She heaved an enormous sigh of relief. Just knowing she was on the right track loosened the tension squeezing her chest.

She parked on the opposite side of the road and switched off the engine. It appeared she had guessed right, that Webb had hidden the DX3 inside MegaTron. The big question was, how did he plan to retrieve it, knowing that the security staff would recognise him from the trouble he'd caused earlier that week. Rogue considered waiting for him to return to the car, but for all she knew, he had already recovered the device and joined up with Savik's crew. Or worse, he could be back in the hands of the VerKoll security guards, locked up in some warehouse, never to see the light of day again.

She hopped out and approached the Audi from behind the camper van, in case Webb was slouched down in the driver's seat. The car was empty. Using her own key, she popped the trunk. It was clear that Webb had rummaged through her stuff. A quick inventory check revealed that some cash was missing and the second Gerber knife. The sight of clean clothes and the first aid kit helped Rogue decide her next move. She stuffed a few things into a carrier bag and returned to the Volvo. If Webb didn't arrive back by the time she'd dressed her wound and changed out of her dirty clothes, then she'd go look for him.

As she chewed a protein bar, she unwound the layers of tape from around her arm and slipped off her jacket. Carefully, she prised the material of her t-shirt away from the bullet wound and pulled it over her head. Blood had clotted over the entry point, halfway down her tricep. Her fingertips found the exit on the opposite side of her arm. It was leaking, but slowly. She rubbed the blood between her fingers, but didn't detect any bone fragments. With luck, the bullet had just drilled through the muscle, bypassing the humerus. She took a couple of antiseptic wipes, cleaned the wound, then applied dressings front and back, and secured them with adhesive tape.

Looking in the mirror, Rogue hardly recognised herself. There was purple bruising above her left eye, swelling below the right, and blood caked under both nostrils. Her hair was matted with a cocktail of dust and sweat. Several strands had escaped her ponytail and were plastered onto her forehead. Parting her lips, she was relieved to see all her teeth still in place. She used a few more wipes to clean the blood and dirt from her face and hands, then secured the loose strands of hair back into the ponytail. Finally, she swallowed a few painkillers to ease her growing collection of aches, all the time watching the Audi in case Webb returned.

A few minutes later, after pulling on a clean set of clothes, Rogue climbed out of the Volvo and followed the footpath towards MegaTron. A moist, refreshing breeze drifted across the plaza. Soft lights and clinking glasses from a couple of all night bars gave the area a relaxed mood. After the strain of the previous twenty-four hours, Rogue found it calming to be part of a normal world, though she remained alert for the police or the green uniforms of the VerKoll security guards.

As she proceeded up the side street, the Samsung phone in her pocket rang. It was Savik. Rogue's stomach flipped, terrified that Webb had already contacted his boss. Once that happened, it was game over for Agnetha.

Rogue pressed the answer button, held the phone to her ear, and waited.

"Miss Garde, you have done well so far."

"Meaning what?" said Rogue.

"I know of your actions in VerKoll last night. Although, with your reputation, I expected a more clinical operation."

"I got the job done. That's all that matters."

"I want to speak with Jason Webb."

"That's not possible right now."

"It is not a request." Rogue detected a menacing edge in Savik's voice.

"Webb was out of it when I found him, delirious. Once we got to the car, he passed out and I couldn't wake him. Believe me, I tried. Fresh marks on his arm suggest they drugged him."

"Why don't I believe you?"

"Maybe you have trust issues," said Rogue. "Either way, I've kept my part of the deal. Just make sure you keep yours."

"Let me be clear." Savik's tone dropped deeper and his words became slower. "I need the DX3 and Jason Webb. Without both, all you will get back is a corpse."

"I get it," said Rogue. "Let me be equally clear. If you harm Agnetha, I will hunt you down and end your worthless life."

"You disappoint me, Miss Garde. My information tells me you are calm, very focused. But you are hot tempered and arrogant. Remember what is at stake here."

Rogue dug her nails deep into her palms and forced her mouth to stay shut.

In that moment of silence, she heard a door creak open, then a voice in the background. "Sir, there's someone here to see you."

"Not now, get out," bellowed Savik.

Rogue was deafened, but held the phone to her ear, straining for any snippet of useful intel.

Savik cleared his throat and spat out. "Deliver that device and Webb to me at noon, or you will regret this day forever." He ended the call before Rogue could respond.

She stared off into the distance. Savik was right. She was letting her emotions get in the way. He didn't know her and yet he saw through her so easily. She'd been in worse situations, missions for MI5 where the odds were stacked against her, but back then, there hadn't been a personal crisis distracting her. Now, no matter how she tried, images of Agnetha tied up in a cold damp cellar swamped Rogue's thoughts, clouding her judgement. It was her fault that Agnetha had been kidnapped, and her bad planning that had let Webb get away. Instead of being in control of the mission, she was chasing long shots and hoping for the best. She needed to get her act together, or she'd lose everything.

Rogue pocketed the phone and hurried up the cobbled street. Ghoulish masks surrounded the entrance to MegaTron, reminding her of the ghost train at a theme park. As she read the admittance fees, her phone buzzed. It was Marcus.

"I found him. He's not in MegaTron," blurted Marcus.

Rogue turned and walked back down the steps. "Go on."

"Most of the game arenas have their own app, so I checked out MegaTron and downloaded theirs. But before I could search for Webb, it forced me to create an account. Even then, it wouldn't show me his location unless I was a friend of his."

"Get to the point, Marcus," snapped Rogue. "Where is Webb now?"

"Sorry. He's on the move, somewhere between MegaTron and the plaza, on foot. The app is slow to refresh, so he could be a little further on."

"He's heading back to the car," said Rogue, as she sprinted back down the street, searching for Webb, wondering if he was still wearing the navy Astro Logistics jacket.

"He's just taken a left turn," shouted Marcus. "Last one before the plaza, a narrow lane."

As Hugo turned to leave, his head jerked back and his legs flew out from under him. For a moment, he seemed suspended in the air before crashing to the pavement. He let out a long moan as the impact knocked the air from his lungs. Webb thought he saw the outline of someone standing over Hugo. He rubbed his eyes and tried to clear the fog in his brain. When he looked again, Hugo was getting back to his feet, but before he fully straightened up, his assailant lashed out, kicking him in the midsection. He clutched his stomach as a fist smashed into his face. Hugo staggered sideways and fell again. He used the wall for support as he struggled up.

"You had enough yet?" A woman's voice, one Webb thought sounded familiar.

Hugo reached into his pocket. Webb heard a click as a knife flicked open. Hugo closed on the woman, sweeping the blade back and forth. Moving in a circle, she sidestepped his attacks until she reached the opposite side of the lane. She grabbed a lid from a trash can and charged at him, shielding herself from the knife with the metal lid. She added punches and kicks, forcing him back against the wall. Then she pinned his knife hand against the concrete and kneed him in the groin. When he doubled over, she followed with an elbow to the back of his head. Then she dropped the lid, grabbed one of his wrists with both hands, and twisted his arm to its limit. He screamed and let the knife fall. She bent the arm behind his back and marched him over to Webb.

"A friend of yours?" asked Rogue.

"Not anymore," said Webb. He reached for Hugo's pocket, but Hugo kicked out.

"He's got the DX3. It's in his inside pocket."

Rogue forced Hugo's face against a boarded-up window, pushing up hard on the arm still twisted behind his back. Patting his pockets, she found the Decryptor and held it up.

"That's it," said Webb, reaching for it.

Rogue dropped it into her inside pocket.

"He took all my money as well," complained Webb.

Rogue tilted her head at him. "Your money?"

The wail of a siren interrupted them. They both looked back to the street in time to see an ambulance and a police car speed past.

Rogue turned back to Webb. "Is that something to do with you?"

The image of the knife sticking out of the guard flooded back. Webb shuddered at the memory. "A security guard from VerKoll."

"Dead?" asked Rogue.

Webb shrugged, trying and failing to appear casual. "It was him or me."

Rogue relieved Hugo of the money he took from Webb, then released her grip and shoved him away. "If I were you, I'd disappear before the cops cordon off the area."

Hugo knew when to quit. He shuffled off, nursing his injured arm.

Rogue turned to Webb. He stood there, unsure of how things were between them. She walked up to him slowly, her eyes locked on his.

"About the car," said Webb. "I thought the cops had you. There was no point me waiting around."

In a flash, she grasped his throat and squeezed tight. "I should finish you now and tell Savik I found your useless corpse in this laneway."

Webb couldn't think of anything to say and doubted if he could have got the words out.

Rogue tightened her grip and watched his eyes bulge. "Next time you cross me will be your last."

She released him and waited a few seconds while he caught his breath. Then she held out her hand. "Key for the Audi, and your phone."

Webb rooted in his pocket and handed over the key. "The guards took my phone in Verkoll."

"Then what's that in your pocket?"

Webb followed Rogue's eyes and saw the telltale shape of his new phone bulging in his trouser pocket. He sighed, fished it out, and surrendered it.

"Move." Rogue prodded him to walk ahead of her.

"Where are we going?" Webb already knew the answer and wasn't looking forward to facing Savik after all the trouble he'd caused.

Back at the square, Rogue opened the front passenger door of the Audi and waited for Webb to get in. Then she locked the car, just in case Webb tried to make a run for it. Rogue was in no mood to go chasing after him. She made her way around to the driver's side and sat in. As she started the engine and shifted into reverse, the rear door opened and she felt the cold steel of a gun pressed hard into the back of her neck. Her eyes snapped to the rear-view mirror. A familiar face filled the reflection. The man from the alley in Geneva grinned back at her, the same man who had callously put a bullet in the shoulder of the young girl from the hotel kitchen.

Chapter 30

On hearing the rear door of the Audi close, Webb twisted around. "Coburn." It was more a statement than a greeting.

Coburn drilled the barrel harder into the base of Rogue's skull, forcing her to lean forward. "I don't need you anymore, so think twice before you react."

Fire ripped through Rogue's bloodstream. She'd been on a high after recovering Webb and the Decryptor, then got careless and hadn't followed her own rules. She gripped the steering wheel tighter and forced herself to remain still. In those milliseconds, her mind raced through multiple options, calculating angles and speeds. It told her the muzzle of the gun was one centimetre off the centre of her skull, that he was leaning to one side and wasn't wearing a seat belt. She fed her brain new scenarios, but every simulation led to her being shot dead. In the end, her brain over-ruled her gut. She took a slow deep breath, then exhaled the adrenalin and dropped her shoulders in submission.

"A wise choice," said Coburn. "Now, slowly reverse out of this parking spot."

"Where are we going?" asked Rogue. Any conversation would tell her more about the man. Even his tone and hesitations could give her vital information, details she could use to stay alive.

"Onto the motorway. Drive towards Basel."

Rogue digested the words. He said 'towards', not 'to'. He had plans to dispose of her along the way, somewhere quiet.

Coburn moved the barrel of the gun down to Rogue's shoulder, allowing her to rotate her head as needed. Rogue tapped the GPS and searched for Basel, then started the directions. It was eighty-five kilometres from Zurich, a journey that would take about an hour. She glanced at the fuel gauge. It was still three-quarters full. She would have very few opportunities to regain control. Shifting gear, she backed out of the spot and drove away from the square.

Webb settled back into his seat, facing the windscreen. "Bit late to the party, Coburn."

"You look the worse for wear," said Coburn.

"Yeah, those guards did a number on me. But you look OK."

"I presume you have the device?"

"How come you weren't part of the rescue team?" said Webb.

So that was it, thought Rogue. Coburn's job was to protect Webb, and he'd screwed up.

"The device, where is it?" demanded Coburn, a little too loud for the confines of the car.

Webb opened his mouth to say something, then changed his mind. He jerked a thumb in Rogue's direction. "She has it."

"Get it," instructed Coburn.

Webb half turned, then hesitated.

"She won't bite." Coburn dug the muzzle of his gun firmer into Rogue's shoulder blade.

Webb carefully reached into Rogue's pocket and pulled out the DX3.

"The boss says you need to activate it as soon as possible," said Coburn.

Webb turned the black box over in his hand, examining it for damage. "What?"

"Stella got a message from Meerkat, something about VerKoll changing the access codes."

Webb held up the DX3. "Not possible. This little baby generates single use disposable codes. The hacks in VerKoll can't do anything about it."

"I'm just passing on the message. It's your neck in the noose."

"What do you mean?"

"After your screw-up, you're no longer in the boss's good books." Coburn took out his phone with his free hand and selected a number from his recent calls list.

"It's me," said Coburn. "I ... yes, we have it ... leaving Zurich now ... I told him, but ... I know ... yes, boss ..."

As the call went on, the voice on the other end grew louder and angrier. In the mirror, Rogue could see Coburn was holding the phone away from his ear.

Coburn handed his mobile between the front seats to Webb. "The boss wants to speak to you."

"Mr Savik," said Webb, his head turned to face out the side window. "That makes no sense ... right ... yes, I understand."

Webb ended the call and tossed the phone over his shoulder into the back seat.

"That went well," sneered Coburn.

"Meerkat held back, didn't give us the full story," muttered Webb.

"Surprise, surprise. Now what?"

"I need a computer," said Webb, picking at a scab on his thumb.

"An internet cafe?"

Webb shook his head. "It has to be a secure connection. And something fast."

"So where do we find that?" said Coburn.

"Let me think."

Coburn jabbed Rogue with the gun. "Follow the signs to the motorway, but stay off it for now. Just drive around."

Rogue wondered how far they'd go beyond the city limits before Coburn would tell her to turn down some deserted country road. He'd enjoy putting a bullet in her head. She came to a crossroads managed by traffic lights and stopped. There was a police car on the opposite side. She thought of several ways she could draw their attention and get pulled over, but she needed to stay with Webb, at least until she could take back the Decryptor. If she could get that, it would give her some leverage. She needed something to ensure Agnetha's safety.

"Don't get any ideas," said Coburn. He had seen the cops too and read her mind.

Rogue waited for the lights to change to green, then eased forwards, avoiding eye contact with the driver of the patrol car.

"So, Mr Hacker, where to?" said Coburn, as they drove away from the city.

Webb exhaled loudly as he studied his phone. "It's only 7 am. There aren't too many options. We could wait for a computer store to open and buy a laptop with a Wi-Fi dongle. That would be the most secure option."

"We don't have time for that. The boss said you need to act now. We should break in somewhere and use their computer."

"Yeah, sure, we just knock on someone's door," said Webb, waving the apartment blocks on each side of them.

"Everyone has a computer nowadays. Offices, shops, cafes. I bet that undertaker over there even has one."

Webb chewed his lower lip. Coburn was right. Why hadn't he thought of that? In theory, anywhere with a computer and an internet connection would do.

"A private house would be best," said Webb finally. "The computer wouldn't have much of a firewall and no logging of internet traffic."

"You over-think everything college boy," said Coburn. "It makes no difference, we just smash the thing to bits when we're finished with it. No computer, no logs."

Webb turned to face Coburn. "Most business computers go through a shared router which logs everything into the cloud."

"Fine then, a house. Find one set apart from the neighbours, with less chance of us being noticed," said Coburn. "And don't pick a rich area, too much security."

"And how the hell will I know that?" shouted Webb. He was finding it hard to think straight. His head pounded and judging by the ache in his chest, he was convinced several of his ribs had been cracked.

"Size of the house, number of cars outside, maybe a swimming pool out back, use your bloody imagination," said Coburn.

As Webb used the satellite view on his phone's map application to scour residential areas on the edge of the city, Rogue relaxed a little. They had presented her with the opportunity she desperately needed. She imagined the layout of a typical house. Downstairs, there'd be a kitchen, living and dining areas, maybe a conservatory. Upstairs would be the bedrooms and possibly a home office or study. A laptop could be in any room, a desktop most likely in the office or study. If she were selecting a target, she'd find a bungalow. Entry and exit would be easy from any part of the house. And one without dogs. She wondered how Coburn would play things. He'd want to go in first and secure the location before setting Webb loose. And there was no way he'd leave Webb to watch her in the car. Which meant he'd tie her up first and throw her in the boot.

Webb continued to stare at his phone, mumbling to himself every few seconds. They'd left the built-up areas of the city behind them and were approaching a roundabout with signs for Baden, Brugg and Basel.

Coburn jabbed the muzzle of the gun into the back of Rogue's head. "I told you to stay in Zurich. Drive around the ring road until Merlin here finds what he needs."

Rogue took the third exit off the roundabout onto a route which would bring them in a clockwise circle around the city. There was nothing she could do until they stopped somewhere.

As they crossed a bridge over the Limmat river, Coburn's phone rang. "Yeah … not yet … just pulling in to a place now … of course."

He ended the call and prodded Rogue's shoulder. "Turn in to that business centre on the left."

Rogue flicked on the indicator and drove between a pair of red brick pillars. She slowed down to match the twenty-five kilometre speed limit and crawled over a series of ramps.

"Pull over to that signpost," ordered Coburn.

Rogue braked beside a billboard showing a map of the complex. Office buildings hugged the outer perimeter of a square. In the centre, clusters of benches surrounded a few cafes and food trucks.

"These are all commercial units. I thought we had decided on a private house," said Webb.

"I'm not wasting any more time. Pick something on that list or I'll do it for you," said Coburn impatiently.

Webb lowered the window. As he read through the names, Rogue studied the map and committed the road layout to memory.

"Dammit Webb, hurry up. I do not want another call from the boss."

Webb threw his hands in the air. "I'm trying, but most of them are in German. It's pure guesswork."

Coburn tried to see the names, but he was on the wrong side of the car. He wasn't prepared to slide across the seat and take his eyes off Rogue. "Just pick one."

"Fine," said Webb, turning away from the window. "There's two that should have plenty of computers. Strut-Technik and KollerPrint. They're the last two units on this stretch of road."

Being a Sunday, there appeared to be no activity in any of the offices or warehouses. Several had vans parked outside, but it looked like each premises was empty. When Rogue reached the businesses Webb had selected, she pulled in to the kerb.

"There's a light on in KollerPrint, and a van parked out front," said Rogue. "Strut looks better, all dark and an empty car park."

"Agreed," said Coburn.

Rogue pulled into Strut-Technik, then turned the car around and parked close to the building, facing the exit. She switched off the engine and looked in the rear-view mirror.

Webb released his seat belt and opened the car door. "What about her?"

"Check the boot, see if there's a rope or something to tie her up," said Coburn.

Webb grinned at Rogue. "Not sure about a rope, but I saw a bunch of cable ties."

When Rogue glared back at him, he turned and jumped out of the car.

Coburn pressed the gun into Rogue's neck. "Lean forward, head against the steering wheel, hands behind your back, wrists overlapped."

Rogue did as he said.

Webb appeared at the driver's side of the car, holding a bunch of cable ties and a length of tow rope.

"Use a cable tie to secure her wrists. And make sure it's tight," instructed Coburn.

Webb opened the car door and tentatively reached in, expecting Rogue to spring into action.

"And make it quick, we haven't got all day," snapped Coburn.

Webb slipped one band around Rogue's overlapped wrists, slid the tapered end into the slot, and pulled it tight.

"Pull it again, hard," said Coburn.

Webb yanked the free end, causing Rogue to wince as the rigid plastic bit into her wrists. As soon as Webb stood back, Coburn jumped out of the car. He took another cable tie from the holdall and threaded it over the first one, taking no chances.

He waved the gun at Rogue. "Get out."

She swung her feet onto the ground, leaned forward, and stood up.

Coburn turned to Webb. "Remove everything from the back, including the toolkit. Put them on the back seat."

Webb trudged to the rear of the car. When he had finished, Coburn shoved Rogue around and motioned for her to climb in. After securing her ankles with more cable ties, Coburn removed her phone, keys and the knife strapped to her shin. Then he slammed the lid, leaving Rogue in darkness.

Chapter 31

Locked in the boot of the Audi, Rogue strained to hear Coburn and Webb. The back door of the car was still open and muffled words drifted in through the rear shelf. It was clear from the tones that Coburn was in charge.

The doors slammed shut, and she heard the locks snap into place. Their footsteps quickly faded, leaving her alone in the confined darkness.

Coburn had taken her knife and removed everything from the boot, including the tyre changing kit. Rogue traced her hands along the panels, searching for a metal edge she could use to cut or break the plastic ties, but there was nothing sharp enough. She tried biting into the hard plastic between her wrists, but only succeeded in hurting her teeth. With all her experience, she couldn't believe there wasn't a way to break free.

She lashed out at the rear door with both feet in hope and frustration. When the plastic panel cracked, she continued her assault until it shattered and fell away.

Then she fumbled around in the recess, hoping she might release the locking mechanism by disconnecting it from the car's battery. It turned out to be a waste of both time and energy. The cluster of wires she found came away easily, but the door held firm.

Cursing her predicament, she lay down again. She had to get free somehow. Once Webb finished activating the Decryptor, they'd leave Zurich and Coburn would find a remote location to kill her.

Reaching her arms up, Rogue tested the rear shelf. It felt fragile. She kicked one side until it broke free from its slot, then turned and did the same with the opposite end. With the shelf free from its moorings, some daylight seeped in. A volley of kicks buckled the shelf in half. Manoeuvring onto her knees, she dragged it aside and wriggled over the back seat, landing headfirst.

Liberated from her prison, she still needed to free her hands and feet. Stuffed behind the driver's seat, she found the holdall with the rest of her supplies, including the knife and phone Coburn had taken from her. She quickly sliced through the cable ties, got out of the car, and stretched her limbs.

It was 7:29 am and although a Sunday, there was some activity in the surrounding area; the clatter of a compressor, someone hammering metal and the drone of a lawn mower. Apart from the Audi, she was relieved to see the car park was still empty. She needed to engage Coburn and Webb without trying to protect any innocent bystanders.

Coburn had a gun, and Rogue knew from the confrontation in Zurich that he wouldn't hesitate to shoot. If that happened, time would be critical. Anybody hearing the gunshots would report them, first to the local security service and then the police. She would have to get Webb and the Decryptor away from the business park before either arrived.

Staying close to the wall, she made her way around to the front entrance. The lock on the white PVC doors had been forced, probably with the wheel brace from the Audi. She stepped into a small lobby. Office doors on each side faced an oversized marble reception desk. Beyond the desk, stairs rose to the next level.

Instinctively, she looked for security cameras and alarm sensors, and found both. She would have heard the alarm sounding from inside the Audi, which meant Coburn must have disabled it. As much as she disliked him, she had to admit he was resourceful.

Slow, heavy footsteps crossed the floor up above.

Just one set.

Rogue heard Webb's voice.

She started up the wooden stairs, staying tight against the wall, hoping to avoid any creaking boards. Five steps from the top, she paused and crouched down.

Wooden shelving split the open plan area into three sections, the centre one facing the stairs. Coburn's voice drifted from the far right.

Rogue darted into the middle section and took cover behind tall shelving laden with files. On top, potted plants and framed photographs provided adequate cover. She peered between two large ferns. Both men had their backs to her, Webb seated at a computer, Coburn standing behind him with a gun hanging by his side.

Coburn looked at his watch. "How much longer?"

"Stop asking me that. And stand somewhere else. I can't think straight with you hovering over me," said Webb.

Coburn marched to the windows overlooking the street below, scanned left and right, then returned to Webb's side. "We're running out of time. I thought you were an expert with these things."

Webb swivelled around to face him. "If you stopped pacing up and down, I'd be able to think straight!" He moved to another desk and turned on the computer.

"What was wrong with that one?"

"Password protected, same as the others," said Webb, flicking through a desk diary.

"So hack them."

"Takes too long, much quicker to find where they've written it down."

"Why that one?" shouted Coburn. "Have you any system, or is this just random guesswork?"

"It's a salesperson's desk. The others belonged to accounts. In my experience, sales people are less security conscious." He pulled a hardback diary from the drawer, flicked through the first couple of pages, then jumped to the back. "You could help by checking over ... never mind, I found it." Webb typed in a combination of numbers and the computer screen came to life.

"About bloody time," said Coburn. "So how long before you're done?"

"Fifteen minutes, maybe twenty."

"That security van will be around again soon. He slowed down the first time, obviously didn't expect to see a car here on a Sunday." Coburn walked back to the window.

"Well, if they stop to investigate, use your charm to get rid of them," replied Webb with a smirk.

Coburn grunted and headed for the stairs.

Rogue ducked down, crawled under a desk, and hid behind a set of drawers. She listened for Coburn's footsteps descending the wooden stairs. Once he reached the lower floor, she would make her move. The sound of his shoes on the wooden floor seemed to stop short of the stairwell. Ten seconds passed and still Coburn hadn't moved.

Rogue strained her ears for the sound of his breathing or the rustle of his clothes, trying to determine if he had stopped or was silently padding around the office. She checked that she hadn't left a boot or part of her jacket sticking out where he might see it. She tried to relax, but her calves were cramping. Still, the only sound was Webb tapping on the keyboard.

As the ache spread along her legs, Rogue squeezed her calves and resisted the urge to stretch her legs out.

A deep cough startled her. It sounded less than a metre away, but being under the desk, she couldn't be sure.

Coburn cleared his throat and spat out. A deep thud came from the floor below. Without a word, Coburn started down the steps, slowing as he reached the halfway point, then continued on. Rogue straightened her legs, flexing the cramp out of them.

An unfamiliar voice floated up the stairwell. "I saw the door open. Is everything OK?"

Rogue stood up and checked on Webb. He was busy typing and had his back to her. She crept over to the window and peered through the vertical blinds. There was a Heckler security van parked out front. Both seats were empty. If the driver was alone, Coburn wouldn't hesitate to put him out of action. She hadn't much time. Her goal was to leave with Webb and the decryption device. She'd prefer Webb to be conscious and mobile, but she'd need to disable him before Coburn returned.

Rogue slid out her knife and padded up behind Webb. Too late, she saw her reflection in his computer screen.

She quickened, but he'd already looked around and seen her. If he called out, Coburn would come running. As Webb pushed back his chair, Rogue flipped the knife, caught the blade between her fingers, and threw it, aiming for his shoulder. Even if she missed, it might distract him long enough for her to subdue him.

Webb reacted quicker than Rogue expected. He kicked at the desk, propelling himself and the wheelie chair across the wooden floor. Rogue's knife flew by him and clattered onto the computer's keyboard.

Webb tried to stand up while the chair was still rolling, but he lost his balance and toppled sideways against a pedestal, sending a stack of glasses crashing to the floor. As he scrambled to his feet, he yelled out to Coburn.

Rogue closed in fast and caught him with a punch to the jaw. Webb's eyes swam. He fell back against a partition, then slid to the floor. She retrieved her knife and hurried to the top of the stairs, expecting Coburn to come charging up. A door banged shut as the security guard returned to his van.

Rogue ran to the computer Webb had been working on, knowing she only had seconds to find the DX3. The screen was a mass of white text on a black background. Rogue hoped that Webb hadn't completed the job he'd started.

Behind her, footsteps pounded up the wooden stairs. Frantically, she searched for the Decryptor. It had to be connected to the computer box sitting under the desk, but it wasn't plugged into any of the slots at the front of the machine. She dragged it out and checked the ports on the back. It wasn't there either.

Next, she rifled through the items on the desk, scattering the keyboard, mouse, pens, and everything else onto the floor. Finally, she spotted the Decryptor behind the monitor. Webb had used a cable to plug the device into a port on the side of the screen.

Rogue's peripheral vision detected movement to her right. She grabbed the Decryptor and turned in time to see Webb hauling himself off the floor. She instantly regretted not hitting him harder.

He saw the DX3 in her hand, grabbed an umbrella from a coat stand, and charged at her.

At the last second, Rogue ducked left and caught Webb in the solar plexus with the butt of her knife.

He groaned and sank to his knees. The roar of a gun exploded around them and a bullet embedded itself in the lights above Rogue, showering her with broken glass.

"Drop it," yelled Coburn. He had her cold. He could have shot her dead if he wanted.

Rogue's priority was still Agnetha. To secure her release, Rogue needed the DX3 as a bargaining chip. Whatever else happened, she needed to keep it away from Webb and Coburn.

She launched her knife at Coburn, distracting him for a valuable second, long enough for her to sprint for cover. He fired repeatedly, following her path to a cluster of tall filing cabinets, bullets ricocheting off the grey steel.

Rogue spotted an emergency exit in the far corner. She knew she could cover the distance in less than three seconds, but she'd be an easy target. Instead, she veered left, but ended up in a cul-de-sac of desks and partitions. Grabbing a pair of wheelie chairs, she used all her strength to send one, then another, speeding at Coburn as he rounded the corner.

He dodged the first, but the second cracked into his knee and knocked him off balance. While he was distracted, Rogue buried the Decryptor in a huge potted plant standing on the floor, then climbed onto a desk and vaulted over the partition.

As she headed for the stairs, she spotted Webb, armed with her knife, but still trying to clear the dizziness from his head.

Coburn doubled-back and parked himself at the end of the next row, waiting for Rogue to appear. She realised it was pointless to keep climbing shelving and dodging desks. The security guards would have heard the gunshots and called the police. Rogue needed a course of action that would further her own goals.

Raising her hands high over her head, she dropped to her knees.

"Kill her. She's nothing but trouble," said Webb, spitting blood onto the carpet.

Coburn closed in on Rogue. He tilted his head sideways and stared at her, aiming at her chest. "Are we done here?" he called back to Webb.

"Almost, but then she showed up and tried to kill me," scowled Webb.

"What are you waiting for? Get back and finish the job," ordered Coburn.

Webb spat on the floor and shuffled back to the computer.

Coburn turned to Rogue. "You, face down on the floor, arms out in front."

Rogue reluctantly followed his instructions and hoped she'd made the right choice. As she stretched out on the carpet, Coburn bent down and pinned the muzzle of his gun into the base of her skull.

Chapter 32

With Coburn's gun pressing Rogue's face into the floor, she found it difficult to breathe. At least he hadn't pulled the trigger. Maybe he was under orders from Savik. If Coburn's boss wanted the pleasure of killing her himself, it meant there had to be something in a previous mission that linked her to Savik. So far, she had failed to identify it.

Coburn moved behind Rogue and kicked her legs apart. She raised her head a little and looked across at Webb.

He was cradling his jaw, rotating it left and right, grimacing with each movement. "I think she cracked a bone or something."

"Hey," shouted Coburn. "You can feel sorry for yourself later. Finish what you were doing and make it quick. We should be gone from here by now."

"We would be if she hadn't turned up," persisted Webb as he edged closer to Rogue.

Coburn came back into Rogue's view but stayed beyond her reach. He glared at Webb. "Finish that computer crap before the police show up."

Rogue pasted a smirk on her face and watched Webb, hoping he'd make eye contact with her. She needed a distraction and if she could goad him into confronting Coburn, that might do it.

Webb hesitated, but held Coburn's stare. A second passed, then another before he turned and marched back to the computer. Rogue followed him with her eyes, but he collected the fallen chair and wheeled it back to the desk. After picking up the mouse and keyboard, he sat down and started typing. Rogue knew what was coming next.

"The DX3," shouted Webb. He hunted around the desk for it, then searched on the floor.

Webb leapt off the chair, toppling it over. "She must have taken it. Search her."

Rogue received a sharp boot in the ribs from Coburn. "Hand it over."

"I don't have it," said Rogue.

Coburn drove the heel of his boot down on her wrist.

"You're wasting your time," she grunted. "I haven't got his DX or whatever it's called."

"Where. Is. It," said Coburn.

"It must be in her pocket," said Webb.

Coburn knelt down and jammed the muzzle of his Sig into the back of Rogue's hand. "Search her," he ordered Webb. "Carefully."

Webb circled around behind Rogue. After emptying the contents of her jacket pockets, he patted her jeans, front and back. He stood up, perplexed.

"Search her socks and boots," said Coburn.

Rogue shifted her body weight onto her left side and tensed her right leg. When Webb probed her right sock, she kicked upwards, hard and sharp. Her heel connected with some part of him. It wasn't solid like bone, but it did hurt him.

Webb yelped and jumped back. As Coburn's head snapped around to see what had happened, Rogue wrenched her hand from under his gun. Coburn reacted instantly and pulled the trigger, but Rogue's hand was already gone. As Coburn sprang back, he swept his gun around, searching for his target.

It was a move Rogue had expected. She rolled in close and caught him with a boot in the chest. He recovered quickly and lashed an elbow at her face, but she deflected the blow, wrapped her legs around his neck, and dragged him to the floor.

His gun hand jabbed blindly for her head. She gripped his wrist and forced it backwards, angling his gun away. He fired twice, the bullets drilling into the wooden floor. Rogue squeezed her legs tight, drew Coburn's head down further, then twisted his arm back until the elbow joint popped. His gun dropped to the floor.

Rogue unhooked her legs and booted him in the head. He groaned but didn't surrender. Letting himself fall back, he kicked out, narrowly missing her face. They both rolled in opposite directions and got to their feet, his right arm hanging limply by his side.

Webb was standing, waiting, holding a chair over his head. He charged at Rogue. She grabbed the legs of the chair, swivelled, and diverted his momentum into Coburn. As the two men untangled themselves, she grabbed Coburn's gun and fired a shot over their heads. Both men stopped, exhausted and beaten.

Rogue aimed at Coburn. "Get on the floor."

He dropped to his knees and rested his injured arm on his lap, his face bathed in sweat and rage.

"Face down, you know the drill." She waved the gun at him.

He eased himself onto the floor with one hand, grunting from the pain. Rogue kicked her knife away from him, then picked it up and slid it into her belt. Webb had gathered himself into a seated position on the floor and was rubbing the back of his head.

Rogue walked over to the potted plant and retrieved the Decryptor. After cleaning it on her trouser leg, she slipped it into an inside pocket.

She kicked the soles of Webb's boots. "Get up. We're leaving."

He shook his head. "You have what you came for. What do you want with me?"

"You want a dislocated elbow, too?" She jabbed his ankle bone sharply with her toe. "Move."

Webb looked at Coburn, got nothing, then scowled at Rogue. She returned his look with added venom. Webb slowly got off the floor.

"Unplug the cables from those computers," she said, pointing at a desk. "Use one to tie his wrists, the other for his ankles."

Webb pulled the power leads from a computer and looped one around Coburn's ankles.

"Tighter," said Rogue.

Webb yanked on the cable and secured it with a double knot.

"Wrists behind your back," said Rogue to Coburn.

He brought his arms around, but there was a sizeable gap between his hands. "I can't. My arm isn't working."

"Force them together," she said to Webb.

Webb looked at her open-mouthed, then slowly stooped down and drew Coburn's arms closer until his wrists were only centimetres apart. Agony spread across Coburn's face, but he stayed quiet.

Webb tied off the knot and stood up. "Happy now?"

Rogue pulled a cable from another computer screen.

"Turn around," she said to Webb.

He looked at the cable. "What, you don't trust me anymore?"

She shoved him against a cabinet, roughly jerked his arms back and tied his wrists together, then pulled him to a chair and sat him down. "Stay."

After checking Coburn's knots, Rogue found a scarf on a coat stand and use it to gag him. She considered securing him to a desk or something heavier, but she was out of time. Anyway, she'd be well on her way to Basel before he got free and found transport.

Shoving his gun into her belt, she patted Coburn's pockets for her phone and the keys to the Audi. She also took his phone. It had Savik's number on it and she needed to talk to him, to let him know she had Webb and the Decryptor.

She stood back and looked around. Whoever occupied the office would have quite a mess to clean up. She'd have preferred to wipe off her fingerprints, but she'd touched too many surfaces. She grabbed Webb's ear, hoisted him off the chair and propelled him towards the stairs.

At the top step, he paused. "Where are we going?"

Rogue pushed him forward, then grabbed the collar of his fleece as he toppled over. "To meet your boss."

Chapter 33

Rogue was edgy. Nothing in the previous twenty-four hours had gone according to her plans. Quite the contrary. The combination of pain, blood loss and fatigue had left her drained, both physically and mentally. As she took the stairs to the Strut-Technik lobby, she realised that she had to rescue Agnetha within the next few hours. Otherwise, she wouldn't have the energy or the concentration to get the two of them out alive.

As always, time was Rogue's biggest obstacle. Webb hadn't completed whatever convoluted computer hack he had started, but Rogue couldn't decide if that strengthened her position or not. She had the Decryptor that Savik was so keen to get his hands on, but if Webb didn't use the codes before the VerKoll guys disabled them, the device would be useless. Rogue had encountered lunatics like Savik before. He valued power and wealth above all else. People, including Webb, were expendable. If the VerKoll technicians managed to remotely disable the DX3, then Savik would just kill Agnetha and find another way to advance his plans.

Half way down the stairwell, Webb doubled over.

"What's wrong?" asked Rogue suspiciously.

"I'm gonna throw up," he said, clutching his midsection.

Rogue poked him in the ribs. "It can wait. Any minute now, this place'll be swarming with cops."

Webb looked back at her, sceptical.

She jabbed him again, harder. "Move it. Somebody will have heard those gunshots and called the police. It might already be too late."

Webb straightened up and continued down the steps at a slightly quicker pace. As they crossed the lobby, Rogue caught their reflections in the floor-to-ceiling mirrors. They were both dishevelled, weary and moving with difficulty, like wounded extras from a war movie. When Webb opened the door to the car park, Rogue heard the distant wail of a police siren. Webb needed no further encouragement. He hurried to the Audi and sat into the front passenger seat. Rogue had planned to secure him in the back seat, but there wasn't enough time.

As she opened the driver's door, Coburn's phone rang in her pocket. The caller's name on the screen said one word. 'Boss'. Rogue needed time to think before talking to Savik, but he was a control freak, a man who thrived on information and would vent his frustration on whoever was near him. If that person was Agnetha, then Rogue couldn't risk provoking him. With the phone still ringing, she dropped into the driver's seat, jammed the barrel of the Sig into the flesh of Webb's cheek and showed him the Caller ID.

"One word from you and it's lights out. Understand?"

Webb pressed into the headrest, but his eyes narrowed and flared back at Rogue. She raised a questioning eyebrow and held his stare, waiting for his brain to catch up. Webb blinked, then looked away, but she knew what was going through his mind. He was way out of his depth and needed an ally. He didn't trust Rogue, but whenever Savik's name was mentioned, she could see his eyes flooding with apprehension.

The phone stopped ringing.

As a chill ran up Rogue's spine, the unnerving silence was shattered by multiple police sirens. Slapping the Audi into gear, she screeched out of the car park. Savik would call back. Rogue was sure of it. Almost. But for now, she had to focus on evading the police.

It was impossible to tell which direction the sirens were coming from. Recalling the map of the business park, Rogue gambled and drove away from the main artery towards a second exit at the rear. Watching the mirrors for flashing lights, she followed the road as it hugged the perimeter of the complex. At a junction, a sign indicated routes to the city or the motorway. Rogue chose the motorway. A hundred metres further on, she bounced over a series of ramps and left the business park.

Coburn's phone rang again.

Rogue hit the speaker button, shot a warning at Webb, and waited for Savik to speak.

"Where the hell are you?"

Rogue got straight down to business. "I have Webb and I have the Decryption device. We're leaving Zurich now."

"You! Where is Coburn?"

"We'll arrive on the outskirts of Basel within the hour. Send me coordinates for the meeting point."

As Rogue followed the signs for the motorway, there was silence on the other end of the line. She counted the seconds. One, two, three, four. A heavy bang, then shattering glass. Five, six, seven, eight, nine. When he finally spoke, his breathing was laboured.

"You come alone. You come on time. Or you will find her corpse."

The line went dead.

Rogue's heart was pounding inside her chest. Her logical brain knew she had got it right, giving Savik what he craved most. But her heart desperately wanted assurances that Agnetha was unharmed and begged Rogue to ring Savik back. She gripped the steering wheel tighter and resisted the urge. Asking Savik for anything would be a sign of weakness. When the time came for the final showdown, Rogue needed him to respect her, to treat her as an equal.

Without warning, a dark shape loomed from the right, bearing down on her at speed. The truck's horn bellowed like a train. To her left, car brakes screeched as a Land Rover steered away from her. Webb wrapped his arms over his head and screamed. Rogue floored the accelerator and turned the Audi away from the oncoming collision. As she braced for impact, her eyes locked on the red traffic lights she'd missed. The Audi surged forward and mounted the pavement. Directly ahead, a group of stunned teenagers blocked her path. Rogue swerved back onto the road, narrowly missing a cyclist. She straightened the wheel and sped away, taking a quick series of left and right turns in case anyone tried to follow.

"Have you got a death wish?" demanded Webb, his voice trembling.

Rogue turned into a shaded alley behind a row of shops and came to a stop. As she lowered the window for air, Coburn's phone beeped. It was a message from Savik with a GPS reference. She clicked it, then zoomed in on the map. The meeting point was a house in a remote rural area, a few kilometres from the EuroAirport outside Basel. The satellite image showed a farm house set in from the road. Off to one side was a large structure resembling a barn. The closest neighbour was two kilometres away and the nearest town was a further seven. It was the perfect location to dispose of a dead body. Or two.

Rogue took a drink of water, then poured some into her palms and massaged her face, trying to clear the fog that had her so distracted. Then she returned the bottle to the storage tray.

"What about me?" asked Webb.

Rogue had been so consumed by the near collision with the truck, she'd forgotten that the person beside her had urged Coburn to kill her only half an hour earlier. Webb's hands were tied, but otherwise, he was free to move about. She got out of the car, took the holdall from behind the passenger seat and threw it in the boot. All that remained on the back seat was the bag of groceries Webb had purchased at the service station. She emptied them out, checking there was nothing he could use as a weapon.

Then she opened his door. "Get into the back seat."

"I need a drink. And something to eat."

He scowled at her like a stubborn teenager, but his slumped posture and gaunt face let him down. Rogue knew she could force him out, but didn't want to risk a confrontation in a public place.

"Move, then you can have whatever you want," said Rogue.

Webb's eyelids were drooping, and she knew he just wanted to sleep. But he was cold and shivery too.

Rogue tried again. "Get in the back and I'll give you a blanket. You can sleep all the way to Basel."

Webb exhaled loudly and stared at Rogue. Then he unclipped the seat belt, got out, and obediently sat in the back of the car.

"Give me your phone," said Rogue.

Webb handed it over without further objection, then selected a can of Sprite and chocolate bar from the items strewn on the seat. Rogue retrieved the blanket from the boot and a few more cable ties from the holdall. Looping several cable ties together, she secured his hands loosely to the steel frame under the front seat, then repeated the process with his ankles. He could sit back or lie down if he wanted to, but there wasn't enough freedom for him to attack her from behind. After taking a Sprite and two bars for herself, she dropped back into the driver's seat. She popped open the can and savoured the sparkling liquid against the back of her throat. In the mirror, Webb finished the remains of his snack. He caught Rogue looking at him.

"How come Savik sent you to break me out? Doesn't sound like you two are old friends."

"I didn't have a choice. He kidnapped my niece."

"Sounds like him alright."

"Tell me about him," asked Rogue.

"He's a tough guy, with plenty of money and connections."

"So, which are you after?"

"You need connections to get ahead in life," said Webb defensively.

Rogue shifted around to face him. "True, but you gotta be careful who those connections are. Pick the wrong ones and your life can be very short."

"I'll be OK."

"Not when the Russian government come after you."

"What've they got to do with this?"

Rogue took the DX3 from her pocket. "VerKoll is registered in Switzerland, but their operation is funded by the FSB."

"Who?"

"The Russian Secret Service, formerly the KGB."

Webb froze, the can of Sprite halfway to his mouth.

"First, they'll take it back, or render it useless, whichever." Rogue leaned closer to him and lowered her voice a notch. "After that, they'll make an example of whoever took it." Rogue turned back to face the front, unwrapped a bar of chocolate, and bit off a chunk.

"You're just winding me up. Anyway, you're the one who broke in there and shot up the place."

"It's not my first rodeo Jason, I can take care of myself. But if I were you, I'd be watching my back from now on. It's not if they come knocking. It's when."

Rogue started the engine and pulled on her seat belt.

Webb sat forward, his words tumbling out. "It's only a set of codes. Given enough time, my guys would eventually hack the Anchor servers without them."

"They don't care about the codes. It's the principle. Those guys have a longstanding reputation to keep. Anyone who threatens that must be dealt with."

Rogue eased down the narrow alley and joined the morning traffic. Webb sat back, lost in thought. Rogue wondered whether Anchor was a company or the name of a computer. It sounded familiar. She stored it away with the other scraps of information she had. What she'd told Webb about the Russians was only half true. Yes, she could take care of herself, but against an organisation that powerful, she'd need a bargaining chip.

Rogue darted a glance in the mirror. Webb was picking at a scab on his chin, but his attention was elsewhere.

She switched her focus back to the road, still angry at herself for missing the red light earlier. On the outskirts of the city, she joined the A3 and headed west for the canton of Basel-Stadt.

She felt a little better, being on the road again, and more importantly, on her way to Agnetha. Their holiday in Geneva had faded into the distant past. All that remained was the horrible moment when she discovered Agnetha had been abducted. That memory would haunt her forever.

Rogue wondered how Agnetha was coping and what conditions she was enduring. Rogue had been captured several times over the years, but MI5 had trained her how to survive. For Agnetha, the experience would be radically different. Before Geneva, the girl had led a protected and insulated life, but after her ordeal with Savik, she could be traumatised for years to come.

As Rogue sped along the motorway, she took on the responsibility for whatever emotional challenges Agnetha would endure in the years ahead. For the first time since Tasha's death, Rogue dreaded being alone in the world. She couldn't, wouldn't, put Agnetha's life at risk ever again.

Chapter 34

The traffic was light when Rogue merged onto the motorway. In the mirror, she could see Webb asleep, his head lolling over one shoulder. She switched into the fast lane and did her best to stay within the speed limit. As she drove along, her mind drifted to previous missions with Tasha, then mulled over the difficult time she endured after her friend's death.

Rogue's job with MI5 had been a handy number compared to the stress of running her own security agency. Not for the first time, she chastised herself for being a fool. Her old boss, Charles Dent, had extended an olive branch more than once, but her stubborn independence wouldn't allow her to go back. Now she wished she still had their support, not for her own benefit, but for Agnetha. No matter how Rogue flipped it in her head, she just wasn't equipped to be a parent, a mentor, or whatever Tasha was thinking when she registered Rogue as Agnetha's next of kin.

As they passed Giebenach, Rogue's phone rang. It was Arnold Hunter.

She took the phone off speaker and kept her voice low so that Webb couldn't listen in on the conversation.

"I'm just checking in," said Hunter.

"It's good to hear a familiar voice."

"Your meeting with my colleague was successful?" Hunter was going through the motions, giving Rogue an opportunity to signal if she was under duress.

"I met with Odette. She had everything I needed."

"Excellent. Do you need a clean vehicle?"

"Not right now, maybe later, but I don't know where exactly. The coordinates they sent me might not be the final destination."

"What part of the country?" said Hunter.

"West of Basel, just over the French border. I'm sending you the details now." Rogue tapped her phone a few times and waited for Hunter to receive the message.

"Hmm. It's conveniently close to the airport. What's your ETA?"

Rogue glanced at the dashboard clock. "Thirty-three minutes. Sorry, I should have phoned you earlier."

"I'm familiar with the area. There's an old construction depot five kilometres south of your target. I'll have something there for you. Do you require support?"

Against all his rules, Hunter was offering Rogue fire power, mercenaries for hire.

"This is a solo run, but thanks."

Hunter coughed. "It's just, well, there's more at stake this time."

Rogue was taken aback. She couldn't recall Hunter ever offering unsolicited advice. Then she remembered he'd lost his daughter in similar circumstances. He hired Tasha to track down the killer, and then Hunter had finished the job himself.

Rogue tried not to let the enormity of the situation she was in blur her focus, but it was becoming increasingly difficult. Doubt picked at her resolve. Since Tasha's death, Rogue had insisted on working solo. When MI5 tried to force a new mission partner on her, she resigned. Maybe that had been a mistake. Rogue shifted in the car seat and shook off her misgivings. It was imperative she trust her own methods. If she allowed any shred of weakness to seep in, she'd lose everything.

"I appreciate the offer, Hunter. Really."

"OK then. You know how to contact me."

"I'll call you when we're clear," Rogue assured him.

"Stay safe."

"Always."

Rogue hadn't noticed the time passing by until Hunter had phoned. Now that she was closer to the showdown with Savik and his welcoming party, her shoulders tensed up. She leaned on the accelerator. The build-up was always the hardest part of a mission, but once the action started, her confidence would return tenfold.

As she approached the outskirts of Basel, her phone rang again. This time, it was Marcus. She hoped he had found some useful intel on Savik. Once again, Rogue held the phone to her ear instead of using the car's hands-free system.

"Hi Marcus."

"Hey Rogue, I've done some digging on Goran Savik. Born in Leskovac, Serbia, he has a twin brother Lazar who has a rare auto immune condition since childhood. When their father died in a mining accident, Goran left school and became an enforcer for the local drug runner."

Rogue's lungs tightened as she listened to Marcus. His voice was urgent, racing through the details.

"As Lazar got older, his health deteriorated, and they needed serious money for treatments. Goran helped expand the local drug business to surrounding towns and used his earnings to enrol Lazar in a medical implant program, but the debts continued to grow, so eventually Goran moved to Belgrade and joined a major crime gang."

Something in the way Marcus paused for a breath told Rogue he was about to drop a bombshell.

"Who do you think was a leading figure in the same gang?"

Rogue could only think of one person. "Kaznov."

"Savik is Viktor Kaznov's cousin," said Marcus slowly.

Rogue said nothing for a few seconds, allowing the information to sink in. "It doesn't add up. If Savik was after revenge for me killing Kaznov, he could have done it in Geneva."

In the silence that followed, Rogue knew Marcus was thinking the same as she was. If Savik was anything like Kaznov, he wouldn't avenge his cousin by just killing Rogue. He'd punish her by targeting Agnetha. In that moment, Rogue realised that she'd fully expected Agnetha to survive the next few hours, even if Rogue herself didn't, but Savik's family connection to Kaznov changed everything. She would have to change her approach and go on the offensive much sooner that she had intended.

"You still there, Rach?" asked Marcus.

"Did you find anything else on Savik?" asked Rogue hopefully.

"Not much. His name pops up every six of seven months over a four-year period, as a mercenary for a variety of revolutionary groups in Eastern Europe. Two years ago, he was spotted in London. He's on the Drug Squad's watch list as a player but has never been caught with anything. He was charged with assault twice, but not convicted. On one occasion, his victim spent three weeks in intensive care. His regular pub is the Black Hammer."

Marcus left the last bit of intel hanging for Rogue to pick up.

"Dimitri Mitrovic owns the Black Hammer," said Rogue.

"Yep, Kaznov's uncle. Looks like Savik is following in Kaznov's footsteps."

"More like taking his place."

"It all adds up," said Marcus. "Mitrovic has history with you and Tasha, and he knows about Agnetha. The question is, how did he find out that you were in Geneva?"

Rogue thumped the steering wheel. She couldn't help but conclude that she had been careless. Her silence told Marcus what she was thinking.

"Don't beat yourself up, Rach, Mitrovic has contacts everywhere. It's impossible to watch every step you take."

"All this time, I believed she was safe. I should have killed Mitrovic when I had the chance."

"What about our assets in France and Germany? They could meet you in Basel. I'm sure Dent would authorise it."

"No. It's too risky, Marcus, especially in Switzerland. If anything went wrong, you and Dent would be out of a job."

"I know, but it's Agnetha," said Marcus, "I'd risk anything for her, you know that."

"Don't worry, I'm not totally solo on this."

"Really? OK. But be careful."

"I will. Thanks for the intel."

"Keep in touch." Marcus hung up.

On the French side of Basel, Rogue left the motorway and joined the much quieter D105. Up ahead, banks of dark cloud crept in from the North and cast a grey gloom over the industrial units on each side. As the road wound along the southern boundary of the EuroAirport, the voice of the SatNav informed Rogue that she was five kilometres from her destination. Rogue's stomach tightened. She tightened her grip on the steering wheel and tried to concentrate on the mission. The problem was, for all the information she had about Savik, none of it pointed to any specific weakness she could use against him.

As a strong wind whipped through the roadside trees, Rogue opened both front windows down fully. A welcome blast of fresh air washed the staleness from the cabin, but it failed to penetrate the tangle of anxiety that tightened around her chest. She had no doubt the next few hours would be rough, that nothing would go according to any plan she could make. As the Audi bounced over a speed ramp, she heard a thud from the back seat. In the mirror, Webb grimaced and rubbed his forehead.

As she left the airport complex behind, the landscape changed to open fields, with an occasional clump of trees obscuring the view. Light rain spattered the windscreen, triggering the automatic wipers. The Sat-Nav guided her through a series of turns until she found herself on a minor country road, with dense forest on one side. According to the map, the farmhouse was only two kilometres further on. Rogue pulled over where a wooden gate led to a forest trail and switched off the engine. In the back seat, Webb groaned as he attempted to straighten himself, hampered by the cable ties around his wrists.

He looked through the side window. "Where are we?"

"Outside Basel. A few minutes from the coordinates."

Rogue watched him in the rear-view mirror. He seemed to relax, half smiling to himself. Then he frowned, and the smile faded. Rogue knew he was thinking about Savik, that his boss would blame Webb for the MegaTron fiasco and the death of the man in the Geneva apartment. Rogue waited for the realisation to sink in. He slumped deeper into the seat, his mind no doubt scrambling for plausible excuses and people to blame. Rogue allowed herself a half smile, then got out and opened the boot.

The rear shelf lay broken in half after her escape outside Strut-Technik. She did her best to stick the two pieces together using duct tape, then slotted it back into place. Next, she took the remaining slabs of C4 and secured them together. After adding a timer with the delay set to five minutes, she switched off the safety feature. That meant she could start the countdown by clicking the activation button, something she could do by touch alone. Placing the black holdall on the ground, she carefully tucked the explosives into a side pocket, then ordered Webb out of the car. He refused, demanding to know what she had planned for him. Rogue had no time for diplomacy. Without warning, she punched him in the jaw, then dragged him from the back seat, bundled him inside the boot and slammed it shut.

Next, she reclined the front passenger seat and cut a slit in the side of it. Peeling back the black leather, she pierced the foam, then reached in and gouged out a space large enough for the C4 rig. She squeezed the explosive into its new home, making sure the timer switch was accessible. Then she took the Verkoll De-cryptor and slid that in too. She placed a sliver of black duct tape over the damaged upholstery and reposi-tioned the seat so that it was less obvious. After stuff-ing the holdall behind the driver's seat, she pulled back onto the road and drove the short distance to the farm.

As Rogue rounded a bend, she found herself on a hill overlooking the property. She stopped the car and used the binoculars to get a quick mental snapshot. The satellite image had suggested a two-storey house at the end of a long driveway with a large barn off to one side. Now she could see that the farm house still existed, but the windows were boarded up and a portion of the tiled roof had collapsed. A new bungalow had been built in front of the barn, but a row of portable cabins and stacks of building materials suggested it wasn't yet complete. The chances were that Agnetha was being held in one of the three cabins. Alongside them stood a black SUV and a silver Mercedes. Rogue followed the farm boundaries and memorised three exit points she could use in an emergency, then drove down the hill and stopped outside a pair of ornate steel gates.

One gate opened half way. A man in a high vis jacket and safety helmet trudged out and, holding his jacket back to reveal a gun, he gestured for Rogue to wind down the window. He said nothing, just looked from her face to his phone, then marched back through the gate, his phone raised to his ear. It wasn't long before both gates rolled inwards and he beckoned Rogue to drive through. He pointed towards the house, then began closing the gates behind her.

The Audi crunched along the loose stones of the driveway. Low hedging lined both sides until it opened into a wide semicircle. To the right, a bulldozer and a dumper truck blocked a track leading to the old farmhouse. On Rogue's left were the cabins she'd seen from the road and, beyond them, the new bungalow.

When she was thirty metres short of the cabins, Rogue killed the engine and placed both hands on top of the steering wheel as a gesture of good faith. Hostage exchanges were highly volatile. Parties on both sides were on alert, both expecting a double-cross. One wrong move would kick off a barrage of bullets, with no winners.

There was no sign of life, but her sixth sense told Rogue that she was being watched through the sights of a gun. She peered through the windscreen, looking for any clue that would tell her where Agnetha was being held. The rain had stopped, but the turbulent clouds gathering overhead suggested that more was on the way.

The dashboard clock showed two minutes past ten. Next to the clock was the photo of Agnetha in the Jardin Anglais. Rogue angled it to catch the light and promised her niece that she would soon be safe, then slipped the photo into an inside pocket close to her heart.

As the seconds turned to minutes, Rogue tapped her fingers on the steering wheel. Savik was playing games with her. It took all her willpower not to leap out and clear the cabins one by one, gunning down any opposition until she found Agnetha. But this was Savik's playground, and she needed him to feel in control, at least for now. He had to make the next move.

Rogue jumped as a thud reverberated through the car from behind. She whipped around, expecting to see a truck or a tractor. Instead, a muffled shouting came from the boot. It was Webb. Rogue cursed. She should have knocked him unconscious, but that would've complicated the exchange.

She settled back into the seat and scanned the windows of the three cabins again. A bin overflowing with wrappers and polystyrene cups flanked the door of the last one. Agnetha would be in the first or second, probably the latter as it would be harder to breach if Rogue mounted a rescue attempt.

The door to the first cabin opened. Rogue's heart thumped harder, her knuckles white as she squeezed the steering wheel tighter. Two men descended the steps, both armed. The first was stocky and moved at a slow and determined pace, his jaws chewing in time with each step. A jagged scar curved across one side of his bald head and disappeared behind an ear.

The second man took a path several metres to the left of the first. He carried an Uzi sub-machine gun, but his lazy swagger and scraggly beard suggested a lack of formal training. As they drew nearer, Rogue detected the shadow of a third man creep up the wooden door from inside the cabin and pause. Something in her gut told her it was Goran Savik.

The bearded man stopped a few metres in front of the car and aimed his Uzi through the windscreen at Rogue.

The second gunman approached the driver's door of the Audi, but kept a safe distance. He levelled his Sig pistol at Rogue. "Get out slowly, hands high."

Maintaining eye contact, Rogue eased back the lever and opened the door fully. Keeping her hands in plain sight, she swung her legs over the ledge, leaned out, then stood up. The gunman backed away and gestured for her to walk ahead of him, towards his colleague. Rogue slowly made her way to the front of the car.

"That's far enough," said the bearded man. "Keep your hands where I can see them. Becker, frisk her."

Rogue stretched her arms up, palms facing forward. Becker frisked her from behind, starting with her arms and working down. He was methodical, thorough, experienced. Even with his partner covering him, he was cautious. When he reached her calf, he removed the knife without comment.

Satisfied, he stepped into her view and nodded. As Rogue gradually lowered her arms, the two men stepped back and took up positions a short distance away from her, their backs to the cabins.

Rogue turned her attention back to the open door of the first cabin. It took all her self-control to be patient and play by their rules. The door creaked loudly as the shadow moved and the man responsible for kidnapping Agnetha stepped down onto the gravel.

He strode purposefully towards Rogue, his long black coat swinging open at his sides. Underneath, Rogue glimpsed a shoulder holster over his white shirt. His face revealed nothing, even his eyes seemed to be fixed on some point off in the distance.

He came to an abrupt halt between the two gunmen. Only then did he look at Rogue, staring at her through sunken eyes that overflowed with vengeance.

Chapter 35

"Where is Jason Webb," snapped Savik.

Rogue recognised his voice from the phone calls. "He's in the back of the car. I want to see Agnetha."

Deep creases formed on Savik's forehead, his dark eyebrows almost touching. He took a step closer to Rogue. "Give me the device. Now."

Rogue stood as tall as she could, but still had to look up at him. "Not until I see Agnetha."

Savik curled his fingers into fists, opened them, then clenched them again. "This is not a game where we take turns. I could kill you now."

"Isn't that your plan, anyway?" prompted Rogue. "You'll take what you want, then execute me."

His eyes flared. "You won't die so easy."

Rogue nodded back at him. "I get it. You want revenge for your worthless cousin, Viktor. You really should thank me. I could have let him rot in prison, but I did him a favour by putting a bullet through his brain."

Savik looked around him and shook his head. "You're not in England now. There is no backup, no MI5." He spat out the acronym. "You are all alone."

But she wasn't. Agnetha's face flashed into her mind. Rogue's stare wavered, her eyes drawn to the middle cabin.

Savik jumped on it. "You have a weakness and I exploited it so easily."

Rogue widened her stance. "I'm tired, so let's get this over with. Webb is in the boot of the car."

Savik turned his head to the last cabin in the row. Rogue locked her eyes on the door and held her breath, her chest thumping with alternate beats of hope and fear. Movement registered in her peripheral vision, but her obsession with seeing Agnetha delayed her reaction.

Savik's fist struck Rogue's jaw like a steam engine. The force spun her like a rag doll and slammed her into the Audi. The gunshot wound in her shoulder erupted and her vision swam, blurring the three men surrounding her. She clamped her eyes shut and dug in, demanding her legs to support her. She refused to give Savik the satisfaction of falling into the dirt.

Rogue pushed herself off the bonnet and faced him as her dizziness cleared. The two gunmen tensed, their eyes flicking between Rogue and their boss.

Savik covered the distance to her in three long strides. "That was from my uncle."

Rogue rotated her head slowly, testing her jaw and neck. Her eyes blurred again, forcing her to look down until her vision cleared. She saw the uppercut coming, but he was too close and she couldn't avoid it. Her teeth crunched together as she toppled back, landed on the bonnet and slid to the ground.

"And that's from Viktor, God rest his soul." Savik drew a cross on his forehead with his thumb.

Rogue sucked in a deep breath and braced for a boot to the midsection. Now wasn't the time to fight back. It was better that Savik vent his anger on her than on Agnetha.

"Get her up," shouted Savik.

Rogue spat a glob of blood onto the ground and ran her tongue around her teeth, counting the gaps. Still only two, souvenirs from previous missions.

Becker grabbed her by the hair and pulled her up to standing. She steadied herself and peered at Savik through half-closed eyes.

Savik turned to the bearded gunman. "Frack, get Webb out here, now."

Frack went to the Audi and opened the boot. Rogue could hear grunts and moans, but didn't look back, her eyes uncontrollably drawn back to the cabins.

Savik began pacing, his impatient steps carving a channel through the loose stones. He flicked his wrist to check the time. "What's taking so long?" he bellowed.

"He was tied and gagged. I had to cut him free," explained Frack, as Webb crunched slowly along the gravel.

"Where is the Decryptor?" demanded Savik.

Webb stopped in front of Rogue. "She has it." He glanced at Savik and noticed he was massaging the knuckles of his right hand. As he turned back to Rogue, she licked a trickle of blood seeping from her bottom lip. Webb grinned. "I see you've met my boss."

Rogue read Webb's mind before he'd even formed the thought himself. When he dropped his shoulder and swung, aiming a right hook at her jaw, she stepped to one side, punched him in the stomach, then hooked his ankle and sent him flailing to the ground. Webb spat out dirt as he scrambled to his feet and charged at her, but he lacked coordination and she easily sidestepped and let him pass.

Webb was exhausted, but stubborn. He grabbed the barrel of Frack's Uzi and tugged, but the gunman was much too strong for Webb and resisted.

"Enough," commanded Savik.

Webb turned to face him. "We don't need her any-more. Give me a gun and I'll do it myself."

Rogue's instincts kicked in. Webb was standing in front of Frack, trying to take his gun. Both Savik and Becker were distracted by the tussle. It was the perfect opportunity for Rogue to attack. In an instant, a sequence formed in her mind. Three strides to Frack, a punch to his throat, take his Uzi, then kill Becker and Webb in a single sweep. Using Frack as a shield, swivel around to face Savik, who will have drawn his own gun and will shoot. Frack's body would take the bullets, allowing Rogue to finish off Savik.

But Rogue stayed where she was. They outnumbered her four to one. If she was dead or even badly injured, Agnetha would be on her own, defenceless. Rogue had promised Tasha she would protect Agnetha and she would do her utmost to keep that promise.

Frack looked to his boss for orders. As Savik studied Rogue, it felt like time stood still. She tried to read his thoughts. He wanted revenge and no loose ends. Letting Webb do his dirty work would be convenient. But it wasn't the right time, not yet. Savik curled his lip, glanced at Frack, and shook his head.

Webb was still pulling on the barrel of the Uzi, but making no headway. Frack suddenly stepped in closer. As Webb stumbled backwards, he released his grip on the gun. Fuming, he squared up to Savik, refusing to lose face in front of Rogue and the two gunmen.

"What's the story with you and her?"

Savik shoved Webb away, surprising the younger man with his strength. "Enough! Except for you, we wouldn't be in this mess."

"It wasn't my fault, it was Coburn. I had it all under control in MegaTron until he started a fight with the security guards."

"Well, now it is out of control." Savik looked at his watch. "We need to leave here. Where is the Decryptor?"

"I told you. She took it," said Webb.

"Hand it over. Now," Savik said to Rogue.

"Not until you bring Agnetha out here."

Savik gestured at Frack. "Do it."

The gunman walked towards the cabins.

"And make it quick," bellowed Savik.

Rogue's eyes were glued to Frack as he jogged the short distance to the middle cabin. He took a key from his pocket and slid it into the lock. Rogue knew that things would move fast now. Once Savik got the Decryptor, he'd want to leave Basel and return to London.

She surveyed the men around her. Savik was pacing again, restless. Becker eyeballed Rogue, focused and fully aware of the danger she presented. He'd cut her down without hesitation. Webb had found a bottle of water in the Audi and was slouched over the bonnet, nursing his wounded ego, avoiding eye contact with Savik. Webb took another slug from the water bottle, then launched it across the yard. Rogue's throat constricted as the remains of the clear liquid trickled into the dirt. She'd inhaled a mouthful of dust when Savik knocked her to the ground and her tongue felt like sandpaper.

Minutes passed, and Frack still hadn't reappeared. After checking his watch yet again, Savik yelled across the yard. A muffled voice drifted from inside the open cabin door, brief and incoherent. Rogue held her breath.

A moment later, a hooded figure emerged, her wrists bound. Rogue didn't recognise the over-sized grey hoody or the black tracksuit bottoms. Only the few strands of blond hair trailing from beneath the hood and the pink runners suggested it was Agnetha.

The girl tentatively reached one leg forward and stepped down. Rogue inhaled sharply when Agnetha stumbled, but Frack's tight grip on her hoody prevented her from falling. A muffled groan carried across the yard as he yanked her upright, then prodded her forward. Agnetha was limping, favouring her right leg.

Rogue took a step towards them, but Becker blocked her path and stuck his gun in her face.

Savik moved a safe distance from Rogue, then shouted across the yard. "For God's sake, remove the hood."

Frack hesitated, looking at Savik momentarily for confirmation before realising his boss didn't intend leaving any loose ends. It didn't matter if the girl saw Savik's face. Frack untied the cord and tugged the hood off. Agnetha raised her palms to her eyes, shielding them against the daylight.

As they drew level with Savik, Rogue was shocked by an ugly bruise under Agnetha's left eye and bloody streaks on her wrists. The ever-present smile in her eyes was gone, replaced with apathy and defeat.

"Which one of you hit her?" demanded Rogue. She detected a grin forming on Frack's face and charged at him, but Becker stepped in and rammed the barrel of his gun into her ribs. Rogue dropped to one knee, but quickly got back up and glared at Savik. "Let me go to her."

"Give me the device, then you can have your reunion."

Rogue turned back to her niece. "Neta, are you OK?"

Agnetha peered at Rogue through dark eyes as tears trickled down her cheeks. "I'm sorry," she mouthed, her words barely audible. "I tried, but … " A tsunami of tears swept her voice away as her body shook.

Savik drew a gun from inside his coat and yanked Agnetha in front of him. Wrapping his thick fingers around her throat, he pulled her close and pressed his gun against her temple.

"And so, the endgame. It is your move," he said to Rogue.

"It's alright Neta, don't worry, I promise this will all be over soon," said Rogue.

Agnetha's eyes darted to the gun, then back to Rogue, pleading for help.

Rogue dragged her attention back to Savik and flicked the switch in her mind that shut down her emotional centre and engaged mission mode. She locked onto his eyes and saw a little fear creep into them, a little doubt.

"The device," demanded Savik. He pulled his hostage tighter, lifting her off her feet. Agnetha's eyes bulged, her open mouth fighting for breath.

"Stop, please," pleaded Rogue, her hands up, palms facing Savik. "Let her breathe."

Savik relaxed his grip around Agnetha's throat a little, enough that she could suck vital oxygen into her lungs.

"It's in the car," said Rogue.

"You two, go with her and stay close," Savik shouted at his men. "Watch her hands. One mistake, shoot her in the head."

Both men followed Rogue to the Audi. She opened the rear door. "It's hidden inside the upholstery of the seat."

Becker adjusted his position, so he had a clear view inside the car. "Use one hand, keep the other behind your back."

Rogue levered the seat back, peeled away the black tape covering the incision she'd made earlier, and slid her hand inside. She looked back and held Becker's attention as her fingers delved further into the foam. His eyes flicked back and forth between Rogue's arm inside the car and her free hand behind her back, unsure which posed the most danger. Frack stood a few steps away, covering his partner.

When Rogue felt the hard plastic casing of the Decryptor, she eased it back a little, then reached in further. Her fingers closed on her second target.

"Found it. Just need to get a hold ... "

Becker leaned in a little, his eyes focused on her arm, expecting her hand to reappear with a gun.

Rogue's index finger explored the familiar row of buttons on the detonator. If she got it wrong, it would trigger an instant explosion, destroying the car and Agnetha in a ball of flames. She found the raised symbol that identified the activation button, clicked it and felt a one second pulse as confirmation.

"Got it." Rogue withdrew her arm, gripping the Decryptor with her fingertips on the way out. In five minutes, the explosives would destroy the car and anyone near it. She looked between the front seats at the dashboard clock and memorised the time.

Becker backed away. Rogue offered him the device, but he gestured her towards Savik. "Move."

Rogue walked to the front of the car. Savik was still using Agnetha as a protective shield.

"Take it," said Savik to Webb. "There's a laptop in the first cabin. Make it fast."

Webb snapped the device from Rogue's outstretched hand and made a big show of examining it from every angle.

Savik frowned. "Has she tampered with it?"

Webb scowled at Rogue. "It looks alright."

"For both your sakes, it better be more than just alright," said Savik.

Webb was about to protest, but thought better of it and hurried off to the cabins.

"Tie her up, then prepare to leave," said Savik. He turned his back on Rogue and followed Webb, dragging Agnetha roughly behind him.

"We had a deal," shouted Rogue. "Let her go. You have what you need."

Becker rammed the muzzle of his pistol into the small of Rogue's back. "You heard the boss. Move."

The countdown in Rogue's head told her that two and a half minutes had already elapsed. She had hoped to be near Agnetha when the bomb went off, but that was out of her control now.

The gun drilled into her spine. "Move, or I'll finish you right here."

The two gunmen escorted Rogue to the second cabin. As she climbed the steps, she pretended to trip and landed face down on the floor.

"Clumsy fool. Get up and sit on that chair," said Becker. He remained outside the cabin, taking no chances.

Rogue looked at her watch. Sixty-three seconds left.

Chapter 36

Rogue remained on the cabin floor and rubbed her ankle vigorously, trying to use up time. She stole a glance at her watch. In forty-two seconds, the C4 would detonate and blow the rented Audi to pieces.

Becker stepped into the cabin and stamped on Rogue's shin. "Sit on that chair."

Burning as many seconds as she dared, Rogue stood up, brushed off her clothes and lowered herself onto an old wooden chair. A coil of rope lay in a heap under it. One section was frayed and stained red. Rogue's mind flipped back to Agnetha's angry red wrists.

Becker moved behind her and lifted the rope while Frack remained outside, watching closely.

"Do what you want to me, but please, don't harm my niece," pleaded Rogue.

"Hands behind your back."

"She's only nineteen. She's no threat to any of you," persisted Rogue, counting down the seconds in the back of her mind.

"Tell that to the man bleeding out on your apartment floor," hissed Frack from outside the cabin.

"What did you expect? That she'd just let you kidnap her?"

"Enough talk," snapped Becker. "Cross your wrists behind your back or I'll knock you unconscious and do it myself."

Rogue believed him. Reluctantly, she obeyed, but left a gap between her hands. He looped the rope around them and pulled tight. Rogue tried to maintain the gap, but he yanked the rope, pulling her wrists close together. In her head, she continued counting down the seconds. She estimated there were only five left.

Becker took a second length of rope and hunkered down in front of her. As he threaded the rope around her ankles, Rogue braced herself. The last seconds on the timer clicked to zero and the C4 explosives ignited.

Rogue turned away and tried to hide her face as the eruption tore the Audi apart and sent a hailstorm of glass and metal in every direction. Still outside, Frack took the brunt of the force and smashed into the cabin wall.

Inside, a chunk of metal clipped the back of Becker's head. As he keeled over, his gun went skating under a stack of shelves. Dazed, he rose to his knees. Rogue lashed out and caught him in the throat with the heel of her boot. He hovered in mid-air, stunned. Rogue kicked him again, this time in the face. He crumbled to the floor, blood streaming from his nose.

Outside the cabin, Frack pushed himself off the ground, his face and neck a bloody mess. When he saw the Audi on fire and realised what had happened, he twisted around to face the cabin. Rogue jumped off the chair, but her hands were tied behind her back, restricting her movements. Frack reached for his Uzi, but the barrel was trapped beneath him. Rogue stepped through her arms and brought her hands in front, her eyes glued to him as he rolled off the Uzi and grabbed the barrel.

She scanned for a sharp edge to slice the rope, then remembered the knife Becker had taken from her when he'd frisked her. He was still on the floor, groaning. His eyes fell open when she dug into his pocket, but he didn't resist. As she pulled the knife clear, her sixth sense screamed. She threw herself sideways, avoiding a stream of bullets from Frack's Uzi.

Rogue gripped the sheath between her teeth. As she pulled the knife free, she kicked at the open door. It swung shut as Frack's submachine gun erupted again and a barrage of bullets peppered the timber like a swarm of killer bees. Rogue was cornered and of no use to Agnetha trapped inside the cabin. Savik would quickly take control of the situation, lock them both inside and then torch the place.

Rogue needed to go on the offensive. Squeezing the handle of the knife between her knees, Rogue feverishly worked the rope along the blade, desperate to free her hands. One by one, the individual fibres snapped.

Her brain screamed at her to move further back into the cabin, that the door was about to disintegrate under the constant barrage of bullets. Just as the last strand snapped, the door cracked in two.

Still lying on the floor, Becker stretched beneath the wooden shelving, his fingers scrambling for his gun. Rogue dropped down low as Frack fired another burst, but his Uzi snagged in the broken timbers of the door and skewed his aim.

Beside Rogue, Becker's hand reappeared with his Sig pistol. She lunged at him and sank the blade of her knife through the back of his hand.

As Frack shouldered his way through the remains of the shattered door, Rogue snatched Becker's fallen Sig and fired blindly. Frack squeezed the trigger of his Uzi and dropped low to avoid Rogue's bullets, but in doing so, he hampered his own aim.

Becker prised Rogue's knife from his hand and swung the blade at her face. As she rolled away, bullets from Frack's submachine gun drilled into the floor all around her, tugging at her jacket. With nowhere to hide, she was an easy target.

Rogue stopped moving. In the gloom, it took Frack a second to register where she was. Rogue found his outline, silhouetted by the morning sunlight, and emptied the Sig's magazine into his chest. The Uzi slipped from his grip and clattered to the wooden floor. As he fell back into the yard, Rogue sensed movement to her left.

Becker was back on his feet and charging at her. She hooked her foot around the wooden chair and swung it into his path. Unable to slow down, he toppled over it and landed face first. Rogue hadn't time for a prolonged fight. Desperate to find Agnetha, she dived on him and pummelled the butt of her empty Sig into his skull. Without waiting to check whether he was alive or dead, she sprang up and made for the door.

On the way, she took Frack's Uzi and ripped spare magazines from his belt. As she reloaded, she felt blood seeping through the cotton of her shirt. She pulled it up. Two wounds, one below her ribs, the second a little higher, both leaking. If she couldn't stem the flow, she'd pass out from blood loss. Spotting a roll of grey insulation tape on the shelves, she wound several layers tight around her waist. Outside, a car engine burst into life.

Rogue rushed out to the yard as a silver Mercedes jammed to a stop. She expected to see another of Savik's men driving, but it was Webb behind the wheel. The door of the adjacent cabin swung open, and Agnetha stepped out, her face ashen, her mouth quivering. As she descended the steps, Savik emerged behind her, his gun pressed to the back of her head.

"Get back or I will kill her," growled Savik, drilling the barrel in harder. "You know I will do it!"

Rogue raised the Uzi and aimed at his head.

Savik crouched down behind Agnetha, shoved her towards the waiting Mercedes and pulled open the rear door.

"I won't let you leave," said Rogue. "You won't take her from me again."

"Then shoot now and kill both of us," said Savik.

Rogue switched the machine gun to single shot mode. She had a partial target, two centimetres of Savik's right temple, three at a stretch. As she tightened her finger against the trigger, she felt the resistance of the spring behind it. She could take out a man's eye with a Glock, but she wasn't as confident with the Uzi, especially when Savik had a gun pressed to Agnetha's head.

Cold beads of sweat gathered along Rogue's forehead. Agnetha reminded her so much of Tasha, her liquid hazel eyes, and soft apple cheeks. Rogue wondered what Tasha would do in the same situation. Maybe she'd convey a signal to Agnetha that only the two of them shared, a countdown to action. In those agonisingly slow milliseconds, Rogue wished she had spent more time with her niece, that they knew each other much better.

A crunching penetrated the background hum of the car's engine, enough to set off the alarm in Rogue's brain. She whipped around, snapped an image, and returned to her target. Savik had mirrored her actions, but lagged half a second behind. In that brief moment, she had a larger target, a corner of his skull the size of a tennis ball. But as he moved, so did Agnetha, her body welded to his. Rogue had a clear shot, but it was still too much of a risk.

The crunching noise grew louder, the sound of boots on gravel. Rogue recalled the image and recognised the security man from the gate. He was armed and was closing in fast.

"Shoot her, shoot her," screamed Savik.

The guard fired a shot, then another, the rounds thudding into the cabin walls behind Rogue. She swivelled and dropped to a crouch in one fluid movement, took aim, and fired twice, hitting the guard in the chest. He sank to his knees and got off another shot, but his aim was wide. As Rogue fired another volley to finish him, the Mercedes took off, spraying a cloud of grit and mud into her face.

Savik and Agnetha were in the back seat. If they got away, Rogue knew she'd never see Agnetha again. She sprinted after them as Webb spun the car in a tight arc towards the driveway. Rogue waited until the last second, until she had a clear view of Webb, then took aim and fired several times. The bullets shattered the side window and turned the windscreen into a white haze.

Webb kept going, but the tyres struggled for grip on the loose stones and the car skidded. Rogue switched her aim to the front wheel and continued firing. As the tyre shredded, Webb lost control and ploughed the

Mercedes into a mound of sand. Rogue raced after them, trying to see Agnetha in the back seat.

A rear door opened and Savik stumbled out. When he spotted Rogue, he scrambled frantically for his gun. Rogue was about to shoot, but just in time, she noticed Agnetha right behind him. As Rogue closed in, Savik recovered his Sig from inside the car and opened fire. Rogue weaved left and right, but his bullets were dangerously close. She returned fire, but had to aim low to avoid Agnetha.

Savik faltered and shifted his weight to his left leg, but kept firing. His aim was wild now, distracted by the pain in his leg. Rogue stopped shooting when she saw Agnetha loop something around Savik's throat. His head jolted back, and he grasped at the noose with both hands.

Rogue's head spun as the blood loss from her wounds took its toll. She tried to cover the last fifty metres, but her vision blurred and she tripped and went sprawling across the gravel. Rising to her hands and knees, she gritted her teeth and tried to squint through the sickening haze. When her vision cleared, she saw Savik had broken free from the noose. He swung an elbow at Agnetha, catching her on the side of the head. Stunned, she fell back, her body limp.

Savik clambered out of the Mercedes and hobbled towards Rogue, his Sig pistol aimed at her gut. He couldn't miss. Rogue's eyes latched onto the Uzi she'd dropped, lying just millimetres from her fingertips.

She had nothing to lose. Hoping to catch him by surprise, she whipped it up and squeezed the trigger, but Savik fired first. Both guns clicked the hollow sound of empty magazines.

Savik dug into his coat pocket and pulled out a fresh clip. Rogue jumped up and charged at him, yelling as loud as she could. He pressed the release button, letting the empty fall away. Rogue was closing fast. She considered a two footed kick but knew she hadn't the energy.

Savik shoved in the fresh magazine, but it jammed part way in. He yanked it out, twisted it around, and tried again. This time, it slid home. As he raised the Sig to fire, Rogue pivoted on one leg and slammed a boot into his groin. As he stumbled backwards, bullets whizzed over Rogue's head. She lashed out again, connecting with his elbow. Savik howled and dropped the Sig.

Rogue kicked the gun and sent it skating underneath the car. Savik swung at Rogue, but she ducked and countered with a volley of body shots. Savik was tough but out of condition and was soon wheezing, unable to catch his breath. Doubled over, he yelled out to Webb.

Rogue turned to the Mercedes and saw Webb lying over the steering wheel. Agnetha was still in the back seat, blood trickling from her nose. Savik was to blame for everything that had happened to Agnetha and for the horrible nightmares that she might endure for years to come. Even though Rogue knew it wouldn't change anything, she wanted to make Savik suffer.

She launched a barrage of punches, pummelling his stomach and head until he fell down, his face covered in blood. As Rogue stood over him, her lungs pounding in her chest, Agnetha screamed, then sprang forward, flailing her arms in panic. Rogue rushed to the car and pulled the door open. Agnetha jolted back against the seat, gasping for oxygen. She was suffocating.

Chapter 37

Agnetha sagged limply against the seat, her eyes barely open. Rogue placed two fingers on the side of the girl's neck. Her pulse was slow and erratic, her breathing worryingly shallow. Rogue called her name, gently at first, then more urgently.

Agnetha's eyelids lifted. She turned to Rogue and tried to speak, but got a fit of coughing. Rogue folded her forward and placed one hand on the girl's forehead as she fought for air. Her coughing stopped abruptly, replaced by a desperate sucking noise from her throat.

Rogue hooked her hands under Agnetha's armpits and dragged her from the car. Unable to breathe, Agnetha panicked and tried to break free, swinging wildly. Rogue wrapped her arms around Agnetha's waist. With one fist above the girl's navel, Rogue pressed in and up, forcing the air from Agnetha's lungs and hopefully dislodging whatever obstruction was choking her. Rogue repeated the manoeuvre again, watching Agnetha's face in the wing mirror. After the third attempt, the blockage shifted, and Agnetha breathed freely.

Rogue lowered her gently, then hunkered down and hugged her. Tears rolled down Agnetha's cheeks. She tried to speak, but only fragments emerged.

"Tooth," said Agnetha, pointing to a small white shape in the dirt. She opened her mouth wide and curled her lips up, revealing the jagged edge of a broken molar. Savik had broken it when he punched her. Agnetha coughed and spat out blood. A tidal wave of love, remorse, and outrage overwhelmed Rogue. Unable to find the right words, she sat on the ground, wrapped her arms around Agnetha again, and wished she could magically transport them both to a happier place.

A groan came from inside the car. Rogue jumped up in time to see Webb regain consciousness. She yanked open the door as he righted himself in the seat. Webb looked at Rogue, but there was no sign of recognition. His eyes squinted, then blinked slowly. There were cuts and bruises on his face, but it was impossible to tell which injuries happened when he drove into the sand.

After ensuring that Webb wasn't armed, Rogue stood back and surveyed the scene. The front wheels of the Mercedes were buried in the mound of builders' sand. It would probably start, but Rogue had shot out a tyre on the driver's side. As for her rented Audi, the explosion had ripped it apart. The doors lay mangled on the ground and a column of smoke drifted from the smouldering wreck. It wouldn't be long before a passing motorist notified the police.

She ran across the yard towards the SUV she'd seen from the road, a black Citroen. On her way, she passed Savik lying motionless on the ground. Rogue had unfinished business with him, but it would have to wait.

Whoever owned the Citroen had left the keys in the ignition, ready for a quick getaway. Rogue threw it into gear and looped back around towards Agnetha. As the crashed Mercedes came into view, Rogue expected to see Savik in the dirt where she had left him. Instead, he was staggering around the back of the car, steadying himself against it. Rogue screeched to a stop between Savik and Agnetha. The girl was still on the ground, elbows on her knees, hands cupped under her chin.

A warning bell rang deep in the recesses of Rogue's brain, but she ignored it. The two bodyguards were dead and Savik was in no shape to be a threat. Rogue checked Agnetha's vital signs again. Her breathing had improved, but her heart rate was slow.

Rogue's sixth sense screamed louder. She snapped her head up and scanned the yard, then the building site beyond. Nothing moved or registered as being out of place. Savik was still propped against the Mercedes, looking directly at her, expressionless and beaten. But something in his eyes worried her. Rogue's brain, overworked and overloaded, finally caught up with her gut instinct and dragged her attention back to the driver's seat in the Mercedes. It was empty. Webb was gone.

She whipped around and saw him bending down, reaching into the sand. Rogue tried to see what he was doing, but his body obscured her view. As he lifted a dark, shiny object, she saw it was a gun. As she raced to intercept him, she screamed in a desperate effort to distract him.

Webb sprang up and levelled the Sig at her. Rogue stopped dead. Only a few metres separated them. Close enough that he wouldn't miss, but too far for her to tackle him.

"I think you have used up the last of your cat's lives," said Savik, as he limped towards them.

Webb's hand was trembling, and he was blinking repeatedly, his vision unclear after the impact of the crash. Rogue needed to disarm him before Savik reached him and took the gun. She pointed back at Agnetha, who was lying on the gravel.

"Agnetha's hurt, Jason. She needs a doctor. Please, just lower the gun and let me take her to the hospital."

Webb's eyes flicked beyond Rogue, squinting, but the gun never moved. Rogue heard Savik drawing closer, dragging his injured leg.

"Jason, you should leave. Get out of here before the cops arrive," urged Rogue.

Webb half nodded. The idea of ending his ordeal, even to lie down somewhere safe and comfortable, appealed to him. Rogue took a step forward, her hand outstretched. His arm dipped slightly, but maybe just from exhaustion.

"Don't be a fool, Webb," yelled Savik. "She's trying to trick you."

Webb jumped, startled. He took a step back and adjusted his aim, pointing the gun at Rogue's face. In seconds, Savik would take control. Rogue had to do something, but rushing at Webb would be suicide. Instead, she turned and hurried back to Agnetha.

Flopping down beside her niece, Rogue gently lifted her head. "I'm here Agnetha. You're safe now."

A sharp breeze whipped up and blew sand into their faces as drops of rain began falling. Agnetha was shivering, her face worryingly pale.

Savik appeared at their side. He had the Sig in his hand, the same one Rogue had sent skidding under the car during their fight. Before she could plead for Agnetha's life, Savik waved them towards the bungalow.

"Bring her into the house," said Savik.

"She's hurt. She can't walk."

"Carry her or drag her corpse," said Savik. "I don't care, just do it."

"One of you could help me," said Rogue, not expecting any cooperation from Savik or Webb. She manoeuvred Agnetha into a seated position, then looped her arm around the girl's waist and hoisted her up. Fire erupted in Rogue's side and she almost dropped Agnetha again. She felt the wound on her side pulsing as blood oozed into the makeshift bandage.

Savik just stood there, his lip curled in a sneer. He seemed to take a perverse pleasure in other people's suffering. Rogue looked from Savik to Webb. Both were in terrible shape and eager to leave, but not before taking care of the loose ends. Rogue cursed. Only for that gun, she and Agnetha would already be miles away.

Switching to her weaker left side, Rogue gritted her teeth and trudged across the yard, carrying Agnetha. Webb went ahead of her. Savik followed several paces behind them.

Agnetha was too exhausted and confused to realise the gravity of the situation. "Are we going home, Rachel? I don't feel well."

"Soon Agnetha, soon, we're going to the house first, out of the rain."

"Is that your house?"

"Come on, one step in front of the other," encouraged Rogue. Agnetha tried to walk, but kept dozing off. She was a dead weight and Rogue's grip around her was slipping.

Savik took out his phone and selected a number. Rogue only caught snatches of the conversation but enough to realise he was calling for reinforcements. It gave Rogue a glimmer of hope. She just needed an opportunity to overpower him.

On reaching the house, she mounted the steps, hauling Agnetha up one at a time. Rogue paused for a breather in the hallway until Savik prodded her in the back with the pistol. She lifted Agnetha again and struggled into an enormous kitchen which spanned the rear of the bungalow.

From outside, the house looked finished, but inside, the brickwork and wiring were still exposed between the timber uprights. The kitchen windows were boarded up and the only source of daylight was through frosted glass in the back door. One corner of the floor was covered with sheets of insulated plaster board.

Rogue took in her surroundings in a second, picking out items she could use as a weapon. A screwdriver perched on a windowsill, rolls of electric cable sitting on the floor and a handsaw resting on a toolbox.

Rogue guided Agnetha to the stack of boards in the corner and eased her down. Agnetha was barely conscious and unable to sit up. Rogue helped her lie flat and placed a folded sack under her head. Agnetha wasn't shivering as much, but she was still deathly pale. Rogue took another set of overalls and spread them over her like a blanket.

Savik shuffled in and perched himself against a ladder, the Sig aimed at Rogue. "Sit down on those crates."

"Agnetha needs a doctor," demanded Rogue.

"Webb, find something to tie them up."

Rogue took a step towards Savik. "Didn't you hear what I just said?"

He swivelled the gun and pointed it at Agnetha. "Sit, now," he barked.

Rogue sucked in her anger, reversed to an upturned crate, and dropped onto it. Despite everything, Savik appeared to be alert. Rogue wondered what he was thinking and how long she had left to live. Agnetha's eyes were shut, her breathing shallow. She mumbled something, but Rogue couldn't make sense of it. Risking Savik's wrath, she hurried across the room and shook Agnetha gently.

"Agnetha, wake up."

When Agnetha's eyes opened and she saw Rogue, her cheeks rose with a half-smile. But when she saw the gun in Savik's hand, her smile evaporated and tears welled in her eyes.

"It's OK, don't worry," assured Rogue.

"It's all my fault, I'm so sorry." Her words tumbled over each other.

Rogue shook her head. "No, it isn't. Don't say that."

Agnetha nodded feebly, lips pressed together in resignation.

"Enough of the family reunion," snapped Savik. "On that crate, now, ankles crossed, wrists behind your back."

"Don't worry, I'll get us out of here," whispered Rogue. "But you need to stay awake and be ready. OK?"

"I'll try," said Agnetha, her lips quivering.

Rogue returned to the upturned crate and sat down. Webb stood watching them, a sneering grin on his face. He approached Rogue with a roll of builders tape and a knife. Rogue looked over at Savik.

He shook his head. "Don't try anything. I will kill you."

Webb wound the industrial tape around Rogue's wrists.

Rogue eyeballed him. "He's going to kill us, and you are an accessory. Do you really want murder added to industrial espionage?"

"Now, secure her to those timbers. And hurry," ordered Savik.

Webb moved behind Rogue, looped a length of tape through her arms, and secured the other end around a vertical wooden beam.

She lowered her voice. "Remember those Russians I told you about? The FSB? Every heard of the Lubyanka prison?"

Webb flinched and threw a glance at his boss.

"Get on with it. She's playing mind games with you."

Webb sliced the tape from the roll and backed away.

"The girl too," said Savik.

Agnetha locked eyes with Rogue and swallowed hard. As Webb taped Agnetha's wrists, Savik stood up and walked behind Rogue. She ignored him and kept eye contact with Agnetha, trying to comfort her.

Rogue had a bad feeling, but she was helpless to stop it. She sensed Savik behind her and saw the alarm in Agnetha's eyes a second before she felt the impact on the back of her head. Waves of nausea and darkness flooded Rogue's senses, shutting down her consciousness. Agnetha blurred in the distance, shimmering like a ghost, her mouth strangely misshapen, then disappeared. Rogue's brain sent a last message to her vocal chords, to tell Agnetha everything would be alright, but no words emerged.

Chapter 38

Rogue was trapped in the depths of a recurring nightmare. Tasha was alive, but Rogue could never get close to her and as the nightmare came to its inevitable conclusion, Rogue saw the barrel of the sniper's rifle glisten through the open window and release its messenger of death. As she raced to save Tasha, Rogue heard someone yelling her name. The voice was urgent and hysterical enough to wrench her from unconsciousness. Dragging her eyes half open, she shivered under the familiar cold sweat of her night terrors. She let her lids drop again and waited for the shivering to abate, but the voice yelling her name intensified. As the fog cleared, she shifted uncomfortably, the surface underneath her hard and unfamiliar.

"Rachel, wake up. Aunt Rachel." The same panicked voice, shrieking her name.

Rogue sat up with a start and tried to stand, but her hands were pinned behind her. Across the room, she saw Agnetha propped up against the wall, her face screwed up in pain as she fought to free her wrists. The same black tape bound her ankles. The throbbing at the back of Rogue's head reminded her of what had happened and where she was. She tugged in vain at her own restraints.

"He's going to set the house on fire," screamed Agnetha. "We're going to die."

Rogue's nostrils flinched, recognising the petrol vapours. She turned and saw Webb spraying the raw timber struts from a plastic drum. There was no sign of Savik. "Webb, what the hell are you doing?"

Rogue strained with every muscle to pull free. She tugged one way, then another, but the tape securing her hands held firm. "Listen to me, Jason. You have what you came for. Just walk away. You're not a murderer. Not yet."

Rogue pressed back against the vertical beam, kicked the upturned crate from underneath her, and stood up. Webb continued splashing petrol along the walls, as if he hadn't heard a word she'd said. She wedged one foot against the wooden beam and pulled as hard as she could, trying to stretch the tape and weaken it.

"Dammit, Webb, turn around. Just for one minute. Think about what you are doing. Agnetha is only eighteen years old. Do you want her death on your conscience for the rest of your life?"

Webb was moving progressively closer to Agnetha. Rogue planted both feet onto the cement floor and heaved. The loop of tape curled in on itself, stretched and lengthened, but didn't break. She dug into her memory and recalled the profile of Webb that Marcus had sent her.

"Jason, what about your sister? Jessica, isn't that her name? She's only seventeen. Would you burn her alive too?"

Webb lowered the drum and let it hang from his grip, his back still facing them. He'd already doused two of the kitchen walls with the fuel. If he ignited it now, it would spread to the ceiling in seconds.

"Talk to me, Jason, please."

He turned to face Rogue, but stopped when he saw Agnetha. Her eyes were red from crying and her entire body was trembling. She'd pressed herself as far into the corner as she could and hugged her knees tight into her chest. She'd given up. Webb stared at her, unable to look away.

"Help us," whispered Agnetha. "Please."

Rogue didn't know what Webb's sister looked like, but in that moment, she hoped that Agnetha reminded him of Jessica. Any small resemblance might cast a doubt into his mind.

Savik marched into the kitchen from the hallway. "Is it done?"

He took in the scene and instantly understood what was happening. Marching over to Webb, he snatched the drum from his grip.

"I told you not to engage with her." His mouth twist-ed into a bitter snarl. "She knows every trick in the book. She's like a witch, playing with your mind."

He shoved Webb out of the way. Webb lost his foot-ing and stumbled back onto the sheets of plasterboard beside Agnetha.

"I'll finish this." Savik started towards Rogue with the can of petrol but halfway there, he stopped and cocked his head.

Rogue heard the sounds, too. Sirens. Savik let the drum fall and snatched a paint stained rag from the floor. Petrol flowed freely from the overturned drum and pooled near Rogue's boots.

As he fished a cigarette lighter from his coat, Savik bellowed at Webb. "Get out of here. There's a car wait-ing outside."

Webb shot a look at Rogue, his face contorted with indecision. Rogue mouthed to him, to stop Savik, but he looked away and stared at the floor. Savik grinned at Rogue as he bent down and doused the rag in a pool of petrol.

"Do what you like to me," pleaded Rogue. "But you've no quarrel with Agnetha. Let her go."

Savik stood up and snapped the wheel on the lighter. The flame licked the fabric, then found the petrol and ignited. He tossed the rag onto a stack of floor boards and backed away. "See you in hell."

When Webb leaned across to Agnetha and reached out a hand, Rogue wondered if he'd changed his mind.

Savik turned on him. "If you want to burn here too, that is OK. I am leaving now, with or without you."

As the flames scaled the timbers and ignited the plastic covering of the insulation, Webb withdrew and hurried into the hallway after Savik. Ignoring the darts of pain in her joints, Rogue tugged at her restraints, but it was pointless. Agnetha screamed after Webb, begging him to come back, but the front door slammed shut, sealing their fate.

The fire devoured the raw timber partition separating the kitchen from the rest of the bungalow. Between the square tiles of the partially completed ceiling, electric cables draped down, ready for light fittings. Rogue hoped that the gaps in the ceiling might slow the fire's progress.

She strained her ears for the wail of sirens. Fragments of sound pierced the crackling of the flames, but she couldn't identify them. To have any chance of survival, she'd need to make something happen herself, and fast.

Rogue twisted around to face the wall, then sunk to the floor. Webb had secured her to a vertical length of timber, which sat on another beam running horizontally. She kicked at the junction where they met, trying to dislodge the upright. It wouldn't budge. She drew both legs close to her chest and launched them together. The impact reverberated through her entire body. She lashed out again and again, grunting with each effort from the worsening ache in her lower back.

The length of tape between her wrists and the beam stretched a little with each attack, but progress was agonisingly slow.

Rogue doubled over, her body exhausted, her energy drained. She glared at the wooden beam. A small gap had opened beneath it, revealing the glint of steel nails. Rogue felt heat on one side of her face and was shocked by how fast the fire had crept along the walls towards her.

She glanced across the room. Agnetha was further from the flames, but she wouldn't be safe for long. Her head rested on her chest. At first, Rogue feared she had passed out from the smoke, but then noticed her wrists sliding back and forth. Something glint-ed between them, maybe a piece of glass or a work-man's tool. A dose of adrenalin surged through Rogue's bloodstream.

She turned her attention back to the timber upright. The black tape had stretched considerably from her exertions. It was now a tight narrow band over a metre long. Blood seeped from Rogue's wrists as the tape dug into them. She stood up and charged at the upright, leading with her shoulder. Her head spun as the impact sent spasms through her body. She shook off a wave of nausea and tried again. This time, the top end of the timber separated from the ceiling. Again and again, she threw herself at the upright. Sweat soaked her clothes as her lungs inhaled the fumes.

Rogue paused and squinted through the growing swirls of smoke. Agnetha sensed her and looked back. There was no need for words. They both understood how desperate their situation was, but neither was ready to admit defeat.

Rogue clenched her fists, summoned every ounce of rage from her past, and attacked the beam again. The nails ripped from their mooring and the upright swung free from the ceiling. Rogue gripped it with blood-stained hands and pulled it down until she could slide the twisted black tape over the top. Using the cluster of exposed nails, she punctured holes in the tape between her wrists, then severed the remaining slivers on the raw timber. As she broke free, molten drops from above slid down the back of her neck, scorching her skin.

She ducked and ran across the kitchen to Agnetha. As she scrambled onto the stack of boards, a section of the ceiling crashed to the floor and lodged itself in the doorway, blocking the hallway and their only way out. Rogue wiped sweat and dust from her stinging eyes and turned to Agnetha. The poor girl was trying to cut through the tape on her wrists using a rusty blade, but her hands were trembling and the angle was so awkward that she'd made little progress. Her fingers were torn and bloody, and she could hardly see what she was doing through a mixture of smoke, blood, and tears.

"Here, let me do it," said Rogue. She eased Agnetha's fingers apart and took the blade. Agnetha shrank back as Rogue expertly sliced through the tape. She grabbed Agnetha's arms and tugged, but Agnetha resisted, pressing herself further into the corner.

"What's wrong?" asked Rogue, anxiously checking for injuries.

Agnetha's eyes darted around the room at the advancing flames. She shook her head, jerked her hand free from Rogue's grasp and pulled her legs in tight.

Rogue shimmied closer and placed her palms on Agnetha's cheeks. "Agnetha, look at me. We can do this, but we have to go right now."

The ceiling above let out an agonising creak. Agnetha shrieked and clamped her eyes shut. Rogue felt her optimism drain away. On her own, she'd ignore the danger and drive forward, either find a way out or die trying. Agnetha wasn't like that. She was young, had never faced a life and death situation. She was terrified. Rogue could try to carry Agnetha, but if she resisted, it would make a difficult task impossible.

Chapter 39

Agnetha sprang forward. The panels behind her had blistered from the heat and scorched through her top. As a breeze blew in from the hall, the flames leapt dangerously close. Rogue grabbed Agnetha and pulled her clear of the advancing fire. The two of them tumbled off the stack of panels and landed in a heap on the concrete floor.

The smoke and boarded windows made it difficult to see anything. All the internal walls were now ablaze. Rogue urged Agnetha into the centre of the room, the only area where the ceiling wasn't consumed by fire. From there, she scanned the kitchen walls, looking for another way out.

The rear of the house was concrete blocks, and the fire hadn't yet ignited the timbers either side of the back door. It was the only option left, but a wall of flames blocked their path. Rogue hunkered down and looked for something, anything, they could use as a shield.

She spotted a tarpaulin spread underneath a pile of paint tins. Grabbing one end, she heaved. It shifted slowly, then snagged. Rogue kicked over the stack of tins. As they rolled away, she yanked the tarpaulin clear, then threw it over Agnetha and huddled in beside her.

Wrapping one arm around the girl's waist, Rogue urged her through an avalanche of burning debris from above. The kitchen was now thick with smoke, and the floor littered with smouldering ceiling tiles. Rogue's throat burned and she could see Agnetha's breathing was heavy and ragged. Fighting to keep their eyes open through the searing heat, they stumbled through the obstacle course, tripping over building materials and tools.

Rogue struggled on, half carrying, half dragging Agnetha through the fumes, praying they were still moving in the right direction. Just as Rogue started to lose hope, her outstretched hand struck a brick wall.

She flattened her palm against the rough concrete. It was cooler, solid, safe. Agnetha pressed her back against the wall and sunk down, searching for cleaner air.

A few steps away, Rogue found the rear door. She turned the handle and pulled, but it stayed shut. She tried again, tugging with all her strength, but it was locked. In desperation, she checked the keyhole, then probed the window sills on either side for a key, stabbing her torn fingers on discarded nails and a myriad of sharp objects. It wasn't there.

Rogue took a few steps back, then launched herself at the door, but her light frame just bounced off it. She was wasting valuable time. Wiping rivers of grimy sweat from her face with her sleeve, she tried to think. The glass window in the upper half of the door was cracked but still intact. It was double or treble glazed and not very wide. She looked over at Agnetha and wondered if she was slim enough to squeeze through.

A stack of heavy duty plastic cases stood to one side. Rogue clicked open the top one. Inside was an electric saw with a selection of blades. She shoved it aside, let it topple to the floor, and flipped opened the next case. Another electric saw, this one with a circular blade. They were useless without a power source.

The third box held a hammer gun with two battery packs. She hefted out the gun, shoved in a battery, and pulled the trigger. It whirred and clicked, but nothing emerged from the nozzle. Flipping it over, she realised the nail cartridge was missing.

She unsnapped the lid of the last case. It was packed with cartridges, but they all gaped up at her, each one empty. She tossed the case over in frustration. The empties tumbled out, revealing a second row underneath, all full. She grabbed one and slotted it into the nail gun.

Agnetha screamed.

Rogue spun around.

Agnetha was lying on the floor, the tarpaulin in a heap beside her. Drops of hot plastic were streaming from above, singeing her arms.

Rogue rushed over and draped the grimy canvas back over Agnetha. The tarpaulin was so badly scorched and burnt through that Rogue had to double it twice. Even then, there was barely enough to protect Agnetha's head and shoulders.

Squatting down, Rogue scraped the burning resin from Agnetha's arms, then moved her closer to the back door. Flames licked through the dense smoke, searching them out. Agnetha was coughing hard, inhaling more charred particles with each breath.

Rogue tugged her shirt up over her mouth and grabbed the nail gun. Through half-closed eyes, she pressed the nozzle against the glass window of the back door and fired. A volley of nails embedded themselves in the thick glass, but the pane held. Switching to the perimeter, she traced a line just inside the wooden frame, firing continuously until the gun clicked empty.

She hit the eject button and let the spent cartridge fall away, then slammed in a fresh one and resumed her attack on the glass. Black smoke thickened around her, hot and sickening, stinging her eyes and raking her throat. She squinted through streaming eyes, barely able to see the glass.

When the gun emptied a second time, she reversed her grip and pounded the centre of the pane with the handle, heavy with the weight of the battery pack. Cracks spread along the line of holes she'd made and the glass shattered.

A gush of cold air from outside sucked the fire all around Rogue, burning her legs. She continued hammering around the jagged edges, clearing as much as possible. Then she took the tarpaulin from Agnetha, pushed it through the gap and draped it over the remaining shards of glass. Agnetha squeezed up against Rogue, drinking in the fresh air from outside.

Rogue bent down, interlaced her fingers, and urged Agnetha to step up and crawl through the window. Agnetha grimaced, reluctant to squeeze her bony frame through the narrow wooden frame, edged with broken glass. An explosion erupted somewhere in the smog, showering them with splinters and dirt. Rogue screamed at Agnetha to get out.

Agnetha pressed both hands on Rogue's shoulders and hoisted herself up. Reaching her arms through the window, she pulled herself into the opening. When Rogue felt Agnetha's weight shift forward, she wrapped her arms around the girl's legs and heaved.

As Agnetha's bare shoulders wedged tight against the window frame, shards of glass tore into her flesh. Sobbing with pain, she wriggled and pulled her body in an effort to escape. Rogue felt the resistance and pushed harder, trying not to think of Agnetha's injuries.

The girl's torso barely moved. Rogue heard Agnetha yell but couldn't make out the words. Rogue's vision blurred, and she fell to her hands and knees. Through the haze, she could see Agnetha squirming and kicking as she struggled to free herself. Rogue called out to her, urging her on.

Thick black smoke billowed around Rogue as her head swam and she lost all sense of direction. Desperate to stay conscious, she bent down lower and sought a pocket of clean air as she fought the urge to close her eyes and give up. Rogue looked for Agnetha, but she'd been swallowed up by the smoke, her cries lost in the roar of the fire.

Rogue's chest tightened as she envisioned Agnetha still wedged in the shattered window pane, midway between living and dying. Up above, the rafters cracked and groaned. As she tried to stand, a beam tore from its mooring and plunged down on top of her. Somehow, Rogue's legs reacted and threw her clear. Her shoulder slammed into a wooden bench, snapping her head against the concrete. A stream of tiles and timber fell from the ceiling, burying her from the hips down.

Rogue lay there, broken, haunted by the image of Agnetha's legs thrashing wildly, scorched and blistered. Fanned by the air being sucked in through the roof, the kitchen was rapidly turning into a furnace, swallowing every remaining pocket of oxygen. In that moment Rogue recognised a belief that lived deep in her soul, that she would die before her time. It was her destiny. She didn't deserve any better.

Amidst the snapping and crackling inferno, Rogue heard a voice calling her name. She paused for a moment, doubting her ears, convinced that the fire was playing tricks on her senses. Tears welled in her eyes. She had failed. Memories flooded back of missions with Tasha. The two of them never gave up, one always saving the other. If only Tasha could be there now, for her daughter, to save Agnetha.

Again, a voice penetrated the fire. It was louder, demanding. Rogue thought she recognised Tasha's voice. But Tasha was dead. It had to be Agnetha crying for help. Rogue prised her shoulders off the floor. Twisting around, she dragged her legs clear of the rubble. She pushed up onto her knees, inhaled a cocktail of smut and charred wood, and forced herself to stand up.

Unsure which direction to go, Rogue closed her eyes and tried to focus on sounds, searching for Agnetha's voice in the roaring fire. It was gone, swallowed up. Rogue shuffled forward, kicking through the obstacles in her path. The floor rumbled, and Rogue heard a loud crash. At any moment, she expected the roof to collapse and bury her. Ignoring her body's plea to give up, she forced herself onwards, one step at a time.

Up ahead, shards of light penetrated the billowing blackness. She hoped it was light from the broken window, beckoning her to freedom. A deep tremor rippled through the floor, followed by an eerie silence.

As Rogue stopped and listened, an explosion shook the room. She was thrown sideways as the back door flew past her and crashed to the floor.

Rogue's skin burned as air sucked from outside fed the flames, and the temperature soared. Smoke billowed and swirled through the doorway. The heavy wooden door was gone, but something large was blocking the opening.

Staying close to the floor, Rogue crawled on all fours until her fingers closed around cold metal. She recognised the teeth of a digger bucket, several of them embedded deep into the door frame. Someone had used the construction vehicle to break down the door and the huge bucket lay wedged in the gap. The air outside was hot and littered with burning debris, but compared to inside the inferno, it was lifesaving. Rogue gulped it in and blinked the smoke from her eyes.

As she clambered over the steel bucket and onto the engine, a second explosion blew out the sheets of board covering the kitchen windows. Wooden daggers peppered the side of the digger, some of them finding Rogue's bare arms. Her hands lost their grip, and she fell off the digger onto the gravel.

Rogue lay on the hard stones, unable to move. Every bone in her body was a dead weight, pinning her to the ground. Smoke and flames billowed from the bungalow, but through them she glimpsed a patch of blue sky she never expected to see again.

Sucking air into her clogged lungs, she mentally scanned herself for damage. Every muscle and tendon twitched and stung, and she found it difficult to distinguish one part from another. As the ringing in her ears subsided, she recognised the sound of gunfire.

Rolling onto her side, she spat out a glob of charred phlegm and peered through the smoke. The shots were muffled, but she guessed they came from the front of the house. That meant the police had arrived in time to stop Savik from escaping.

Reaching one hand for the wheel arch of the digger, she hauled herself up. The bright yellow metal of the vehicle jarred her memory, and she remembered the kitchen door caving in. In that same instant, she thought of Agnetha and whipped around to face the cab.

Agnetha was draped over the steering wheel. Rogue hoisted herself inside. Agnetha had twisted her hair into a makeshift bun and Rogue winced at the cuts and burns disfiguring the girl's face. Gently, she helped Agnetha to sit up.

"Agnetha, it's time to go." Rogue gently put an arm around her shoulders and kissed her on the cheek.

Agnetha's eyes opened a little, and she frowned, as if trying to remember something. Rogue hated having to ask any more of her niece, but it was too dangerous to stay where they were. Savik and his men were still free and, if possible, Rogue wanted to avoid dealing with the police.

She licked her fingers and carefully rubbed grit and ash from around her niece's eyes and mouth. "Agnetha, it's me, Rachel."

A half smile formed on Agnetha's lips. Her eyes glistened, then released a few tears.

"It's OK, we're safe. You saved me," said Rogue. "But we have to go now."

Agnetha looked around at the burning house. Her smile faded and her head dropped. As she examined the cuts and burns on her fingers, her shoulders sagged.

Rogue cradled her hands under Agnetha's chin and tilted her head so that their eyes met. "Hey, we're in this together. You and me, a team."

Agnetha's lower lip curled in. She bit into it.

"We can do this Agnetha. You're so strong, just like your mum." Rogue took a step back. "Ready?"

Agnetha nodded tentatively, then slid across the seat. Rogue reversed out of the digger and helped her down.

Chapter 40

A huge barn faced the rear of the house. Rogue took Agnetha's hand and the two of them half ran, half hobbled away from the inferno. Rogue's left ankle throbbed with every step, and the skin on her hands and face was raw and blistered. The gunfire coming from the far side of the house was sporadic. Rogue guessed Savik was saving his ammunition while he conjured up an escape plan. The police would bide their time until reinforcements arrived. A SWAT team would soon surround the farm with a chopper overhead for support. Rogue needed to be well gone by then.

The door of the barn was slightly open. Rogue and Agnetha hurried inside and left the noise of the fire and the gunfight behind them. Rogue ran her hand along the wall, found a row of switches, and flicked them all. A random selection of bulbs spluttered into life and delivered a depressing yellow glow.

Animal stalls occupied one half of the vast space. They were all empty. Open shelving lined the back wall, laden with tools, cardboard boxes and empty beer bottles. Off to one side, Rogue spotted a familiar shape under a stained white sheet. Seizing one end of the cover, she pulled it clear. Underneath was a Mitsubishi pickup, the faded yellow bodywork eaten with rust, the tyres bald and a little soft.

The driver's door groaned as Rogue opened it and sat in behind the wheel. Her fingers reached for the ignition, but the key was missing. She quickly searched the usual places. Dashboard, sun visor and storage areas. Nothing. The floor was littered with cigarette butts, but the half closed ashtray looked empty. She yanked it out and found a single grubby key sitting inside.

The pickup started on the first turn, backfired, then died. Rogue tried again, revving gently, this time waiting until the engine settled before driving forward. The needle on the fuel gauge sat barely above the red zone. It would have to do. Rogue left the engine running and got out.

Agnetha had sat herself down on a bale of straw and was drinking water from a tap. Rogue ran to the double doors and cautiously stuck her head out into the yard. The gunfire was louder, much closer than before. She heaved one sliding door back until there was enough room for the pickup to get through. Then she called Agnetha to join her and started back to the Mitsubishi.

Agnetha was sitting with her eyes shut and her arms wrapped tightly around her.

Rogue went over and placed a hand on Agnetha's shoulder. "We have to go."

Agnetha shuddered. Her eyes flicked opened, then shut again as she pressed the heels of her hands into her temples.

"What's wrong?" Rogue took a tissue from her pocket and moistened it under the tap.

"Headache." Agnetha let her hands fall to her lap.

Rogue wiped some of the grime and ash from Agnetha's face. Underneath, her cheeks were red, like sunburn, but Rogue couldn't see any serious injuries. She ran her fingers slowly through Agnetha's matted curls, feeling for cuts or bumps. Agnetha took a hold of Rogue's arm and stood up.

Rogue kissed her on the forehead. "We're nearly there."

Arm in arm, they limped over to the pickup. Rogue wrestled the passenger door open and hoped the creaking wouldn't alert anyone outside. After helping Agnetha to climb in, she made sure the door was closed firmly, then hurried around and got behind the wheel.

"Put on your seatbelt and crouch down," said Rogue.

Agnetha shifted on the seat, trying to avoid the metal springs sticking through the torn leather. She found a worn grey blanket on the floor and folded it into a makeshift cushion, then clicked home the safety belt. "Is that gunfire? How will we get past it?"

Rogue eased the Mitsubishi to the doorway and braked. "Don't worry, we're not going anywhere near the bullets. There's another way out." Rogue hoped the side gates she'd seen on the satellite image were still there and not blocked off. "Ready?"

Agnetha pressed her lips together and nodded, but her hands were trembling. Rogue knew she couldn't guarantee anything, but she'd use every trick she knew to get Agnetha to safety. It sounded like the gunfire was originating from a point halfway between the house and the main road. Rogue planned to drive by the front of the house to a set of wooden gates that opened onto a side road.

As they left the safety of the barn, Agnetha folded down and wrapped her arms around her head. Rogue pressed the accelerator and swerved around the gable end of the house. Up ahead, a group of armed men huddled behind two cars that were blocking the driveway. In the distance, she counted three police cars and a black van. A fire truck had stopped a safe distance behind them.

As she rounded the house, Savik detached himself from the group and ran towards her. Coburn followed, his right arm in a sling. When she didn't stop, Coburn balanced a shotgun over his injured arm and fired, spraying the pickup in lead pellets.

Rogue spun the steering wheel and drove through dense smoke surging from the burning house, her eyes searching the yard beyond for the exit to the side road. Savik planted two bullets in the driver's door and roared at Rogue to stop. She crouched down and floored the accelerator as bullets peppered the side of the pickup.

As Rogue sped past the bungalow, the rear tyres struggled on the loose gravel, but she kept her foot planted on the pedal. As the wheels catapulted stones and dust at Savik and Coburn, bullets and buckshot continued to plough into the tailgate of the pickup.

A hundred metres beyond the house, Rogue spotted the wooden gates. She shouted at Agnetha to hold on. Agnetha yanked her seatbelt tighter, then ducked her head between her knees and gripped a metal bar underneath the seat.

A bullet thudded into the glass behind Rogue's head. She ducked as a second one drilled through and embedded itself in the windscreen. A crack spread across the glass, then forked in several directions. Rogue peered through the growing spider web and ran her eye along the narrow gap between the wooden gates. Two bolts and a heavy chain held them together. Rogue would need speed to break through, but the road on the far side was narrow. She couldn't afford to overshoot it and bury the pickup in a ditch.

Flashing a glance in the wing mirror, she saw that Savik and Coburn were some way behind, but hadn't given up. As she coaxed a little more speed from the aged pickup, a black van jolted to a stop outside the gates. Several figures in visored helmets and protective vests leapt out. The armed police split into two groups and took up positions at each end of the gate.

One man stepped into view and raised a gloved hand, demanding Rogue to stop. Two more figures, both wielding rifles, took up positions on either side of him. Rogue gripped the steering wheel tighter and held her course.

A warning burst flew over the pickup. Rogue roared in frustration. On her own, she'd take her chances. But with Agnetha beside her, she wasn't prepared to take the same risks. She hit the brake and heaved on the steering wheel. The tyres did their best to turn, but the threads were down to the minimum. The rear bucked wildly and threatened to spin out of control.

Rogue eased off the pedal and gave the wheels some freedom, then prodded the accelerator every alternate second. The pickup pulled into the turn, lost traction and skidded again. Gritting her teeth, Rogue fought with the pedals, waiting for the tyres to grip. As valuable seconds passed and the Mitsubishi devoured the distance to the armed police, everything blurred. Rogue felt powerless, suspended in time.

Sunlight reflecting off a rifle snapped Rogue's eyes back to the police manning the gate. Agnetha's side of the pickup was totally exposed. At the risk of toppling over, Rogue pulled harder on the steering and screamed at Agnetha to get down on the floor. The suspension groaned and leaned, shifting its weight to the driver's side. Fifty metres from the gate, the gravel gave way to a patch of tarmac. Finally, the tyres tightened their grip and completed the turn. As Rogue sped back towards the house, a hail of bullets ripped through the tailgate. Up ahead, Coburn dived for cover behind a stack of cement blocks.

Rogue dug into her memory for the satellite image of the farm and recalled a border of tall hedges separating the property from a neighbouring field. Beyond the hedge, a dirt track hugging the perimeter led to a side road leading away from the farm. As she sped towards the end of the house, Coburn reappeared from his hiding place, the shotgun levelled at her.

Rogue jerked the steering wheel towards him. He grinned as shell after shell exploded at the pickup. Movement in her peripheral vision rang alarm bells. It was Savik. Feet planted wide apart, he opened fire at her. Rogue was caught in a crossfire. Glass showered into the cabin as the bullets hissed over her crouched torso, shattering the side windows.

As she closed in on Coburn, he turned to run, but tripped and stumbled. The pickup's steel bars slammed into him and tossed him in the air like a rag doll. He landed on the bonnet, his head hanging awkwardly to one side. As he slid away, the Mitsubishi's wheels spun on wet sand and Rogue lost control. The pickup ploughed into a stack of overflowing sandbags and shuddered to a stop.

In the distance, Savik's men were holding off the police, but it wouldn't be long before the reinforcements at the side gate stormed the property.

Rogue turned the key in the ignition, her fingers slipping with sweat. The engine started, spluttered, then cut out. Gritting her teeth, she tried again, her eyes searching for Savik, sensing his threat all around her. He'd cost her precious time and her chances of escape were now down to zero.

The pickup started again, this time settling into a steady rumble. Rogue gunned the engine and pulled away. As she left the burning bungalow behind and sped towards the old farmhouse, the clatter of machine guns erupted in her wake.

Just beyond the ruins, the concrete gave way to tall grass. Rogue flicked on the wipers and sprayed the windscreen, trying to get a better look at the wall of green that lay ahead. A combination of dense hedges and trees created an imposing barricade much taller than the pickup. It was impossible to gauge the depth, but wherever Rogue looked, no light penetrated from the far side. All she could hope was that the track she'd seen on the satellite photo still existed. The map was three years old. Since then, the field could have been planted with crops or filled with livestock.

Rogue yanked her seatbelt tighter and braced herself as she drove the Mitsubishi into the dense forest of leaves and branches, knowing if they got trapped inside, they would end up in a police cell.

Chapter 41

Rogue braced herself as the pickup charged into the jungle of hedges and trees. Branches thicker than her arms lashed against the bodywork, gouging and scraping the windscreen into a web of frosted glass. Younger branches found their way through the shattered side windows, swiping and stabbing at Rogue's face and neck. She fought the urge to cover her face. She needed to see ahead once the wheels hit solid ground again.

Rogue's arms and shoulders burned as she wrestled with the violent bucking and jerking from the steering wheel. As the pickup bounced over gnarled roots and jagged rocks, her foot slid off the accelerator pedal and the speed suddenly dropped off.

She stood up and planted all her weight onto the pedal. Beside her, Agnetha screamed as she was flung around the cabin floor. Rogue urged her to protect her head, but her warnings were drowned in the clattering noise all around them.

Sunlight blinded Rogue as the pickup broke through the hedges and shot clear. She jumped on the brake and swung the steering, hoping to find the narrow dirt track hugging the field's perimeter. Through the web of dirt and leaves mashed into the windscreen, she glimpsed a swaying field of green. For endless slow-motion seconds, the pickup sailed through the air, the wheels spinning freely. Finally, the front end thudded onto packed earth and slammed her back onto the seat.

When the rear of the Mitsubishi crashed to the ground, Rogue was thrown sideways. As the steering wheel spun freely, it twisted and bounced through deep troughs and stony ridges. Rogue clambered back into position and regained control, desperate to prevent the pickup from toppling over. Gradually the tyres found some grip, and she managed to drive in a reasonably straight line, but the windscreen was so badly scarred that she couldn't see which direction to follow. She tried using the wipers, but the blades and one of the arms had been sheared off. Eventually, she eased off the power and came to a gradual stop, hoping that the engine wouldn't cut out.

Rogue tried to open the door, but it jammed, and she had to kick it several times to force it open. Then she climbed onto the seat, stuck her head out and looked back towards the farmhouse. So far, nobody had followed them. The area surrounding the pickup was covered in green crops, but on the far side of the field,

Rogue spotted a large trailer. As a plan formed in her mind, she unhooked a branch from under the remaining wiper blade and used it to clear the debris from the windscreen. As she dropped back inside the cab, Agnetha uncurled herself from the floor and crawled onto the passenger seat, wincing with each movement.

"Agnetha, are you alright?" said Rogue, as she debated whether to struggle on through the field or reverse back to the narrow track.

Agnetha groaned. "I think so. Just feel like I've bumps and bruises everywhere."

Before Rogue could reply, a bullet pinged off the roof. She screamed at Agnetha to get down, then searched every direction for the shooter. A second round shattered the remains of her wing mirror.

The shots were coming from the farm. Ducking low, Rogue drove off, doing her best to steer the pickup towards the trailer. The shooter put several bullets through the cabin's rear window, showering Rogue and Agnetha with glass fragments.

As Rogue bounced the pickup across the ploughed ridges, intense beeping noises drew her attention to the dashboard. A pair of red lights flashed angrily. The engine was overheating and the oil level was dangerously low. There was nothing Rogue could do about them, but the beeps seemed to get louder and faster with every second as she urged the pickup nearer to safety. Finally, she drove in behind the trailer and stopped, but kept the engine running, terrified it might not start again.

Rogue folded over the steering wheel, mentally and physically drained. The raised metal sides of the trailer protected them from the shooter's line of sight. But for how long? The police would soon surround the entire field.

Agnetha turned to face Rogue, still cowering from the gunfire.

Rogue leaned over and drew the pale-faced girl close to her. "I'm sorry. So sorry," she whispered. Pulling back a little, she looked at Agnetha, expecting to see pain and fear.

Instead, Agnetha's eyes smiled back at her, filled with trust and love. "You rescued me, and now we're together again. That's all that matters."

Rogue couldn't resist smiling back. "We saved each other, remember?"

Agnetha wrapped her arms around her aunt's neck. As Rogue tightened their embrace, she took in their surroundings and calculated the odds of escape. They were isolated in the middle of a field. The shortest route to the gate was approximately six hundred metres across rough terrain. The pickup was ready to collapse, and Rogue doubted it would survive another trek across the unforgiving ridges of the field.

A path bearing the thread of the abandoned trailer's large tyres snaked off to her right. Once it reached the boundary, which was lined with tangled gorse and tall trees, it followed the perimeter to a second gate on the opposite side of the field. It was a considerably longer route, but a much smoother surface.

The shooting had stopped, but Rogue knew the police wouldn't let her go. Looking at the dashboard, she saw the needle on the temperature gauge had dropped a little. She pulled the release lever for the bonnet, then jumped out and looked around for something to wedge it open. Grabbing two blocks of timber from beneath the trailer, she lifted the bonnet and placed one block on each side. Then she lowered the bonnet lid onto the blocks and hoped the increased airflow might cool the engine down some more.

Rogue climbed back into the pickup, shifted into gear, and released the handbrake. She looked over at Agnetha. "No matter what happens, stay down low until I tell you."

Agnetha tightened her seat belt, nodded firmly, then folded herself down flat onto her legs, hands clasped over her head. Rogue gunned the engine, turned the Mitsubishi onto the track, and floored the accelerator. The temperature needle quickly crept back into the red zone as they raced over the hardened surface, Rogue's focus constantly drawn to the rear-view mirror.

As they drew close to the trees without being shot at, her face paled. The shooter was waiting until they left the protection of the trailer. Once she reached the trees and turned towards the road, he'd have a clear shot.

Instead of slowing for the ninety-degree turn, Rogue sped up. In the seconds it took the pickup to reach the junction, she scanned a stretch of gorse hedging between two trees and spotted a weakness. There was a patch where daylight pierced the foliage. Beyond it, more trees and bushes gave way to another field.

It was a gamble. It was also the best option available to her.

Rogue shouted a last-minute warning to Agnetha, then mounted the bank, willing the battered Mitsubishi up and over. Their speed carried them down the far side and across a grassy track, through more gorse and into the next field.

Rogue braked, reversed back onto the track, then sped off. She was driving in the opposite direction she'd originally planned, away from the route she had taken earlier that morning to the farm, but she didn't care. She was beyond exhausted, her body and mind running on autopilot. She had to just trust her gut. It had kept her alive before and would do so again. It had to, for Agnetha's sake.

As Rogue approached the end of the track, it straightened out. In the distance, she saw a truck pass by. Her path to the road was clear, unobstructed by gates or hedges.

At the end of the track, she turned onto the narrow road and sped away from the farm, watching nervously for the police, hoping they were still busy with Savik and his men.

Chapter 42

Rogue drove on instinct, away from the farm, the police, and Savik. She and Agnetha were another step closer to survival and safety. As she urged the pickup around the tight bends, her eyes rarely left the rear-view mirror. Once the police had overpowered Savik and his crew, Rogue was certain they would send a patrol after her. She just hoped she had gained some valuable time by cutting through the fields.

Rogue's next problem was knowing which turn to take. She tried to recall the map of the area, but she'd memorised the main routes, not the back roads. For all she knew, the road they were taking might loop back around to the farm entrance.

Every few seconds, the Mitsubishi skipped a beat, dragging Rogue's attention to the warning lights. The engine had settled to an acceptable rumble, and the temperature was hovering inside the red zone, but she knew the old pickup was liable to give up at any moment.

Apart from the mechanical problems, the multitude of bullet holes and shattered glass would attract unwanted attention. Rogue needed to dump it before joining any major routes monitored by traffic cameras. As she drove past houses and farms, Rogue kept an eye out for a replacement vehicle. Something parked on the side of the road would be preferable, away from windows and guard dogs.

Agnetha had dozed off, exhausted from her ordeal of the previous few days. She had multiple cuts and bruises, but they would heal. Rogue was more concerned with the effects of the fire, particularly any damage to Agnetha's lungs. Checking in to a hospital wasn't an option. At least not for Rogue, who had a gunshot wound. She could drop Agnetha at a clinic somewhere, tell her to feign amnesia, spin a story about a house fire, but she'd be taking a huge risk. If the medical staff contacted the police, they'd drop Agnetha into another nightmare.

Exiting a bend too fast, Rogue hurtled towards a crossroads. She stood on the brake as a passing SUV brushed the pickup's bumper, the driver blaring the horn as he flew past. The rear of the Mitsubishi lifted and bounced to a stop. The engine whined, then cut out. Agnetha lurched forward, straining against the seat belt, then whipped back into the seat.

Rogue's face broke out in a sweat. She'd almost killed them both. As she twisted the key in the ignition, she glanced over at Agnetha. "Are you OK?"

The engine turned over but didn't catch. Red and amber lights flooded the dashboard display. The fuel needle sat deep in the danger zone, but it hadn't quite reached the empty mark.

Rogue stared at the console, her hand resting on the ignition key, waiting and hoping. One by one, the warning lights blinked off until only the battery alert remained.

"Where are we?" asked Agnetha, as she massaged her neck.

The rear-view mirror was empty and the main road quiet, but for how long? All around them were dense trees and hedgerows, with no sign of a quiet cottage where they could steal a car. Rogue held her breath and turned the key a second time. A dry click and a sharp hum, then nothing.

"I'm not sure. How are you doing?"

"Tired and sore. And a little hungry." Agnetha's voice was raspy, an octave lower than usual.

Rogue looked into Agnetha's eyes. Despite everything, she seemed more calm and lucid than earlier. Rogue felt her chest relax a little, and without thinking, turned the key again. The engine spluttered into life. She quickly shifted into gear, checked there was no traffic coming, then drove across the junction and under the cover of more trees.

She could cover more distance on the motorways, but the bullet holes decorating the pickup would be like a beacon to the police, not to mention the doubts she had over the engine lasting much longer.

Hunter's words echoed around her mind as if he was sitting in the back seat. "There's more at stake this time." "You know how to contact me."

The thrum of a helicopter rotor penetrated the branches overhead. Rogue shifted in her seat and leaned on the accelerator.

Agnetha straightened up and winced as she pulled the seat belt tighter.

"This nightmare will be over soon, I promise," said Rogue, as she wondered how Agnetha would be in the days and months ahead. She glanced over at her niece, needing to know but afraid to ask. Agnetha smiled back.

Rogue raised an eyebrow.

Agnetha blinked as her eyes welled up. "I was thinking of mum. You remind me so much of her. She was indestructible too."

Rogue swallowed hard. She'd been in awe of Tasha, her ability to switch from assassin to mother in an instant. In the months and years after Tasha's death, Rogue had felt inadequate and out of her depth in her efforts to take care of Agnetha.

"You wouldn't be in this mess except for me," said Rogue. She swallowed again. "Savik used you to get to me."

Agnetha shook her head as she traced a jagged gash on her palm. "I failed you both. You and mum taught me so much, but I fell on the first test."

A siren wailed some distance behind them.

Rogue wanted to pull over and comfort Agnetha, but time was against them. She reached for Agnetha's arm and squeezed gently. "Don't you ever believe that. You didn't fail us, Agnetha. All you've gone through in the past few days, I've seen grown men crumble. Your mother would have been so proud of you, so proud. And so am I."

The engine skipped a beat, then another. Rogue knew she couldn't keep driving and hope for the best. First, they needed another vehicle. After that, somewhere to clean up before trying to get across the border into France.

Rogue thought of Hunter again. Something told her he wasn't far away.

"The truck doesn't sound very good," said Agnetha, worry etched on her face.

"We need to dump it, find something else. Check the glove box."

Agnetha popped it open. "What am I looking for?"

"Anything useful. Maps, sat nav, cash."

Agnetha reached in, dragged the contents onto her lap, and began sifting through them.

"Mostly useless bits and pieces. Pens, a notebook, a dirty rag, a few sticky toffees, a rusty screwdriver, and one glove," said Agnetha, dropping the items on the floor. "What about this old phone?" she said, holding it up.

"Try it. See if it works."

Agnetha flipped the lid on the phone. She turned it over in her hand, found the power button, and held it in. The screen lit up, then went dark again. "The battery is dead, I think. It came on but died. I don't see a charger in this lot," she said, stretching back into the glove box.

Rogue rooted around the storage compartment in the driver's door, but only found an oily rag and a roll of insulation tape. "Try the door pockets."

Agnetha pulled a bunch of wires from the storage area beside her. She tried the first two, but the plugs were too small. Then she found a match. "Got one. This fits," she said excitedly.

"Plug it in here," said Rogue, pointing to an adapter protruding from the cigarette lighter.

Agnetha disentangled the cable from the nest of wires and slotted it in. She stared at the small black screen expectantly. Several seconds passed, then a grainy logo appeared. "It's working!"

"Let's hope we can get a signal out here," thought Rogue aloud. She ran names in her head, deciding who she could ask for help. Hunter was the obvious choice, maybe the only one. No one else was close enough or had the type of resources she needed. When they came to another staggered junction, Rogue pulled in.

"I have a dial tone," said Agnetha, holding the phone to her ear. "It's working."

Rogue took the phone and keyed a number from memory.

Hunter answered after two rings. "You took your time."

"I've been a little preoccupied."

"Black smoke is never a good sign."

"You're nearby?" said Rogue, astonished.

"How is she?"

Rogue looked at Agnetha and wondered if she'd ever recover. "Safe."

"That's a winner."

"It is."

"Do you need a safe house?"

"And a medic. After that, transport, cash, a phone."

Hunter's deep laugh brought a grin to Rogue's face. "What's your location?"

"Best I can tell, we're five or six kilometres south-east of the target, approaching a crossroads." Rogue looked around for a landmark. "There's a water tower away to my right."

Hunter was silent while he checked a map. "You've got fields and three hills to your left?"

Rogue peered through a gap in the trees. "Roger that."

"Proceed through the crossroads, watch for a V on the road and take the left fork. Continue for five kilometres, then take a right at a T junction. Drive another... seven to a narrow bridge. Immediately after that, on the left, you'll find a service depot. Wait there."

"Got it," said Rogue. "I owe you one."

"No, this is a favour I owe to an old friend," replied Hunter.

The call ended.

Chapter 43

Rogue handed the phone back to Agnetha, shifted gears, then eased the last few metres to the junction.

"Well?" said Agnetha, louder than she'd intended.

Rogue's eyes darted to the rear-view mirror. "What?"

Agnetha twisted and looked at the road behind them. "Who were you talking to? And why do you keep looking in the mirror?"

Rogue crossed the main road, scanning left and right for flashing lights. "To meet someone."

"You don't sound very sure of him."

"I'd trust him with my life."

"But?"

Rogue looked in the mirror again, then rubbed her eyes. "He normally uses other people in the field. I didn't want to drag him into this."

Agnetha pulled the worn blanket from under her and wrapped it around her shoulders. "Isn't that better, that he's coming himself, instead of some stranger?"

"Yes, I suppose so. I'm just overthinking it, that's all." Rogue rolled her shoulders and settled back against the ripped upholstery.

"So after we meet him, what then?"

The road ahead divided in two. Rogue veered onto the left fork, grateful for the cover of the dense trees overhead. "We swap the pickup for something less conspicuous, then get far away from here."

Agnetha found a clean piece of windscreen and stared at the road ahead. "Back to Geneva?"

"We'll see. You've been through a lot and your first term doesn't start for another week."

"What about the apartment? Our clothes and other stuff are still there."

"Everything is safe. It's been put into storage. And I arranged for the apartment to be cleaned. By now, it'll look like we were never there."

Agnetha said nothing, but Rogue could hear the anxiety in her breathing. It wasn't her belongings that Agnetha was thinking about. It was the man she'd stabbed and left bleeding on her bedroom floor.

"Don't think about it, Agnetha. Just for now. We're running on empty, so we need to use our reserves to stay safe. We'll deal with all that another day."

"Can you teach me? To move on. To pretend that none of it ever happened."

Rogue's stomach turned as old wounds surfaced, twisting into a familiar knot of grief and regret. She pulled into a gateway, then twisted around to face Agnetha.

"I wish I could, but it doesn't work like that."

Agnetha fingered the weals on her wrists and shuddered. She tried to smile, but deep shadows filled her eyes.

Rogue leaned in closer and took her hands. "These wounds will heal Agnetha. It'll take a little longer to shake the memories of what happened, but you are Tasha Ryll's daughter and you have her strength."

Agnetha's head dropped. "Do you ever forget Mum's voice?"

"Sometimes," admitted Rogue. "But I have ways of remembering."

Agnetha raised her gaze a little.

"I imagine she's in the next room and I call out to her, to ask her something. It's uncanny, but I always get an answer. And it's usually a really good one." Rogue raised Agnetha's chin. "Try it."

Chattering voices filtered in through the broken side window. A couple of teenagers cycled by. One of them looked back at the battered pickup, but kept going.

"We need to get moving," said Rogue.

The sun was high in the sky and breaking through the clouds in places. Rogue flipped down the visor and took a right at the next T junction. Ditches lined both sides of the road, interrupted by the occasional gateway into a field or house.

A minute later, Rogue came to the bridge Hunter had referred to in his directions. It was an old stone humped back, just wide enough for vehicles to cross in one direction at a time. Rogue considered blowing the horn, but preferred not to attract any attention. Slowing to twenty kilometres, she crawled over the rise. The road beyond was dead straight and empty.

On the left, she spotted the construction depot. It was basic, nothing more than a wooden shed alongside a wire fence enclosure. Rogue eased the Mitsubishi pickup onto the packed earth and stopped, but held her foot over the accelerator while she surveyed the site.

A rusty padlock hung limply from the shed door, and a web of ivy smothered the two small windows. Inside the enclosure, a cement mixer lay on its side next to mounds of sand and loose stones. She doubted anyone had worked there all year. Overhead, ancient trees cast a sad gloom over the depot. Rogue could see why Hunter had chosen it.

She reversed under an umbrella of low-hanging branches. Anybody crossing the bridge wouldn't see the pickup until they had driven past. It also gave her a perfect view of vehicles approaching from the opposite direction.

The clock on the dashboard was stopped at 2:05. Rogue lifted the phone from the centre console and pressed a random button. The screen lit up. 12:41 pm.

She tried to listen for sirens and helicopters, but it was difficult to hear anything over the trundling of the

Mitsubishi's diesel engine. Nevertheless, she kept it running.

Rogue checked the phone again. Only a minute had passed. She placed her hands on top of the steering wheel and began tapping.

"Mum used to do that," said Agnetha.

Rogue dragged her eyes from the road. "Do what?"

Agnetha pointed to Rogue's fingers. "Play piano scales on the steering wheel."

"She could play the piano?" said Rogue, surprised.

Agnetha laughed. "No, but whenever she collected me from music lessons, she'd be doing that with her fingers when I'd get in the car."

Rogue resumed watching for traffic. "Your mum always looked forward to seeing you when we returned from missions. I remember one time she left a debriefing like a tornado. Our boss was furious. I'm sure she broke every red light on the way to your school."

"What was it like? Working with Mum. I know it was dangerous, but," Agnetha shrugged. "She never told me about the missions. Every time she got back, I'd ask her, but she'd change the subject and give me whatever she'd bought at the airport or some all-night store."

"This world, Agnetha ... it's very different."

"You don't have to protect me Rachel, I'm not little Neta anymore. I know what Mum did for a living. I'm proud of her. And of you."

Rogue turned in the seat. Even battered and bruised, Agnetha was beautiful. Rogue hated that she'd dragged her niece into an underworld of evil, and exposed her to the people and experiences that Tasha had battled so hard to shield her from.

Rogue sighed.

"What? Talk to me," said Agnetha.

"You're right to be proud of your mother. The world needs people like her to balance the evil. But she would never want you to grow up believing that force is the answer."

12:46 pm.

Rogue's fingers tapped a little faster. The longer she waited, the more likely they'd be found by a police patrol or trapped inside a chain of road blocks. Without a gun, Rogue felt very exposed. She peered back into the flat bed of the pickup. A tarpaulin stretched from one side to the other, concealing whatever was stored underneath.

"This man we're waiting for. Did he know Mum?" asked Agnetha hopefully.

Rogue said nothing, unsure how to proceed. She had very few memories of her own mother and would love to know more. Was it right to hold that connection back from Agnetha?

"His name is Hunter. Arnold Hunter. Yes, he knew Tasha." She turned to face Agnetha. "That's the only reason he's helping us now."

"What do you mean?"

"He provides supplies and services during the early stages of a mission, before things heat up. Once the bullets start flying, he stays out of it."

"Sounds a little mercenary to me."

"Quite the contrary. He'd rather ensure the safety of his contractors than make tons of money."

The breeze carried the low hum of an engine in through the window. Rogue craned her head forward. It seemed to come from the road ahead, but the wind could play tricks.

Two seconds later, a grey SUV rounded the bend, coming towards them. It slowed, turned off the road, and stopped just beyond the shed. It had a Volvo badge on the grill, but the driver's face was obscured by the reflecting sunlight.

"Wait here," said Rogue. She got out and stood by the bonnet. Her gut tightened into a knot. Without a gun, she was at the mercy of whoever was behind the wheel of the SUV.

Chapter 44

The driver's door swung open. A tan boot crunched down into the dirt and a man stepped out.

Rogue couldn't tell for sure if it was Hunter or not. Sun glasses and a peaked cap obscured his face, and his loose jacket and dark trousers concealed his shape. Rogue tensed and changed her stance slightly, ready for action.

The man did a quick sweep of his surroundings, then proceeded slowly towards Rogue. Despite his best efforts to disguise his old injury, Rogue recognised Hunter's walk. Judging by the tension in his jaw, the pain from his hip had worsened considerably since they'd last met. Rogue's breathing eased a little, and she went to meet him.

As they drew closer, Hunter's hand shot inside his jacket and pulled out a gun. He raised it and aimed directly at Rogue's head.

She slowed and stuttered, confused, betrayed.

A shot rang out, then two more, so close together the second sounded like an echo of the first. Rogue's jaw dropped open as she stared at Hunter, waiting for her brain to register where she'd been hit.

Hunter's free hand clutched his chest. Then he arched forward and dropped to one knee. Realising what had happened, Rogue sprinted to him, sliding and dropping the last few metres as he collapsed. She whipped the Beretta from his hand and rolled towards the wooden shed as more shots rang out, splintering the rotten timber above her.

Pressing into a narrow gap beneath the shed, she sought out the gunman. The narrow bridge was empty, but the trees on either side provided ample cover for a shooter. Suddenly, she remembered Hunter had aimed directly at her. He had seen someone directly behind her.

Rogue's body chilled as she snapped back to the Mitsubishi pickup. Through the windscreen, she saw Agnetha, her face contorted and her arms gesturing frantically. A shadow moved above the cab and two more bullets drilled into the woodwork over Rogue's head.

Squinting against the sun, she returned fire, but couldn't pick out the shooter. She shuffled backwards, took cover by the side of the shed, and called out to Hunter.

There was no reply. Rogue watched his chest but couldn't detect movement under his jacket. She considered making a dash to the Volvo, but Hunter had probably taken the keys. Skirting around the rear of the shed was an option, but Rogue couldn't afford to take her eyes off Agnetha. If the gunman took her hostage, it was game over.

Before Rogue could decide her next move, the pickup jerked forward, stopped, then reversed. Agnetha was at the wheel. She was trying to unbalance the gunman in the back. As Rogue looked on, he clambered over the side of the pickup and yanked open the driver's door. At that moment, sunlight sliced through the trees and lit up his face. It was Savik.

Rogue jumped up and fired, but he ducked behind the cab door. She dropped to the ground and let off a volley of shots, aiming at his legs. Rogue heard him grunt, then both his feet disappeared as he climbed inside the cab.

Terrified he would hurt Agnetha, Rogue sprinted towards them, half expecting to be gunned down.

As she closed in, she searched for Agnetha through the windscreen, but all she could see was Savik's arms swinging erratically inside the cab.

The passenger side door creaked open and Agnetha tumbled out, landing in a heap. Savik darted across the seats after her. Time seemed to slow down as Rogue watched Agnetha hurl something into the undergrowth.

As Savik jumped down, he reached for Agnetha with one hand, shooting at Rogue with the other, but his injured leg collapsed and his shots flew past Rogue. As she took aim, Agnetha scrambled to her feet and ran into the clump of trees.

Rogue had a clear shot.

She fired. The first bullet found Savik's shoulder, the second buried itself in his stomach. He staggered, then dropped to the ground.

Rogue stuffed the Beretta into her belt and hurried over to Agnetha. Overwhelmed by relief, she pulled her niece into a tight embrace and kissed her on the cheek.

"I'm OK," said Agnetha. "What about Hunter? Is he dead?"

Rogue's head jerked around as she uncurled herself from Agnetha. As she started towards Hunter, she found herself staring into Savik's gun, his eyes blazing, his mouth twisted with hatred.

As Rogue's fingers wrapped around Hunter's Beretta, Savik pulled the trigger.

His gun clicked empty.

Rogue lashed out and kicked the weapon from his hand. His mouth opened, but the words collapsed into a gurgling wheeze. He coughed, spluttered blood, then fell back. As his head thudded on the damp earth, he grinned up at her. A deep, hoarse laugh escaped between his lips.

Rogue looked across the yard to where Hunter lay motionless. She turned back to Savik and fired. A red rose blossomed on his forehead.

Then she ran to Hunter. At her touch, he opened his eyes and grimaced.

"How bad is it?" said Rogue, searching for blood.

"Hurts like hell, but I think this saved me." Hunter pulled his shirt open, revealing a kevlar vest underneath.

Rogue looked at him wide eyed.

Hunter prised a nine millimetre bullet from the vest and flicked it away. "You know me, take no chances. Where did that shooter come from?"

Rogue offered a hand to Hunter. "Last I saw him was back at the farm. He must've climbed into the back of the pickup during the skirmish with the police."

Hunter pulled himself up. "Speaking of police, that gunfire will attract attention. We'd better hit the road."

Rogue handed him the Beretta. "I want to torch the pickup. Agnetha's prints are all over it."

"OK, but make it real fast. I've got some supplies in the car you can use."

As Hunter headed back to the Volvo and opened the boot, Agnetha appeared beside Rogue, her arms wrapped around her shoulders. Rogue guided her to the car. Hunter appeared with a fleece jacket and offered it to Agnetha.

"This is Hunter, the friend I told you about," said Rogue as she draped the jacket around Agnetha's shoulders and opened the back door of the car. "You sit in. We'll be leaving in a minute."

Agnetha slid her arms into the sleeves and buttoned it up. It was several sizes too big, but she stuffed her hands into the pockets and drew it tight around her.

Rogue took a can of petrol from Hunter and followed him to the pickup. While he rigged a detonator and attached it to the fuel tank, she doused the seats and dashboard with petrol. As she climbed onto the back and splashed the rest of the petrol over the tarpaulin, Rogue noticed Agnetha wandering over to them, reluctant to wait on her own in the Volvo.

As Rogue made her way down, pain ripped through her side and she lost her footing. Hunter had been watching her and stepped in to break her fall.

"You'll need to take it easy for a day or two," he said, as Rogue steadied herself.

"And then some," she muttered.

"I'm all set. Are you ready?"

Agnetha was trembling as she stared down at Savik's corpse. Rogue stepped in front of her, blocking her view. Rogue was used to death and violence and couldn't imagine what Agnetha was feeling or thinking.

"You go with Hunter and get into the car."

Agnetha's eyes widened in alarm. "Aren't you coming with us?"

"Give me two minutes. I need to finish up here." Rogue nudged Agnetha towards the Volvo.

Hunter appeared beside them and handed the timer to Rogue. "How long?"

"I'll set it for ten."

Concern flooded Agnetha's pale face.

"You can trust Hunter," said Rogue. "He was a good friend to your mother."

"Call me Boomer," said Hunter, smiling. "It was your mother's nickname for me."

"I promise I'll only be a minute," said Rogue. "But I need you in the car, ready to go."

Agnetha glanced at the timer in Rogue's hand. "OK."

Rogue searched Savik's pockets and retrieved her phone. Once Hunter and Agnetha were safely inside the Volvo and Rogue heard the engine start, she set the timer to ten seconds, started the clock, and ran. A moment after she landed in the passenger seat, Hunter drove off at speed.

Rogue counted down the seconds as they hit the tarmac and left the depot behind. She watched the fireball in the wing mirror, hoping it was the last action she would see for some time.

As they leaned into a bend, Rogue twisted around and wished she'd sat in the back. Agnetha had curled up on the seat with only her face visible, the rest of her lost in Hunter's jacket. For a moment, Rogue thought she was looking at Tasha. As they bounced over a railway track, Agnetha's eyes popped open. She smiled at Rogue, then her lids slid down again.

"She'll be OK," said Hunter.

Rogue swivelled back to face the road. As light rain spattered the windscreen, she lowered the window and inhaled deeply. "I hope so," she sighed.

"I can see it in her eyes. She's a survivor, just like you and Tasha." Hunter nodded reassuringly. "She'll do alright."

The End.

AUTHOR'S NOTE

Thank you for reading Extreme Force. I hope you enjoyed Rogue's latest mission. If you did, and you have a moment to spare, I would really appreciate a short review on the site where you purchased your book. Every review makes a huge difference in spreading the word, so that new readers discover the ROGUE Thriller Series.

I've been a fan of mystery and crime stories for as long as I can remember and often dreamed of someday writing my own novel. In 2017, I dipped my toe into the world of creative writing with Hard Choices, the first book in the ROGUE series. Having enjoyed that experience, I eagerly dived into writing the sequel, Extreme Force.

My journey from brain-storming the first ideas to publishing the finished book has been a fantastic adventure. I've loved creating the characters and have learned so much about the process of writing. Rogue is an intriguing protagonist, and one I am still getting to know. I hope you enjoyed reading this book as much as I enjoyed writing it.

Follow me on social media or check my website for news of new book releases :

Instagram – @HarryBrooksAuthor
Facebook – www.facebook.com/HarryBrooksAuthor
Goodreads – www.goodreads.com/harrybrooks
Website – www.harrybrooksauthor.com

ABOUT THE AUTHOR

My name is Harry Brooks. I was born in Dublin, Ireland and now live with my wife in Co. Kildare.

When I'm not writing, I enjoy listening to podcasts, walking in nature and having a coffee in my favourite cafes while reading a good book.

People often ask me questions about my writing, such as how I got started, where I get my ideas, and how I keep track of all the story details. During the early stages of writing Extreme Force, my friend Ciara posed some of those same questions. Soon afterwards, she wrote these few words describing her image of me when plotting out my books—

> *Harry sat on the rocks overlooking the harsh sea, pen in hand, a pensive look on his face. With flashbacks of his first success fresh in his mind, he wondered, 'How can I top this?'*
>
> *A thriller it had to be. A shoulder tensing, eye pinching, mouth gasping, epic, but about what? The one thing that always starts it is the name, that main character that makes you analyse every part of their personality. The*

mystery, that troubled background, those secrets, that past mistake still haunting every thought.

He began to write.

It's true. My principal character, Rogue, did set the ideas flowing for me. Rogue is an intriguing character and one I am still getting to know as I begin writing the third book in the series.

ACKNOWLEDGEMENTS

The journey of planning, writing and publishing a book is often sparked by the author's enthusiasm for an idea, with little thought for the inevitable potholes, forks and hills along the way. It is during these challenging times that the support of friends and colleagues is invaluable. Without their help and encouragement, I am sure this book, Extreme Force, would still be a work-in-progress.

Thank you to my amazing wife, Geraldine, who listened enthusiastically to my ideas and patiently to my predicaments as I navigated my way through the story. She devoted many hours to reading my completed manuscript, all ninety-seven thousand words of it, and contributed insightful and invaluable feedback. Most of all, she allowed me to follow my dream.

Thank you to my friend and writing buddy, Ian. Our weekend writing sprints, monthly coffee catchups, and regular updates kept me on the right track.

Thank you to my friends who generously offered their time as advance readers for this book. It helped me sleep at night, knowing people other than me had read the final version, and I hadn't somehow lost large chunks of the story.

Thank you to my colleagues in writing groups for their support and encouragement while I was working on this book.

Thank you to my cover designers, 100Covers, for their expertise and patience, and for doing a great job.

And finally, the lifeblood of many authors - coffee and cake. I would not have finished this book without litres of lattes and Americanos, and plates of Danish pastries.

Hard Choices

by Harry Brooks

Book 1 in the ROGUE Thriller Series

A routine operation quickly turns bad. With time running out, MI5 turn to a former special agent for help.

Enter Rogue, who left MI5 after her partner Tasha was murdered by Viktor Kaznov, a member of the Vipers drug cartel. Rogue has spent the past five years building her own covert security business and using its resources to protect Tasha's daughter, Agnetha, from Kaznov.

Unfortunately, some of Rogue's operations involved cooperating with enemies of the British government, dealings which could put Rogue herself behind bars. Only the chance of killing Kaznov could persuade Rogue to team up with her old boss.

Success will mean freedom for Tasha's daughter. But failure will land Rogue in prison and lead to certain death for Agnetha.

Hard Choices is a fast-paced thriller packed with non-stop action.

www.harrybrooksauthor.com